D1732783

NIGHTSTALKERS

Sanctum

(1st Edition)

by Jasper T. Scott

JasperTscott.com
@JasperTscott

PREVIOUSLY IN THE SERIES

Note: this is a comprehensive summary of the events in book one of this series, *Nightstalkers: The Extinction Event.* If you mostly recall what happened in that book, feel free to skip ahead to Chapter One where a much briefer summary has been incorporated.

Nightstalkers (Book 1) Synopsis

May 13, 2024

Adam and Kimberly Hall are living a quiet suburban life in Austin, Texas with their daughter, Crystal, and their dog, Bowser, when the Specters arrive. The invasion begins with a meteor shower that wipes out more than half of Earth's population. Deadly alien predators come crawling out of the lesser impact craters and begin hunting the survivors.

After an initial encounter turns deadly for his neighbor, Harry Cooper, Adam flees Austin with his family and his neighbor's wife and son. They get as far as the interstate when a crashing fighter jet causes Adam to roll his truck off the freeway. His wife Kimberly is killed in the accident. They abandon the scene and convince a passing motorist to pick them up. An old Army buddy of Adam's owns a ranch in Texas Hill Country. If they can get to it, they should be safe.

Eight years later...

March 16th, 2032

For almost a decade, Adam and Crystal have been living on Rick Jackson's ranch with their former neighbors Carla and Connor Cooper and the Brooks family, who picked them up on the interstate the night of the invasion.

Every day is a struggle just to survive. Dangerous bands of raiders roam the wastes during the day, and packs of primitive alien predators known as "stalkers" come out to hunt at night.

The actual invaders, known as Specters, have never been seen, but their space ships are visible drifting across the stars at night. They seem to be waiting for their terraformers to make Earth more suitable for them to inhabit. Meanwhile, human civilization has been reduced to a handful of walled-off safe zones rebuilt around the cores of old inland cities. America has reformed into the Republic in the south, and the Coalition in the north.

One night Adam is out mending a fence with Rick when they see a damaged Spec lander fly overhead and land half a mile away. With so little known about the actual invaders, Adam and Rick realize that this could be a unique opportunity to learn more about them.

They follow the lander and hide in the trees, watching as an armored figure emerges. They can't see its face, but it seems to have human proportions. While they're still watching, a pack of stalkers emerges from a nearby burrow. They leave an albino stalker cub at the feet of the armored figure, like some kind of sacrifice.

Having seen enough, Adam and Rick turn to leave, but the stalkers hear them and give chase. Knowing they can't outrun the monsters, Rick stands his ground, giving Adam a chance to escape. Adam is reluctant to leave, but Rick insists that someone has to tell the governor of the Republic what they saw.

Adam barely makes it back to the ranch alive. Stalkers attempt to break in, but they are repelled by the ranch's fortifications. Adam tells the others what happened to Rick and what they saw. Then, in private, after his daughter has gone to bed, he convinces Owen Brooks to join him on a dangerous mission to reach the Travis Safe Zone so that they can tell Governor Miller what he saw. Owen's wife

Sophie says that it's too dangerous, but Adam insists they have to go. Rick can't have died for nothing.

Later that night, Adam is contemplating Rick's death, and his late wife, Kimberly. Carla Cooper knocks at the door and joins Adam in his room. She kisses him, revealing a romantic interest in him, and giving him an added reason to make it back from Travis alive.

Adam isn't sure that he's ready to move on, but he's beginning to feel something for his old neighbor. Their spouses have each been dead for eight years. Maybe it's finally time to let them go.

The next morning, Adam is packing supplies into the back of Rick's old F350 in preparation to leave the ranch. Owen Brooks returns with Connor Cooper from checking on their cattle. Stalkers took a few last night, but the herd is mostly intact.

Adam and Owen say their goodbyes. Crystal is mad at her father for leaving. She runs away crying. Connor Cooper, who has a crush on her, follows her to the stables.

Adam and Owen drive away, promising to return before sundown tomorrow night. When they reach the perimeter fence, Adam has to get out to open the gates. As they're driving away, he and Owen both hear something. Not seeing anything in their mirrors, they decide that it must have been a bump in the road.

In reality, it was Connor and Crystal sneaking into the back of the truck. With a custom truck topper built over the back and their supplies blocking the rear view mirror there's no way for Adam to see them hiding back there.

As they turn onto the highway to Bexar, Adam and Owen see a Spec Terraformer in the distance, blocking the way through Bandera. They decide to turn north and go through the Kerr Safe Zone instead. But Owen warns that Medina, which lies between them and Kerr, is a raider town. He says that they should turn back, but Adam is determined to press on.

They almost make it through Medina before running into a blockade on a bridge. An armed band of raiders ride up on horses behind them, and two more jump out from behind the blockade. A firefight ensues, and three of the raiders are killed. Crystal and Connor help by firing rifles out the back, and Adam discovers that they are hiding back there. They crash through the blockade and continue to Kerr. Along the way, they discover that Crystal was injured by a piece of shrapnel. They bandage her leg, making plans to see a doctor in Kerr and to ask the mayor for a Ranger escort to get them the rest of the way to Travis.

In Kerr, while waiting to see the doctor, Adam has a run-in with a Ranger Sergeant who appears to have been beating his wife.

They see the doctor and learn about a critical

food shortage in the city. Adam knows that the ranch has an exclusive contract to trade with Bexar, but the doctor wants them to consider trading with Kerr instead. Owen isn't sure that they should break their contract—Bexar has better goods for trade.

They go see Mayor Maloney of Kerr who invites them for lunch. The mayor also mentions the food shortage and tries to get Adam to commit to trading with Kerr in exchange for an escort to Travis. Adam gets a bad vibe from the mayor, but he agrees to think about it. As a token of good will, Maloney assigns one man to escort them: Sergeant Curtis of the night watch. It's the same sergeant that Adam ran into while waiting to see the doctor. Adam is about to decline when Owen accepts the offer. After the mayor leaves, Owen explains that if the mayor is planning to coerce them into trading with Kerr, it's better that they find out now.

They go to the restrooms before continuing on their way. As they're coming out, they see two of the raiders from Medina enter the restaurant. Adam realizes the raiders must have followed them. They duck into the ladies' room and hide in one of the stalls. One of the raiders comes in, obviously looking for them, but Adam manages to get him to go away. Rather than risk walking out the front door to their truck, they decide to sneak out the window in the ladies' room.

Just before all of them can escape, raiders burst back into the restroom and discover them. They flee to their truck, narrowly escaping the raiders. Sergeant Curtis joins them by the north gate, and then they're on the road to Travis.

Adam is troubled by the fact that the raiders followed them. He knows they won't be able to catch up on horseback, but what will happen when they have to drive back this way tomorrow?

The raiders are detained for causing trouble. Their leader, Devon Santos, speaks with Mayor Maloney, explaining that one of the three raiders that Adam and the others killed in Medina was his cousin and also the niece of Esteban Santos, the infamous leader of the Sinaloa Syndicate in Mexico. Devon strikes a deal with the mayor: he'll take care of the current occupants of Sunny Valley Ranch, and then Mayor Maloney can send his people down to take over the ranch and supply Kerr with food.

On the way to Travis, Adam and the others run into trouble with stalkers. They manage to escape relatively unscathed, reaching Travis just as the sun is setting. Rangers treat their injuries at the gates and then escort them to the Governor's Mansion. They meet Governor Miller and Adam tells him what he and Rick saw last night at the ranch.

The governor seems troubled by the possibility of human collaborators working with the invaders. He promises that they will speak more about it in the morning. In the meantime, they are invited to stay the night at the mansion.

Both Adam and Owen realize that the governor didn't seem completely surprised by their news. They wonder if maybe *he* is collaborating with the invaders, but they decide to play dumb to avoid getting themselves into trouble.

The next morning they are escorted to the Capitol building by a Ranger Lieutenant, who takes them down into the basement, and from there down a secret staircase into a bunker. The bunker turns out to be compromised and infested with stalkers. The lieutenant locks them inside, and they realize that the governor is trying to get rid of them.

Adam finds a gun buried in the rubble inside the bunker just before the stalkers reach them. They run frantically through the facility, looking for another way out. They find one, but they have to hold a door to keep the stalkers from following them. Adam insists that he and Sergeant Curtis hold the door while Owen leads Crystal and Connor to safety. Sergeant Curtis rejects that plan and abandons the door, leading the charge for safety. Adam tells Owen to follow him up with the kids, arguing that someone has to stay behind to hold the door. Owen reluctantly agrees. They reach the top of the chamber and begin climbing out through a crack in the walls and ceiling. Far below, the stalkers overwhelm Adam. One of them paralyzes him with a stab from the stinger in its tail, and Crystal watches from above as they appear to devour her father.

Owen and Curtis lead the kids out. They discover that they have emerged just outside the walls of Travis. Hiking away on foot, they reach the south gate where they came in. Owen and Sergeant Curtis re-enter the city to get their truck back, assuming that the governor's treachery won't be public knowledge.

They manage to get their vehicle back, but Rangers try to stop them just before they can retrieve their guns. They smash through the gate at the guard post and begin looking for alternate routes back to Kerr to avoid more run-ins with Rangers on the way home.

Devon and his band of raiders arrive at Sunny Valley Ranch. They manage to get the upper-hand, capturing Carla Cooper as well as Sophie and Emily Brooks. They tie them up and wait for the others to return.

Hours later, Adam awakens underground in a stalker den to discover that he's not dead, but he can hear and see stalkers eating a dead Ranger not ten feet away. Another man wakes up screaming beside him. Adam tells him to be quiet, then notices that one of the man's arms has been bitten off. The man introduces himself as Casey Jones.

Casey and Adam get to talking while Adam struggles to recover the feeling in his limbs. Casey explains that he was on his way north to Chicago when stalkers captured him. He tells Adam about a rumor that the Coalition has captured one of the Specters' spaceships and they're using it to smuggle people to safety on another planet, code-named Sanctum.

Adam doesn't know if he believes the rumor, but Casey insists that it's true. His brother's family already left for Sanctum.

Filled with a newfound sense of hope and purpose, Adam is determined to escape the stalker den alive. He wants to take Casey with him, but Casey says that he's in no shape to run.

Adam sees the dead Ranger's sidearm and Casey provides a distraction while he scrambles to reach it. Adam shoots and wounds several of the stalkers and then escapes into the labyrinthine tunnels. He comes to a dead-end sealed with a metal door.

Just before the stalkers can tear him apart, the door opens and Adam falls inside. He finds himself confronted by an armored figure like the one he saw with Rick. They speak briefly, and Adam learns that the man inside the armor is a human and that it is none other than his old neighbor, Harry Cooper—Carla's husband. Harry doesn't seem to remember Adam. He is looking for human candidates for "integration therapy." Seeing a pair of bio-luminescent growths on Harry's skull, Adam can only imagine what that might entail. Yet some remnant of Harry must still be in there because he recognizes the names of his wife and son, whom he identifies as ideal candidates for integration therapy.

Adam reluctantly agrees to lead Harry back to the ranch, and Harry takes him aboard a Spec Lander. Once aboard, Adam has a change of heart. He realizes that he can't lead Harry back. He'll capture everyone and turn them into mindless slaves just like him. But then Harry attaches a pair of alien creatures to Adam's skull, and he finds himself powerless to resist Harry's interrogation.

Crystal, Connor, and Owen finally make it back to the ranch just as night is falling. They secured a proper Ranger escort in Kerr, led by Sergeant Curtis.

When Crystal and the others knock on the front door, they realize that it's a setup and the Rangers are in on it. They are captured and tied to chairs in the dining room with Sophie, Emily, and Carla.

Devon Santos begins a game of Russian Roulette to find out who shot his cousin. Eventually, Connor admits that it was him, but Crystal insists that she did it. Devon seems determined to kill all of them, anyway. Unable to stomach the Raiders' sadistic games, Sergeant Curtis and the rest of the Rangers retreat upstairs.

Adam and Harry arrive and land quietly outside the ranch. Harry engages a cloaking shield in his armor, effectively vanishing. He attacks the Rangers on the second floor of the house, killing several of them, including Sergeant Curtis.

Adam sneaks out to assess the situation. He realizes that his daughter and the others have been taken hostage by a combination of raiders and Rangers, and he looks for a way to help them. He manages to secure an assault rifle from one of the dead Rangers and uses it to join Harry's assault.

As the firefight continues, Sophie demands that someone untie them and get them out of the line of fire. One of the Rangers does so and takes them upstairs, and the raiders lock them inside a bedroom.

Left to their own devices, Crystal reveals that her dad installed hinges on the bars across the windows so that they can be opened in case of a fire. She unlocks the bars and they sneak out onto the roof, but a stalker chases them back into the bedroom. They don't manage to shut the bars in time, and they're forced to blockade themselves in the en-suite bathroom.

The stalker begins shredding through the door to get at them.

Downstairs, Devon, the leader of the raiders, is growing desperate as Harry picks off the last of his men. He gets some heavier firepower from the armory in the basement and uses it against Harry as he breaks down the front door. Harry appears to succumb to a combination of grenades and incendiary shotgun rounds.

At the sound of the commotion upstairs, Devon sends one of his men and a Ranger up to investigate. The Ranger is gutted by the stalker, but the raider kills it with incendiary rounds, lighting the room on fire in the process.

Crystal and the others come out of the bathroom to find the room ablaze. Downstairs, Devon uses a stick of dynamite to deal a killing blow to Harry. The house is collapsing and on fire. Devon flees, but Adam intercepts him on the way out, beating him badly and leaving him unconscious on the ground. Adam runs into the burning building to find Crystal.

Upstairs, the only other surviving raider is just about to lock the hostages in the bedroom when Adam barrels into him from behind. After a brief scuffle, Adam shoots the raider in the shoulder, but the man takes Crystal hostage and uses her as a shield. As the raider is dragging her out, Harry comes up from downstairs and kills him.

Harry is still alive, but missing an arm from

the dynamite blast. His armor has sealed it off to keep him from losing too much blood. Carla and Connor realize who he is, and they share a brief but confusing reunion. Harry isn't the same man anymore. Adam leads them out of the burning building.

Once outside, Crystal remembers that her dog, Bowser, is locked in the basement. She dashes in to save him, and Adam runs after her. Devon ambushes Adam at the top of the stairs. Just before Devon can kill him, Bowser attacks. Crystal steals Devon's gun and shoots him in both knees, leaving him to burn.

On their way out of the house, Adam gets trapped by collapsing debris. The heat of the blaze causes the alien growths on his head to fall off. Harry lifts the debris off him, but Adam's legs are badly burned. Harry insists that they go to his ship where he proceeds to treat their injuries with advanced Specter medical tech.

When he's done, there is a brief stand-off as Harry insists that they be submitted to integration therapy. Adam shoots Harry, hitting one of the alien creatures attached to his skull. It shrieks as it dies, and suddenly Harry seems to return to his old self. He warns them that they need to leave, saying that others will come to investigate after he dies.

Harry dies in his wife's arms, and the second alien growth detaches from the other side of his skull, leaving a gaping hole in his head. The creature tries to latch on to one of them, but they quickly kill it before it can.

Fleeing the alien vessel, they pile into the truck, and Adam drives over to the stables to free the horses. A stalker intercepts him on his way back to the vehicle, but Owen crashes into it, and Adam jumps in on the passenger's side. While they're driving away, Crystal shoots and kills the stalker.

They drive on, looking for a safe place to spend the night. Finding an abandoned gas station, they lock themselves in the back room and discuss what their next steps should be. Adam shares what he learned from Casey in the Stalker den, about the captured Specter starship in Chicago and the colony on Sanctum.

They wonder if it's true and also how they can possibly make the twelve-hundred-mile journey to Chicago. They almost died several times on the way to Travis, and Chicago is ten times as far. Yet Adam is determined that they have to try. With their home burned to the ground, and Rangers and Raiders alike now after them, joining the Coalition could be their only hope.

PART ONE: FINDING REFUGE

CHAPTER ONE

March 19th, 2032
Texas Hill Country

Adam's forearm ached from squeezing the hand pump to pipe fuel down from one of two diesel drums in the back of the truck to the aging F350's bone-dry tank.

While he worked the pump, Adam watched a vivid sunrise seep into the clouds, turning them blood-red. Birds flitted between the tops of trees and the decaying buildings around the gas station where they'd spent the night. The birds were up and chirping, making the morning seem almost cheerful, but a heavy weight rested on Adam's shoulders.

A lot had happened in the last three days. He'd lost his oldest surviving friend, Rick Jackson, to stalkers. They'd learned that the Specters were taking human captives and turning them into mindless slaves. They'd driven up to Travis to tell the governor of the Republic about it, and he'd tried to have them killed—no doubt because he was somehow involved.

Then Adam was captured and dragged down into a stalker den. While he was down there, he'd heard a rumor from another captive that the North American Coalition had stolen a Specter starship in Chicago and they were using it to smuggle people to safety on another planet, code-named Sanctum. Adam managed to escape the stalkers' den with the help of his old neighbor, Harry Cooper, who had spent the last eight years since the invasion as one of the Specters' slaves.

Harry flew him back to the ranch in one of the Specter's landers, where they discovered that Sunny Valley had been taken over by Raiders and corrupt Rangers from the Kerr Safe Zone. With Harry's help, they defeated the raiders and Rangers and rescued their people, but the ranch was burned to the ground. Harry wanted to turn them all into alien slaves like him, but Adam shot him in the head, and they fled the ranch.

Now they were contemplating the drive to Chicago to join the Coalition and find out if the rumors about Sanctum and the stolen Spec starship were true.

Adam wasn't sure what to think, but after everything that had happened at the ranch, it wouldn't be long before they were wanted throughout both the Republic and the Syndicate. That left only one safe place for them to go—north, to the Coalition.

"We almost ready to go?"

Adam turned to see Owen Brooks stepping through the shattered doors of the gas station. The others were right behind him. Bowser ducked between their legs with an excited yip, and then the nine-year-old Golden Retriever began sniffing energetically around a patch of dried blood on the pavement.

Adam frowned, wondering if someone else had tried to hide here before them, only to get ripped apart by stalkers. Or maybe that blood was the work of Raiders.

"Just fueling up," Adam replied.

Crystal and Connor split off from the others, holding hands as they followed Bowser. Adam watched his daughter go with a frown, wondering if he could trust her with Connor. Especially now. Connor was obviously holding a grudge after Adam had shot his father. But the man that Adam had killed wasn't his father. He'd barely remembered Connor, or his wife Carla, and he'd been obsessed with turning them into slaves of the Specters just like him.

Owen walked over to stand beside him, while Carla and Sophie hung back with Emily by the entrance of the gas station.

"So? What's our play here?" the former accountant asked. He ran his hands through thinning mid-length brown hair. He was six-feet-tall and skinny as a rail after years of hard-living on the ranch. His hollow cheeks did little to conceal the jutting curves of his skull, making him look like he already had one foot in the grave.

After the battle at the ranch, Adam felt about as good as Owen looked.

"We head for Chicago," Adam answered, nodding to Owen. He studied Carla in the background, hugging her shoulders against the cool morning air and looking small and lonely as she watched her son walking Bowser with Crystal.

Carla noticed him looking at her, and she flashed a smile. At thirty-six she was the youngest of the adults in their group, but she could have passed for twenty-six in a heartbeat. While hard-living had made Owen look old and tired, it had done little to diminish Carla's beauty. Her romantic interest in him was giving him more to live for than he'd ever thought possible. Adam never thought he'd get over Kimberly's death, and he still hadn't, but maybe moving on didn't have to mean forgetting.

Diesel fuel came gurgling out of the tank, splashing Adam's boots. He cursed and stopped squeezing the hand pump.

"All full," he announced as he withdrew the nozzle and fed it back through the narrow slit in the soldered metal sheets at the top of the truck topper.

Owen pointed to the small of Adam's back where he had tucked their only remaining weapon—a Glock 17 with just three bullets left in the clip. "What happens if we run into trouble along the way? It's got to be at least a thousand miles to Chicago from here."

"More," Adam replied.

"So..." Owen trailed off meaningfully. "We ran into a lot of resistance on the way to Travis, and that was *before* we killed a squad of Rangers. This time it'll be worse. We'll have to stay off the main roads, and that means running into scavs and raiders. There's no way in hell we'll make it without guns."

"No, we won't," Adam agreed. "We'll need to gear up along the way."

"That's a great idea," Owen drawled. "You know where we can do that?" he asked. "After eight years of raiders and scavs taking anything of value from the wastes, it's not like we're just going to find a cache of weapons lying around somewhere."

"Actually, we might," Adam replied.

"If you're thinking about going back to the ranch, forget it. The fire will have destroyed everything in the armory. Not to mention how much debris we'd have to remove just to get access to the basement."

Adam shook his head. "I'm not talking about the ranch."

Owen's eyebrows lifted in question. "Then

where?"

"There was a full Ranger outpost in Bandera."

Owen's eyes widened, then narrowed suspiciously. "Was. Now there's a Spec terraformer in its place."

"Yeah, and because of it, all of the Rangers' hardware will still be right where they left it. We just have to find a way to get past the terraformer."

"Because that's so easy. It'll shoot us from a mile away."

"Not if we can stay out of its line of sight."

"If there's a way to do that, Rangers would have already found it and recovered their gear."

"Maybe not," Adam argued. "That terraformer hasn't been there long. If Rangers are going back there, they might still be planning their mission."

"And if you're wrong, we'll be risking our lives for nothing."

"Do you have a better idea?"

"No."

"Then I'd say it's worth a shot."

Owen turned to regard his wife, Sophie, standing some twenty feet away with Emily and Carla. "We can't take everyone. It's too dangerous."

"No," Adam agreed. "Just you and me. We stay light and move fast. If all goes according to plan, we'll be back before lunch."

Owen blew out a weary sigh. "Sophie is *not* going to like this. Just look at what happened the last time we went on a mission together."

"I could go on my own," Adam suggested.

Owen snorted. "You could also die on your own. Our odds are better with two than one. And besides, if you do find a cache of weapons, you can't carry them all on your own. You tell your daughter about what you're planning?"

Adam shook his head. "Not yet."

"She's not going to like it either."

"Nope," Adam agreed. "We'll tell our families together. Come on."

CHAPTER TWO

Up ahead the bristling bulk of the Spec terraformer painted a deadly shadow across the faded blue line of the horizon, blocking the road to Bandera. Having gotten as close to the alien monstrosity as he dared, Adam pulled off the road and into an old RV park. The rusting remains of a few RVs and cars still dotted the spaces between empty lots. Adam pulled into a patch of overgrown brown grass that was surrounded by thick trees and bushes.

"We'll go from here," Adam said.

"This is too dangerous," Sophie objected. "We'll find another way to get supplies."

"There isn't any other way," Adam replied while meeting her gaze in the rear-view mirror.

"I'm going with you," Crystal added.

He twisted around in his seat to regard his daughter directly. Bowser fixed him with a goofy grin, seeming to agree with Crystal's sentiment. "You're staying right here, young lady."

Crystal scowled and crossed her arms, and

Bowser stopped grinning. "You're going to get yourself killed."

Sophie nodded her agreement, and Emily slowly shook her head, her eyes fixed on her father. Sandwiched between Sophie and Crystal with Bowser standing on her legs, Emily looked more like a kid than a seventeen-year-old girl. She had curly black hair that she'd gotten from her grandmother, and warm brown eyes that were all Owen's.

"We'll be fine," Adam said, nodding to Crystal. "And you going with us isn't going to make it any safer. Sophie, if you run into any trouble here, I want you to drive back to the gas station. We'll meet you there." He pointed to the keys, still dangling from the ignition.

Sophie sighed and nodded, reluctantly giving in.

"Owen? Let's go." Adam retrieved his Glock from the door, then popped it open and hopped out. Tucking the gun into the waistband of his jeans, he walked around to the back of the truck and unlatched the custom-built armored metal doors where the tailgate should have been. They were freckled with dents and ragged holes from their encounter with raiders in Medina two days ago. Carla and Connor were in the back, sitting on sleeping bags for cushions, with their backs propped against the diesel drums.

Adam reached in for a backpack full of basic

survival gear and slung it over his shoulders. "You should go sit up front with the others," he suggested.

Carla and Connor stood and came shuffling out, their backs hunched from the low ceiling.

Adam helped Carla down, she stumbled and fell against him in a way that seemed almost deliberate. Connor glared at them as he stalked away, muttering, "murderer," under his breath.

"Ignore him," Carla whispered. "That wasn't Harry you killed."

Adam nodded. "Maybe not, but I don't think Connor sees it that way."

"He'll come around. You just worry about staying alive out there."

Adam nodded, and Carla stepped up on her toes to kiss him. His lips moved feebly against hers, then with more insistence as she bit his lip. Sparks flew in Adam's brain, reviving parts of him that he'd left for dead a long time ago.

Owen cleared his throat meaningfully.

Carla pulled away from Adam, her hand trailing down his chest as she went.

Owen reached into the truck for a second pack of basic supplies. "We need to hurry. We might not be the only ones making plans to raid Bandera," he warned. "And I don't need to tell you that we're in no position to fight over it, so we need to make sure we're the first ones there."

"Agreed," Adam said.

Owen zipped open his pack, checking the supplies. Adam shrugged out of his to do the same. Inside he found a canteen full of water, some purification tablets, a compass, a barbecue lighter, a hunting knife, a hand-crank flashlight, a candle, a blanket, some beef jerky, two old protein bars from before the invasion, and a first-aid kit.

"It's not much, but it'll have to do," Adam decided. Reaching in, he pocketed the compass and clipped the canteen to his belt.

"If we were well-stocked, we'd be on our way to Chicago already," Owen replied, adding a canteen to his belt as well.

Adam spotted a big green duffel bag with spare clothes bleeding from the open zipper. He dragged it over, emptied the clothes on the truck bed, and stuffed the empty bag inside his pack, thinking they could pack it full of guns and ammo.

"How long are you planning to be gone?" Carla asked, sounding suspicious now that they'd made such a thorough inventory of their supplies.

Adam looked at her as he shouldered the bag once more. "Three, maybe four hours. We'll be back in time for lunch."

"Well, we won't be eating one unless you find some food," Carla pointed out.

"There should be plenty of MREs at the outpost," Adam replied. Carla made a face, and Adam smiled. "Beggars can't be choosers," he said. Reaching for her hand, he squeezed it before setting out toward the trees. Owen hurried to catch up.

Just before they waded into the shadows, Adam turned back and waved. He couldn't see anyone through the sun glinting off the spider's web of cracks in the windshield, but he was pretty sure that they could see him.

Adam waded through the bushes and pushed low-hanging branches aside as they made their way to the edge of the RV park. They had a long journey ahead of them if they were going to get to Bandera and back before lunch.

Adam scanned their surroundings for signs of danger, but all he saw were more trees, dry grass, and scrappy bushes. The sound of cicadas buzzing and birds chirping filled the air. He pressed on through the trees for a few more minutes, eventually coming to the end of their cover.

"Halt," Adam whispered as he crouched behind the trunk of a big oak tree. Up ahead he saw the shadowy bulk of the terraformer hovering some twenty feet above the highway. The air beneath it was a swirling maelstrom of debris getting sucked into whatever alien machinery was busy recycling the debris into useful compounds.

"Now what?" Owen whispered.

Adam studied the terrain ahead. There was

a church between them and the terraformer, and a few more trees scattered about the grounds, but no real cover to speak of. Certainly not enough to make Adam feel comfortable about approaching a heavily fortified enemy position. Looking away from the road and to his right, he saw more of the same scrappy copses of trees and bushes that they'd used to get this far.

Adam pulled out his compass to take a bearing to the Terraformer—only to find that the needle on the compass was spinning like a helicopter's rotors. "Great," he muttered.

"What's wrong?" Owen whispered, leaning over Adam's shoulder for a look at the compass. "What on Earth?" he muttered.

"There must be some strong magnetic fields around that thing," Adam said. He pocketed the compass with a frown and nodded to a copse of trees in the exact opposite direction of the terraformer. "I think that's roughly south. We'll head down that way until we lose sight of it and see if we can circle around behind."

"Out of sight, out of cross-hairs. Sounds good to me," Owen replied.

Adam carefully stood and retreated into the cover of the trees, then he turned and walked due south. He kept pulling out his compass along the way, periodically checking to see if it had stopped spinning. After about half an hour of walking, the needle finally stopped spinning, but it was pointing to the terraformer as due north, which of course wasn't accurate.

They reached a lazy river with thick walls of trees growing along both banks, and the buzzing of the cicadas was joined by croaking frogs and chirping crickets. Adam stopped and leaned against a tree trunk to drink from his canteen. Owen stood beside him, gasping between gulps of water.

"Unless I miss my guess," Adam began while taking another sip from his canteen, "That's Medina River. It should take us to Bandera if we follow it." Adam absently massaged his bad leg. The calf was aching where he'd taken a bullet at the end of his tour in Afghanistan, but the pain was only about a three out of ten. Nothing he couldn't grin and bear.

"Lead the way, Sergeant."

Adam frowned at the reference to his old Army rank. He didn't think of himself as a soldier anymore.

They pushed on down the river, venturing farther and farther from the RV park where they'd left the others. The landscape gradually changed from the lush, familiar greens of trees and grass around the river to something else entirely. Something alien.

Adam came to a sudden halt and slowly drew the Glock from behind his back. The transition between familiar and unfamiliar flora was punctuated by gnarled gray branches of terrestrial trees that had mysteriously dropped all of their leaves, and by patches of greasy black grass and shrubbery that looked like it had either been burned or covered in tar.

Beyond that were exotic alien plants that seemed to be made of glass, and which shimmered in a variety of colors. Massive, crystalline spires jutted to the sky, glowing and pulsing with waves of internal light. Short, fat blue trunks and crusty green growths littered the ground, hissing with steady puffs of respiration. Another kind of tree soared to impressive heights with smooth black trunks and giant canopies of rose-bud-shaped leaves, while others were like massive ferns, with feathery white fronds. Still more looked like giant mushrooms. Thick, dangling sheets of black moss seemed to fill every available gap that wasn't already blocked by the rose-bud trees or the mushrooms and the crystalline spires. Together, the foliage formed high walls and a dense canopy that almost entirely blotted out the sun, plunging the ground below into a quasi-twilight.

Adam glanced back the way they'd come, to the bright blue sky peeking between the more familiar greens of the foliage growing along the river.

Here at the border between two worlds, the droning of insects and frogs had grown ominously silent, leaving far more alien sounds to punctuate the air: a brittle humming noise that seemed to modulate up and down in frequency, the steady hissing of the plants' breathing, and a few piercing shrieks that Adam thought might have been stalkers.

"That terraformer did all of this?" Owen whispered.

"Hard to believe," Adam agreed.

In all of his trips through Bandera to reach the Bexar County Safe Zone, he'd never seen an alien jungle like this one. This was new, and it was his first time seeing one of them up close. He'd heard stories from others about what the terraformers left in their wake, but it was hard to imagine how something like this could be planted in a matter of just a few weeks or months. Maybe there were whole jungles like this one already pre-grown and sitting on conveyor belts inside those terraformers, just waiting to be rolled out like sod.

But that wouldn't explain how fast they spread. Once a jungle like this one was planted, it doubled in size every month, which was where people got their estimates of fifty to a hundred years before the Specs would have terraformed the entire Earth.

"Can we go around it?" Owen asked.

Adam looked up from the river bank, but he could see no end of the jungle. On their side of the transition zone long brown grass and scattered trees tracked back up to the highway where the terraformer was. The trees were too sparse to provide consistent cover. On the other hand, the alien foliage would make excellent cover, but there was no telling what other kinds of trouble they might encounter in there.

On seeing that jungle, Adam began to fear that there might not be anything left of the Ranger outpost and that they'd come all this way for nothing.

"We'll follow the jungle back up to the road," Adam decided. "We can duck into it for cover if we need to."

Owen eyed the shadowy depths of the jungle dubiously. "Yeah… let's hope we don't have to."

Adam nodded his agreement. Not a lot was known about those jungles because the people who ventured into them never came back out. He could only imagine why. The going theory about stalkers hunting at night was they couldn't stand daylight. It was too bright for them. But in there, safely covered by an impenetrable canopy of alien flora, the stalkers would feel free to hunt at all hours of the day and night.

Adam turned away from the river and followed the dead black band of grass in the transition zone like a road back to the highway. He couldn't see the terraformer yet. Hopefully, they were far enough away now that it was no longer a threat.

But after about five minutes of walking up from the river, Adam saw a dark black shadow come seeping through the trees, and he ducked behind an old, rusting RV.

Owen peeked around the back bumper. "It hasn't shot at us. Maybe it doesn't care? Probably doesn't consider us a threat."

"We can't risk it," Adam replied. He peered across the dead black grass into the obsidian depths of the jungle, then followed the ragged line of unfamiliar foliage up to the highway. It formed an unbroken wall across the road, disappearing endlessly into the distance. The Ranger outpost was on the other side of that jungle.

"We'll have to go through," Adam decided.

Owen gaped at him. "Are you crazy?"

Adam shook his head. "You said it yourself. We can't get to Chicago without guns, and it's not like we can trade for them. Even if we had the credits, the safe zones will shoot us on sight once they learn that we killed a squad of Rangers."

"It was self-defense," Owen objected.

"Good luck proving that. Mayor Maloney will deny sending them to take over the ranch, and it'll be our word against his."

"With seven of us all singing the same tune, someone's bound to believe us," Owen argued. "Maybe not in Kerr, but we could go to Bexar.

We have a history with Mayor Ellis. He might want to help us when he hears our story."

Adam wiped a trickling bead of sweat from his brow off on his sleeve. "Bexar is on the other side of that." He pointed again to the jungle.

"We could drive back toward the ranch, then head south through Tarpley, down to Hondo, and east through Castroville."

Adam frowned. "Those roads aren't patrolled. Or even cleared. It'll be slow going, and we'll run the risk of running into more raiders."

Owen pointed to the wall of darkness ahead of them. "It's either that, or we risk running into stalkers in there."

"If we're quiet, maybe they'll stay in their dens."

"That's a hell of a thin hope to hang onto. What if we get turned around in there and we can't find our way out? Your compass doesn't even work properly."

Adam pulled it out of his pocket and saw the needle spinning furiously once more. He tucked it away with a deepening frown and stared hard at the shadowy barrier in front of them. They were so close. The temptation to push on was overwhelming. But damn it, Owen was right. It was too dangerous. Guns wouldn't do them any good if they were dead.

"Fine," Adam ground out.

Owen released a breath, and his shoulders

sagged. "Thank God."

"Don't thank Him yet," Adam replied. "We still have to make it to Bexar." He turned and crept away from the RV, heading back the way they'd come.

***

"Was that truck there yesterday?" a man asked in a heavy Southern accent.

"I don't think so," another one answered in a smoother baritone.

"That means someone drove it here," the first one said. "Check the front, see if you can find the keys. I'll look in the back."

"Copy that," the baritone replied.

Crystal crouched in the sweaty darkness of the back of the truck with the others, doing her best not to breathe. She had both hands wrapped around Bowser's snout. He was struggling to break free.

A muffled *woof* sneaked out. Carla's eyes flared wide, and she held a trembling finger to her lips. Connor scooted over, adding his hands around Crystal's to better muffle Bowser's growing concerns.

Emily and Sophie were crouching by the back doors, peeking out through the bullet holes.

They'd locked all the doors, but that wouldn't stop a determined effort to get in.

A few minutes ago, they'd seen these two swaggering down from the road with their cowboy hats and stolen assault rifles. Stolen, because if they were Rangers, they'd be wearing old Army fatigues, not jeans and dirty T-shirts.

Sophie had almost driven off, but those men had a Humvee parked at the entrance of the RV park, and they'd left a guy behind to man the machine gun on the roof. If Sophie had tried to drive away, she'd only have gotten them captured or killed. Hiding was their best option, but they might have only delayed the inevitable.

The handle of the back door jiggled and the doors rattled loudly.

Another muffled woof escaped Bowser's lips. Crystal cringed, expecting the man outside to hear it and call the alarm.

"It's locked," the Southern man said. "What about the front?"

"Same," the one with the deep voice called back. "I could break a window, but I don't see any keys."

"Think you can hot-wire it?"

"I don't know. Maybe."

"You know what, don't trouble yourself. Someone drove it up here and locked all the doors before they left."

"What are you thinking?" Baritone replied.

"I'm thinking they went down to the river to wash up and re-fill their water jugs. That's not gonna take 'em all day, so we wait here for them to come back."

"I like it."

"Come on. Those trees look like good cover to me."

A low growl rumbled out of Bowser's chest.

Crystal listened as the men's voices receded into the distance. The baritone laughed boomingly at something the Southern guy said.

Carla stood up to peek out the narrow slits at the top of the truck topper. "One of them is hiding in the bushes," Carla said. "The other is running back up the road to the Humvee."

Sophie joined her at the gap to see for herself. "This is not good," she whispered.

Crystal wanted to look, too, but she couldn't afford to release Bowser. If he barked, even once, those two would come running back and break in. Or they'd just fire their rifles indiscriminately through the back until all of them were dead.

"What do we do?" Emily squeaked in a thready whisper.

Everyone looked at her, and Sophie slowly shook her head.

"We have to warn my dad," Crystal said.

Carla nodded her agreement.

"Anything we do will reveal us," Sophie argued. "We can't sneak out with them watching the truck."

"Then we wait until Adam and Owen are close," Carla suggested. "And we call out a warning."

"That'll just start a firefight," Connor muttered. "And Adam has what, like two bullets left in that Glock?"

Sophie cringed. "The only way this works is if our people get a drop on theirs."

"Maybe my dad or Owen will realize that something is wrong, and we won't have to warn them?" Crystal suggested.

Sophie fixed her with a grim look. "If they don't, they're going to walk straight into a trap."

CHAPTER THREE

Up ahead, Adam saw the dirty, discolored sides of moldering RVs dotting the golden pools of sunlight between the trees.

"Almost there," Adam breathed, stopping to massage his leg. Feeling both legs prickling and tickling with sweat, he pulled up a pant leg to check on the burns on the backs of his legs. Just one night after Harry had coated them with that clear, viscous fluid from the alien lander's medical supplies, his burns were almost completely better. He could see fresh pink skin where before there had been ragged black and red flesh.

Owen stopped beside him to regard the healing wounds. "Still hurts?"

"Itches," Adam replied. Straightening, he pulled in a deep breath and let it out in a shaky sigh. "Let's go. We've got a long drive ahead of us."

Adam was already imagining just *how* long that drive would be. Technically, it wasn't that far to the Bexar Safe Zone, but the roads would be blocked by everything from fallen trees to derelict vehicles—and maybe even a few deliberate roadblocks.

Adam stepped out of the shadows into the blazing sunlight. He squinted and put a hand to his brow, wishing he still had his old leather cowboy hat.

The dry golden brown grass came up almost to their waists, rustling loudly as they waded through it. Somewhere a crow or a raven squawked, and Adam flexed a sweaty palm on the grip of his pistol.

Feeling suddenly exposed, he glanced about warily. They pulled alongside the entrance to a baby-blue mobile home with broken windows and a slumping roof. A small black shadow flitted through the air, landing on the porch and drawing Adam's gaze there. A human arm was dangling through the railing. A crow was perched on the elbow, picking strips of glistening red flesh from the man's biceps. A second crow landed beside it and began fighting for the scrap of meat.

Adam's heart rate spiked. He froze and brought his gun up in a steady two-handed grip, sweeping for targets.

"What is it?" Owen whispered.

Not seeing any signs of trouble, Adam sprinted quietly for the mobile home.

"Adam, what's wrong?" Owen asked as he hurried to catch up. They reached the railing, scaring off the crows with a flurry of wings and angry cawing. Owen appeared to notice the dead man lying on the porch and he promptly threw up an arm to cover his nose from the pungent stench of decay. "Shit," Owen mumbled into his sleeve.

Adam studied the corpse with a grimace. The smell was pretty strong already, but he could tell from the relatively pristine state of the body that this man hadn't died that long ago. Despite the heat, the body hadn't even started to bloat yet. Then Adam noticed something else, and he stiffened.

"What is it?" Owen asked.

Adam gestured to the man's chest. At first glance, it was hard to tell how he'd died, but the gleaming brass bullet casings scattered around the porch were a clue, as were the four roughly symmetrical circles of blood that had soaked into his dirty gray shirt.

"Someone shot him," Owen realized.

"Yeah," Adam agreed. "A day or two ago, at most." He dropped to his haunches to pluck one of the empty casings off the porch and study it, but he already knew what caliber it was. He held one up for Owen to see.

"What caliber is it?" Owen asked.

"Five fifty-six," Adam replied. "Fired from an M4 carbine if I had to guess."

"Rangers?" Owen whispered, glancing around suddenly.

Adam nodded. "Or someone who took their weapons."

"Rangers wouldn't shoot an unarmed man," Owen replied.

Adam straightened and arched an eyebrow at him. "You mean like they wouldn't team up with Raiders to steal our ranch?"

Owen frowned.

Adam shook his head. "It doesn't matter who killed him. We need to get out of here before they come back. Stay low and quiet, we're going to sneak around through the trees." Adam nodded sideways to indicate a thicket of young oak and elm trees behind the mobile home.

Adam moved quickly to the back corner of the house. He stopped to peek around it and make sure they were clear before running across the overgrown backyard to the trees.

They fought through the underbrush as quietly as they could to get back to their truck. As soon as Adam saw it come peeking through the branches, he knew that something was wrong. All the windows were rolled up, and the cab appeared to be empty. If Crystal and the others were inside, they'd have the windows down to get a breeze flowing.

"Where are they?" Owen whispered.

"Hiding, I hope," Adam replied. He raised his Glock again in a two-handed grip and pushed down a sweaty surge of dread. "Stay here," Adam added.

"I'm coming with you," Owen said.

Adam regarded him steadily. "You're unarmed."

"My family is on the line, too, damn it!"

"Keep your voice down!" Adam hissed. He shook his head. "If you want to help them, then stay here. I'm trained for this, you're not. If you put one foot wrong, it'll all be over."

Owen licked his lips. "What if whoever it is already took our families and left?"

"They didn't. Our truck is too valuable to leave behind, and Sophie has the keys."

"Well, maybe everyone just got out to stretch their legs? Or to go to the bathroom. We could be panicking over nothing."

Adam nodded. "I hope so, but we can't afford to make assumptions. Stay here, I'll sweep the area and come back if I don't find anything."

"Be careful," Owen said.

Adam nodded and spent a moment scanning the trees for the best path through. Seeing one, he moved quickly, watching his steps to avoid snapping fallen twigs and branches or crunching through piles of dead leaves. When he was about halfway around the truck and the clearing, he spotted them: two men lying in the underbrush with M4 carbines trained on the truck. One was an African American man, the other Caucasian with shaggy blond hair shining the same color as the grass where the sunlight found it. Both looked young, maybe in their twenties, and neither of them was wearing a Ranger uniform.

They hadn't spotted him yet. Their attention was fixed on the clearing and the truck. They probably figured they had the element of surprise. And they would have, too, if they hadn't left that dead man lying on his porch surrounded by a constellation of spent cartridges.

Crouching behind a tree for cover, Adam considered his options. He could shoot them from here, but they were still about twenty-five feet away. Odds were that he'd miss with at least one shot, and he only had three bullets. Plus, as soon as he fired that first shot, those two would start firing back, and their rifles were a hell of a lot more accurate.

Sneaking up behind them was the better option, but if either of them heard him coming it wouldn't end well. Adam hesitated, feeling torn. Maddening trickles of sweat slithered down his spine. A mosquito buzzed around his ear, and then—

A strident *woof!* sounded from the back of the truck. The two men in the woods shifted their aim to the vehicle and Adam cringed.

A flicker of movement in the clearing caught his eye. Owen was walking out with his hands raised in plain view of the two men skulking in the trees. Adam muttered a curse under his breath. *Get back into cover, you idiot!*

Owen called out in a shaky voice. "I'm unarmed! Don't shoot!"

The raiders in the trees shifted their aim away from the truck once more, having identified Owen as a greater threat than the dog in the back of the truck.

"I don't want any trouble," Owen went on blithely. "If you need supplies, I'd be happy to share."

Adam began creeping around the clearing once more, determined to take advantage of the distraction that Owen was providing.

Maybe it wouldn't be so hard to sneak up behind them, after all.

But then a familiar *crack* split the air. Adam spun around just in time to see a puff of pink mist erupt from Owen's shoulder. He dropped like a sack of rocks, and another *woof!* erupted from the back of the truck. This time the sound was joined by a woman screaming—probably Sophie reacting to Owen getting shot.

The Caucasian man lying in the shadows pushed up to his feet and stepped into the sunlit clearing. "All right, come on out!" he ordered, waving his rifle vaguely from the hip at the back of the truck. "I'm going to count to three. One…"

Bowser was barking steadily now.

Realizing he was out of time, Adam burst into motion. He sprang to the edge of the trees, raised his gun, and planted his feet, one behind the other.

"Two!"

Sighting down the barrel of the Glock, Adam let out a slow breath to steady his aim.

"Three!"

The doors at the back of the truck flew open just before Adam squeezed the trigger.

"Wait! Don't shoot!" Carla shouted. "We're coming out."

Adam grimaced, torn between shooting the raider now and biding his time to make a more covert approach.

The raider's aim shifted to the back of the truck as Carla came out. When the man didn't immediately open fire, Adam realized that he still had time to turn this around. His eyes darted to the one still lying in the bushes, covering his buddy, and Adam edged away from the clearing, moving quickly and quietly through the trees and making sure to keep his footsteps as quiet as possible.

CHAPTER FOUR

Crystal shimmied out of the back of the truck, holding tightly to Bowser's collar to make sure he didn't do anything stupid. He was usually pretty docile, but that gunshot had spooked him. If he attacked one of those raiders he'd get his stupid butt shot off.

Connor scooped Bowser into his arms, giving Crystal a chance to clamber down, and then she and Connor rounded the back doors of the truck behind Sophie and Emily. Carla led the way to meet the young man who'd addressed them. She had both of her hands raised high above her head just as Owen's had been when that raider had shot him. Crystal stopped with the others a few steps back from Carla.

"You can have the truck," she said. "Just let us go."

The raider was tall and lanky with shaggy blonde hair and a pimply face. He was aiming an old army rifle at them, and he had a giant pistol holstered to his hip. His buddy was in the trees, lying on his stomach and sighting down the barrel of a matching weapon. The one in front of them whistled and grinned crookedly at them, revealing yellow teeth. He licked his lips and looked Carla up and down.

"Well, aren't you a pretty thing."

Bowser growled and squirmed in Connor's arms, and Crystal's stomach clenched up as a cold weight settled inside of her.

But Carla didn't even register a reaction. Maybe she was used to the way men spoke to her. Crystal was beginning to realize just how unfair the world was. Men only had to worry about physical violence, but women had to fend off sexual threats, too.

Sophie glanced back at where Owen had fallen. She was biting her lip, her eyes brimming with unshed tears, while Emily was already crying and stifling her sobs.

"You have the keys?" the pimple-faced raider asked.

"Sophie?" Carla prompted.

Emily's mother fished into her jeans pocket and produced the keys with a metallic jingling. She stepped forward and handed them to Carla.

"Toss them over," the raider said.

"Not yet," Carla insisted.

The pimple-faced raider sneered and raised his rifle, sighting down the barrel. "Okay, how about this, hand them over, or I'll shoot you."

Carla smiled thinly at him and cocked her

arm back, holding the keys high. "If you do that, I'll throw them into the trees and make you play needle in a haystack."

"You won't be throwing anything after I shoot you."

"Maybe I won't, or maybe I'll find the strength for one final act of spite. You really want to find out?"

"Bitch," the raider muttered.

"Let us get to the edge of the clearing, and we'll throw the keys to you from there."

"No deal. You could just run away."

"If we take the keys, then you'd have a reason to chase us, and my bet is you'd catch up pretty quick. This way everyone gets what they want, you get our truck and our supplies, and we get to walk out of this alive."

Crystal wanted to object and point out how they needed those supplies to survive, but then she remembered their plan. Keep them talking. Delay. If Owen was back, then her Dad was here, too, and he had to have a plan.

"What about your friend?" the raider jerked his chin to Owen.

"We'll take him with us," Carla said.

The raider sneered. "He's just going to slow you down."

"We're *not* leaving him," Emily gritted out in an icy whisper.

The raider's eyes flicked to her, then back to Carla. "Suit yourself. All right, you've got one minute. Get a move on."

Carla nodded and turned away from the raider, moving quickly. The rest of them followed her, rounding the back of the truck to reach Owen. Crystal noticed that Carla chose a path that put the vehicle between them and the raider. But it didn't last long. He moved over to keep them in his sights.

They reached Owen's side and found him face-down in the tall grass. His shoulder had been ripped apart, with the back of his shoulder blade a gaping bloody ruin of shattered bone and glistening, dark red muscle. A sticky crimson stain had seeped into the dirt and grass around him, and he wasn't moving. Sophie stifled a sob as she fell to her knees beside him.

"Owen," she said, touching his arm and shaking him gently.

Emily had stopped crying. Now she looked pale with shock, staring down at her father with a slack jaw and wide eyes. Suddenly she seemed ten years younger, a little girl realizing that her daddy wasn't immortal.

Owen groaned, and stirred feebly, mumbling something.

"Thank God, he's alive," Carla whispered.

"Help me get him up," Sophie said. Carla dropped to her haunches and together they turned him over. Crystal gasped at the sight of Owen's ashen face. Blood was bubbling steadily from both sides of his shoulder.

"Hey! I said one minute, remember?" the raider called to them.

"We have to stop the bleeding!" Sophie shouted back at the raider.

"I can put him out of his misery if you like!" the raider quipped.

"Fuck you," Sophie muttered under her breath.

"Here," Connor handed Bowser back to Crystal, and she sagged under the dog's weight. He shrugged out of his long-sleeved button-up shirt, leaving just his dirt and grass-stained white undershirt below.

Sophie took the shirt and worked quickly to tie it around Owen's shoulder. It wasn't even close to good enough as a tourniquet. He was still bleeding through it. Owen's eyelids fluttered and he groaned again. "I feel cold," he said.

"Stay with me, Owen," Sophie urged. Looking up, she stared hard at the back of the truck. "We need the field dressings from the med kit."

"Ten seconds!" the raider announced.

"I don't think he's going to let us get them," Connor muttered.

"If we don't, then Owen is going to die!"

Carla released a heavy sigh. "We should have grabbed them when we got out."

"I'll do it," Sophie insisted. "Keep pressure on

the wound." She jumped to her feet and started back toward the vehicle.

Crystal apprehensively watched her go. If her Dad was out there, he needed to act *now*.

"I hope you're coming over here to hand me the keys!"

"I need a bandage to stop the bleeding!"

"Those are *my* bandages now," the raider replied.

"He'll die without it!" Sophie insisted, not skipping a step.

"Not my problem!" the raider said, raising his rifle and taking aim.

Carla glanced anxiously over her shoulder. "She's going to get herself killed."

Bowser yipped and struggled to free himself from Crystal's grip. She squeezed him tight and buried her face in his fur, not wanting to see what happened next. "It's going to be okay, Bowie. It's going to be okay…" she whispered.

CHAPTER FIVE

Adam crept across the last few feet of ground at a snail's pace, easing each foot down with such deliberate care that he was barely moving at all. The dark-skinned raider was lying right in front of him. Adam heard the second raider warn the others that they had ten seconds left, and he knew that he was out of time.

He considered shooting the man, but that would provoke an immediate reaction from the one in the clearing. If he could take this one out silently it would be much better, but doing that presented a far greater risk, and he needed to get even closer to be able to do it.

Gritting his teeth, Adam eased through the last couple of feet until he was almost standing beside the raider. He'd made sure to sneak up on the man's right side since that cheek and eye were pressed to the stock and scope, reducing his peripheral vision on that side.

Having closed the distance between them as much as he dared, Adam flipped his Glock around, clutching the barrel like the handle of a hammer. He dropped to the ground and brought it down as hard as he could into the back of the raider's skull. The man had only a fraction of a second to react. He began to roll over—

And then the Glock cracked into his skull, and his body went limp. He collapsed into the bed of dead leaves with a bloody gash on the back of his bald scalp. Adam tucked the Glock into the waistband of his jeans and snatched the army carbine away from the unconscious raider. He whipped it up and quickly aimed down the scope to the other raider's back.

"Not my problem!" that man shouted to Sophie, who was moving quickly toward the open doors at the back of their truck.

Adam lined up a spot directly between the raider's shoulder blades.

"He's my husband!" Sophie cried. "Please!"

"Tough shit, lady!"

Adam squeezed the trigger. The rifle went off with an ear-splitting report, and the raider cried out, firing his weapon as he fell. His shot went wide, plinking into the back of the truck, but Sophie hit the ground anyway, taking cover.

Adam stepped out of the trees, moving quickly and scanning for more targets as he went. Not seeing anyone, he sprinted into the clearing to check on the raider he'd shot. The man was lying face up, his eyes staring, and blood bubbling from his lips. The exit wound was off to the right of his heart, but it was hard to imagine that he'd live through the injury. His rifle lay beside him, but his hands weren't even twitching toward it. Adam kicked the carbine away from him, just in case, and then ran the rest of the way to reach Sophie. She was busy digging around in the back of the truck. By the time he arrived, she was already pulling out thick pads of gauze, and two Army-issue hemorrhage control bandages still sealed in gray plastic.

"About time you showed up," Sophie groused at him as she ducked out of the truck, and ran back to Owen.

Adam hurried after her with a frown, glancing about warily as he went. He shot a quick look at the man he'd left in the trees. Still not moving. He wondered absently if he'd accidentally dealt that raider a killing blow with the Glock.

"How could you let him go out on his own?" Sophie demanded.

"I didn't," Adam replied. "I told him *not* to come out."

They reached Owen's side and Sophie tore the bandage open with her teeth. Crystal met his gaze with an anxious look. Bowser squirmed in her arms, panting and grinning. Failing to break free, he woofed stridently.

Adam patted him quickly on the head. "It's okay, boy," he whispered, and then his gaze drifted back to Owen as Sophie and Carla worked to bandage his ruined shoulder.

The rattling roar of a truck's engine caught Adam's attention, drawing his gaze to the dirt road running through the RV park. An army-green Humvee came rolling into view with a fifty-caliber *"ma deuce"* mounted on the roof.

"Everyone get down!" Adam roared. Crystal and Connor dropped, but Emily took an extra second to follow suit. Adam tucked the carbine hard to his shoulder and aimed down the sights. Seeing a hint of a shadow behind the windshield, he fired twice in quick succession, starring the glass with two bullet holes. Despite that, a moment later, someone jumped up behind the turret and the barrel swung into line with him. Adam fired twice more. Blood misted the air around the gunner. He slumped over the roof, and the machine gun tipped up to the sky.

Adam relaxed his stance and let out a shaky breath. Glancing back at Owen, he saw that Sophie had just finished applying the field dressing.

"We need to move," Adam said. "Can he walk?"

Sophie shook her head. "He shouldn't."

Adam grimaced. "Connor, help them carry Owen."

The boy nodded, and Emily scrambled to her feet to add her hands to the task. Between the two of them and Sophie and Carla, they hoisted Owen into the air, drawing an agonized cry from his lips. Like that, they crab-walked back to the truck with Adam leading the way and keeping them covered.

They'd scarcely made it ten steps before Adam realized that something was wrong. The man he'd knocked out was missing.

Adam cursed under his breath, swinging the rifle around and checking for signs of an ambush. The clearing was empty. No sign of him anywhere. Had he run off to get reinforcements, or…?

An electric prickle of dread raised hairs on the back of Adam's neck. That was his only warning. "Contact!" he shouted even before he understood why.

The others darted behind the truck, stumbling along under Owen's weight. Adam ducked behind the open doors at the back just as a bullet zipped past his ear from the direction of the trees.

He dropped to the ground and peeked around the rear wheel, popping off a shot of his own to make the shooter keep his head down.

"You didn't *kill* the other one?" Sophie hissed.

Adam didn't reply, focusing instead on finding the missing raider.

"Help me get Owen in the cab," Sophie grunted, nodding sideways to indicate the doors on their side.

They shuffled down the length of the truck, and Connor spared a hand from Owen to yank open the back door.

Owen cried out again as his weight shifted. Another crack of rifle fire shattered a window, and Carla screamed. This time Adam spied a hint of movement in the shadows. Aiming quickly he fired back—

And heard a muffled cry erupt from the trees. He fired again for good measure, but couldn't see if the second shot hit.

"Got him," Adam decided a moment later, and then he sprang up from the ground and hurried over to see how the others were doing.

They began sliding Owen into the back seat. Owen did his best to help them, but he looked very weak. Sophie squeezed in behind him, and Connor slammed the door.

"We'll get in the back," Crystal said. Connor nodded, and Emily started after them.

"Let me take Bowser," Carla suggested. She took the dog from Crystal, then went for the front passenger's side door.

"Wait," Adam breathed as Crystal started for the back end of the truck. He realized that he couldn't be a hundred percent *sure* that the other raider was dead, and they needed that second carbine.

He led the way and peeked around the back end of the truck again to check that they were clear. Not seeing any signs of movement in the trees, or from the road, he stepped out of cover, waving over his shoulder for the kids to follow. They climbed up and Adam shut the doors behind them.

With everyone in except for him, Adam hurried for the trees.

"Where are you going?" Carla called after him, her head popping out the shattered driver's side window.

"We need that other rifle!" he explained. Reaching the dead Caucasian raider, he stopped to collect a gleaming colt python revolver from the man's hip. He noticed that the weapon was intricately engraved. Some kind of collector's piece.

The dying man gurgled something, blowing bloody crimson bubbles with his lips. Adam noticed how his arms were moving feebly to staunch the blood, but his legs weren't moving at all. He'd probably been paralyzed when Adam's bullet severed his spine.

Adam was tempted to put the kid out of his misery, but this raider hadn't given a damn about Owen or any of the rest of them. He didn't deserve an easy death, so he tucked the revolver into his belt and moved on. Reaching the trees, he discovered that the dark-skinned raider was also still alive. Gutshot, and sobbing from the pain. His back was propped against a tree trunk, while the other rifle lay discarded at his feet.

"Help me," the man croaked. "Please, man. I got a son. He's only five. He needs me."

Adam stooped to recover the second carbine. Frowning deeply, he regarded the man with hooded eyes. "Does the kid have a mother?"

The raider seemed to guess where Adam was headed with that, and his eyes flew wide. "Please! I can't leave them. Not like this."

"You should've kept your head down," Adam replied. "You were going to be fine, just a bump on the head and a bad headache. That would've been it. Can I see the damage?"

The man grimaced and he pulled his hands away from his stomach, revealing a glistening red loop of his intestines that he was struggling to hold inside of his pelvis.

Adam slowly shook his head. "Listen, I couldn't help you if I wanted to." He nodded to the man's stomach and aimed the carbine in his right hand at the raider's head. "You want to go the easy way or the hard way?"

The man swallowed thickly. "Oh shit. Oh shit. Please, don't. Please! You've gotta do something. Get help. Someone's gotta be able to fix this."

"What's your name?" Adam asked, feeling sick to his stomach from the man's begging.

"Jaden. Jaden Nelson."

Adam nodded and dropped to his haunches, putting on a smile and pretending to have a change of heart. "All right, I'm going to help you, Jaden. You don't deserve it, but I'm going to help you anyway. You're gonna see your kid again."

Jaden let out a ragged sigh and nodded. "Thank you."

"I'm going to go back and get a trauma bandage for you, all right?"

"Sure, man. Just hurry, please."

"I will," Adam replied, and with that, he pulled the trigger. The bullet tore straight into Jaden's heart. His jaw dropped in shock, but the light quickly left his eyes, and then his head slumped and his chin hit his chest before he could say a word.

Adam turned and fled into the sunlit clearing, his heart heavy and his throat aching with a familiar grief. He strode quickly past the other raider, not even tempted to repeat the mercy-killing with him.

Reaching the truck, he climbed in behind the steering wheel and quietly handed the two carbines over to Carla. She slipped on the safeties and placed them at her feet. Standing on her lap, Bowser regarded him with sad, drooping jowls, as if even he understood the grim weight of what Adam had done.

"He wasn't dead," Carla guessed.

"No," Adam replied.

Sophie handed him the keys, and he stuck them in the ignition, glowing the engine and then drawing a blast of hot air from the vents. Adam cranked the wheel around to get them pointed toward the road.

"How's Owen?" he asked as they drove away.

"Not good," Sophie muttered. "He lost a lot of blood while we were dealing with the raiders."

Adam sucked his teeth angrily as he drove past the Humvee, its engine still rattling away as it idled on the dirt road. He thought briefly about checking it for more supplies, but he had no way of knowing if these raiders had reinforcements coming, and Owen was in bad shape. Delaying any more than they had to could cost him his life.

"We're driving down to Bexar," Adam decided. "They can treat him there."

"What about Kerr?" Sophie asked. "You saw a doctor up there for Crystal, and the road should be clear now that we dealt with the raiders from Medina."

"Kerr sent those Rangers to take the ranch from us, and then we killed them. Even if their buddies at the gates don't recognize us, Mayor Maloney will hear that we're back, and he'll do whatever he can to cover up his part in things. We'd be lucky to get out of there alive."

Adam met Sophie's gaze in the rear-view mirror. He could tell from how pale and frightened she looked that Owen might not make it if they pushed as far as Bexar. He needed a miracle to live through this, and they both knew it.

CHAPTER SIX

"What about a direct transfusion?" Adam asked as he turned left onto the main road, heading back toward Tarpley. He caught a glimpse of the terraformer to his left, a bristling black mountain in the middle of Texas.

Sophie appeared to think about it. "I'd need an IV kit and someone with the same blood type."

"Remind me, what is his blood type?" Adam asked.

"He's a universal donor," Sophie said. "O negative, but that means he can only receive blood that's the same type as his."

"Fantastic," Adam muttered. "Well, I'm O positive."

"AB positive," Carla said.

Adam glanced in the rear-view mirror for Sophie's answer.

"A positive," she added.

Carla twisted in her seat to look at the small black window at the back of the cab. "What about Emily?"

"She's O positive," Sophie said. "Same as Adam."

"And Connor is the same as me," Carla put in.

"Crystal is A positive," Adam said. "Same as her mother." He grimaced, realizing that none of them could help Owen. "So we need to find a donor *and* an IV kit," he concluded. "How rare exactly is O negative?"

"Rare," Sophie lamented. "Only about one in ten people have it. It was always in short supply at the hospital where I worked."

"So we would need to find a settlement with at least ten or twenty people just to find one who could donate," Adam concluded. "And that's assuming they would agree to it."

"I'll be okay," Owen whispered. "I just need to rest. Can I have some water?"

Sophie produced a canteen and unscrewed the cap. "Here." She helped raise his head so that he could drink. Owen took a few sips and then laid his head back, gasping from the exertion of that simple act. "Easy," Sophie whispered.

Adam focused on the road, scanning both sides for any hint of a building that might have medical supplies. The nearest place that might have what they needed was the old volunteer fire station in Tarpley, but they would have been picked clean years ago. Hondo was their best bet. As a mid-sized town, it was bound to have a camp of scavengers living there. If they could find them, the scavs might have the supplies they needed. "Hang in there, Owen," Adam said. "We're going to find help."

He reached the turn to Tarpley and continued down Ranch Road 470. Adjoining roads periodically snaked away to various ranches and country homes, all of them abandoned, including now, Sunny Valley Ranch. They'd personally scoured at least a dozen of those places over the years, raiding them for building materials more than anything. Unfortunately, they'd lost all of their supplies when the ranch had burned down. They'd had IV kits and even a few spare bags of blood in the basement fridge. Ironically, it had been Owen's blood that they'd stored, now that Adam thought back on it. But maybe Owen was right. Maybe he just needed to rest.

***

Adam's heart slammed frantically in his chest as he drove up and down the streets of Hondo. Owen was unconscious now, and Sophie was muttering frantic prayers in the back. Considering she wasn't a religious woman, she had to be desperate.

It had taken them almost two hours just to get here, thanks to all of the debris on the road. Adam had to get out twice to physically remove fallen trees and power lines with the truck's winch. On several other occasions they'd had to push the debris aside with the truck's bull bar.

"Come on..." Adam muttered to himself, scanning the boarded-up one and two-story buildings for signs of life. At least the streets in town were clear. Hondo was one of the stops along the trade routes between the surrounding ranches and Bexar.

"We should pull over somewhere and search for supplies," Carla whispered from the front seat beside Adam. "Maybe we'll get lucky. Do you see any clinics or pharmacies?"

Bowser had his head out her window, and he was panting steadily into the hot, dry air.

Adam shook his head. "Anything worth taking is long gone. We'd have to find a place that hasn't been hit. Or an active camp of scavs."

Hondo didn't have a reputation as a raider town, but at this point, Adam would have been grateful even to see a raider waving a gun at them. At least that would mean that the town wasn't completely abandoned.

Adam crossed a set of railroad tracks and turned onto the main highway running through the town. This one was four lanes rather than two, and the buildings on either side of the road grew further apart, buffered by old, crumbling parking lots and fast-food franchises. Adam drove past a burned-out Shell station, followed by a Sonic drive-in.

Precious minutes slipped by with no sign of life anywhere. At this point, their best bet would be pushing on for the Bexar County Safe Zone.

"Hey, what about that?" Carla pointed to a familiar blue sign with a yellow 'spark' on it that looked vaguely like a sun.

Adam eased his foot off the accelerator. "Walmart? That's the first place scavs would have hit."

"Exactly," Carla replied. "Walmarts were used as shelters for a while. They were easy to fortify. Big spaces with relatively few windows, plenty of supplies, and clear sight lines all around."

"Those supplies would have run out years ago," Adam pointed out.

"The edible ones, sure," Carla replied. "But what about the rest? And they're still more defensible than houses. If there is a group of scavs here, that's where they'd be."

Not having anything better to go on, Adam nodded and turned off at the Walmart sign. They passed a few warehouse-style buildings before coming to a sprawling brown and blue one with peeling paint. The giant parking lot was completely empty, and a wall of cars were parked end-to-end in a crude fence around the perimeter. Ramshackle wooden and sheet-metal ramparts had been constructed on the roofs of those cars, and a pair of chain-link gates had been soldered to the backs of two old delivery trucks to block the road leading into the compound.

Adam hit the brakes, bringing them to a stop while they were still about thirty feet from the gates. "Looks like you were right," he said while leaning over the steering wheel and struggling to peer through the cracks in the windshield.

"Can you see anyone guarding the wall?" Sophie asked from the back.

Adam shook his head. "No. It could be abandoned."

"Pushing those cars together is a lot of work to go to just to walk away," Carla replied.

"Yeah, maybe," Adam agreed. "But that's what scavs do. They're nomads, always moving around."

"Not all of them," Carla said.

He looked at her with eyebrows raised, waiting for her to explain how she knew so much about the habits of scavengers. She'd barely left the ranch in the last eight years.

"I met one in Bexar a couple of years ago," she said. "We got to talking over a few drinks."

The way she said it made Adam think those drinks had led to something more. An echo of some old emotion rippled through him. Jealousy. He hadn't felt that since Kimberly had died, and she'd been good about making sure that he never had a reason to be jealous.

Adam made a gimme gesture to Carla. "Hand

me one of those carbines," he said in a voice that was more gruff than he'd intended.

Carla matched his frown and reached for one of the two M4s at her feet. Adam pulled back on the charging handle to check the chamber. Still loaded.

"I'll be back in a minute," he said.

"Be careful," Carla put in.

"Hurry," Sophie added.

Adam opened his door and used it for cover as he slid out and crouched behind it. He flicked off the safety on the weapon and peeked around the edge of the door.

"Hello?" he called out, then waited for a response from the walls.

But the only sound was the wind rustling through nearby trees, and the cicadas buzzing.

Adam tried again, "We don't want any trouble. We drove down through Tarpley, and we ran into raiders on the way. My friend got hurt. He needs medical attention. We've got supplies for trade—guns, fuel, and credits." He still had about eighty republic credits left after their ill-fated trip to see Governor Miller in Travis. It wasn't much, but hopefully it would be enough to get Owen the treatment he needed.

Adam waited for a handful of seconds more, hoping to hear someone call back to him from the walls.

But no one did.

Despair clawed inside Adam's chest. He glanced back at Carla. She looked as defeated as he felt.

He tried one more time, "We've got a trained ER nurse! If you've got any wounded of your own, she could take a look at them for you."

Still no answer.

"It must be abandoned," Adam muttered, glancing back over his shoulder. "We need to keep moving."

"Wait," Sophie said from the back, peeking around the side of the driver's seat. "If there are people in there, they don't know that *we're* not raiders. They're probably too scared to reveal themselves. Tell them where we came from and where we're headed."

Adam frowned and nodded. "We came from Sunny Valley Ranch just west of Tarpley. We were on our way to trade with Bexar when we saw a terraformer blocking the way through Bandera."

This time, a woman with a high, reedy voice answered. "Show me your hands!"

Adam raised both of his hands above the door, but one of them was still holding the M4.

"Drop your gun!" the woman screamed at him.

Adam dropped his hands to set the carbine on the cracked asphalt beside him. He gave it a shove, sending it rattling away.

"Now come out where I can see you! Get the

others to do the same, and leave the rest of your weapons in your vehicle."

Apprehension trickled into Adam's gut. If they did as she said, then they'd be at the mercy of these scavengers. It would be better if just one or two of them went in with Owen and the rest stayed out here with their guns and the truck.

"No," Adam called back. "Just me, and the nurse, and my wounded friend. The rest will stay with our vehicle."

A long pause followed. For a minute Adam was afraid that the woman was going to reject his terms.

"Fine! Let's get it over with!"

Adam slowly straightened from behind the door with his hands raised above his head. Sophie's door popped open and she came around the hood with her hands raised. Adam studied the wall, looking for signs of the woman he'd been speaking with, but she was doing an impressive job of staying hidden.

Sophie opened the door on Owen's side. "Adam, I need your help."

He nodded and slowly backed over to her. Together they pulled Owen out with their hands under his back and shoulders.

Adam quickly realized that it would be easier to carry Owen on his own, so Sophie backed off.

"Get my rifle," he said, nodding to it.

Sophie looked confused.

"Give it back to Carla. We're not leaving it lying there."

Sophie nodded uncertainly and used the driver's side door for cover as she did what he'd asked. Adam looked to Carla and said, "Head straight up to the highway and get the kids in the cab with you. At the first sign of trouble, you burn rubber and get the hell out of here."

Carla nodded mutely as Sophie shut the door. Carla struggled to push Bowser off her lap and then climbed over the center console and slipped in behind the steering wheel. She reached into the driver's side door and passed their leather money bag of credits through the broken driver's side window.

"How long should I wait for you?" Carla asked as Sophie took the bag of credits.

"Give us an hour," Adam replied. "If they're good people, we'll come back for you."

"And if they're not?" Carla whispered darkly.

A muscle in Adam's jaw twitched. "Then you floor it to Bexar and don't look back."

CHAPTER SEVEN

Two armed men stepped into view at the gates, one of them carrying a pump-action shotgun, the other a scoped Remington hunting rifle. The one with the shotgun hung back while the one with the hunting rifle came forward to open the gates. Adam's gaze lingered on the one with the shotgun. He was a big guy with darkly tanned skin and thick arms covered in tattoos. He wore dark glasses, and a red bandana around his head like he'd stepped straight off a Harley. But what most caught Adam's eye was the black leather vest with red-rimmed yellow patches all over it. He scanned them quickly: *1%ER, ROAD CAPTAIN, EXPECT NO MERCY,* and *BANDIDOS.* That last one put all of the others into their proper context. This guy had belonged to the infamous Bandidos biker gang before the invasion. Unless he'd stolen that jacket, which was also possible.

Adam looked to Sophie to check if she'd noticed the man's ostensible criminal ties, but if she had, she was covering her reaction.

At least the man with the Remington wasn't wearing a Bandidos vest. He was tall and skinny, pale-skinned with a sunburned nose and cheeks, and stringy, shoulder-length black hair. He looked to be in his mid-thirties, while the Bandido was probably closer to his mid-forties like Adam.

"Where's the woman I spoke with?" Adam asked as the man with the Remington opened a padlock and unwrapped a heavy chain from the gates.

The Bandido jerked a thumb to his right. "Nelson—" he growled in a gravelly voice that perfectly matched his gruff exterior.

That name provoked an uneasy quiver in Adam's gut. Where had he met a *Nelson* recently?

The man with the Remington rifle opened the gates, and a young African-American woman with hollow, haunted eyes and jutting cheekbones stepped into view. Suddenly Adam realized where he'd heard the name. That young raider who'd been begging for his life outside of Bandera. He'd said that his name was *Jaden Nelson.* Adam's blood turned to ice, and his guts clenched up. Was this his *wife,* the mother of his five-year-old son? It couldn't be, *could* it?

The young woman looked to the Bandido as if asking him for permission, and Adam realized that he was in charge.

The Bandido nodded. "Go ahead, ask 'em."

The woman met Adam's gaze and her words came out in a tumbling rush. "You mentioned Bandera earlier. Did you see anyone up there? A dark-skinned man about my age, mid-twenties, tall, with a shaved head and a thick beard."

The description fit. So this *was* Jaden's wife. *Holy crap,* Adam thought. *What are the odds?* He did his best not to react and looked to Sophie as if deferring the question to her.

Her brow was knitted with apprehension, but she shook her head. Adam looked back to the woman at the gate. "I'm sorry. We didn't see anyone like that."

The woman's face fell, and her lips began to tremble. "Are you sure? Did you see anyone else? He was with two others about the same age. One had blonde hair, the other brown."

Adam sighed. "I'm sorry, ma'am."

"All right, that's enough," the Bandido said with a cutting gesture. He jerked his chin to Owen. "Can't you see that this man is bleeding out? There'll be time for questions later." He looked back to Adam. "Come on in."

Nelson shrank back, looking chastened.

"Thank you," Sophie said as she and Adam walked through the gates. The skinny man with the hunting rifle shut the gates behind them and began rattling the chain and padlock once more.

"We don't have much in the way of supplies,"

the Bandido explained as he led them toward the Walmart. "But we'll share whatever we can. It's on the house if you'll lend us your skills."

Adam was surprised by the man's generosity, especially considering his gang's reputation for criminal behavior. But maybe that was his mistake. Old stereotypes had no place in this world. The slate had been wiped clean, and everyone was starting over.

The Bandido went on, "We've got a few men laid up in our infirmary who could use an ER nurse."

Sophie nodded. "I'll do the best that I can. How many people live here?"

Adam felt his arms weakening under Owen's weight. He adjusted his grip, hefting him higher. He checked for a reaction from his friend, but Owen was out cold, his arms and legs dangling limply.

"Why you wanna know?" the Bandido asked Sophie.

"Because my husband needs a blood transfusion," she explained. "And his blood type is rare."

The man regarded her steadily from behind his dark glasses. "Well, you sure ain't shy. Y'all just got here and you're already asking us to spill our blood for you."

Sophie set her jaw. "It's just a transfusion."

"Fifty-six," the Bandido said.

Sophie let out a sigh. "Good. Then at least a

few of them should be O negative. Do you have any IV kits?"

"Those plastic tubes and needles?"

Sophie nodded.

"Yeah, we got a few in the infirmary that we pulled from a Walgreens a while back. Fair warning, they're used, but we sterilize them between uses by piping rubbing alcohol through."

Sophie let out a shaky sigh. "That will do just fine, thank you."

"What's your name?" Adam asked.

"Robert Burks, but call me Bobby. What about you?"

"Adam Hall. This is Sophie Brooks and her husband, Owen."

"Good to meet you," Bobby said. "You know the rest of your group is welcome to join us. We're not cannibals or anything like that."

Adam smirked. "That sounds like something a cannibal would say."

"Hah! I suppose that's true. Well, the invitation's open if you change your mind."

"Thank you," Adam replied. "We'll see how long it takes for our friend to recover. If we're still here by dusk, we might just take you up on the offer."

"That would be wise," Bobby agreed.

Adam stared dead ahead at the entrance they were headed for. The glass doors had been boarded up completely with a combination of corrugated sheet metal and plywood. Two improvised wooden doors stood open to the darkened interior of the Walmart. The remnants of white letters above the entrance read:

Ho e & Ph rmacy.

Adam drew in a deep breath as they passed through the doors, bracing himself for what they might find inside. His eyes adjusted quickly to the shadows, picking out the pale glow of working lights beyond the second set of doors.

"You have power here?" Sophie asked.

Bobby nodded and flicked his eyes up to indicate the ceiling. "Solar. One of our crew hooked it up for us a while back."

"And water?" Sophie asked as they stepped through the second set of doors.

"We've tapped a few local wells," Bobby explained as he led them past the cashier registers and the empty aisles of the pharmacy on their left.

Adam noticed that the aisles had been rearranged into U-shaped cubicles with sheets drawn across the openings for privacy. A few people sat in lawn chairs in front of them, while others were walking about with guns slung over their shoulders, pushing shopping carts full of supplies.

"Infirmary's this way," Bobby nodded sideways to indicate the fresh produce area at the far right end of the supercenter.

When they drew near, Adam saw that the produce bins had been pushed along the far wall to make room for more cubicles with old Army cots inside. They walked down an aisle with four cubicles on either side. Sheet curtains were drawn across three out of the eight, while the open ones were furnished with a collection of familiar medical equipment. It looked vaguely like a couple of the field hospitals that Adam had seen during his tour in Afghanistan. Bobby stopped in front of one of the open cubicles. This one had an IV bag half-full of clear liquid already hanging from a hook beside an empty cot.

"You can treat your man here," Bobby said. Adam hurried in and laid Owen out on the cot.

Sophie ran straight to the bag of clear fluid beside the cot. "Is this saline?" she asked, cupping it in one hand to read what was written on the bag.

"Yes, ma'am," Bobby answered. "I'll see if I can rustle up a blood donor. O negative, you said?"

Sophie nodded quickly. "Yes." She was already busy untangling the IV line trailing from the bag of saline. She held up the cannula at the end. "Do you have something I can use to sterilize this?"

Bobby pointed to a rolling metal tool cabinet behind her with red sides and silver drawers.

"Second compartment from top. Is there something you'd like to offer the blood donor? Not sure I'll get anyone to give you their blood for free."

Sophie patted her pocket and their last eighty credits jingled enticingly. "How about forty credits?"

Bobby's eyebrows shot up. "Well, shit, now I wish I was the donor." He nodded. "I'll be back soon."

Sophie didn't reply. She retrieved a bottle of rubbing alcohol and a bag of cotton balls from the tool cabinet. She sprayed alcohol liberally over the needle, then opened the IV, letting saline dribble onto the floor before spraying it again.

"That'll have to do," she muttered, shutting the valve. "Hold his arm out straight for me."

Adam picked up Owen's left arm and Sophie rolled up his sleeve. She began hunting for a vein on the inside of his elbow, but Adam couldn't see any.

She wiped his arm with more alcohol, then stuck the needle in. Not finding the vein she tried two more times before she was satisfied.

"Hold it there," she said. "I need to find some tape."

Adam took over holding the IV in place while Sophie went back to the tool chest. She pulled open a few drawers, sending the supplies clattering around noisily. A moment later she returned with a roll of silver duct tape and a pair of hook-nosed scissors that were used for cutting stitches.

She sliced off a big square of tape and pasted it over the IV to hold it in place.

"There," Sophie sighed, stepping back to admire her work.

Owen still wasn't waking up, but Adam could see his chest rising and falling in a steady rhythm. As long as he was alive, he had a chance.

Sophie adjusted another valve and the saline solution began dripping faster into the little plastic chamber below the bag.

"Will that be good enough?" Adam asked.

"For now," she replied. "He still needs blood, but this will buy us time."

Adam nodded and glanced furtively at the open curtain. Not seeing anyone out there, he stepped to Sophie's side and whispered directly into her ear, "That man they asked about at the gate is one of the three that I killed."

Sophie's eyes widened sharply. "How do you know?"

"Because he told me his name. It's the same as that woman from the gate. Nelson. They were married."

Sophie's eyes darted to the open curtain, double-checking that they were still alone. "Then these people are raiders, not scavs," she whispered.

Adam nodded grimly.

"If they find out that we killed their people…" Sophie trailed off ominously.

Adam grimaced. "That's why I'm telling you. They can't find out how Owen got shot. At least, not the real story."

Sophie started to reply, but whatever she was going to say was cut short as Bobby returned with a teenage boy with reddish blonde hair and freckled cheeks.

"I've got your donor," Bobby announced, smiling broadly. He was holding the kid's arm up in a meaty fist, leaving Adam to wonder if the boy was a *willing* donor.

Adam stepped back, watching as Bobby led the kid to a folding lawn chair beside the cot and made him sit down. Sophie found another IV kit in the tool cabinet and an empty bag of saline that she muttered, "would have to do."

"I'll leave you to it," Bobby said, stepping back out of the cubicle. "I've sent our doc over to assist you. His name's Henry."

"If you have a doctor, then what do you need me for?" Sophie asked.

"I may have misspoken. Henry was a pharmacist, not a doctor. He'll get you briefed on what our people need when you're done here."

Sophie nodded absently as she hunted for a vein in the kid's arm.

Adam said, "Thank you."

"Don't mention it," Bobby said as he stepped out and pulled the curtain shut.

"Will it hurt?" the kid asked, staring wide-eyed at the needle.

Sophie hesitated. "Have you ever gotten an injection before? A vaccination?"

"Before the invasion, for Covid."

"Well, this is about the same as that. It's just the needle going in that hurts, and not too much. Just a little pinch."

"Okay," the kid replied.

Sophie hesitated, regarding him warily. "Are you sure that you're O negative?"

"Y-yeah. My old ID card had my blood type on the back."

"Do you have it with you?" Sophie asked.

The kid shook his head. "I lost it in the invasion."

"You couldn't have been more than seven or eight years old," Sophie insisted. "I need you to be sure about this. If you're wrong, giving your blood to my husband will kill him."

The kid hesitated, and his eyes darted to the curtain, looking suddenly frightened.

"What is it?" Adam whispered. "Did Bobby threaten you?"

"I'm O negative," the kid insisted, and his brow dropped an angry shadow across his eyes.

Sophie pulled back, shaking her head. "It's not worth it."

"Can't you test his blood?" Adam asked.

"Not without proper lab equipment, and I doubt that they have any of that here," Sophie replied.

"Hey, I told you, lady. I'm O negative."

A short man with glasses, olive-colored skin, and thinning brown hair pulled the curtain aside and stepped into their cubicle. "Hello, I'm Henry," he said as he walked over to join them by Owen's side. The pharmacist pushed his glasses up higher on his nose. "I hear your friend needs a blood transfusion?"

Sophie frowned. "Yes, but we can't afford to make a mistake. I need O-negative blood. If he gets anything else…"

Henry's unruly eyebrows drifted up. "That's unfortunate." He nodded to the teenage boy. "Sean? You're O negative?"

The kid nodded defiantly.

"That's a strange thing for a kid to remember after all these years," Henry said.

"It was on the ID card that my parents got me when I was in school," Sean explained.

"Back or front?" Henry asked.

"What?" The kid blinked stupidly at him.

"Was your blood type on the back or front of the ID?"

His brow wrinkled. "What does that matter?"

"It matters," Henry insisted.

"Front."

"Get out of here."

Sean balked at him. "Fine," he sneered and jumped up from the chair.

Henry regarded them with a small, pitying smile. "Sean isn't exactly the most honest person in this camp. I heard you offered credits to the donor?"

"Forty."

"That was a mistake," Henry said. "These are desperate times. May I take a look at him?" the pharmacist asked.

Sophie shrugged and nodded. Henry pressed two fingers to Owen's neck and waited for a handful of seconds. "His pulse is weak but steady."

"His lips were blue a minute ago," Sophie said.

"It does look like some of the color is coming back," Henry said. "You might not need a transfusion, after all." He studied the blood-soaked bandage around Owen's shoulder. "What was the injury?"

"Gunshot," Adam put in.

"I see…"

"No lung involvement," Sophie explained quickly. "The bullet passed straight through."

"Well, that's something, at least," Henry sighed.

"He needs stitches to close the wounds," Sophie said.

Henry peered under Owen's wounded shoulder. "Well, it looks like the bleeding has stopped, so let's not add to the trauma just yet."

"We're not going to do anything?" Adam asked incredulously.

Henry pointed to the bag of saline. "You already have. Now all that's left is to wait. While we do so, perhaps you could help me with some of our people? Robert mentioned that you were a nurse."

Sophie nodded. "I worked in the ER for twelve years at St. David's in Austin."

"That's quite the résumé," Henry replied, already moving for the opening of the cubicle.

Sophie glanced over her shoulder. "Adam, would you watch Owen, please?"

"Of course."

She breezed out with the pharmacist and Adam dragged the lawn chair over to Owen's side. He sat watching the steady dripping of saline solution and wondered how long they'd have to wait for him to recover. He wasn't eager to spend the night in a raider camp, but they might not have a choice.

At least the compound was well-defended, so stalkers wouldn't be a problem. As long as these raiders didn't find out what had happened to their people in Bandera, they'd be okay.

CHAPTER EIGHT

"Come *on*, Bowser," Crystal groaned. She threw her head back and stared up at the clear blue sky as if to ask God *why*. She had Bowser tied to an improvised rope leash. He was sniffing around eagerly by the side of the parking lot, having found an interesting scent, but he was taking his sweet time to follow through and do his business.

Carla had parked their truck around the back of an old restaurant with rotten siding and peeling, barn-red paint. They'd parked right between two rusting cars to make their truck seem less conspicuous.

After waiting there for an hour and a half in the sweltering heat, Carla had shut off the engine to save fuel. The A/C was barely working anyway, and with the driver's side window shattered, all that tepid air was just flowing out.

Not long after Carla shut off the engine, Bowser began to whimper and whine. Thinking that he was thirsty, they'd poured some water from one of their canteens into a plastic container from the first aid kit. Bowser had guzzled it dry and pawed at the container for more, so they'd refilled it two more times.

By the time they were done, Bowser found a new way to pass the time: lunging at the broken driver's side window. To avoid a messy accident in the truck, Crystal and Connor had decided to take him out for a walk, improvising a leash from some rope in the back.

As soon as Bowser got out, he'd lifted his leg enthusiastically against the big metal signpost for the restaurant, but now he was taking his time to handle the rest of his business.

He tugged insistently on his leash, his nose leading the way through the overgrown grass along the highway. Crystal and Connor followed him, muttering and sweating in the mid-afternoon sun.

Connor warily watched the horizon with one of the two M4s that Crystal's dad had taken from those raiders. She'd tucked the engraved revolver into the waistband of her jeans to keep her hands free for Bowser's leash, but it was too big and heavy and she kept worrying that it would fall out. The revolver still had all six bullets, which was three better than the Glock her dad had left behind.

Bored by Bowser's endless sniffing, Crystal drew the weapon and studied the gun's stylized engravings. "It's kind of pretty," she said, running her fingers over it. There were tongues of flames and repeating patterns that looked kind of like four-leafed clovers. The handle was made from some reddish wood, and it was also engraved and stamped with a miniature black horse rearing up on its hind legs.

Crystal heard the muffled rumbling of an engine in the distance. For a moment, she thought it was Carla starting up the truck again, but then she realized that it was coming from the highway. She looked sharply in the direction of the sound and saw a heat mirage shimmering in front of a convoy of multiple glinting vehicles. Connor cursed and yanked his rifle up to peer through the scope.

"Rangers," he muttered. "Looks like... three trucks," he said. "We'd better go."

Crystal yanked sharply on Bowser's leash, but he dug in with all four paws, threatening to slip out of his collar. "Bowser, come on!" Crystal urged.

He tugged his head free, and Connor snapped into action, switching his weapon to a one-handed grip and lunging to grab Bowser.

Spooked by the sudden movement, the dog darted away with a defiant *woof!*

"Bowser, get your stupid butt back here!" Crystal called after him.

But he wasn't listening. He went streaking for a clump of trees and bushes on the other side of the highway, taking full advantage of his freedom to run like he used to on the ranch. He wasn't accustomed to a leash.

Crystal tore after him.

"Christie, leave him! He'll come back," Connor shouted.

But she couldn't do that. Bowser was family. What if he got himself run over by one of those trucks?

Crystal sprinted across all four lanes of the highway. Bowser had stopped on the shoulder with his tail up and his head held high. He was staring intently at the approaching vehicles.

"Bowie, get over here!" Crystal hissed as she drew near. She held out the leash, planning to slip the collar over his head again.

But Bowser took one look at the rope and bolted, running straight at the approaching vehicles. Crystal ran after him, screaming for him to stop.

Connor pulled alongside her, gasping for breath. "This is stupid!" he muttered. "What if they think we're going to attack them? We're armed!" He patted his rifle for emphasis.

"I'm not leaving him!" Crystal insisted. "He chases cars! He could get run over!"

Bowser reached the approaching vehicles and began barking and snapping at the wheels, proving that Crystal's fears were justified. The lead vehicle of the three Army trucks swerved away from him and slowed right down, and then the other two followed suit.

Crystal caught up to Bowser a moment later. She tucked her revolver into her belt and jumped on Bowser, falling on her knees beside him. This time she managed to wrangle the collar over his head.

"You kids should be more careful," a smooth voice said from the truck.

Crystal looked up to see a Ranger with spiky blonde hair aiming his rifle out the open passenger's side window. The barrel was directed at Connor, not her.

Crystal yanked Bowser back, away from the trucks.

"Where'd you get that carbine, son?" the Ranger asked, nodding to Connor and smiling coldly.

A sharp spike of fear lanced through Crystal. She'd forgotten that Connor was carrying an old Army rifle, the same as the ones the Rangers used. They were probably wondering if he'd killed one of theirs and stolen it.

CHAPTER NINE

"We found it," Connor said.

"Yeah? Whereabouts?" the Ranger with spiky blonde hair asked.

Connor looked at Crystal. She shrugged and said. "Close to Bandera. The guy it belonged to was dead."

The Ranger's expression hardened. "Because you killed him?"

"He wasn't one of you," Connor explained.

"Oh?"

"They were wearing civilian clothes," Connor added.

"They. There was more than one?"

Crystal nodded. "Raiders, we think."

"So what killed them?"

"Looked like stalkers," Connor lied. "There wasn't much meat left on the bones."

"I see. Where are you from? You got a camp around here?"

Crystal realized that the man was still suspicious of them. He probably figured they were raiders and that they *had* killed a few

Rangers to get Connor's gun.

"We were just passing through," Connor replied. "We were headed for Bexar."

"On foot?" the Ranger pressed. "We just came from there. I could probably spare a vehicle to take you."

Crystal hesitated. She couldn't leave without her dad. Not to mention Carla, Emily, and the others.

"Uh, that's okay, sir," she said.

"I'm afraid I'm gonna have to insist," he said. "Put your weapons down nice and slow and let's see your hands."

Crystal balked at the order. "Have we done something wrong?"

"That's what we're going to find out, sweetheart. We have reports of a raider camp in this area, and one of our patrols went missing in Bandera, right where you claim to have found that carbine. So, I'm thinking that maybe your people killed ours and stole our gear."

"That's not true," Crystal insisted.

Connor was already laying his rifle down by the side of the road.

"Hurry up, girl. And don't think I can't see that Colt Python peeking out of your belt."

Crystal reached for the gun.

"Slowly," the Ranger insisted.

She plucked it from her belt and laid it down gently beside Connor's rifle.

"You're making a mistake," Crystal said.

The young man opened his door and stepped out, keeping them covered with his carbine.

Bowser growled as the man approached.

"Your dog bite?" the Ranger asked, hesitating.

Bowser woofed as if to confirm that he did.

"Only assholes," Crystal replied.

The man grinned at her. "Cute. A raider with a sense of humor. Look, we can cut a deal. You lead us to your camp, and we let you go."

"We're not raiders," Connor said.

The Ranger just smiled. "Either way you're gonna lead us there. It's just a matter of how many fingers and toes you want to have left by the time you do."

"We really don't know who you're looking for," Crystal insisted. "We're not with any camp. We came from a ranch near Tarpley."

"Oh? Just the two of you running a ranch all by yourselves?"

"With my dad and his Mom and a couple of others," Crystal explained.

Bowser's lips peeled back in a snarl, and the Ranger stopped just out of reach of his snout with his rope leash pulled taut.

"So where are they now?" the Ranger asked.

A sharp whistling sound ripped through the air, and the driver of the Humvee slumped against the wheel, hitting the car horn with a long, sustained *beeeeep...*

A rattling roar of rifle fire answered from the

Rangers' convoy, followed by, "Contact!"

The one in front of Crystal swiftly ducked and took cover behind his truck. Then came a *skirshhhh... boom!* and one of the Humvees exploded in a fiery rain of shrapnel.

Connor yanked Crystal down hard, and they flattened themselves to the shoulder. Crystal's ears were still ringing from the explosion. She watched the Humvee in the middle of the convoy reverse in a hurry, spinning its wheels to get away. The Ranger who'd been speaking with them snapped off a few shots around the hood of his vehicle and screamed something into his radio.

Bowser struggled to break free again, dragging her in the direction of the trees below the highway.

"We have to get out of here!" Connor shouted into one of Crystal's ringing ears. He recovered his rifle, and she scrambled to reach her revolver. Then she let Bowser drag her down the embankment.

A bullet zipped past Crystal's cheek and she dove into the tall grass in the ditch beside the highway. Connor landed beside her, and they pressed ahead, crawling on their hands and knees. Zipping bullets and the roar of gunfire chased them, splintering tree trunks and kicking up clods of dirt. Even Bowser was keeping his head down, slinking on his belly for the safety of the trees.

As soon as they reached the foliage, they jumped up and dashed through a thick wall of bushes to hide behind a couple of skinny saplings. Crystal peered through the branches to see that the Humvee in the back of the convoy was still on fire, while the lead vehicle was surrounded by a ragtag group of men and women carrying rifles and shotguns. The missing truck in the middle of the convoy was roaring back the way it had come with two raider pickup trucks in hot pursuit.

A man standing on the back of one of them held an RPG to his shoulder. A rocket shot out on a fat white tongue of smoke and fire. Another *boom* split the air, but more distantly this time, and the fleeing Humvee exploded in a burst of flames. It ground to a halt just a few seconds later.

Blinking in shock, Crystal glanced back at the lead vehicle and the Ranger who'd spoken with them. He was surrounded by raiders. Crystal thought she recognized one of them as the man her father had spoken to at the Walmart. He was wearing the same leather vest with yellow patches all over it.

The Ranger with the spiky blonde hair slowly raised his hands, and the raiders took his guns. Another two Rangers were escorted over, their hands also raised. A brief conversation ensued between them and the one with the leather vest. Crystal couldn't hear any of it.

Suddenly the one with the leather vest drew a pistol and shot one of the Rangers in the head. Crystal clapped a hand to her mouth to stifle her reaction, and Connor muttered a curse.

The other two Rangers cried out in alarm, suddenly struggling to get away.

The raider in the leather vest shot one of the remaining two Rangers, leaving just the blonde-haired man. Bowser gave a belated *woof,* and then one of the raiders shouted a warning and pointed to the trees.

"Damn it!" Connor muttered while backing deeper into cover and pulling Crystal along with him.

"Come on out!" the one with the vest said. "We can see you hiding down there."

Connor glared at Bowser, and Crystal did, too. "You really are dumb, Bowie," she muttered.

He regarded her with drooping jowls, and then he grinned and began panting noisily.

Connor straightened and stepped out of cover with his hands up and his rifle dangling from its shoulder strap. "We're from the white Ford!" he explained. "A couple of hours ago you let three of ours into your compound so they could treat a wounded man. His name's Owen!"

"Yeah, I remember!" the man with the leather vest called back. He waved to them. "Come on up here. You're not in any trouble."

Crystal tucked her revolver back into her jeans to avoid looking like a threat, then followed Connor back up to the highway. She had to drag Bowser most of the way. He *really* didn't want to go back to the scene of all those loud noises.

The Ranger with blonde hair glared at her as she approached. "You lied! You *are* with them."

The raider in the leather vest flipped his shotgun around and slammed it into the Ranger's stomach. He doubled over with a *whuff* of escaping air. "Shut up! No one's talkin' to you."

Crystal gave the raider a hard look. "What are you going to do with him?"

"That's none of your concern. Where is your truck and the rest of your people?"

Connor hesitated for a second, then pointed to the parking lot of the restaurant.

"You'll have to come back with us. It's not safe out here." The raider made a few hand signals to his people and they began dragging away the dead Rangers.

A rattling roar of machinery erupted from an old motel across the parking lot from the restaurant. Moments later, Crystal saw an old yellow bulldozer rumbling into view.

"What are you going to do with *that?*" Connor asked.

Metal treads clattered across the pavement, gouging out bits of broken pavement as it went.

"We're gonna bury the evidence," the raider replied. "How do you think our camp has stayed hidden? Of course, it was easier back when all of the traffic went through Bandera. Now it looks like Rangers are determined to clear out Hondo and establish a new outpost here. At this rate, we're gonna have to relocate."

The captured Ranger glared at him. "You'd better do it fast. When my team fails to report in, Bexar will send a whole company to flush you out. Hondo will be crawling with Rangers by this time tomorrow."

"I imagine that's true," the raider replied, sighing heavily. "Which is why we have you— Major... Hunter, is that right?" the raider asked, reading the Velcro patch on the man's uniform. Hunter glared stonily at him, and the raider smiled. "Should've left the soldiering to the grunts, Major. You're far too valuable to risk your neck out here in the wastes." The raider's gaze slowly slid away, and his smile faded when he noticed Crystal and Connor still standing there. "Nelson!" he snapped his fingers and a gaunt, dark-skinned woman appeared.

"Yes, Bobby?"

"Take these kids and the rest of their people back to the camp, would you? We don't need them loitering around here to point the way for Rangers when they come back."

"Yes, sir," the woman replied. She gestured impatiently to Crystal and Connor, and they joined her by the hood of the Humvee. "Where's your vehicle?" she asked.

Connor pointed to it, and Crystal noticed that Carla was peeking around the back fender with their other carbine. When they looked her way, Carla straightened and waved to them.

"Let's go," Nelson growled, striding quickly off the road to reach Connor's mom.

Crystal pulled alongside her. "You're raiders, right?" she whispered.

"What of it?" Nelson asked.

"We thought you were scavs."

"Same damn thing," the woman snorted. She looked annoyed to have been sent on a baby-sitting errand.

"It's not the same," Connor insisted. "Scavs don't kill people unless they have to. They only fight in self-defense, but raiders are murderers and thieves."

"This *was* self-defense," the woman replied. "And you'd be surprised what a so-called scav will do when their back's to the wall."

"You shot first," Crystal pointed out.

"No, *they* did. You just weren't there when it happened."

Crystal regarded her with a deepening frown. "What's your name?"

"Nelson."

"I meant your first name."

The woman regarded her stonily before gritting out, "Kasey."

"Nice to meet you, Kasey. I'm Crystal. And this is Connor."

Connor shot her a questioning look as if he didn't get why she was introducing them. Something told her that it might help to keep them alive. It's harder to shoot someone you know than someone you don't.

Kasey appeared to notice the revolver peeking out from the back of Crystal's shirt, and she abruptly stopped walking. "Where did you get that?"

"Get what?" Crystal shook her head, playing dumb, but icy dread was already flooding her veins.

"The gun." Kasey pointed to it and then yanked Crystal's shirt up to fully reveal the stylized engravings on the revolver.

Kasey stopped cold and yanked it out. She spent a moment examining the weapon before her fist hardened on the grip and her upper lip curled. She whipped the revolver up and shook it at Crystal's chest. "Where the fuck did you get this?!" she screamed.

Bowser snarled warningly at the raider, but she didn't seem to notice.

"We found it," Connor explained smoothly, using the same excuse that he had with the Rangers.

"Where? In Bandera?"

Connor frowned. "Yeah. In an abandoned Humvee. Why?"

"Abandoned?" Kasey asked, arching an eyebrow at them.

"Is something wrong over here?" Carla asked, striding over quickly from the truck with her carbine casually aimed.

Kasey glanced back at her with a sneer, then nodded to Crystal. "This gun. It belongs to a friend of mine."

Carla stopped beside her, still casually aiming her carbine. "We found it," she said, repeating Connor's lie. "We just assumed that whoever it belonged to was already dead."

Kasey scowled and stared long and hard at them, her eyes flicking suspiciously to each of them. "Let's go," she finally said, turning toward the truck and storming away.

Crystal let Kasey get ahead of them, and then she released a shaky breath and whispered, "What was *that* about?"

Connor shot her a warning look and shook his head. Carla looked shaken.

Crystal realized that if Kasey recognized the gun, it meant that she'd known the man who'd shot Owen. Maybe he was a friend of hers. Or worse, a family member. Goosebumps prickled her arms, and the hairs rose on the back of her neck. It felt like she was walking into a trap. She recalled watching the guy in the biker vest execute those two surrendered Rangers, and her apprehension blossomed into full-blown dread. If these raiders found out how they'd actually come by that revolver, she knew they would be next.

CHAPTER TEN

Adam couldn't believe it. He watched with an ache in his throat and stinging eyes as Sophie slowly tore the duct tape off Owen's arm and pulled out the cannula.

"I'm sorry," Henry said. He stepped back from checking Owen's pulse and slowly shook his head. "I'll leave you two alone for a minute."

Adam watched him go, then looked back to Sophie and Owen. He half-expected to see Owen sit up with a sudden gasp, but his face was gray, and his lips were once again blue.

Sophie held his arm up, his hand dangling limply from the wrist, and she stared sightlessly at the old mechanical watch on his wrist.

Adam remembered that she had bought it for Owen for their 15th anniversary. He grimaced, stepping over to her and laying a hand on her shoulder.

"He loved that watch," Sophie sniffed, smoothing a thumb over the chipped glass face of it. "He said it was the best gift that I'd ever given him. And that's including the set of carbon fiber golf clubs that I bought before the invasion." Her smile faded with the memory. She quietly undid the clasp of the watch and slipped it into her pocket. She laid his arm back down, straight at his side, and stepped over to the head of the cot. Leaning down, she kissed him gently on the lips.

Adam shook his head angrily. Owen had been getting better! The color had been coming back in his cheeks. They'd hooked him up to that saline drip, and it had looked like he'd turned a corner.

But they'd conveniently forgotten that it had taken hours to get him here. He'd lost several pints of blood in the back of the truck, let alone what he must have lost in that clearing while they'd been dealing with those raiders.

Sophie looked back at Adam. Her dirty cheeks were streaked with tears, and her wavy brown hair was greasy and matted with Owen's blood. "What am I going to tell Emily?" she croaked.

Adam opened his mouth to answer—then promptly shut it as the curtains flew open with a rattling shriek from the rusty curtain rod.

A pair of armed raiders appeared in the opening. They shoved Crystal, Connor, Carla, and Emily ahead of them, but the raiders remained standing by the entrance. Bowser came barreling in, tugging to the end of his rope leash and jerking free of Crystal's grip.

"What happened?" Adam demanded, looking from Crystal to Connor, then finally to Carla for the answer.

Bowser spun in happy circles around Adam's legs, oblivious to Owen's passing, but then he began sniffing energetically at Owen's blood on his hands and he padded over to check the cot. He lifted his head and sniffed the air around Owen, and then his snout shut abruptly, and his jowls drooped, and he lay down beside the cot.

Smart dog, Adam thought.

"Rangers happened," a familiar dark-skinned woman snarled belatedly at him. "We dealt with it."

"How's Owen?" Carla asked, stepping quickly toward his bed. Emily followed with her brow knitted and her curly hair bouncing lightly.

Sophie's face crumpled anew and she shook her head.

"What?" Emily shrieked. "No!"

Sophie broke down sobbing and hugging her shoulders while Emily stared blankly at her dad's lifeless face.

Adam could feel the air thickening with grief, making it hard just to breathe.

"Dad?" Emily croaked. She shook him lightly by the arm, then waited for a reaction as if she couldn't believe that he was really gone. Tears sliced steadily down her cheeks, turning dust to muddy rivers. "No! Dad! Answer me!"

Crystal and Connor gathered around, laying their hands on Emily's shoulders and whispering how sorry they were. Carla folded Sophie into a hug, and the other woman sobbed against her shoulder.

A flash of movement caught Adam's eye, providing a welcome distraction. That dark-skinned raider was striding purposefully toward him. She grabbed his arm, her fingernails digging into his biceps like talons.

"Hey!" he objected and tried to jerk his arm free.

The woman produced a familiar-looking revolver with elaborate engravings.

"Where did your daughter get this?"

Adam froze, hesitating. "We found it in Bandera," he explained.

The woman's eyes narrowed. "You *found* it?" She demanded. "Where?"

Adam hesitated and glanced pointedly at Crystal, wondering what, if anything, she had already told this woman. Crystal noticed him looking her way and her eyes flashed in warning.

She strode over from Owen's cot. "Is everything okay, Dad?" she asked in a grief-thickened voice.

"Just fine," Adam managed with a tight smile.

"Kasey wanted to know where we got

that gun," Crystal explained, looking pale and frightened. "I told her how we found them in an abandoned Humvee near Bandera."

"Would you shut up?" Kasey snapped at her. "Did it look like I was talking to you?"

Adam scowled. "Hey, watch how you speak to my daughter."

The raider smiled sweetly at them, her eyes flicking from Adam to Crystal and back. "If something happened to Jaden, and I find out that one of you had something to do with it..." Her lips twisted into a cruel sneer. "Let's just say that there are worse ways to die than to be ripped apart by stalkers."

Adam met her gaze calmly. "Noted."

Sophie was glaring daggers at Kasey's back. With Owen's death still so fresh, she had more than her share of blame to lay with the Raiders who'd shot him.

But Kasey had her back turned, so she missed the deadly look that Sophie was giving her.

Before any of them could say another word, a thundering roar drew their eyes up to the ceiling of the Walmart.

"Is that a helicopter?" Crystal asked.

But it wasn't just any helicopter. From his time in the Army, Adam could say with reasonable certainty that this was a Black Hawk. And more than one.

A tall, skinny raider with long, stringy black

hair pushed past another raider at the entrance of the cubicle. Adam recognized him as one of the ones from the gate. He was wearing a camo-print jacket and hefting a scoped Remington hunting rifle. "Nelson, we've got Rangers inbound!"

Kasey cursed and spun away from Adam to address him. "ETA?"

"A minute, maybe less."

The sound of chopper blades thumping intensified, reaching a crescendo before tapering off into the distance. Everyone stared breathlessly at the ceiling.

"Maybe they don't know where we are?" the man with stringy hair suggested.

"Those Rangers must have called for backup before we took them out," Kasey muttered.

Moments later, the *whup-whup-whupping* of rotors came thundering back, and this time the sound lingered directly overhead. Heavy thumps hammered on the corrugated ceiling, one after another.

"Shit!" Kasey hissed. "They're going to come in through the roof!" She sprinted for the exit, and in a blink, all three raiders were gone.

Adam's eyes darted between the bright rectangles of skylights in the ceiling. Shadows flitted around the edges of the nearest one just before it exploded with a jagged rain of glass. Echoes of the same sound rippled throughout the Walmart as a dozen different skylights shattered.

Shouts of alarm went up through the supercenter, followed by the tinny clattering of grenades landing on the polished concrete floors. Then came the distinctive *pop* and hiss of smoke gushing out. Adam sincerely hoped that it was just smoke and not tear gas, but either one would be a significant irritant in an enclosed space like this.

Moments later, fits of coughing erupted from the raiders in surrounding cubicles. Adam was already breathing into his sleeve in anticipation.

Carla fixed him with an urgent look. "We have to get out of here!"

"Wait!" Adam ground his teeth, debating their options. If they ran out of here now, they risked getting caught in the crossfire. This cubicle wasn't much for cover, with no ceiling, and a curtain across the entrance. But the walls were made from old, empty metal shelving units, and that was a whole lot better than nothing.

Thick walls of smoke came curling into their cubicle, and Adam's throat and eyes began to burn. Soon all of them were coughing, and Bowser began sneezing uncontrollably.

Long black ropes spooled down from the ceiling, followed by armored Rangers zipping down those lines, firing precision bursts as they went.

Screams erupted from dying raiders, along with scattered return fire.

"Everyone get down!" Adam shouted above the rising tumult. He hit the ground and forced Bowser down beside him just as stray bullets came zipping into their cubicle and plinked off the shelving units. Still sneezing, Bowser wriggled free and tore out of cover.

"Bowie!" Crystal screamed between coughs.

"Leave him!" Adam shouted. "He'll find an exit!"

Gunfire rattled and roared on all sides of them, punctuated by the dying screams of the raiders.

Adam lay face-down on the floor with the others, making a cage around his face with his arms in a vain attempt to keep the smoke out of his lungs. It didn't work.

"Keep your heads down!" Adam croaked, just in case any of them thought to do otherwise.

An eternity seemed to pass before the gunfire faded to sporadic pops, then finally to ringing silence. Adam risked looking up, but couldn't see anything through his swollen eyes.

"Is everyone okay?" he asked.

"I think so," Crystal managed between sobs and coughs.

Connor grunted something unintelligible and Sophie screamed for Emily to reply. She shouted back that she was fine.

"We have to get out of here!" Carla gasped.

Now that the gunfire had ceased, Adam was inclined to agree, but the smoke from those grenades still hadn't fully dissipated, leaving them blind. Feeling their way to the exit would be next to impossible, and Rangers could still mistake them for hostiles.

Just as he was about to suggest that they try groping for the exit with their hands up, someone jerked him to his feet, and Adam found himself standing before a blurry figure in black armor and a gas mask. The others were yanked to their feet one after another by more soldiers in matching armor.

Adam threw up his hands. "Don't shoot! We're not with them!"

"Who are you?" the one in front of Adam demanded.

"We're ranchers out of Tarpley!"

"What are you doing here?"

"We came looking for help to treat one of ours for a gunshot," Adam explained.

"You picked the wrong people to ask for help. Let's go."

They were half-dragged and half-shoved from the cubicle. Adam stumbled through shifting curtains of smoke, tripping over dead raiders and colliding with overturned shelving units as he went.

Eventually, they made it outside and collapsed in the parking lot, desperately gulping lungfuls of fresh air between racking coughs. Adam had used smoke grenades plenty of times to signal choppers in the Army, but he'd never used them in an enclosed space. No wonder the Rangers were wearing gas masks.

Soldiers passed out bottles of water, which helped somewhat to soothe Adam's irritated throat. Moments later, the Rangers dragged them back to their feet and shoved them toward three Black Hawks idling in the parking lot.

Bowser was barking and sneezing and running in agitated circles around them. The Ranger holding Crystal cursed as he nipped at the back of one of his legs. "Stupid mutt!" the man roared, rounding on Bowser with his carbine raised.

"Don't shoot!" Crystal cried. "That's my dog!"

"It's just a fucking Golden!" another Ranger shouted from the open side of one of the choppers. Adam noticed that whoever it was, he wasn't wearing a mask or body armor—just regular combat fatigues. "Grab his leash and let's go!"

The one who'd been bitten grumbled something and dove for Bowser's leash on the next pass. He caught it, which led to a furious struggle between the soldier and Bowser's snarling, snapping jaws.

Crystal took the leash and ended the struggle by yanking Bowser away. "Easy, boy," she soothed. "It's okay. I'm fine, see?"

Bowser settled down with that. They reached the nearest Black Hawk and the Rangers shoved them inside.

"Good to see you made it out alive," said the man who'd saved Bowser's life.

Adam didn't recognize him. He had spiky blond hair and an easy smile. His name tape read, Hunter, and he was wearing an Army major's insignia.

"I take it you've met?" Adam asked as he sat down opposite the Ranger.

"We have." He thrust out a hand. "Major Hunter."

Adam accepted the handshake. "Former Army Sergeant Adam Hall."

"Pre-invasion? Or active duty during the event?" Major Hunter asked.

"Pre-invasion." Adam slapped his bad leg. "Honorable discharge."

"Lucky you. Most of our active duty personnel died in the first year after the Specs arrived."

A couple of Rangers bustled in and the chopper's rotors sped up to a thundering roar, making further conversation impossible.

Bowser crawled under Adam's seat, cowering there to escape from the noise.

Adam laid his head back with a weary sigh. He spotted the headset dangling beside his ear but decided not to put it on, grateful for the break. There would be time for questions and answers later. Right now, he was just happy that they were alive and breathing—painful as the latter might be.

Then Adam winced as he remembered who was missing from their group.

Owen.

It was day one of a twelve-hundred-mile journey to Chicago, and they'd already lost someone. If that was any indication of what was to come, they were never going to make it.

Adam wasn't the kind of man who gave up easily, but he didn't believe in stubbornly adhering to a plan no matter what the cost. The best way to keep all of them alive and breathing was to leverage whatever goodwill they'd banked up with Mayor Ellis in Bexar and ask him for asylum.

That was assuming, of course, that Ellis never found out about the Rangers they'd killed at Sunny Valley, and that Governor Miller hadn't already put up wanted posters with their faces on them.

Adam grimaced and yanked his headset on.

"Ready to chat now, Sergeant?" Major Hunter asked with a bland smile.

Adam nodded. "I'm an open book. What do you want to know?"

"Let's start with the basics. What were you doing in a camp full of raiders?"

"One of our people needed urgent medical attention," Adam explained. "We were short of supplies, and we thought they might have what we needed. We didn't know that they were raiders at the time."

"I see. And did your man make it?" the major asked.

Adam shook his head.

"I'm sorry to hear that. Well, that checks out. We found the body, and that blonde girl gave me the same story on the road right before my convoy was ambushed. And none of your people shot at any of ours, so that stands in your favor. We'll take your statements at the Ranger station. You might spend a night or two in lock-up while we sort through the paperwork, but so long as we don't learn anything new to contradict your story, you'll be free to go after that."

"I might be able to shortcut the process for you," Adam said.

"How's that?"

"We're old acquaintances of Mayor Ellis."

Major Hunter arched a bushy blond eyebrow at him. "Is that so?"

Adam nodded.

"All right. Let's get you to the mayor, then." Major Hunter peered over Adam's shoulder, and raised his voice to speak with the pilot, "Change of plans, Lieutenant! Take us to city hall."

"Yes, sir!" the pilot replied, and the helicopter banked ever-so-slightly to the left.

Adam didn't miss the worried look that Crystal shot him. The last time they'd dealt with the mayor of a safe zone, things hadn't exactly gone their way. Mayor Maloney from Kerr was as corrupt as the governor.

But this time would be different. They went way back with Mayor Ellis. Adam wouldn't exactly call him a friend—a business associate, maybe—but from the handful of times that they'd met, he'd gotten the impression that Ellis was a decent guy—a rare breed of leader who was looking to use his position to make a positive difference in the world as opposed to leveraging it for personal gain. Adam just hoped that if it came to it, Ellis wouldn't side with Governor Miller to protect that position.

CHAPTER ELEVEN

After about fifteen minutes of flying over the seemingly endless, overgrown wastes of San Antonio's moldering suburbs, the helicopter reached the Bexar Safe Zone. High walls of corrugated metal sheets guarded the perimeter of what used to be downtown San Antonio. Ramshackle wooden guard towers were erected on the roofs of nearby buildings, and ramparts ran along the walls with Rangers pacing along their length.

Like most safe zones, Bexar was built around the old core of the city to take full advantage of high rises for their defensibility. Stalkers could tunnel under a safe zone's walls, or find a way into its sewers, but the stairwells of apartments and office buildings were easily barricaded to protect their inhabitants at night. Far more easily, anyway, than the windows and doors of old wooden homes.

The helicopter set down in a relatively empty parking lot between the mayor's office and city hall.

As the steady thumping of the rotors died down to a whistling whine of fading engine noise, Major Hunter ripped off his headset and stood up. "Let's go."

Adam removed his headset and grabbed Bowser's rope leash before handing it to Crystal. He followed the major out with her and Connor right behind him. Carla, Sophie, and Emily came next, with the latter two still noticeably distraught over Owen's death. A pair of Rangers were the last ones out, keeping wary guard from the rear.

Adam squinted against the glare of mid-afternoon sun as he followed Major Hunter across the sun-dappled asphalt to a simple two-story building with a restaurant on the corner. The side that contained the mayor's office was guarded by a pair of Rangers in combat fatigues. The guards adjusted their stances and their rifle barrels drifted up as Adam and the others approached, but at the sight of the major they appeared to relax.

One of the men saluted and came to attention as Major Hunter stopped before him. "Sir!" he said.

"At ease," Hunter replied, returning the salute. "We're here to see Mayor Ellis."

"He's in his office, sir."

"Good."

The guards pulled the doors open, and Major Hunter led the way in. Bowser lifted his leg against a tree on the sidewalk, leaving a steaming puddle of piss in their wake. Adam lingered, waiting for him to finish.

"Hey, you can't take that animal in here," one of the Rangers warned.

Adam scowled but nodded to Crystal. "Tie him to that tree."

She looked horrified.

Bowser regarded him with drooping jowls, then started panting relentlessly.

"He needs water. And food," Crystal objected.

"So do we," Sophie growled.

The second Ranger softened. "I can give him some water from my canteen, but he's gotta stay out here."

"We can stay with him," Connor offered as Crystal cupped her hands and the Ranger poured water into them for Bowser to drink.

"Fine," Adam sighed. He turned and hurried through the open doors to meet the major inside a familiar-looking office space.

The building was well-lit with a handful of glaring overhead light fixtures that added to the muted glow from the curtained windows. Eight desks with partitions between them adorned the interior of the building, each of them covered in messy stacks of papers and big brown boxes of files. Only two people staffed those desks, both of them women.

The dark-haired girl sitting closest to the entrance looked familiar from Adam's previous visits, but he didn't recognize the buxom blond by the entrance of the mayor's office. Her desk had an actual working computer on it, and she was tapping away at the keyboard while a Xerox machine beside her spat out copies of something. The world's telecommunications systems were in shambles, and working technology was hard to come by, but the handful of computers and printers that had survived the Specters' initial EMP attacks still held vital roles in government, business, and health care.

Adam wondered if there was a copy machine out there somewhere up in Travis regurgitating wanted posters with artists' impressions of him, Crystal, and Connor after they'd escaped from the Governor's trap. Hopefully not, but maybe he should grow a beard just in case.

As they approached the wooden doors to Ellis's office, that plump blonde woman looked up from her screen and promptly stepped in front of the major to bar his way. She was a lot younger than Adam had expected. Prettier, too. She wore a vest and a white button-up shirt with a simple, woven gray skirt. She pushed a pair of black-rimmed glasses up on her nose and planted hands on her hips. "Where do you think *you're* going?" she demanded.

"We need to see the mayor," Hunter explained.

"Not without an appointment. What's your name? I might be able to sneak you in for a meeting tomorrow morning—assuming of course that your business merits the mayor's attention..." She trailed off with eyebrows raised, waiting for the major to elaborate.

Major Hunter frowned and looked past her to the doors. "And who will be the judge of that?"

The woman smiled. "His senior executive secretary, Emma Koch."

"Fine, and where is she?"

"Standing right in front of you," she declared.

Major Hunter frowned. "I haven't seen you here before."

"I'm new," she explained.

"What happened to Helen?"

Adam recognized the name of the mayor's previous secretary, an elderly woman with thinning gray hair who never seemed to be able to remember his name.

"She couldn't keep up with the work," Emma explained. She stepped back to her desk and flipped open an appointment book. "Now, let me see where I can squeeze you in... your name, please."

Major Hunter shifted impatiently from one foot to the other. "Major James Hunter," he replied, his gaze fixing on the doors to the mayor's office.

"Okay, Major... James... Hunter..." Emma said while scribbling his name into the book. "Now, what did you say your business was?"

While she'd been busy writing down his name, Hunter had quietly snuck around her to the doors of the mayor's office.

"Oh no you don't!" Emma cried, beating him to the doors with surprising quickness for her ample frame.

The major reached around her and wrenched the doors open, sending her stumbling away.

"Guards!" the woman shouted, but they were too far away for the ones standing outside to hear her, and the two Rangers that Hunter had brought with him were unlikely to side with a petty functionary.

Mayor Ellis looked up from his desk with a giant chocolate-frosted donut in one hand and his round face comically sketched in alarm. His mouth was full and hung halfway open with chocolate frosting smeared all across his upper lip.

"Guards!" Emma cried again.

Mayor Ellis scowled and set the donut on a plate in front of him. He yanked a white napkin from the collar of his shirt and dabbed the frosting from his mouth. "It's okay, Mrs. Koch. Let's give the major a chance to explain himself."

Adam stood awkwardly in the background

with the others, listening as Major Hunter briefly explained what had happened with the raiders in Hondo. Then he turned and pointed to Adam.

"We found these five in their camp. They claim to know you personally."

At that, Mayor Ellis stood up, somehow managing to look both startled and happy to see them at the same time.

"Adam Hall!" he thundered.

"You *know* this man?" the mayor's secretary asked, sounding surprised.

"Of *course,* I know him! He's one of the illustrious heroes who keeps Bexar fed by risking life and limb herding cattle outside the safety of our walls. Please, come in, Adam!"

He squeezed past Major Hunter to enter the office, and the mayor made a shooing gesture to his secretary who quickly retreated and shut the doors.

"Please, sit down, Adam," Mayor Ellis said, gesturing to a pair of chairs in front of his desk.

"Thank you," Adam replied, but he pulled out a chair for Carla before sitting himself.

She smiled her thanks, and then Adam sat down beside her. With only two chairs, Sophie and Emily remained standing by the doors. Adam spent a moment staring at the mayor, trying to gather his thoughts. Ellis didn't seem to notice how tired and dirty they were, their clothes ripped and stained with blood and smelling of smoke from the fire that had devoured Sunny Valley Ranch.

"So, tell me, Adam, what can I do for you?" the mayor asked, with his brow furrowing all the way up to his receding hairline.

Adam launched straight into it, explaining how raiders had attacked Sunny Valley Ranch, attempting to take it for themselves. He changed the story with regard to the corrupt Rangers from Kerr, claiming that they'd tried but failed to drive the raiders off. Ultimately the two groups had wiped each other out, and stalkers had taken care of any survivors. "We narrowly escaped with our lives," Adam finished. "But Rick and Owen didn't make it."

Ellis looked aghast. "And the ranch?"

Adam shook his head. "The house and the stables burned to the ground. We had to let the horses go. Our cattle are still out there, but we're in no position to tend the herd anymore. I suggest you send a detachment of Rangers to round them up and drive them over to the next nearest ranch."

Ellis sat back in his chair. "We'll be sure to do that. What will you do now?"

"I was hoping you might have a place for us here," Adam said. "You know we don't mind getting our hands dirty, and we're hard workers. Just give us a roof over our heads and three square meals, and put us to work."

Carla looked at him, her green eyes wide.

Adam hadn't shared his change of plans with any of them yet, so this was the first they had heard of it.

Ellis began stroking his baby-bottom-smooth jaw. "We could also help you rebuild the ranch. It wouldn't take too much to get a basic shelter erected, and then you could go right back to doing what you do best."

"Without Rick and Owen, we'd be short-handed," Adam explained. "And the truth is, the Syndicate is gunning for us after we killed their people. We need a safe place to lie low until they forget. And what could be safer than a Republic safe zone?"

Ellis sighed. "You're not giving me much of a choice here."

"If I felt that we had one, I wouldn't be asking for asylum."

"Hmmmm. Well, I'm sure we can find something for you around here. Major Hunter —"

"Sir?"

"Would you please escort our guests to the Drury and get them checked in?"

"Yes, sir," Hunter replied.

"Thank you," Adam said, rising to his feet with Carla. "You won't regret taking us in."

"I'm sure that I won't," Ellis replied, smiling tightly up at them.

Adam nodded and turned to leave. Major Hunter opened the doors, and led them out, striding quickly through the office and drawing a beady-eyed glare from the mayor's secretary as they went. Adam caught a flicker of movement in his peripheral view and noticed the other two Rangers that had come with them from the helicopter once again falling in behind them.

Moments later, they burst back out into the blinding light of day, joining Crystal and Connor once more. Bowser looked happier now that he'd had something to drink. He pranced over and licked Adam's hands.

They crossed the parking lot to the street and followed Major Hunter down the sidewalk.

"Where are we going?" Crystal asked.

"To a hotel. It's only a few blocks from here," the major replied.

Connor groaned and muttered something about his feet.

Carla pulled alongside Adam and leaned close to whisper in his ear, "We're going to *stay* in Bexar? What happened to Chicago?"

Adam shook his head. "We'd never make it. I was a fool to think that we could."

"*Now* you come to that conclusion?" Sophie erupted from just behind them. Adam glanced back to find her scowling angrily at him.

"You got Owen killed by convincing him to blindly follow along with your reckless schemes, and *now* you decide to play it safe?" Sophie sneered. "How convenient."

Adam nearly tripped over a piece of rubble. He stopped walking and turned to properly face his accuser. "I'm sorry about what happened to Owen, Sophie. I really am. If I could go back and do things differently, I would."

"It's not fair to blame Adam for what happened," Carla added.

He noticed the kids and the other two Rangers hanging back and keeping their distance from the developing confrontation.

Sophie crossed her arms over her chest, and her lips twisted bitterly. "Fair? You want to talk to me about fair? I'm a widow because of him!" She jabbed a finger at Adam's chest.

"That's enough, Sophie," Carla said.

"No, it's okay," Adam said, shaking his head. "Let her vent."

"You don't believe me?" Sophie challenged, fixing Carla with a brittle smile. "Just look at his track record! In Afghanistan he got his entire squad killed, but somehow, Adam survived. When the Specs came, he got your husband captured, and then he rolled his truck off the road and killed his own wife. Just two nights ago, he left Rick to be torn apart by stalkers, and the very next day he leads my husband, your son, and his daughter on a suicide mission to Travis where he almost got all four of them killed! Somehow, they survived, but then what happened? He leads us all on another suicide mission to Bandera and raiders kill Owen.

"It's time to face facts: Adam is a lightning rod; anyone standing too close to him is going to get struck down sooner or later. If you're not careful, Carla, you and your son will be next."

Major Hunter came striding over, looking annoyed by the delay. "Are you done?" he asked. "I've got places to be."

Sophie snorted. "*Done* is an understatement. Emily? Let's go." She stormed past the major with her daughter trailing meekly behind her.

Hunter's gaze lingered on Adam. "Is that true?" he asked.

Adam worked some moisture into his mouth. "Which part?"

"That you got your squad killed in Afghanistan."

He hesitated. He was still struggling to recover from Sophie's unexpected attack. She'd aimed one too many blows below the belt, leaving him reeling.

"Of course, it's not true!" Carla answered for him. "He was honorably discharged. He took a bullet that shattered his leg, but somehow he still managed to drag one of his men to safety. He saved that man's life and earned a medal for it."

"No, I didn't," Adam whispered, shaking his head. He'd told Carla and her husband the story a few times over dinner at each other's houses

in Austin before the invasion. He'd explained how he'd been discharged from the Army, and what had happened to his leg. In the process, he'd mentioned the other survivor from his unit—Private Aaron White, but he'd never meant to paint himself as a hero, and he wasn't.

"You *didn't* save him?" Carla demanded, her outrage redirecting to him as she began to suspect that maybe he'd told her a lie all those years ago.

But some truths could be just as misleading as lies. "Aaron was paralyzed from the waist down by the shrapnel in his spine," Adam explained. "He took his own life a year later."

Carla frowned. "That's not your fault."

"No?" Adam smiled bitterly. "Either way, you have to admit that Sophie has a point." He jerked a thumb to where she and Emily were standing about twenty feet down the road, hugging each other—an island unto themselves. "People *do* seem to have a bad habit of dying around me," Adam finished.

Major Hunter sighed. "All right. You people have obviously been through a lot. My advice is don't be too hard on yourselves, or each other. Your friend will come around. She's just grieving. Anger is a part of that. It comes in waves."

Adam nodded. "Yeah." He knew all about grief.

"Let's get y'all situated at the hotel so you can

wash up and get some rest," Major Hunter said. "Tomorrow we'll see if we can figure out where we can use you." Major Hunter went striding down the sidewalk, leading the way once more.

Adam and Carla fell in behind him, keeping a respectful distance from Sophie and Emily.

"Don't listen to her, Dad," Crystal whispered. Adam glanced over his shoulder to see his daughter smiling grimly at him. She and Connor were walking hand-in-hand. Bowser was back to panting up a storm, looking about as exhausted as Adam felt. "It wasn't your fault," Crystal added.

Adam nodded and looked back to the fore, pushing the guilt aside to focus on more imminent concerns.

Resting up at a hotel sounded like heaven after everything that they'd been through. Making a life for themselves here in Bexar might work out for the best in the end. Following a rumor to Chicago so they could book a spot on a mythical spaceship to run away to another planet sounded impossibly far-fetched. Bexar was real, and so far, Ellis didn't seem to know anything about what had happened in Travis between them and Governor Miller. As long as it stayed that way, they'd be fine.

No, we'll be better than fine, Adam decided. *We'll be safe.*

CHAPTER TWELVE

Curious timing, Ellis thought to himself as he crossed the parking lot to City Hall. Adam Hall and the rest of the survivors from Sunny Valley had pitched up on his doorstep on the *same* day that he was supposed to check in with Governor Miller.

He took the elevator up to the top floor of City Hall and strode quickly down the corridor to the communications room. He shut and locked the door behind him, then pulled out a rolling office chair and sat staring at the shortwave radio system. He took a minute to steady his pulse and collect his thoughts.

The governor's orders had been clear: send Rangers to Sunny Valley Ranch and make sure that no one had escaped alive. Ellis had done exactly as the governor had asked, although he'd given his Rangers orders to bring them back *alive* to Bexar.

As fate would have it, they'd arrived too late. The ranch had already been burned to the ground by the time the Rangers arrived. If the corpses they'd found were any indication, there'd been some kind of altercation between a group of raiders and a squad of Rangers from Kerr. Yet mysteriously, there'd been no sign of the civilian ranchers. Until now, that is, when they'd pitched up on Ellis's doorstep, requesting asylum.

The problem was that they were also fugitives. *What to do?* Ellis wondered while absently tapping his chin.

The governor had accused Adam Hall, Owen Brooks, and several others of treason. But Ellis felt that the governor had overreacted—a knee-jerk reaction from a guilty conscience. It wasn't as though Adam had gone to Travis to accuse Miller of being a collaborator, but now there could be no doubt. So far the governor hadn't made their fugitive status public, so it was conceivable that they could safely hide out here in Bexar and Miller would be none the wiser —even more conceivable once Ellis reported to the governor that his Rangers had found everyone at Sunny Valley dead, killed in a shootout between the Rangers and raiders.

That would keep them safe for a while. Maybe even long enough for Ellis to use them to bring Miller down.

Initially, Ellis had sympathized with the governor's position. The Specs required a steady supply of human recruits for whatever it was they were up to, and at some point, the demand had outstripped supply. People had gotten too good at battening down the hatches and hiding from stalkers. And on top of that, the stalkers were an unreliable source of recruits. After all, they still needed to *eat*.

So the Specs had begun blatantly abducting people from the safe zones with their ships. It only had to happen a couple of dozen times before panic had set in and begun to spread, rocking the Republic to its matchstick foundations and threatening to burn everything that the governor had built to the ground.

Left with no choice, the governor had played the only card he had and made an unholy alliance with the Specs. He found ways to quietly funnel recruits to them, all the while ensuring that the residents of the safe zones still felt *safe*. And that was key. The illusion of safety, if not safety itself, had to be preserved. But it meant that the people in the know —people like Governor Miller, Thomas Ellis himself, Mayor Maloney of Kerr, Mayor Billings from Dallas, and tens or hundreds of others— all had to shoulder a heavy burden of truth.

And the truth was, Governor Miller's willing collaboration was the only thing keeping the Specs from coming down from orbit and forcing the issue.

Ellis grimaced at the thought of their ships roaring down from orbit en masse. Yet maybe that was what needed to happen. At the very least, people would know the score, and then they could establish a more impartial system of sending people to the Specs. They could draw names. Or ask for volunteers. Or maybe they'd develop some set of criteria that everyone could agree upon.

But for any of that to happen, the people had to know the truth, and then they had to make Governor Miller pay for hiding it.

Ellis was in a good position to make that happen now that Adam had shown up and could bear witness to the governor's cover-ups. But Ellis couldn't afford to be hasty, either. Ellis had to recruit an army to his cause before he exposed the governor's lies. Then he would lead that army to Travis and take the Governor's mansion by force.

Ellis smiled thinly to himself. Miller had made a mistake. By secretly funneling recruits from the safe zones to the Specs, he had broken the cardinal rule: *don't shit where you eat.*

Miller had cherry-picked single men and women and orphaned children, making sure that the ones who disappeared were the ones who were least likely to be missed. But he'd based his criteria on a dangerous assumption —just because someone is alone, it doesn't mean that no one cares about them. Miller had focused on sending newcomers and refugees to the Specs, and that was what had ultimately led to them taking the only woman that Ellis had ever loved—Valentina Flores.

Ellis had loved her from afar, taking his time to insert himself into her life in a natural, organic way. A smart, beautiful, independent woman like Val would have nothing less. She wouldn't fall for him just because he was the *mayor* of Bexar, and she was too independent to allow herself to be caged by any man. But instead, thanks to Governor Miller, she had been caged by the Specters, and now Ellis would never see her again.

It might seem like a small thing, a pathetic excuse for a revolution that could kill thousands in its course, but to Ellis, Val was *everything*. She was pure of heart and soul in a way that others could only pretend to be. She had founded the *Nightingales* and had served as their first Proctor for many years.

They were an anonymous, volunteer-based group dedicated to bringing in survivors and refugees from the wastes. They wore these ridiculous *Day of the Dead* masks, even when they met amongst themselves. That way, no one would ever know who had saved them, and no one would owe them any favors. Val believed in doing good for goodness' sake, and not for ego or reward. So when people had begun disappearing inexplicably from the safe zones, most of them being the very ones that the Nightingales had rescued, it was inevitable that Val would look into it.

She must have discovered something damning about the governor, because Miller had suddenly turned on her organization, declaring publicly that they were in league with the Syndicate, and that they were bringing in Syndicate raiders, not refugees.

The governor sent Rangers searching for them home by home, in many cases finding the masks that identified their association with the Nightingales.

In a move that the Governor had probably intended to look merciful, the Nightingales were exiled rather than executed. They were forced to leave their homes and families in the middle of the night with nothing but the shirts on their backs, while others fled in daylight with better preparations. Ellis had discreetly helped Val and her conclave to escape Bexar before they could be discovered. But now, just a week ago, an informant from Val's conclave had returned to Bexar with the news that she and her entire group had been captured by the Specs.

It was hard to believe, and even harder to accept, that Ellis would never see Val again. He would never have a chance to tell her how he felt. Ellis gritted his teeth. Governor Miller would pay.

Ellis drew in a deep breath and held it for a second before letting it out and with it all of his rage and contempt.

Finally, he reached for the radio mic, pressed the button, and said, "This is Alamo, calling Longhorn. Come in, Longhorn. Over."

Buzzing static answered, followed by a *click* and then the deep, baritone voice of Miller himself, "Go for Longhorn. Over."

"The target was neutralized by raiders before we got there. Over." Ellis waited a beat to see if Miller would buy the lie.

"Are you certain? We cannot afford to leave any loose ends. Over."

Ellis nodded. "Positive. The location was burned to the ground. Over."

"Did you make a positive ID of the bodies? Over."

Ellis considered his response. If he said yes, the investigation would end there, but was it realistic that he'd been able to ID the bodies after a fire? Even after a fire, he probably could have identified genders and ages. So he decided to stick with that. "Yes, sir. We ID'd six civilians. They all died in the fire. Two women, two children, and two adult males. Over."

"Excellent! Were any vehicles missing?"

Ellis chewed his lip. That lie would be easier to verify. Stalkers could conceivably drag away the dead bodies for a snack, but then their truck wouldn't be missing.

"We didn't see any vehicles besides the two Humvees from Kerr. Over."

"The ranchers were driving a white Ford," the governor said. "You didn't see it?"

"No, sir. It was probably taken by one of the raiders who attacked them."

"Or by one of the ranchers who defended against them. Are you sure you identified the bodies? Over."

Ellis scowled. This conversation was getting dangerously close to the truth. "As sure as I can be without having laid eyes on the corpses myself, sir."

"I suppose that will have to do," the governor replied. "But be on the lookout for any survivors. We do *not* want them spreading rumors about us."

"Understood, sir," Ellis said. "If any of them come here, you'll be the first to know."

"Good. I expect nothing less. Longhorn out."

Ellis flicked off the radio and leaned back from the mic with a sigh. Hiding Adam and his people in Bexar could turn out to be more trouble than it was worth.

CHAPTER THIRTEEN

The Drury Plaza Hotel was located right on the San Antonio River, along the city's once-famous Riverwalk. Major Hunter led them down a flight of steps to the river, and then across an old pedestrian bridge to the hotel.

Crystal stopped halfway across the bridge with Bowser to admire the murky green depths of the river. Bowser peered through the railing, wagging his tail as if he'd spotted something down there. Adam joined them by the railing. "This used to be a popular tourist spot," he said. "I took your mother on a boat tour here just before you were born."

Crystal squinted at him. "That sounds romantic."

Adam smiled. "It was. Especially at night with all the restaurants and hotels lit up, their lights shining on the water."

"I wish I'd been alive to see that," Crystal sighed.

"Oh, we still do boat tours," Major Hunter put in from where he stood a few feet away. "If you like, I can look into it for you."

Adam cut him off with an upraised hand. "We don't have any credits."

"Don't worry about it. You're guests of the mayor."

Crystal looked to Adam with eyebrows hopefully raised. "Can we, Dad? Please?"

"Well…" Adam hesitated. With Owen's death still so fresh, it felt wrong to be enjoying themselves, but Crystal had experienced so little normalcy in her life that it was hard to pass up the opportunity to put a smile on her face.

Adam nodded to Hunter. "If it can be arranged, we won't say no."

"Good," Hunter said. "I'll see if I can comp a few tickets for you later tonight."

They continued across the bridge to the other end and down another flight of stairs to a stone walkway along the river. Sophie was waiting for them at the bottom of the stairs with a strained smile and glittering eyes.

"Must be nice, going on a river cruise while your friend's bloated corpse is rotting in a Walmart a hundred miles away. Out of sight, out of mind, isn't that right?"

Adam grimaced. "Shit, Soph. I didn't mean any disrespect. I'll send the kids on their own."

"Emily, too, of course." Sophie was grinning now, her unshed tears shimmering brightly. "I'm sure *that* will make up for losing her father."

Adam hesitated, struggling to put together the right words, but he thought better of it and bit his tongue. Nothing he could say right now was going to make this any better, and if Sophie needed a punching bag, then it may as well be him.

The only thing that could help Sophie now was the grim passing of the days—not that she would forget, but eventually she would learn how to cope.

Sophie spun away from him, still smiling. She quickly caught up with Emily and Major Hunter by the entrance of the hotel, while Adam stood frozen at the bottom of the stairs. Crystal, Carla, and Connor joined him there.

"I'm sorry I suggested it," Crystal whispered. "We shouldn't go."

"No," Carla replied. "You and Connor go. We'll stay and make sure that Sophie and Emily are okay. You punishing yourselves for what happened isn't going to change anything."

Adam sighed. "She's right."

"Well, okay…" Crystal conceded.

"Are you coming?" Major Hunter called from the open doors of the hotel.

Adam nodded, walking quickly to catch up.

Major Hunter led them through the hotel until they reached a dusty but ostentatious lobby with double-story ceilings and a mezzanine that overlooked the lobby from the second floor. Elaborate brass moldings crowned the ceiling, and an ornate stained-glass window loomed high over the main entrance.

The major walked straight to a long wall of desks between ornate columns where a young woman sat leaning back in her chair with her feet up on the desk and her nose buried in a trashy romance novel. Adam smiled as he studied the bare-chested man with a cowboy hat and blue jeans on the cover.

Major Hunter cleared his throat and the woman flinched, almost falling out of her chair.

"Oh, my! I'm sorry! I didn't see you standing there." She stood up quickly and shut the book. "Is there something I can help you with?" Her gaze drifted past Major Hunter to Adam and the others, and then to Bowser who was grinning up at her and panting noisily. Her brow furrowed deeply at that. "Dogs are not permitted in the Drury," she said.

"We'll make an exception. They're Mayor Ellis's guests," Hunter replied.

"Oh, I see. Well… just make sure he doesn't… do anything inside."

"He's house-trained," Crystal said, hefting his leash. "But we'll be sure to take him for plenty of walks just in case."

"Yes…" The woman dragged her eyes away from the dog with a visible effort. Her attention lingered on Adam. He must have looked like hell—covered in blood, dirt, sweat, and soot from the ordeal of the last three days. He tried a weary smile, and the woman glanced hastily back to Major Hunter.

"We're looking for three of the Drury's best rooms," Major Hunter explained.

"Certainly, just give me a moment while I see what's available..." She flipped through an old-fashioned log book on her desk, running her finger down the list of names and signatures. "It looks like we have a few rooms on the top floor above the parking garage, overlooking the river," she said.

"That sounds great," Carla said.

"Oh, yes. They're delightful," the woman replied.

It took another minute for her to find the requisite key cards in a drawer. She didn't waste any time programming them, which made Adam think that they were master keys used by the staff, or else that they had been programmed not to expire. That made sense. Working computers were a rare commodity, after all.

Adam noticed that those dirty plastic key cards had been crudely labeled with a black sharpie to indicate which rooms they belonged to.

The concierge handed them to the major and then directed Adam, Sophie, and Carla to sign the log book for each of their rooms.

"Welcome to Drury Plaza!" the concierge declared brightly once they were done. "Would you like me to get someone to help you with your luggage?" A frown creased the woman's brow as she scanned their group once more, this time searching for their bags.

A whistling wind howled through the lobby from the broken windows.

"We didn't bring any bags," Adam explained.

"Oh, I see," The woman replied, looking them over with a frown. She was probably worried about them sullying the bedsheets with their filthy clothes. "Well, we do have a laundry service if you need it, and terrycloth robes."

Adam smiled and nodded. "We'll be sure to take full advantage. Thank you."

Major Hunter led them away from the desk, cupping the key cards in his left hand and leaving his right to manage his carbine. He led them across the marble-lined lobby. Adam heard another whistling gust of wind, and he looked at the massive stained-glass window above the main entrance of the hotel. It was cracked and broken in a dozen different places, letting in golden shafts of sunlight.

They reached the elevators and Major Hunter hit the call button. A moment later the doors to the nearest one opened and they stepped inside. Hunter tapped the *8* on the flickering control panel, but it didn't light up. The doors shuddered and squealed against tortured mechanisms, slowly grinding shut. Adam waited for the platform to go speeding upward, but nothing happened.

"Ummm… maybe we should take the stairs?" Crystal suggested.

Bowser whined anxiously as the lights flickered again.

"Hang on." Major Hunter hammered the control panel with a fist. The lights on the panel flickered again. This time their floor lit up, and the elevator lurched into motion, speeding steadily upward.

"Just bad wiring," Major Hunter explained. "The city's filthy with it."

Adam nodded uneasily, wondering what other aspects of elevator maintenance had been neglected over the years. He was definitely taking the stairs next time.

The elevator dinged on the 8th floor, and Major Hunter led the way out into a carpeted hall. Sophie and Emily were the first to follow him, nearly colliding with each other in their hurry to exit the elevator.

Crystal started after them, but Adam gently pulled her back.

"Let's give them some space," he suggested quietly.

Carla nodded her agreement, and they waited a few more seconds before leaving the elevator. Adam let Crystal and Connor go first to keep a buffer between him and Sophie. He didn't want to fan the flames of Sophie's grief. He'd become the focal point of her rage, but he didn't blame her. If the tables had been reversed, he would have been looking for someone to blame, too.

As they strode down the hallway, Adam couldn't help but notice the stains on the ragged carpets and the dank, musty smell that pervaded the corridor. He had a feeling that these carpets hadn't been washed since the invasion.

Overhead lights flickered, plunging the windowless hallway into darkness for several seconds. Crystal yelped with fright, and Adam crashed into her in the dark.

She clutched his arm, clinging to him for dear life. Bowser let out a low growl, picking up on their anxiety.

"It's okay!" Major Hunter called out just before the lights flickered back on. "Like I said, bad wiring. On top of that, we've been having problems with our electrical grid lately."

Crystal quickly let go of Adam's arm and reached for Connor's instead. Adam realized with a sharp pang of disappointment that she'd only reached for him by mistake.

"I've heard that some of the other zones have it worse," Adam commented, walking quickly past Crystal and Connor. "Programmed power outages, food shortages…"

"You mean load shedding?" the major asked. "We've got that, too." He stopped in front of room 816 and sorted through the key cards in his hands, looking for the one with the right number scribbled on the back. He fitted it to the slot in the door, and the lock blinked green and beeped. Major Hunter turned to regard them as he opened the door. "Who wants this one?"

"We'll take it," Sophie said, pushing quickly through with Emily.

The major barely had a chance to hand her the key before she slammed the door in his face. Adam heard the security chain jangling on the other side. The major walked on to the next room without comment and opened it. Adam made an after-you gesture to Carla. She smiled and walked in with Connor.

"Dinner is on the house," Major Hunter explained as he handed Carla her key. "The hotel restaurant is right on the riverwalk. We passed by it on the way in. It's open until ten, I believe. It's a buffet, so the food will be fresher if you get there early. I'll see what I can do about the boat tour tonight. How many tickets would you like?"

"Just two," Adam said, holding up that many fingers.

Major Hunter regarded him steadily. "You sure? I can get tickets for all of you."

"It'd be wasted on me," Adam replied. "All I can think about right now is a shower, a soft bed, and a solid eight hours of sleep. Or maybe twelve."

Major Hunter smiled and nodded. "I hear you."

Adam and Crystal followed the major to the next room. Hunter opened the door and handed Adam the key.

"If you need anything, just dial zero. Should still get you to the front desk."

"Thank you," Adam said. He stepped into the room behind Crystal and Bowser.

"You're welcome. Enjoy your stay, Mr. Hall. I'll have those boat tickets sent up to your room for the kids."

"Great." Adam swung the door and it clicked shut. With that simple action, all of the fight abruptly left him, leaving his knees weak and his whole body cold and wracked with pain. He leaned hard against the door, struggling not to pass out. He'd barely had eight hours of sleep in the last seventy-two, and now that he was somewhere safe, his brain had just pulled the plug on whatever emergency reserves were keeping him going.

Adam stumbled down the short entry hall. Crystal and Bowser were busy gawking at the view from the windows. He shuffled over to join them and stood swaying lightly on his feet beside a table with two armchairs.

The sun was sinking steadily toward the horizon, lighting the sky on fire and turning the river to a gleaming ribbon of molten copper.

"Did you stay here with Mom?" Crystal asked suddenly.

Adam blinked. "What?"

"When you came here. You said you went on a boat ride?"

"Oh yeah, we did, but we didn't spend the night. We drove back to Austin the same day—I mean, Travis."

"You drove there and back in one day?" Crystal asked, sounding surprised.

Adam nodded. "It used to be quicker than it is now. The roads were in better shape."

She nodded absently and looked back to the view. "Well, it's a nice hotel."

"Yeah, it is," Adam agreed. He glanced longingly at the nearest bed, and then at the bathroom. "Why don't you go wash up first?"

"Aren't Connor and I going on a boat ride later?" Crystal asked. "I don't have any clean clothes to change into."

"Oh, right. Well, then I guess I'll shower first. You can wait until you get back."

"Okay."

Adam turned away, shuffling past an old bar fridge that wasn't turned on and probably didn't work. Sitting above it was a bottle of red wine with a red bow tied around the top, along with two glasses, a bottle opener, and a gold-rimmed card tented on the counter beside it. Adam flipped the card over and read the message on the other side:

Welcome to Bexar!

-Mayor Ellis

Adam frowned, feeling suddenly like he was being bought—or sold. The mayor obviously made a habit of inviting his guests to stay here, wining and dining them to curry favors—but with whom and for what?

Adam had been to Bexar many times before with Rick and Owen, but they'd never stayed at the Drury before. They'd always paid their way in some cheap rat-infested motel.

So why roll out the red carpet for us now? Adam wondered. Was the mayor just being magnanimous? Or was he planning to ask for something in exchange?

Adam took that thought with him into the shower. Hot water was a rare treat, easing the aches and knots of tension in his muscles. He stood under the pounding spray amidst billowing clouds of steam, remembering the last time that he'd had a hot shower— at the Governor's Mansion in Travis. Miller's hospitality had turned out to be a farce, designed to lull them into a false sense of security before luring them to their deaths in his bunker the next day.

Adam hoped that Mayor Ellis's hospitality

wouldn't take a similar turn.

CHAPTER FOURTEEN

Adam popped the cork on the wine and poured himself a generous glass, then he sat in one of the two chairs by the window to watch the boat that had just pulled alongside the hotel. Adam's stomach rumbled as he sipped his wine, reminding him that he was drinking on an empty stomach. Having already showered and peeled out of his filthy rags, he'd decided to skip dinner, thinking that he couldn't exactly waltz down to a fancy restaurant in a bathrobe and slippers. If he'd been smart, he might have eaten before showering. *Oh well.* Alcohol was a kind of food, wasn't it? Empty calories for an empty stomach. Adam took another sip.

A flicker of movement caught his eye down by the river. He spotted Crystal, the fading sunlight shining gold in her hair. Connor stepped into view beside her. He was carefully helping Crystal into the boat.

Adam frowned, contemplating the scene ruefully. Crystal was practically a woman already, and he'd run flat out of options to delay the inevitable. His days of playing chaperon were coming to an end. Now it was up to Crystal and Connor to decide what came next. For all Adam knew, if things kept progressing between them, he was looking at his future son-in-law.

The boat began pulling away, and Adam sighed and massaged his scratchy, aching eyes with his thumb and forefinger.

A knock sounded at the door. Bowser woofed and raised his head from the bed where he lay. Adam stared at the door for a couple of seconds before he summoned the energy to move. He stood up with a groan. "One minute!" he called, adjusting his terrycloth robe as he went. "Who's there?" he thought to ask just before checking the peephole.

"Carla."

He saw her standing on the other side holding a steaming plate full of food. She hadn't showered yet, but her face was clean, and she looked radiant. "You didn't come down for dinner, so I thought I'd bring some up to you."

Adam's stomach growled again, and he smiled as he opened the door. "I appreciate that," he said.

"Connor and Crystal just left," she explained.

"I know, I was watching them from the window."

Carla smirked and shook her head. "Of course, you were."

Adam caught himself checking her out as she walked in. He forced himself to look away and shut the door, then turned back to see her setting the plate of food beside his wine. Carla picked up the bottle with the bow still tied to it. "What's the occasion?"

"A soft bed, and warm shower, and most importantly, nothing is trying to eat me tonight."

Carla laughed lightly at that and set the bottle down. "How come I didn't get one of these?"

"You didn't?" Adam asked.

"No."

"Well, there's an extra glass," he said. "You're welcome to join me for a nightcap."

"That sounds wonderful."

Adam pulled out the other chair and waited for her to sit down, and then he poured her a glass of wine. Carla smiled as she accepted it from him.

Adam sat once more, being careful to hold his robes shut as he did so.

"You didn't waste any time," Carla said, nodding to him.

He arched an eyebrow at her. "I'm sorry?"

"Showering."

"Do you blame me?"

Carla snorted. "No, I suppose not."

Adam reached across the table and tipped his glass toward hers. "To not wasting time," he said.

Carla hesitated. Her eyes dipped and flashed darkly before she touched her glass to his with a musical *clink*.

She repeated the toast with a small smile, and he realized that she'd taken a meaning from his toast that he hadn't intended. Adam felt his robes stirring of their own accord, and he shifted uncomfortably in his seat. He dropped a hand to his lap to make an adjustment, and Carla's smile widened as she sipped her wine.

Adam cleared his throat nervously and directed his attention to the food she'd brought. There was a nice-looking steak and mashed potatoes with melted cheese on top and a small garden salad on the side. Adam cut a giant piece of the steak and scooped potatoes onto his fork before popping it into his mouth. The food was still warm, and the meat was surprisingly tender and well-seasoned.

"Delicious," he managed just before swallowing.

"It was," Carla agreed while gazing absently out the window at the boat below. It was still taking on passengers from the hotel. "I'm glad we were able to get the kids those tickets. This is like their first date if you think about it."

Adam scowled. "Don't remind me."

Carla laughed and reached under the table to squeeze his thigh. "Oh, relax! They have to grow up eventually."

"Do they?"

"Some would say they already have. Crystal's fifteen and Connor's sixteen."

"Still babies," Adam grumbled.

"What were you doing at their ages? I bet you were already breaking hearts."

Adam frowned. "That's different."

"It's exactly the same."

"It's not the same. I couldn't get pregnant at fifteen."

"But you *could* get someone else pregnant," Carla pointed out. "How is that any different?"

"I guess it's not," he mumbled lamely.

"But you didn't get anyone pregnant, did you?"

"Of course not."

"Then maybe you should trust your daughter and Connor to have just as much sense and self-restraint as you did."

Adam shifted uncomfortably again. "You talk about that stuff with him?"

"You mean you *don't* talk about it with Crystal?"

"Once. When she got her first period."

Carla frowned. "That's great timing."

"Well, I just figured if she got her period then it meant that she could... you know."

"That poor girl. The indignities she must

have suffered without her mother around."

Adam winced.

Carla reacted belatedly to what she'd said as if only now playing it back in her mind. "Oh, Adam, I'm sorry. I should have thought before I spoke. I just meant…"

"I know what you meant," he replied gruffly, but he softened it with a smile.

Carla reached across the table for his hand where it rested on the table, gripping the stem of his wine glass. She held his gaze for a long moment while her thumb gently stroked the back of his hand. "I don't think you do," she whispered.

Once again Adam felt his robes stirring.

"Do you mind if I use your bathroom?" Carla asked.

Adam shook his head. "Go ahead."

Carla stood up and crossed the room. She turned and shut the bathroom door. Moments later, Adam heard the shower turning on. The response from his body was immediate, but this time he didn't try to suppress it. He took another sip of his wine and went on eating, allowing the spreading warmth of a gentle buzz to numb his myriad aches and pains. Somehow, as beaten-up and sleep-deprived as he was, a new impulse had just taken center stage in his brain. He remembered his wife, Kimberly, but this time the memory didn't fill him with guilt, and somehow, he had the sense that she wouldn't blame him. He'd been alone for long enough, and life was too short for wasting.

Adam washed down a man-sized bite of his steak with more wine. Far below, the boat began pulling away with Crystal and Connor on board.

Adam was halfway through his meal by the time the shower shut off. The bathroom door clicked open, and Carla appeared standing there, stark naked and leaning on the door jamb. Suddenly Adam's food was forgotten.

"I couldn't find the other robe..." Carla said.

Adam wordlessly stood from the table and crossed the room, walking quickly to her. He took Carla's face in his hands and pulled her lips to his. She fell against him, warm and soft in all of the right places, and they kissed each other deeply. Adam picked her up and she wrapped her legs around his waist. Turning to the bed, he lowered her gently to it and spent a moment admiring her supple curves while untying his robe and letting it fall to his ankles.

They devoured each other hungrily, starved as they were for the slightest drop of warmth and human contact, having each spent nearly a decade in mourning.

When it was over, Carla was the first to fall asleep. Her head lay on his chest, her long, curly brown hair cascading over him in waves. He gently stroked his hand through her hair while the other lay at his side, his fingers entwined with hers.

Adam lay there, staring up at the ceiling in awe and terror as darkness fell. He'd felt something that went far beyond the physical, a feeling that he used to think a person could only ever find once in a lifetime. And yet, somehow, he'd been lucky enough to find it twice. But knowing how rare it was terrified him. Having something, meant having something to lose.

Adam realized that was what had been holding him back with Carla. It wasn't guilt that he would somehow dishonor Kim's memory, or the fact that he still blamed himself for her death. He hadn't wanted to start something with Carla because he was terrified to go through losing someone all over again. With Crystal, it was bad enough, but now he had two people that he cared about more than life itself.

Adam lay there for a long moment, exhausted, but unable to succumb to sleep. Eventually, the physical need for rest outweighed his swirling anxieties, and Adam's heart rate subsided until it merged with Carla's. He drifted off into a restless sleep filled with shapeless, nameless horrors.

CHAPTER FIFTEEN

The boat thrummed steadily along the river, making Crystal's teeth ache from the vibrations. She was tired, dirty, and cold, but somehow this was heaven. Connor's arm tightened around her shoulders, drawing her close to share their warmth against the encroaching chill of the night.

Crystal glanced about warily at the jagged, gleaming glass of broken windows in old, abandoned high rises, and at the never-ending parade of boarded-up restaurants along the river. There were a handful of pedestrians out walking down the stone paths that flanked the river. Here and there she spotted a dog on a leash, or a couple kissing on a bench.

"This place must have been amazing before the invasion," Crystal whispered.

"Yeah." Connor nodded.

She snuggled against him, and he encircled her with his other arm. Having him so close was electrifying. She wasn't even bothered by the accumulated smell of dirt and his sweat from the past day and a half. Besides, she doubted she smelled any better than he did.

Crystal felt safe with Connor. They'd grown up together. She'd known him since she was seven and he was eight. She still remembered making him play with her Barbies and stuffed animals at her house when his parents came over for dinner. Crystal smiled wanly as the memory brought a fuzzy half-remembered image of her mother to mind. Not wanting to focus on sad things, Crystal set the memory aside to focus on Connor.

Despite her familiarity with him, there was something about him that made her feel more alive than she ever had in her life. It hadn't always been there, but somehow he'd changed in the last couple of years, and she'd begun to see him as more than just a friend. For one thing, in the last year, he'd shot up from her height of five-foot-six to just a hair shy of her dad at six-foot-one. He had thick, shaggy brown hair that she couldn't stop daydreaming about running her hands through, and just the right number of freckles framed his warm honey-brown eyes—eyes that made her melt every time she looked into them.

Crystal thought about the kiss they'd shared yesterday when she'd thought that her dad had died in the governor's bunker. Had Connor just been trying to cheer her up? He hadn't tried to kiss her again since then, so maybe he didn't feel the same way that she did. Or maybe she'd messed up that kiss. Or maybe he secretly liked Emily better. Maybe he thought of her like a sister.

Crystal grimaced and looked up at Connor, quietly studying him. He was busy watching the scenery, but a moment later his head turned and he caught her looking at him.

He flashed a grin. "What's up?" His eyes blazed with coppery embers from the street lights along the riverwalk.

She turned into a puddle. Her mouth popped open to say something, but her mind drew a blank.

Still smiling, he leaned down and kissed her on the lips.

This time, she felt his tongue touching hers, and her whole body flooded with a wash of heat. A tingly tightness began somewhere deep inside of her. Her heart began to race, and her hands grew clammy. When he finally withdrew, her head was spinning. Connor laced his fingers through hers, then he went back to watching the scenery as if nothing had happened.

She experienced a brief flash of annoyance that he could be so calm after leaving her a fluttery mess.

Then Connor's hand tightened suddenly in hers, indicating a different kind of tension. He sat up straight and his arm left her shoulders.

"What is it?" Crystal whispered.

Some of the other passengers in the boat began mumbling and muttering to each other.

Connor wordlessly pointed to something floating in the water.

It was a body, a bloated corpse, lying face-up rather than face-down as if it might just be a fat man out for a relaxing swim. His face was covered with a colorful mask that looked vaguely like a skull.

A woman screamed.

A man said, "It's a Nightingale."

"Is he dead?" someone else asked.

An elderly man stood up from the seat in front of theirs and leaned over the side of the boat to poke the body with his cane. The dead man's bloated belly dimpled grotesquely beneath the cane, but he didn't even twitch.

"Definitely dead," the old man confirmed.

Crystal gaped at the corpse as it drifted by.

"He's wearing a *calaca*," Connor whispered.

"A what?"

"A *skull*. It's a mask that people wear to celebrate the Day of the Dead. My mom took me to one of the festivals in Costa Rica when I went there to see my grandparents."

Crystal frowned. "So that man is—or he *was* —from there?"

"Or Mexico probably." Connor shrugged. "It's not the right time of year for the celebration, though."

An elderly woman with stringy gray hair turned to look back at them from the row of seats in front of them. "He was a Nightingale," she whispered. "That's why he was wearing the mask."

"What's a Nightingale?" Crystal asked.

The old man with the cane sat back down. "Terrorists who were trying to undermine the Republic by bringing Raiders into the safe zones disguised as refugees."

Crystal blinked. "Really?"

The old man nodded gravely. "They're outlaws now, but for a time people thought they were heroes. They wore those masks to stay anonymous. In hindsight, we probably should have realized who they were working for. The damn Syndicate is everywhere these days."

The old woman sitting beside him nodded along with her husband's sentiment.

Crystal couldn't help feeling unnerved by the thought of the Syndicate raiders lurking within Bexar's walls.

"If they're outlaws, what was one of them doing in the city?" Crystal asked.

"I guess he must've snuck in," the old man said. "But don't worry, it looks like the Rangers took care of it."

"You're safe in here, dear," the old lady added. "As safe as anyone can be these days."

Across the aisle from them, on the other

side of the boat, someone snorted. "Sure, safe. That's what they want you to think, isn't it? Just like they want you to think that the Nightingales are the enemy."

"Excuse me?" the old man demanded, peering over the top of his wife's head to address the one who'd spoken.

It was a young man with thinning blond hair and sunken cheeks. He was hugging his shoulders against the cold and rocking gently on the edge of his seat. The seat beside him was empty, which made Crystal wonder why he was even on the boat. The river tour seemed like an activity for couples, not single riders, but maybe the boat also served as a kind of public transit system.

"You want to explain yourself?" the elderly man demanded.

"Never mind," the young man muttered, his eyes already sliding away.

Crystal frowned, and the elderly couple went back to minding their own business. A brittle silence fell, unbroken but for the steady thrumming of the boat's engine.

Crystal tried to sink back into the moment with Connor, but the mood had been spoiled. She couldn't stop thinking about the dead body and that grinning skull mask. Even if they were terrorists, why kill one of them and leave the body to float down the river? Maybe as a warning to others.

The boat ride went on for another hour. They were served drinks and snacks, and Crystal managed to more or less forget about the incident. By the time they returned to their rooms at the hotel, exhaustion was taking over. Crystal's eyes were sinking shut, and she was stumbling and swaying on her feet as if she were drunk. Connor helped her to her room and kissed her good night, leaving her even more unsteady than before. She opened the door with her key card and walked quietly in. Bowser woofed, and she quickly shushed him. Her dad stirred beneath the covers of the other bed but didn't appear to wake up.

Crystal was just about to go take a shower when she noticed that he wasn't alone. Carla was in the bed with him. Then she noticed her dad's bathrobe lying in a puddle on the floor, and she realized that they were *naked.*

She gaped at them in shock, then glanced at the other bed where Bowser was lying with his head between his paws.

A mess of conflicting emotions flashed through her. It felt like her dad had cheated on her mom. But her mother had been gone for so long that Crystal could barely remember her face anymore. It wasn't fair to blame him for moving on. Ultimately, Crystal decided she was happy for her dad. And for Connor's mom. But there was a more immediate concern. Where was *she* going to sleep?! She couldn't just climb into the bed beside theirs, could she?

Awkward!

She had a better idea. Turning back the way she'd come, Crystal stepped lightly down the hall to the door. She quietly opened it and clicked it shut. Walking to Connor's room, she knocked lightly on the door.

He opened it with a knitted brow. "Hey, what's up? I was just about to take a shower…"

Crystal smiled tightly at him. "Yeah, me too. Can I come in?"

"Uhh… yeah, I guess."

Crystal breezed in, and he shut the door behind her. She began pacing back and forth in front of the two beds in his room.

"Is your dad there?" Connor asked.

Crystal nodded. "Yeah, he's there."

"Oh." Connor sounded perplexed. "It's just that I can't find my mom. I thought maybe they went out for a walk together or something."

"Or *something* is more like it."

"Huh?"

"They're both sleeping in my room."

Connor's brow furrowed deeply, and he slowly shook his head. "What? Why would they…" His eyes widened suddenly as he appeared to figure it out for himself. "*Nooo…*" he said, drawing out the word and accentuating it with shock.

"*Yes…*" Crystal replied, mimicking his tone.

Connor snorted a laugh and began shaking

his head. "Well, I guess it's about time."

"You're not upset?" Crystal asked, frowning at him.

"Well... I mean, I was mad, sure. My dad came back and saved us, and then your dad killed him. But it wasn't really my dad anymore. He didn't even remember us until one of those *things* growing on his head died, and even then..." Connor let out a shaky sigh. "I don't know, I guess, I can't blame Adam. My dad was going to turn us into slaves like him. If Adam hadn't shot him, we'd probably be sitting on a Spec starship right now, going through whatever they did to my dad."

Crystal frowned. "Fine, but what does that have to do with him sleeping with your mom?"

"Well, if you're going to have a stepdad, it's probably better if you don't hate his guts, right?"

Crystal gaped at him. "Who's talking about a stepdad? They just had sex. It's not like he proposed or something!"

"Christie, *come on*. My mom's liked your dad for *years,* and after waiting almost a decade to make their move, you really think that this is just a one-night stand?"

Crystal felt a knot of tension forming between her eyes. "I guess I didn't think about it."

"Well, maybe you should, because I'm not the only one who'll be getting a stepparent."

"What does that make us?" Crystal asked.

Connor appeared to think about it. "Well, it's not as though we'll be related."

"Yeah, but still…"

"What's the difference?" Connor asked. "We grew up in the same house, anyway. This will just be more of the same to us."

"Maybe, but… you'll be my step*brother*."

Connor hesitated. "It's just a label. It doesn't matter."

"What if our parents try to stop us from being together?" Crystal asked.

"Because they had sex before we did? How's that fair?"

Crystal felt the heat rising in her cheeks. Up until now, they'd only shared a few kisses. It was all innocent fun. But sex? That was something else. She wasn't ready for that. Was that all Connor was really after?

"Sorry," Connor said, seeming to realize his mistake. "I didn't mean to make you uncomfortable. I'm not suggesting that we should… you know. I'm just saying that so what if we like each other, and if it goes somewhere and someday we get more serious? Is that wrong just because our parents got together before we did?"

Crystal hesitated. "I don't know. Is it?"

Connor shook his head. "It doesn't change anything."

"Our parents might not see it that way."

"My mom's not that conservative."

"My dad might be," Crystal replied.

"Let's not jump to any conclusions. Besides, I'll be seventeen in April. One more year and I'll be an adult. Pretty soon they won't be able to tell me what to do anymore."

"Yeah, you," Crystal replied. "What about me?"

"Let's worry about that when the time comes, okay?"

"Okay..." Crystal glanced at the bathroom. "Do you think I can take a shower here? And uh, maybe spend the night—but not like that," she added quickly.

Connor smiled. "I know what you meant. Go ahead. You can take my mom's bed by the window."

"Thanks," Crystal replied, already moving for the bathroom. She shut herself in and locked the door. A minute later she'd peeled out of her sweaty, dirt-crusted clothes, leaving them in a pile on the floor. She wrinkled her nose and kicked them into the closet beneath the two white terrycloth robes. Her clothes smelled more like smoke than anything, but they were definitely filthy.

Walking to the shower, she turned it on and waited a moment for the water to heat up. While she waited, she studied herself in the mirror, shocked to find that she barely recognized the dirt and soot-covered girl staring back at her.

She probed lightly at the worst of her injuries. She had four stitches in her right leg just above the knee where a piece of shrapnel had sliced her open after fighting raiders in Medina. And she had another dozen stitches in her left arm to seal three parallel gashes where a stalker had sliced her open just before they'd reached Travis.

Crystal probed lightly at the puckered gashes in her arm. They didn't look infected, but she was going to have a couple of nasty scars from that encounter.

Seeing the clouds of steam billowing from the shower, Crystal turned and stepped into the hot spray, letting it wash away the dirt and grime of the past day and a half. When she was done, her head was a lot clearer and she felt more like a human being again. She took a minute to avail herself of a courtesy toothbrush and a tiny tube of toothpaste, and then she shrugged into one of the two robes and tied it tightly around her waist. She stepped out of the bathroom to see that Connor was sitting in the dark in one of the chairs by the window, staring out into the night.

"You can use the bathroom now if you want," she said, quickly crossing the room to the bed that he'd indicated was his mother's. Connor looked over at her as she climbed under the covers and tucked them up to her chin.

"You think that was true, what they said on the boat?" he asked.

Crystal shook her head, pretending not to know what he was talking about. "What do you mean?"

"About the Nightingales. People bringing in raiders disguised as refugees."

"I don't know," Crystal replied.

"That man sitting across from us seemed to think it was a lie."

"But why would the Rangers execute innocent people?" Crystal asked.

Connor slowly shook his head. "I don't know. I hope they wouldn't."

"But?" Crystal prompted, sensing that he hadn't said everything.

"Governor Miller tried to execute *us*, and *we* were innocent."

Crystal winced. He was right. For all they knew, the Nightingales were being treated the same way. "I guess that's true," she muttered.

"Yeah." Connor stood up from his chair. "You should get some sleep."

She nodded wordlessly as he headed for the bathroom. Her gaze was drawn out into the darkness beyond the windows, wondering what terrors might be lurking out there, even within the walls of this supposedly *safe* zone.

Crystal chewed her bottom lip, wondering what to do about the dead man they'd seen. She could tell her dad, but knowing him, he wouldn't leave it there. Did she really want him to go sticking his nose into places where it didn't belong? The last thing they needed was to have to flee Bexar the way they'd fled the ranch. Where would they even go after that? They wouldn't last long out there in the wastes. Mr. Brooks' death was proof of that.

And things were just starting to turn around for them. They were living in the city now, and Connor was talking about a future with her. She could almost imagine having a normal life here, maybe even getting married and having kids of her own someday.

She couldn't risk all of that now. Not for something as fragile and dangerous as the truth. No. She'd swear Connor to secrecy. He'd understand. Whatever was going on with these so-called Nightingales, it was none of their business.

CHAPTER SIXTEEN

"Come in, come in, Mr. Hall." Mayor Ellis waved him through the door to his office with a pudgy hand while the other held a cup of steaming coffee to his lips.

Adam glanced back at Major Hunter. This time, the major shut the door, leaving Adam alone with the mayor. He took a seat in front of Ellis's desk and waited patiently while the man spread what looked like cream cheese on a bagel before taking a giant bite. The mayor began nodding and gesturing with his hands in lieu of words while he chewed.

Finally, he swallowed and spoke, "How have you been enjoying your stay at the Drury so far?"

Adam inclined his head in an appreciative nod as he thought back over the past few days. "Soft beds, warm meals, and hot showers... It's like Heaven. We're very grateful for your hospitality, Mr. Mayor."

"I'm glad to hear that." Ellis grinned and took another bite of his bagel. Once again, he began gesturing with his hands in advance of whatever he was about to say. This time he pointed a finger at Adam and began wagging it, like a parent reprimanding a child. He swallowed thickly. "Unfortunately," he began, "I am going to have to deny your request for asylum."

Adam's jaw dropped and he leaned suddenly forward in his seat. "What? Why? Did we do something wrong?"

"Not here..." Ellis said leadingly. Then his voice dropped to a whisper, "You didn't tell me that the governor was looking for you."

Adam could feel the blood draining from his face. "I... what do you mean he's *looking* for us? Did he put out a warrant or something?"

Ellis leaned back in his chair and folded his hands over his protruding belly. "Perhaps you'd like to tell me your side of the story?"

Adam hesitated. If Mayor Ellis was working *with* the governor as a fellow collaborator, then telling Ellis what he knew wasn't a good idea. Clearly, the existence of human slaves flying around in the invaders' ships was some kind of a big state secret. And for all Adam knew, slaves like Harry were being actively supplied by the Republic.

"There isn't much to tell," Adam insisted.

"That's fine. Don't tell me anything, but then I can't help you, and you'll have to leave my city in the morning."

Adam winced and swallowed thickly at the thought of venturing back out into the wastes again. But the mayor was deliberately leaving a window of possibility open. He was inviting Adam to confide in him in exchange for his assistance, and that implied that the mayor might not be on the governor's side after all.

Adam drew in a deep breath and explained what he'd seen that night on the ranch with Rick, and how Rick had died so that Adam could escape to tell the governor about it. Then he skipped straight to the part about them arriving in Travis and telling the governor, only for them to be lured into his stalker-infested bunker the next morning.

"So…" Ellis tapped his chin thoughtfully. "The governor was willing to kill you rather than risk that you might learn about his arrangement with the Specters."

Adam frowned. "His *arrangement?* What do you mean? Do you know something about this?"

Ellis nodded slowly. "Oh yes, and I'm not the only one who knows. At my level, everyone does. People are disappearing from the safe zones every week. Sometimes even daily. There's always an excuse for what happened to them—a stalker den was discovered somewhere and then cleared. Or else the missing people ventured into the wastes never to return.

"Whatever the case, the people who disappear are always conveniently the ones who are least likely to be missed—refugees, prisoners, orphans, and widows. And when that barrel scrapes dry, suddenly entire families go missing. Poof."

"But…" Adam shook his head. "How? If it's not stalkers that are taking them, then who?"

"As near as I can tell, there's a shadow organization within the Rangers. Some of them are involved, and some of them aren't. But the ones who are, answer directly to the governor."

Adam grimaced, suddenly wondering if he even wanted asylum in Bexar anymore. The wastes were sounding a lot safer at this point.

"Why are you telling me this?"

"So that you'll understand that I am not involved. And because I believe that you can help me get to the bottom of it."

Adam jabbed a thumb at his own chest. "Me?"

"Yes, you. You were with the Army before the invasion, weren't you?"

"That was a long time ago."

"It doesn't matter. With your experience, you're exactly the kind of person the Rangers are looking for. And once you become a Ranger, you'll be a shoo-in for another organization."

"What organization?"

"The Nightingales. Perhaps you've heard of them?"

Adam grew suddenly very still. "I have. Aren't they terrorists?"

"Allegedly, but as they say, one man's terrorist is another man's freedom fighter."

"So, which one are they?"

"I have my thoughts on that, but I'll leave it up to you to decide."

Adam blinked. "Then you're granting us asylum?"

"Conditionally. You join the Rangers *and* the Nightingales, and you'll be my informant in both."

Adam slowly shook his head. "And what if one of *us* is the next to go mysteriously missing? The safe zones don't sound that safe anymore."

"No, perhaps they don't, but being the mayor affords me a certain degree of influence and intel that others might not be privy to. I can keep you safe to a certain extent."

"How?" Adam demanded.

"People who disappear all have certain things in common, and they're never Rangers or the family of Rangers—well, some of them *do* go missing, but for more obvious reasons —like run-ins with stalkers or raiders while they're out on patrol."

"So me joining the Rangers will keep us safe?" Adam asked.

"Precisely."

Adam sighed. "What if the governor

discovers us here in Bexar?"

"Then your heads will roll," Ellis replied. "Maybe mine, too. So be sure that doesn't happen."

"That might not be something I can control. If he's actively looking for us..."

Ellis shook his head. "The governor hasn't issued any warrants, and I don't believe he will. He wants to keep this quiet. And that's the other thing—be sure you keep a low profile yourselves. Don't go shooting your mouths off about whatever you think you know. As far as you're concerned, the only enemies out there are Specs, stalkers, and raiders. Nothing in between. Got it?"

Adam nodded.

"Good." Ellis smiled and took a sip of his coffee. It was no longer steaming, and from the way the mayor grimaced as he drank, Adam suspected that the brew was ice cold. He traded the coffee for another bite of his bagel. Adam waited patiently for him to swallow. "Good luck, Mr. Hall," Ellis finally said. "I'll put in a good word for you with Major Hunter. He's the head of the Ranger regiment here in Bexar, so that should fast-track you to joining their ranks."

Adam glanced behind him to the door, imagining the young man with spiky blonde hair standing out there waiting for their meeting to finish. "Is he... does he know about all of this?"

"You can trust him," Ellis said.

Adam arched an eyebrow at him. "Anyone else?"

The mayor shook his head. "I wouldn't."

"Good to know," Adam replied. It was probably sound advice. In his experience with covert operations like this one, the people you trust along the way are the ones who are most likely to stab you in the back. They'd run a few ops like this in Afghanistan while Adam had been serving there. Invariably they went bad because they'd trusted some local informant who later turned out to be working with the Taliban.

Adam rose from his chair with a tight smile.

"I'll be in touch," Ellis said, returning his smile.

Adam saw himself out, and Major Hunter led him back outside into the fading light. As they continued down the street to Drury Plaza, a vibrant sunset draped the clouds in deepening hues of amber and gold. Once they reached the bridge over the river, the clouds had darkened to crimson, a scene that was reflected vividly on the glassy surface of the water below.

While they were crossing the bridge, Adam dropped his voice to a whisper and said, "Ellis told me about the missing people."

Major Hunter stopped cold and slowly turned to regard him. "Was that all he said?"

Adam shook his head. "He told me that the governor is involved and that he has Rangers working with him. He wants me to join up and see what I can learn."

For a long moment, the major said nothing, but his blue eyes glittered coldly. "Ellis must trust you a great deal to have shared all that."

"I think he knows that I have as much to lose as he does. Maybe more. I have a family. Ellis doesn't."

Hunter nodded slowly. "Sometimes that's the problem—having things to lose. It gives them a way to get to you."

"They?" Adam prompted.

"We call them Vultures."

Nightingales and Vultures, Adam thought, grimly amused by the nomenclature. *Someone's been doing a little too much bird-watching.* "Who are they?" he asked.

Major Hunter took a step closer to him. "They're the ones Ellis wants you to find —Rangers who are secretly abducting people from the safe zones at the governor's behest."

"Isn't that kind of hard to pull off in an organization like the Rangers? Wouldn't it be common knowledge that lieutenant such-and-such is calling in sick or going out on unscheduled patrols, and then conveniently, the next day a bunch of people go missing?"

Hunter smirked. "That's not how it happens. They get to know their targets first. Make their victims trust them. It's not hard. After all, Rangers are supposed to protect citizens, not throw them at the stalkers. But then one night, they pitch up with some flimsy excuse about reports of suspicious activity in the neighborhood.

"As soon as the door opens and the Vulture goes in to look around, a collaborator walks in right behind them, perfectly invisible. As I'm sure you know, their ships have the same cloaking tech, so it's not hard to imagine how they can sneak in and stun everyone and then carry them straight up the ramp of an invisible ship."

"That's how it happens?" Adam asked.

Major Hunter nodded. "Shadows in the night."

"Then what do they need the Vultures for? The collaborators could do it on their own, couldn't they?"

Hunter smiled. "The Vultures pick the targets, making sure that the ones who disappear won't be missed. They're there to ration and cherry-pick the victims to avoid inciting panic. It's a kind of harvest or culling of the herd. Isn't that what you did on your ranch? How did you pick which cattle to send to slaughter?"

Adam mulled it over. "Fair enough, but that means the real enemy is still the Specs. They're the ones abducting people. The governor and his Vultures are accomplices at best."

"What's your point?" Hunter replied.

"Well, what do you think will happen if we uncover this and find a way to stop it? The Specs aren't going to stop taking people. They'll probably just get more brazen about it."

Major Hunter frowned. "Maybe, but at least then everyone will know the score, and no one will have the power to choose who gets taken."

"The Specs will," Adam said.

"You know what I mean," Hunter growled.

"I just don't think that we're attacking the real problem," Adam insisted. "The Specs are the real enemy."

"Do you have an idea about how we can deal with them?"

"Well…" Adam trailed off. "No, but…"

Hunter snorted. "You let me know when that changes. Until then, our job is to find the Vultures and to tie them to the Specs and the Governor. And the next time you breathe a word of any of this to me, it better be because you've made some progress on that. Have I made myself clear?"

"Yes, sir."

With that, Hunter turned and continued across the bridge. Adam followed slowly, feeling more apprehensive than ever. *We never should have come here,* he thought.

But something told Adam that if he tried to leave now, they'd be the next ones to go mysteriously missing. Ellis might genuinely want to get to the bottom of this, but that didn't mean that he was above using the same cover-up tactics as the people he was fighting. It would probably be a simple thing for Major Hunter to throw them to the wolves—or in this case, to the *Vultures.*

PART TWO: BIRDS IN A CAGE

Five years later...

CHAPTER SEVENTEEN

September 9th, 2037
Bexar Safe Zone

Adam stood on the ramparts above the main gate of Bexar, peering through binoculars as the sun sank steadily toward the horizon. Lightning flashed silently within a dark wall of thunderheads, purpling them from within. Adam tracked his binocs down to the dark, glossy canopy of alien trees with their large, rosebud-shaped leaves. Feathery white fans of ferns peeked through in places, but tallest of all were the soaring mushroom-like "trees" that scholars at the University of Bexar called "prototaxites," or *protos* for short. With their bluish-black trunks and the shimmering, iridescent reflections on their caps, the *protos* towered thirty to fifty feet above the glossy black canopy below. And beneath that, Adam knew from bitter experience, was a thriving ecosystem of alien bugs, birds, small woodland creatures, and stalkers.

Adam aimed the binoculars at the near

edge of the jungle and studied the dead, char-blackened husks of alien trees and underbrush, searching for signs of life creeping back in. Periodic, controlled burns were the only way that they'd found to keep the jungles from encroaching on the city.

Ideally, the fires wouldn't be controlled at all, left to completely ravage the alien flora, but somehow it had a built-in defense mechanism against forest fires. As soon as one began, it was as if the trees could *smell* the smoke, and then the entire jungle would begin to *move,* creeping gradually away from the fire to leave a generous firebreak. The process took several days, and sometimes as much as a week, so you couldn't really see the trees moving if you were standing at ground zero, but you could certainly *hear* them—an otherworldly creaking and groaning mixed with the sound of millions of roots writhing through the soil. It was the most eerie, alien sound that Adam had ever heard.

And somehow, the jungle seemed to know which parts it could save, and which parts it couldn't, leaving some areas to burn while the rest of the foliage crept steadily away like a single, giant organism oozing across the earth.

Three years ago, when they'd lit the first fire to beat back the jungle from the walls, Adam had quietly celebrated with the other Rangers. Then they'd sat back and watched it burn for seven days straight, until one day, the fire had suddenly died away to nothing.

There hadn't been any particular reason to explain it, so Mayor Ellis had ordered a team of Rangers to go out and investigate. Adam had been the sergeant of one of the squads he'd sent. They'd taken a pair of eight-wheeled, armored Stryker transports just in case they had to spend the night in the wastes.

But that hadn't happened. After following the old road to Bandera for just a few hours, crossing tens of miles of char-blackened alien jungle, they'd finally come to a break in the devastation: a vast gulf of churned-up red soil with not a scrap of flammable material in sight. And a hundred feet away from that, standing pristine on the other side of the natural firebreak, was a glossy black wall of alien trees. At that moment, Adam could have sworn that the trees were laughing at them.

Since then, one of their jobs as Rangers had been to measure the spread of the jungle, and then every couple of months, to light new fires to control it. Allowing the jungle to get close might not have been a problem if the foliage were benign, but the trees excreted some kind of acid that dissolved artificial structures, making short work of concrete and flimsy sheet-metal walls. To make matters worse, the jungle brought stalkers, and the stalkers had a nasty habit of burrowing *under* the walls.

"Think it's about time to light another fire, Sergeant?" Private Cooper asked.

Adam lowered his binoculars to regard the young man in combat fatigues standing beside him. Beneath his soft Army-green field cap, Connor's head was shaved down to nothing. Warm brown eyes squinted out at the horizon while his hands flexed restlessly on his carbine, eager for action.

At six-foot-three, the boy stood a couple of inches taller even than Adam, and muscles bulged impressively under his rolled-up sleeves. He reminded Adam of himself at that age—a picture-perfect specimen, like he'd stepped right out of a Rangers' recruitment poster.

But what made Private Cooper stand out in Adam's mind wasn't his appearance, it was the fact that he was Crystal's fiancé.

When Connor had turned twenty, he'd revealed his intention to join the Rangers, and soon after that, he'd proposed.

Adam had made a promise to both Crystal and Carla that he'd keep an eye on the boy. So as soon as Connor had graduated boot camp, Adam had pulled a few strings and gotten the kid assigned to his fire team.

Adam belatedly answered Connor, "That's Major Hunter's call, but I suspect he'll wait another week or two. No sense rushing out there any sooner than we have to."

"Yeah, I guess," Connor replied, sounding disappointed, but that was only because he hadn't been out to light one of those fires yet. Adam always rotated him out to the night shift the day before, so Connor had yet to see what it was like out there: the blazing heat and the walls of blinding smoke. Worst of all was how the fires flushed stalkers from their dens, driving them to a frenzy. Ordinarily, stalkers were less dangerous during the day. Not so, when they were fleeing for their lives.

"You think the fires are still working?" Connor asked.

Adam frowned. "Yeah, why?"

Connor shook his head. "Just a rumor I heard."

"What rumor?"

Connor hesitated. "Well..."

Adam raised his eyebrows expectantly.

Connor leaned in close and whispered, "I overheard Major Hunter talking to someone on the radio about how our supply shortages are getting worse. He mentioned how we're cut off on two sides now, and he seemed to think that it's only a matter of time before the jungle has completely surrounded Bexar."

Adam's frown deepened. He hadn't heard that rumor. Was this something that the upper echelons knew about that the grunts on the ground didn't?

Maybe it was just idle speculation. Or

maybe the eggheads at the university had been measuring something between the burns. What if the fires *were* getting less effective? Could the jungle be adapting to their tactics, somehow fortifying itself? Adam couldn't imagine how that was possible, but then again, a few years ago he couldn't have imagined trees uprooting themselves, either.

"Let's stick to worrying about what we know," Adam chided. "Leave the unknowns to the brass."

"Copy that, Sergeant," Connor replied.

But when their shift ended half an hour later and they mounted their bicycles to ride home along the I10, the unstoppable spread of those jungles was all Adam could think about. Life was hard enough without it getting harder all the time. Where would they even go if Bexar was forced to evacuate? To Travis?

The thought of living under Governor Miller's nose was a chilling one. What if one of the Rangers up there recognized him from five years ago? Like Captain Fields. Or that lieutenant who had locked them in the governor's stalker-infested bunker.

Adam kept his head down as darkness fell, pedaling hard up a hill and doing his best to ignore the blinding agony that was radiating up his bad leg.

With his attention almost entirely eroded by the pain, he nearly missed seeing a man-sized pothole that would have sent him flying over the handlebars.

Connor pulled alongside him with the ease and energy of youth. "Careful, Sergeant! I wouldn't want to have to peel you off the pavement."

Adam scowled at the kid's patronizing tone, but Connor missed it in the failing light. "You'd need a damn big spatula for that," he quipped.

"Hah!" Connor breathed. "See you for patrol tomorrow, Mr. Hall." He pulled ahead and disappeared over the top of the hill.

Adam didn't have the breath to spare for a reply. By the time he reached the top of the hill, his lungs were burning and he was gasping for air, feeling the full weight of his nearly fifty years.

He glanced around repeatedly at the abandoned restaurants, outlet malls, hotels, gas stations, and office buildings that flashed by on either side, searching for familiar landmarks. Here and there, a candle flickered in a window, indicating signs of life.

Load shedding was worse than ever in Bexar. The hydro generators on the river were constantly breaking down, and there was never enough fuel to keep the coal and gas power plants running. They had to save what power there was for critical facilities like the hospital. During the day, solar farms increased their capacity, but even those were getting less efficient as time wore on.

When did we go from barely getting by to barely even surviving? Adam wondered.

But he already knew the answer. Ever since they'd lost Sunny Valley Ranch, things had gotten much harder for them. It had been okay for the first year or two. They'd stayed safe inside the walls, working relatively simple jobs in exchange for steady wages that were enough to cover the basics. But now, with food shortages, water shortages, power shortages, and every other kind of shortage imaginable, it was impossible to afford everything. So they'd cut back on whatever they could to focus on the things that they absolutely couldn't live without—like food.

At least we don't have to pay rent, Adam thought, while glancing around at all the darkened windows of abandoned buildings. The population in the safe zones had been declining for years thanks to stalkers, disease, starvation, and a steady wave of mysterious disappearances that was currently worse than ever.

Adam pedaled on for the next thirty minutes, periodically checking his watch to make sure that he'd be home in time for dinner. Like clockwork, Carla had food on the table by seven each night. Getting home to her and eating dinner together was the highlight of every day. Adam smiled as Carla came to mind. Marrying her was the best decision he'd ever made. He'd hate to miss dinner with her, but his bad leg didn't make it easy to cycle the twelve miles of broken roads, up and down hills, from his post at the walls.

And to make matters even worse, the Nightingales had a meeting tonight, which meant that he had another twenty miles waiting for him after dinner. Adam grimaced, questioning for the umpteenth time the wisdom of joining their organization. Not that he'd had a choice.

A gentle roll of thunder punctuated that thought as Adam peeled off the interstate. He raced down the off-ramp and turned left under the overpass, flying through the empty intersections on either side.

After passing five different cross streets, he turned left at an old 7-Eleven to enter the suburb where he lived. He passed a couple of other cyclists heading home after work, and a Ranger officer on horseback.

The majestic facades of large, two-story homes came peeking through walls of overgrown trees. Candlelight flickered in their windows. It was almost fully dark now, and Adam's street was cloaked in shadows, making it impossible to see how badly the homes had deteriorated.

But he knew how they looked in daylight: with their gardens overgrown, paint peeling from their dilapidated siding, and the faded blue and green tarps that were tied with ropes or pinned with debris to cover rotten holes in their roofs.

Adam was grateful for the shelter, such as it was, and for the fact that he wasn't required to pay for it. Residences were assigned to keep people clustered together in groups, but for the most part, the residents of the safe zones were free to choose which groups they wanted to live in. Naturally, Adam had chosen a wealthy suburb that he couldn't have hoped to afford before the invasion. He took a small, smug sense of satisfaction from that. Maybe not everything had changed for the worse.

Recognizing a particular mansion through the gathering gloom, Adam turned into the driveway, aiming for the three-car garage. He saw the curtain in the living room window shiver and caught a glimpse of a familiar silhouette departing the window. That was Carla. She'd been waiting for him, which meant he must be late. Adam grimaced as he coasted to a stop in the open garage door that was closest to the front door. He hopped off the bike, and his carbine swung down from his back with that movement. He put the bike's kickstand down to park it beside Carla's and then walked quickly across the garage to the short flight of wooden steps that led to the house. The door at the top of those steps swung wide just before he reached it.

Carla beckoned to him with a smile. "I kept dinner warm for you."

Adam matched her smile and kissed her at the top of the stairs. "Thank you," he mumbled against her lips.

She nodded and took him by the hand to lead him through to the dining room where their dinner sat cooling on the table.

Adam could see that it was a particularly meager meal. Half a corn on the cob each, and a few spoonfuls of mashed potatoes. No meat.

Adam frowned. "We're scraping the bottom of the barrel again, huh? Didn't you get paid yesterday? I thought you were going shopping after work?"

Carla sighed. "I did..."

"But?"

"Why don't you sit down, and I'll explain."

"Okay..." Adam grumbled. He pulled out his chair and began pushing his mashed potatoes around grumpily before taking a bite. Ice cold. He washed them down with a sip of water, while Carla sat down beside him and began telling him about her day at the state-run supercenter.

She told him about a mother of three who'd come in with her kids, wearing rags and looking like they hadn't eaten in weeks.

Adam winced, already feeling guilty for complaining. He knew where this was going.

"When she got to the checkout, she only had like five things in her cart," Carla explained, "but she couldn't afford any of it, and she had to put it all back."

Adam felt a silent scream building up inside his chest. Somehow he managed to keep it in. Was this what they had come to? Keeping safe from the stalkers only to die in more protracted ways.

"Her eldest was a little girl who couldn't have been more than five or six. She had these sunken, haunted eyes and a coat hanger for shoulders. She started crying when her mother put the eggs back. I couldn't take it, so I paid for their groceries."

Adam set his fork down with a noisy clatter and regarded his wife grimly. He swallowed past a painful lump in his throat and slowly shook his head. "It's okay. They needed it more than us."

"I just thought, we can make it until you get paid, and it's just the two of us now. Our kids don't live with us anymore. Please don't be mad." Tears sprang to Carla's eyes and her lips trembled.

Adam reached across the table and pulled her in for another kiss. Her tears spilled in salty rivers between them. He pulled away, smiling incredulously. "I'm not mad at you, Carla. It's things like this that only make me love you more. But I *am* mad at the situation. We didn't come to Bexar just to slowly waste away into nothing."

"What other choice do we have? It's not any better out there in the wastes."

Adam sighed. "It was, for us, back when we had the ranch."

Carla frowned. "But we don't have it anymore, and the jungles have spread out of control since then. Even if there was something to go back to, Sunny Valley will be completely overrun by now."

"I know." Adam turned to scowl at his plate. Carla reached for his hand, caressing the back of it with her thumb. "We'll be okay. The mayor secured emergency aid from Travis. We'll get re-supplied soon, and we don't have to pay for emergency rations."

Adam considered that as he gnawed on his corn. The governor was understandably loathe to share the Capital's dwindling supplies. He *had* agreed to send aid to Bexar, but it wouldn't be anywhere close to enough to go around. Miller knew he had to do something to put out the fires of discontent before they could flare into a full-blown revolution, but Adam knew, thanks to his association with the Nightingales, that there was nothing the governor could do to stop that revolution now. The wheels were already in motion. It was no longer a question of if, but *when.*

"Is everything okay?" Carla whispered.

"You've been pretty quiet. How was your day?"

"Fine. I'm just tired." Adam managed a tight smile for her benefit. "And…" He heaved a sigh. "I have to go down to the station to interrogate those raiders we brought in last week."

"Tonight?"

He nodded.

"But you just got off patrol!" Carla objected. "Can't someone on the night watch do it?"

Adam shook his head, focusing again on his food to keep her from seeing the lie on his face. Technically they had brought in a group of raiders, and someone *would* be interrogating them tonight, but it wasn't going to be him.

He felt bad for lying to Carla about where he was going, but if he told her the truth, she would only try to stop him, or worse—to *join* him.

"When do you have to go?" she asked.

"Right after dinner," he said.

"Oh." Carla sounded crestfallen. "I was hoping you'd have time for dessert."

Adam perked up at the mention of it. "Dessert? You made something?"

"Well…" Carla demurred, sounding embarrassed. "Not exactly."

"Oh." He smiled. "I get it. Well, maybe I can be a little late."

Carla returned his smile. When they'd both scraped their plates clean, she took the candle from the table and led him up the stairs to their room.

Half an hour later they lay naked in the flickering candlelight, their hearts racing and chests shuddering as a cool breeze blew in from the open window and dried the sweat on their bodies. Physically and emotionally exhausted, Adam wanted nothing more than to lie there with his wife, basking in the glow of the moment.

But it was not to be.

He had a meeting with the Nightingales to get to. Most meetings were optional to attend unless you had something to report since meeting up was risky for everyone, but the proctor of Bexar's conclave had called an all-hands reunion, making tonight's meeting mandatory. Anyone who didn't go would need a good excuse.

"I guess you'd better get going," Carla whispered, patting his chest.

Adam sighed. "Yeah, I guess so," he muttered. He sat up and swung his legs over the side of the bed.

"I'll miss you," Carla added.

She reached up and turned his head to her lips, kissing him once more. "Be careful out there," she added.

"Always," he replied.

Minutes later he was riding down the driveway, once again in uniform with his carbine strapped to his back. There were few disguises better than a Ranger's uniform. No one would think to ask any questions about why he was cycling around after dark, or where he was going. They'd just assume that he was on the night patrol.

As Adam turned off onto the street, he caught a glimpse of Carla waving to him from the bedroom window. He spared a hand from the bike to wave back.

Within minutes, Adam's bad leg was blazing with a familiar angry heat, and his back was aching from a long day of standing on the walls and cycling between Ranger stations.

This meeting had better be important, he thought grumpily to himself.

CHAPTER EIGHTEEN

Carla let the curtain fall back into place at the window and moved quickly to the closet. She traded her nightgown for a pair of black jeans and a faded black T-shirt with a dark gray windbreaker. Hopefully, the dark colors would be enough to conceal her. The encroaching storm would also help. Those heavy clouds made it a particularly dark night, and the street lights on this side of Bexar hadn't been working for years.

A sudden peal of thunder urged her to hurry; she didn't want to be cycling in the rain. On top of that, she was going to be late for the meeting.

But it had been worth it. She and Adam had found precious little time to connect lately, and Carla was about to be sent on a dangerous mission.

Mayor Ellis had finally convinced the governor to send emergency rations to Bexar, but the governor had insisted that they come and get the supplies themselves.

So Carla had been working all week at the supercenter to clean and mobilize their cold storage trucks and to make room on their shelves and in their freezers for the anticipated influx of supplies.

But she'd found out just a few days ago that the Nightingales wanted *her* to join the convoy so that she could infiltrate Travis along with a handful of other operatives, some of whom Carla suspected were coworkers from the supercenter. Just today, Carla's manager had approved her request to join the convoy. She had been meaning to tell Adam, but there hadn't been time. And truthfully, she hadn't wanted to discuss the trip so close to her meeting with the Nightingales, just in case he got suspicious. Adam still didn't know that she was a Nightingale, and she was determined to keep it that way. Fortunately, he had his own business to attend to tonight, so she didn't even have to use her excuse about last-minute preparations for the convoy's departure tomorrow.

She would tell Adam about it in the morning, and if all went according to plan, she'd be back with the emergency rations before dinner. At least, she *hoped* she would. Carla had yet to learn *why* the Nightingales were infiltrating Travis or what she would be doing to help them once she arrived.

Carla hurried down the stairs and across the

hall to the garage door. She shut and locked it behind her before speeding down the stairs and over the cracked and stained concrete floor to her bike. She kicked up the stand and swung her leg over the bar.

Moments later, the cool evening air was racing through her tangled hair as she pedaled quickly down the dark, gleaming ribbon of asphalt to the interstate.

Thunder boomed again, and this time it launched an icy salvo of raindrops that shattered all around her. But those were just the warning shots. Suddenly the sky cracked open, and the air grew thick with a furious assault that cascaded over her like a tidal wave, soaking instantly through her hair, jacket, and jeans, and chilling her to the bone.

***

Crystal lay on her side facing Connor, frowning unhappily at him. Her fingers played lightly with his chest hair while thunder rolled ominously overhead. His chest rose and fell quickly with deep, shuddering breaths, while his heart raced frantically like a bird beating its wings inside of its cage.

He seemed unusually preoccupied tonight, almost as if he'd somehow managed to bring the storm outside in with him.

"Why'd you pull out?" Crystal asked.

"Hmmm?" He looked at her with his thick brown eyebrows innocently raised, as if he didn't know what she was talking about.

"Do I need to go into greater detail?" Crystal demanded. She suddenly stopped playing with his chest hair.

"Oh, that. Uh, sorry, I guess I'm just in a hurry to get going. You know I have all that paperwork waiting for me at the station for those raiders we brought in last week. Speaking of which, I really should get going. I'm going to be late."

"Mmhmmm. You were in a hurry, so you couldn't spare the extra *second* it might take to get me pregnant. Are you really sticking to that story, Mr. Cooper?"

Connor frowned. "Don't call me that. My dad was Mr. Cooper."

At the mention of his dead father, Crystal decided to soften her approach. "Sorry. Connor it is. I thought we agreed that we were going to try for a baby?"

Connor sat up with a sigh. "We're not even married yet."

"But we will be," Crystal insisted. "We're just waiting for a date to go to the courthouse."

Connor stood up and the sheets fell away from his naked body. Crystal admired the way rippling cords of muscle moved beneath his skin. It was like looking at one of those famous old statues, his body chiseled from stone.

Connor caught her smiling slyly at him, and he managed an awkward smile of his own as he went about collecting his clothes from the floor. "Save that thought for later," he said. "Hopefully, I'll be back in just a couple of hours."

"And then we'll try again?" Crystal suggested.

Connor hesitated while pulling on his pants. Eventually, he responded with a silent nod, but his eyes never met hers.

That confirmed it. Something had changed for him. He was no longer on the same page about having kids, but he didn't want to explain why or go into detail right now.

Crystal's brow furrowed into a knot between her eyes. Maybe it was the food shortage that had him second-guessing things. But he'd said it himself, the governor was sending aid. They'd get through this famine just like they had all of the other ones before, and then life would go on as normal.

Connor finished putting on his uniform and went to collect his carbine from the dresser at the foot of the bed.

"Hurry back," Crystal said as he looped the strap over his shoulder and checked the number of spare magazines in his pouches.

"I'll try," Connor agreed.

Crystal sat up then, and the sheets fell away from her bare chest. She shivered from the cool air coursing in from the open window beside her. Her nipples stood painfully erect, and she cupped her breasts, massaging them.

Connor groaned as he watched her. "What are you doing to me? You know I can't stay."

"What?" Crystal smiled crookedly at him, and then she bit her lip provocatively. "At least you already had a good time. I'm not a tease like some people."

Connor snorted and crossed the room in two quick strides to reach her side of the bed. Cupping her face in one giant hand, he leaned down and kissed her passionately. "I'll make it up to you later."

"You'd better."

She intended to make him keep that promise, but not before he told her the *real* reason that he'd unilaterally decided to abandon their baby plans.

Something was wrong. She could sense it, like the electricity crackling in the air outside. Thunder rolled, drawing her eyes to the window—maybe it was just the storm she was sensing. Crystal dragged her eyes away from the window to find Connor emerging from their walk-in closet, now wearing a long, canary yellow raincoat over his uniform. Peeking out of a pocket in the hip, she glimpsed something colorful—

And her breath froze in her chest as she realized what it was.

It was a *calaca*. A skeleton mask.

No...

"I'll see you later. I love you, Christie," Connor said, smiling at her from the bedroom door.

"Love you, too," she mumbled.

The door clicked shut behind him, and she was left to wallow in the horror of what she'd just seen. Connor was a Nightingale! But he couldn't be, could he? Rangers like him had standing orders to shoot Nightingales on sight. And yet somehow, he'd thought it was a good idea to become one himself.

With that discovery slowly gelling in Crystal's mind, suddenly she understood why he might be getting cold feet about having kids. And now, she had them too. The last thing she wanted was to wind up a widow, raising their baby all on her own like her dad had been forced to do with her. Or like his mom had done with him.

Crystal winced as the memories came rushing back. Her mother was still an aching void in her life to this day. She didn't want that for her baby—to never feel whole, always wondering about the piece that was missing.

Another crack of thunder rolled through the open window, bringing with it the first speckles of rain on the window sill.

Crystal had to find out what Connor was into, and how deep it went. Jumping up from the bed, she walked quickly to the closet to get dressed. She picked out the darkest colors she could find, hoping that would keep her hidden while she followed Connor on her bike. But she realized that it wouldn't be enough if he glanced back and saw her face. Or if she snuck into his meeting with the other Nightingales and she was the only one without a mask. She needed a way to hide her face too. Not having a *calaca* of her own, she rummaged around in the closet for something else that she could use. She settled on an old black stocking from the ones she used at the school where she worked as an elementary teacher. She pulled the stocking over her head and used a pair of scissors from the bathroom to snip holes for her mouth, nose, and eyes. Then she put on a hoodie for good measure and ran out of the bedroom.

Bowser was lying at the top of the stairs with his head between his paws, watching the door to the garage. His head came up to watch as she stepped into the hall. He whimpered softly at the sight of her, scared by the thunder.

"Relax, Bowie," Crystal whispered as she walked over to him. His tail began to swish happily across the floor, and she scratched him behind the ear and patted him on the head before running down the stairs to the garage. Bowser followed her there, whimpering again as thunder rolled and shivered through the house.

"You'll be okay," she said. "It's just thunder."

His tail slowly stopped wagging and his jowls drooped as she shut the door in his face.

Crystal ran to her road bike, parked in a rusty bike rack, and went racing down the driveway. She hoped the thinner wheels and lighter frame of her bike would make up for the fact that Connor had a head start.

As soon as she reached the end of the driveway, she saw him. He was already at the end of their street, about a hundred yards away. Thankfully, that canary-yellow jacket made him easy to spot. He made a lazy turn to the right and disappeared behind an old pickup truck.

Crystal urged herself to pedal faster. If she lost sight of him, that would be it and she'd have to turn back and wait for him to come home. Crystal kept her eyes on the road, scanning for any obstacles that might send her careening over the handlebars or puncture a tire, but it was too dark to see more than the fuzzy outlines of cars and trees, let alone smaller obstacles like rocks and potholes. Crystal risked flicking on the rechargeable, battery-powered headlight clipped to her handlebars. It illuminated a wide swath of the street just in time for her to steer around a big chunk of concrete that would have ended her adventure abruptly.

Another boom of thunder split the sky, and this time it brought with it thick, driving sheets of icy rain. Crystal gasped and spluttered as the rain seeped through her clothes and the stocking over her head. Her visibility was down to barely a dozen feet.

Crystal gritted her teeth in frustration and fought the cowardly impulse to turn back and retreat to the warmth of her bed.

But this was too important to ignore. Crystal doubted that Connor had joined the Nightingales recently. Now that she knew what Connor was *really* doing when he said that he had paperwork to get through at the station or that he had to go out on a night patrol, countless other nights just like this one snapped into focus. All this time he had been sneaking out to meetings with the Nightingales.

And that meant Connor's sudden change of heart about having kids might have been because of some mission that they were planning. One that he was worried might get him killed. She had to find out what it was before it was too late.

CHAPTER NINETEEN

Adam's nose wrinkled as he climbed down the ladder into the old, abandoned sewer that would take him under the walls and out into the wastes. But he was grateful for the shelter such as it was. Every inch of him was soaked from the rain.

Adam went splashing down the pipe in at least a foot of sewage and rainwater. He lit the way with a flashlight from his pack. Distorted shadows marched along the curving sides of the pipe as rats squeaked and chittered, darting ahead of him as he went.

Adam followed the twists and turns of the sewer system by heart, having come this way many times before.

Eventually, he came to a particular ladder bolted to the floor below a particular manhole. The location was marked by a few innocuous scribbles of graffiti, one of which was a stylized, grinning black skull—a *calaca,* to be more specific. Just like the mask that he had tucked into his pack.

Adam put his hands to the rungs and climbed. Once he reached the top of the ladder, he heard the splashing echoes of others running through the sewers to tonight's meeting.

At least I'm not the only one who's going to be late, he thought as he cracked the manhole open and peeked outside. It wasn't raining anymore, but there were plenty of puddles, catching his eyes with gleaming scraps of reflections.

It was the middle of the night, several miles beyond the safety of the walls, and stalkers were definitely a concern. But this was the *east* end of the city. The jungles lay to the south and west. Out here, there was nothing but the crumbling, overgrown ruins of abandoned city blocks with their dark, broken windows, and thick snarls of rusting vehicles clogging up the streets.

Not seeing any immediate signs of trouble, Adam pushed the manhole open between two rusting sedans and ran across the street to a vast parking lot with neat rows and columns of old, abandoned army tents. Some of them were completely overturned, having been pillaged by scavs or raiders. Scraps of canvas fluttered in the wind. Bits of junk littered the ground.

Adam moved quickly through the parking lot, with one hand on his carbine, worried that any one of those tents could conceal a stalker or a band of raiders camped out for the night.

Up ahead, the Alamodome loomed impressively large with four massive concrete pillars rising from the corners of its roof. The entrance of the stadium was a curving wall of glass that rose to a height of at least six stories, and beneath that was an underground loading zone. Adam veered left toward the stairs that led up to the pedestrian entrance.

He reached around for his pack and zipped it open to retrieve his mask. He slipped it on and removed the Velcro name tape and sergeant's insignias on his uniform. There wasn't much point in keeping his face covered if he was going to wear those identifiers. That done, Adam hurried up the concrete steps to the main entrance. He headed straight for a wall of busted and boarded-up glass doors.

The Nightingales had secured the stadium years ago. Now it was their primary base of operations and an occasional meeting place for the conclave that operated in Bexar.

Adam slowed to a stop just outside the entrance and shouldered his carbine. He reached for a makeshift metal handle screwed to plywood boards and yanked the door open. From there he passed into a dark, echoing entrance hall. Flickering candles cast long shadows on the walls. Adam slowly raised his hands, knowing full well that guards would be hiding in those shadows, aiming their guns at him.

Adam whistled a particular three-tone melody exactly three times. It was a part of the distinctive song of a real Nightingale, an odd choice as far as code phrases went, but Adam supposed it was as good as anything else. He heard the subtle click and rattle of weapons settling as Nightingales relaxed their guard, but Adam kept his hands raised.

"You're armed," a muffled voice ground out from the shadows of a doorway beneath an old torn and faded poster about a UTSA Football game.

"Do you blame me?" Adam asked.

The speaker stepped out of cover with a silenced Beretta pistol, surprising Adam with the fact that he was also wearing re-purposed Army fatigues. He was a Ranger, but since he was also wearing a stylized skull mask, Adam couldn't tell if it was someone he knew.

"You'll have to leave your weapons here," the man said, gesturing with the barrel of a silenced pistol to a reception desk where a Jewish menorah flickered with nine individual flames.

Adam nodded and began lowering his hands to reach for his weapons.

"Slowly," the Ranger warned.

Adam walked over to the desk, ducking out of the shoulder strap of his carbine as he went. As he drew near, he saw the dull, oily black frames of guns lying in open crates on the floor behind the desk.

He laid his weapons in a particular corner of one of the crates. As he was straightening, the door to the stadium burst open and a woman in a familiar-looking gray jacket burst in, dripping wet. She wore a clean white *calaca* with pink swirls and ruby-red lips painted around the skeleton's teeth.

Adam frowned, wondering where he'd seen that jacket before. The woman froze, staring back at him for the briefest instant before looking to the armed guard.

The man with the silenced pistol had already shifted his aim to her, and he was advancing steadily toward her.

"Identify yourself," he demanded.

The woman whistled the same three-note melody that Adam had, and the ranger relaxed.

"Weapons over there," the man indicated, pointing with his left hand to the desk where Adam stood.

"I don't have any," the woman said in an intimately familiar voice, and Adam's blood ran cold.

It *couldn't* be… could it?

"I'll have to search you to be sure," he said.

Adam gaped at the woman behind his mask, willing it not to be true. But even her silhouette was familiar. He watched the Ranger pat her down with one hand while the other kept the

Beretta squarely aimed at her chest.

"All right, you're clean," the man said, stepping back. "Go on in."

"Thank you," the woman replied, giving Adam's ears another few syllables to process. There could be no doubt about it.

That woman was his wife, Carla.

***

Crystal hid behind one of the trees around the entrance of the stadium, watching as Connor ran across the puddled concrete to a boarded-up entryway.

Having come this far, she was tempted to run right in after him, but along the way she'd begun to doubt the wisdom of her plan. What if these Nightingales were dangerous? What if it wasn't enough to simply cover her face? Her hoodie and stocking mask seemed like a poor imitation at best. Maybe she wouldn't get in unless she was wearing a *calaca*.

Crystal watched until she saw Connor slip through the door before turning around and running back down the steps. Feeling dangerously alone and exposed, she glanced about nervously, hoping that there weren't any stalkers between her and the manhole cover on the other side of the parking lot.

This had been a really stupid plan. Connor had glanced back along the way a few times and seen her from a distance, but he'd probably just assumed that she was a Nightingale like him. She might be able to pull that off from afar, but getting close enough to get into the Nightingales' meeting would be another matter entirely.

Crystal ran across the parking lot, dodging and weaving between tents along the way. She passed down a particularly narrow corridor—

And someone jumped out and grabbed her, knocking her to the ground. Crystal screamed and kicked blindly at whoever it was.

A man grunted in pain, and Crystal scuttled quickly away, but another set of hands seized her before she could escape.

"Help!" she cried, but a hand clapped over her mouth, muffling her voice.

She was jerked roughly to her feet and came face to face with a pair of men in Rangers' uniforms. One of them was almost as short as her at five-foot-six, the other as tall as her dad. They were wearing gas masks, so she couldn't see their faces or any other features to tell them apart.

"Who are you?" the taller man demanded while aiming his rifle at her.

"I'm a Nightingale," she tried, but the way her voice trembled, she didn't sound very convincing.

"Then where's your mask?" the shorter man asked.

"I was going to put it on when I got inside."

"You're going the wrong way," the taller

Ranger said.

"Well, yeah. I forgot something in... in the uh, the sewer," she said, gesturing vaguely in that direction.

"Bullshit," the taller man said. "You're coming with us." He grabbed her arm and began dragging her toward the stadium while the shorter one kept his rifle trained on her.

Crystal stumbled along, feeling numb and cold from the rain. What were they going to do with her? What if they were going to drag her off into some dark corner and then shoot her in the back of the head? Maybe they really were terrorists, just like the governor said.

But then where had these two gotten their uniforms? Were they turncoat Rangers? Something wasn't adding up.

Crystal saw that they were dragging her toward the entrance of the garage below the stadium rather than toward the steps to the main entrance where Connor had gone. Was that where they took people to execute them? To a windowless room deep inside the bowels of the Stadium where stalkers wouldn't hear the gunshots.

Crystal began to struggle.

"Hey, cut it out," the tall Ranger said, tightening his grip until her arm ached.

Crystal turned and kicked him viciously in the shins. He cursed and gave her a backhanded slap that sent her sprawling to the ground. She hit her chin and bit her tongue, crying out in pain as she did so.

"Hey, leave her alone!" the shorter man objected. "She's just a kid." He reached out to help her up.

Crystal hesitated, having seen her chance. She reached for his hand—

And grabbed his sidearm instead.

She pointed the gun squarely at his chest and flicked the safety off. The shorter Ranger froze, stepping back with his hands raised.

Crystal whirled in a quick circle, aiming the gun at the other man.

"Put that down before you hurt yourself," the one who'd slapped her intoned darkly.

"I know how to shoot!" she snapped. "My dad taught me. He's one of you. A Ranger sergeant." Even as she said it, Crystal wondered at the wisdom of revealing who her dad was. These weren't regular Rangers who might find themselves taking orders from him. For all she knew, they weren't Rangers at all, and they'd stolen their uniforms.

The two men glanced at one another, and then back at her.

"Odds are good that we'll survive a bullet from that nine mil, but you won't survive one from my carbine, so why don't you just put that gun down, and we can go inside and talk? If this is some big misunderstanding as you say, then you don't have anything to worry about."

Crystal licked her lips, tasting blood from her tongue. "And what if I lied about being a Nightingale?" she asked. Silence answered the question, telling Crystal exactly what she needed to know. "That's what I thought."

The tall man slowly shook his head. "You've got us all wrong. We'll take you in for questioning. Once we're satisfied that you've told us everything, we'll let you go. You haven't seen our faces, so you can't identify us." The man shrugged as if it was no big deal. "And you don't strike me as one of the Governor's agents, so you've got nothing to worry about. I'm guessing you followed someone here." He nodded to the stadium where Connor had gone.

Crystal flexed her hand restlessly on the gun, not saying anything to that.

"That's it, isn't it?" the taller Ranger pressed. "Who is it? Your dad? Your mom?"

"I'm twenty," Crystal replied. "I live with my fiancé, not with my parents."

"Aha, so you followed him. You probably thought he was cheating on you, right?" The man chuckled darkly. "I bet you wish that were true now."

Crystal struggled to contain her shock that this man had been able to deduce why she was here. "Let me go," she finally managed.

"I can't do that."

"You have to. I have a gun aimed at your chest. Even if the bullet doesn't kill you, the sound of a gun going off will draw every stalker for miles. And that means you can't afford to shoot me either. You wouldn't want stalkers to crash your meeting."

"You *do* make a good point there, sweetheart. I think I'll go for hidden option number three."

The shorter Ranger lunged, revealing that he'd been creeping up on her the whole time that she'd been focused on his partner. He twisted the gun out of her hand just before she could pull the trigger and smoothly holstered the weapon before jerking her arms up painfully behind her back.

"Let's go," he snarled in her ear, sounding considerably less sympathetic this time around.

But Crystal was relieved to see that now they were headed for the steps where Connor had gone.

"Time to find your fiancé," the taller Ranger said. "I just hope for your sake that he's real."

"He won't get in any trouble, will he?" Crystal asked.

"That depends on how you found him here. If he *told* you where he was going…"

"He didn't," Crystal said.

"We'll leave that for the proctor to determine."

CHAPTER TWENTY

Adam sat on a folding chair with at least a hundred others, all of them wearing painted skull masks, all facing the makeshift dais in the center of the evergreen astroturf of the stadium's football field. The overhead lights were on, which meant that the facility had to be powered by some kind of generator. Adam had been here a few times before, but he'd never seen much of the facility, and on those occasions, everyone had been using flashlights. The fact that the lights were working here implied that the Nightingales had more resources than Adam had previously assumed. Fuel for generators was hard to come by.

Adam looked away from the dais, his gaze tracking down the row in front of him until he found Carla. She was seated one row up and three seats to his right. He didn't want to confront her here. That could be dangerous. Instead, he planned to stay close and keep her in sight throughout the meeting to make sure she didn't get into any trouble. He'd wait until they were both back at home to confront her about this, but he had a feeling that when he did, she would just point the finger of blame back at him. After all, he was also a Nightingale, and he'd also been hiding it from her. But the difference was, he hadn't been given a choice. Ellis had forced him to join. It was the only way he'd grant them asylum in Bexar. So assuming that Carla hadn't joined under similar circumstances, he wanted to know *why*.

The proctor of the Nightingales stepped onto the dais between two armed and masked Rangers. The proctor wore a distinctive crimson *calaca*. Traditionally, the masks were white with colorful embellishments, but his was entirely red with black swirls.

Mutterings of anticipation rose through the assembly, then quickly fell into silence as the proctor raised his hands.

"Welcome, Nightingales!" he began, his voice booming across the field as it was both amplified and distorted by a voice changer that was integrated into his mask. "Tonight, I have called you all together for the most important mission since the inception of the Nightingales. It is the culmination of many years of patient waiting and planning. Now, finally, we are…" The proctor trailed off abruptly and his head came up. He seemed to be peering over their heads to something on the other end of the field. The guards standing on either side of him stiffened and raised their carbines.

Adam twisted around with the rest of the audience to see what had caught his attention. A pair of Rangers striding across the field, shoving someone ahead of them.

Alarm trickled slowly into Adam's gut. Whoever it was, they were wearing a black stocking with holes cut out for the eyes and mouth instead of a calaca. Judging by the size and shape of the person's frame, it was a woman, and whoever she was, she was almost certainly a spy.

Dread spiked through Adam's veins as he realized that their meeting could be compromised. He shot to his feet along with several others, and a rising murmur of concern spread through the assembly.

"Silence!" the proctor boomed. "What is the meaning of this? Who is she?"

"We found her skulking in the parking lot. She claims to have followed someone here."

Those murmurs of alarm quickly multiplied.

"We need to get out of here!" someone shouted.

"Wait!" the proctor intoned. "Who did she follow?"

The Rangers dragged their captive swiftly down the aisle to the dais until she was standing directly in front of the proctor.

"Well?" he intoned, now looking to her for the answer.

"My, my fiancé," the woman said in a small, girlish voice. A chill of recognition shot through Adam's veins, but after bumping into Carla here, he didn't believe it. Bumping into his wife and his daughter at the same meeting on the same night was too much of a coincidence. He waited for her to speak again so that he could be sure.

"Is he here?" the proctor demanded.

The woman in the stocking mask turned and briefly regarded the crowd. Her eyes fixed on one of the Nightingales in particular, a tall man in a canary-yellow raincoat.

She nodded. "Yes."

His heart pounding, Adam turned that one hoarsely spoken word over and over in his mind to identify the voice.

"Remove her mask," the proctor said.

One of the Rangers flanking her yanked the stocking off—

And Adam froze, feeling suddenly hot and cold all over. It was Crystal all right, and her chin and lips were bleeding, as if the guards holding her had roughed her up on the way over.

His fists clenched and he ground his teeth, glaring at those men. But Adam had enough sense to deny his first impulse, which was to go running down the aisle to join Crystal in front of the dais. The reaction from the tall man in the yellow raincoat was instantaneous, however. He quickly shoved his way to the end of the aisle where he was sitting and ran to Crystal's side.

It was Connor, of course, which was yet another shock to Adam's system. Adam glanced at Carla to see that her posture was stiff and rigid, indicating that she'd also recognized the fact that her son was here.

"Well," the proctor said, "it would appear that the girl's story is true. She did follow her fiancé here."

"Yes, sir. I take full responsibility," Connor said, bowing his head.

"As you should," the proctor intoned darkly. "Yet now we have the uncomfortable burden of deciding what should be done about this."

Angry mutterings filled the air as people pronounced their judgments.

"Make her join us!" someone said.

"Kill her!" another added.

Adam clenched his teeth, willing the crowd to part so that he could pinpoint the one who'd just said that.

The proctor appeared taken aback by the suggestion. He placed a hand on his chest and slowly shook his head. "Tell me, girl—did you speak to anyone else about where you were going?"

"No, sir," Crystal said.

"And to the best of your knowledge, were *you* followed?"

She shook her head.

"In that case, I don't see any reason to punish you. Please take a seat with your fiancé."

Connor led Crystal away by the hand and they went to sit together in the front row, despite the grumblings and mutterings of the other Nightingales.

"Please, everyone sit down," the proctor said.

Adam sat along with the others, and the two Rangers wearing gas masks hurried back down the aisle to return to their positions outside the stadium.

"Now, as I was saying… we are on the eve of our victory. The mayor has managed to secure emergency rations for Bexar, but the governor has requested that we pick them up ourselves, which we will gladly do. Tomorrow morning a convoy of empty trucks will leave Bexar. All of you will be hiding in those vehicles, armed and waiting to execute a coup once we arrive."

The proctor waited a few seconds for that revelation to sink in. The rumbles of discontent returned, and Adam felt an echo of those same objections building up swiftly in his own chest.

"What are we going to say at work?" someone asked.

"Nothing. You simply won't go. We'll leave your colleagues to fill in the blanks for themselves. Some will think you are sick.

Others might send friends or Rangers to your homes to check on you. When they find that you're missing, they'll assume you were taken, just like all of the Vultures' other victims. But by this time tomorrow night, the Governor will be in our custody, and we will have carpet-bombed his city with the proof of his collaboration with the enemy. Later on, there will be a trial, and some of you will bear witness against him."

More murmurs of discontent spread through the assembly. "I thought we were going to lynch him!" someone shouted.

"Cut off his head!" someone else added. "Put the head on trial."

Laughter followed that suggestion.

Adam frowned. The Nightingales were taking this coup far too lightly. People were going to die. A lot of people.

Adam might have been able to make his peace with that before, when he'd only had to worry about his own skin and that of a bunch of faceless strangers, but after tonight, they weren't so faceless anymore. His wife and future son-in-law were going to be there, too.

The proctor droned on about the details of his plan, but Adam struggled to focus on what he was saying. All he could think about was Carla and Connor lying broken and bloodied in a pile of bodies that were gathered to burn.

Adam went back to listening to the proctor's

plan, hoping that it was a good one.

"Those of us with combat experience will proceed to the governor's mansion where we will begin a direct assault on the compound. With help from a sympathizer on the inside, the engagement will be over quickly. As soon as we have the governor in our custody, we will pretend to smuggle him out in one of two Stryker transports, but both vehicles will be a diversion, designed to throw off pursuit while we sneak him across on foot to a secure room in the basement of the Capitol building.

"Meanwhile, the rest of our operatives will have pasted these posters all over the city." The proctor held one of them up by way of example. It showed a blurry image of the governor kneeling at the foot of the ramp to a Spec lander with a group of civilians bound and gagged behind him, held at gunpoint by Rangers.

Several people gasped and others cursed viciously.

Adam blinked in silent shock, willing the image into sharper focus. The proctor turned and distributed a pile of those posters to the two Rangers standing behind him. They in turn walked down from the dais to distribute the material among the crowd.

Moments later, Adam was staring at one of those posters in his hands. The governor's face was blurry, but still recognizable. He couldn't help wondering how the Nightingales had captured such a damning photograph, leaving him to wonder if it was even real. Before the invasion faking something like this would have been easy. A combination of AI and Photo editing software could have cobbled it together in a matter of seconds. But then the photo wouldn't have been blurry. That one detail spoke to the veracity of the image, as though it had been hastily snapped with an actual telephoto lens.

"This is how we will sway the public once they discover that their beloved dictator has been deposed. And once we have the people on our side, we will come out of hiding and take credit for the coup."

A cheer rose from the crowd.

"We will conduct a legal trial where Governor Miller will be forced to answer for his crimes. Then, finally, we will cede control of the government, and call for the very first democratic election."

The mutterings were back.

The proctor straightened and regarded the crowd balefully with his crimson mask. "Perhaps you feel that we should remain in power."

"Hell yeah!" someone said.

"How do we know that they won't elect someone worse than Miller? We can't take the risk!"

"We can, and we will. The people deserve to have a voice," the proctor declared. "And why wouldn't we give them one? *Our* organization is democratic. You elected *me,* and without ever having seen my face."

"Because no one else wanted the job!" someone quipped.

Snickering erupted in the wake of that comment.

Adam grimaced. He didn't want to see what would happen if these people suddenly found themselves in control of the Republic and then conveniently refused to relinquish control.

"No," the proctor insisted. "You elected me because I know what I am doing, and that is because I am no stranger to leadership."

With that, the proctor slowly reached up...

And removed his mask.

A collective gasp tore through the audience.

And suddenly Adam understood why Ellis had insisted that he join the Nightingales all those years ago. Ellis hadn't really needed an informant in their organization. He'd recruited Adam because that was his job.

Because he was their proctor.

"The time of unmasking has arrived!" Ellis said, his voice no longer distorted by his mask. "From this day forth, we will no longer hide in the shadows! We will walk brazenly in the light of the fires that the governor has set!"

CHAPTER TWENTY-ONE

Adam expected people to cheer in response to the mayor's revelation that *he* was the proctor of the Nightingales, but his big reveal fell flat in the face of the conclave's collective suspicions.

"You're the mayor!" Someone shouted. "You expect us to believe that you don't know who the Vultures are? That you're not involved?"

"Would I be here, if I was?" Ellis challenged. "You know me. Even if you haven't seen my face until today, I have led this conclave ever since our beloved Valentina Flores was taken by the Vultures, and I can assure you that no one was more enraged by her disappearance than I."

Adam remembered her. She predated his arrival in Bexar, but he remembered hearing about her while he'd been living on the ranch. About seven years ago, the Republic had its first election, and Valentina Flores had been Governor Miller's opposition. She'd ultimately lost the vote, but there had been widespread reports that the governor had stolen the election. And considering that he was essentially a military dictator, that was probably true. Her subsequent disappearance had only added to those suspicions.

Mayor Ellis went on for a while, defending himself to the group and answering their questions until grudging acceptance prevailed.

Adam thought back on his investigations into the Vultures over the past five years. Somehow they'd always been one step ahead of him. At one point he'd gotten close enough to overhear radio communications between two of them—"Arbuckle" and "Scout"—but that was as close as he'd ever come to finding the Vultures operating in Bexar.

After that, he'd tried to join them under false pretenses, but they must have realized that it was a trick, and they never took the bait. Whoever the Vultures were, it was too late to find them now. Adam just hoped that Ellis had done his homework to make sure that none of them were at this meeting.

Ellis spoke again, "I would like to invite you to reveal your faces as I have done. After our victory tomorrow, we won't have to hide anymore. The Nightingales won't be persecuted as terrorists; we will be celebrated as heroes, as advocates of truth and democracy, having prevailed over a corrupt dictator and his secret police!"

This time the crowd cheered. Before that positive sentiment could fade, Ellis repeated his invitation, "Those of you who would be so bold, please come up to the dais and remove your masks."

The crowd shuffled their feet as a handful of people went bobbing and weaving toward the aisle. Adam saw Carla moving in that direction, and he followed her. Roughly one in five people took the mayor up on his call to action. Adam stepped up to the dais with them, maneuvering himself until he was standing directly behind Carla, inhaling the rain-washed scent of her hair and perfume. Connor didn't join them on the dais. He stayed right where he was, beside Crystal in the front row of the assembly.

Once everyone who was willing to remove their masks had reached the dais, Ellis stepped back and gestured grandly to them.

"Now, if you please, let us see your faces."

Adam reached up in unison with the others and slowly removed his mask.

Gasps trickled from the crowd below as they recognized some of the ones standing in front of them. It took Crystal a moment to spot Adam. She grabbed Connor's leg and pointed to him—and then to his mother. Connor went suddenly very still, no doubt as troubled by his mother's involvement as Adam had been.

Ellis smiled and nodded. "It's no coincidence that some of you recognize each other," he said. "What is it they say, *birds of a feather flock together?*"

A few strained laughs bubbled through the group, and Adam smirked. *Being a little heavy-handed with the wordplay, aren't we, Ellis?*

"Please, feel free to come up here and join your friends and loved ones. Remember, you are safe here. This group has been carefully vetted, and only our most loyal followers were invited to tonight's meeting."

About twenty others came shuffling down the aisle, convinced by the mayor's reassurances.

"What about her?" someone pointed to Crystal.

She stood up, looking bewildered at having been singled out. "What *about* me?"

But before her accuser could answer, Ellis said, "This young woman followed her fiancé. She wouldn't do anything to compromise his safety. And I think you'll find that he's not the only member of her family who is here tonight. Adam? Would you step forward please?"

Carla spun around to look and spotted him immediately. Shock flickered across her face. "What are you doing here?" she hissed at him.

He smiled tightly as he waded through the crowd on the dais. "I could ask you the same question."

"Adam, please come over here," Ellis insisted.

He did. Now standing beside the stocky mayor, he attempted a more genuine smile. "Five years ago, I granted this man and his family asylum here in Bexar. He came with his daughter, whom you have now seen, and his future son-in-law, sitting beside her. They had learned about the Specs taking human slaves, and they naively went to tell the governor about it, just as any good citizen would. As a reward for their trouble, the governor tried to have them killed, and they were lucky to escape Travis with their lives.

"This man and his family, along with each and every one of you, will take the stand to bear witness against Governor Miller when the time comes."

Adam nodded along with that, and the crowd settled down, once again losing interest in Crystal. Mayor Ellis prattled on for a few more minutes before wrapping up his speech.

When he finished, he divided them into nine groups, one for each of the trucks in the supply convoy. Adam found himself standing in a group with Connor, Major Hunter, and a couple of others that he only recognized from the designs of the masks that they still wore.

"You two must be proud of yourselves," Crystal said as she walked over with Carla from one of the other groups. Her eyes darted back and forth between Adam and Connor, making him wonder which one of them she was mad at.

Connor sighed and finally removed his mask. He took Crystal's hands in his. "You shouldn't have followed me."

"I'm glad I did! Is this why you changed your mind about having kids?"

Adam did a double-take. He hadn't realized they were trying to get pregnant, but maybe they were just talking about it.

"I *do* want them," Connor insisted. "I just... we need to wait until this operation is over, that's all. After that, we can have as many kids as you want. I promise."

"You're afraid that you might get yourself killed," Crystal objected.

Connor looked to Adam for support.

He threw up his hands. "Don't look at me. You shouldn't have joined the Nightingales if you wanted a family. It's bad enough that you joined the Rangers."

Connor scowled. "Look who's talking. You, too," he added, looking at his mother. "It's not like either of you has a family to worry about, right?"

Adam frowned. "It's different for us."

Carla reached for her son's arm. "I joined them to protect you."

Connor jerked his arm away. "Sure you did. Having my mother and my fiancée beside me is going to make me feel real safe as we shoot our way into the capital tomorrow."

Adam's brow furrowed at that. "What do you mean? Crystal won't be there. She's not a Nightingale."

Connor snorted. "You must have missed the part where the mayor said that none of us are going home tonight. What do you think that means?"

"He's right," Major Hunter put in. "She can't go home. She'll have to come with us now."

Adam spun around, searching for Mayor Ellis. He was busy conferring with the leader of one of the other groups. Adam went over there and tapped Ellis sharply on the shoulder.

"Excuse me, gentlemen," Ellis said. "Is there something I can help you with, Sergeant?" he asked as he turned to Adam.

"Yeah, you can send my daughter home."

"I'm afraid I can't do that," Ellis replied.

"Why not?"

"She knows too much."

"Are you kidding? She's not going to talk."

"Maybe not, but she could still be seen returning to her home. Someone could get suspicious. Rangers could take her in for questioning."

"We take that risk every time there's a meeting," Adam growled.

Ellis nodded. "Yes, but surely I don't need to tell you why tonight of all nights, we can't afford to make any mistakes. Rest assured, however, your daughter will have a non-combat role."

"Fine," Adam agreed. "She can go to Travis with us and check into a motel for the night."

Ellis sighed. "Excuse me," he said to the group he'd been speaking with. Then he took Adam aside and dropped his voice to a whisper, "We're going to use your daughter as bait."

"*Bait?*" Adam thundered.

"We need to be sure that the governor will be at his home tomorrow night, and it would be ideal to keep him distracted and focused on questioning your daughter, rather than have him looking out the window where he might see one of our insurgents creeping around. Our man on the inside is going to take your daughter to see him tomorrow night, just before the coup begins."

Adam gaped at Ellis, unable to believe what he was hearing. "Send me instead. You didn't know Crystal was coming tonight. There's no way you could have planned this operation around her. Someone else was going to be the bait, weren't they?"

Ellis frowned. "Originally, there wasn't going to be any bait, but now that Crystal is here, we can't pass up the opportunity. And it's just conceivable that she might have relocated to Travis to give her unborn baby a better life."

Confusion swirled through Adam's mind. "She's not pregnant," he mumbled.

"Isn't she? Her fiancé informed me that they have been trying… Private Cooper?"

Connor glanced over at him. "Yes, sir?"

Adam's gaze flashed back and forth between the mayor and Connor, realizing now that this was a setup. Crystal didn't *follow* Connor here. He'd lured her here! Adam flew across the room and grabbed Connor by the lapels of his raincoat, forcing him up onto tiptoes even though he was both taller and heavier than Adam was. "You led her here!" Adam roared.

"Dad!" Crystal objected.

"Let me go!" Connor squeaked.

"You don't deserve her!" Adam shouted, spraying Connor's face with spittle. "You led her here deliberately, didn't you, you little shit?"

Connor's expression twisted miserably, and this time he didn't say anything in his defense. That was as good as a confession.

"Connor?" Crystal asked quietly. "That's not true, is it?"

"Tell her," Adam demanded. "Tell her how you and the proctor have been talking about her, secretly sizing her up for the part. I just hope you haven't been measuring her for a coffin!" Adam let Connor go with a shove, and he stumbled away.

"Connor?" Carla prompted, looking almost as shocked as Adam felt.

"Don't be too hard on him," Ellis said, joining

them suddenly. "I didn't give him a choice—isn't that right, son?"

Connor looked on the verge of tears. He was staring at Crystal, his eyes red, looking distraught. "It's true," he admitted, "but I never wanted to involve you. I swear!"

Adam scowled. "Yet you did, so whatever happens to her, that's on you. And if something *does* happen to her, I'll *kill* you."

Connor winced, and Carla shot Adam a horrified look, but he was too angry to care.

Connor had wittingly put his own fiancée in jeopardy. *What kind of man does that?* Suddenly, Adam had a whole swath of new reasons to question Connor's fitness to be his daughter's husband.

CHAPTER TWENTY-TWO

"Take it easy, Adam," Ellis chided. His pudgy hand landed on Adam's shoulder, and he turned to glare at it. "We won't let anything happen to Crystal. Our operative on the inside will remain close to her the whole time."

Adam rounded on the mayor, now directing his ire at the mastermind rather than his pawn. "You can't possibly guarantee her safety."

Ellis frowned. "Perhaps not, but we are all putting our lives on the line for this operation. This is bigger than any one person, or their family. We're trying to topple a corrupt and dangerous regime, and there's far more at stake than even you know. Maybe you should ask your daughter whether or not she would like to be a part of that?"

"*Now* we're going to ask if she wants to be involved? Isn't it a little late for that?"

"Perhaps, but I have the power to remove her from the equation. Some of our people will be staying here. If Crystal refuses to join us, she can stay with them until the coup is over."

Adam glared at the mayor. "You promise?" he asked.

"Cross my heart," Ellis replied while making the requisite gesture.

Adam turned to Crystal. "Well? You heard him. You can sit this one out. There's no reason for you to risk your life."

Crystal hesitated, then looked to Ellis. "Is my part important?"

"I believe that it is," Ellis replied.

"Crystal," Adam gritted out. "When we break into the Governor's Mansion, there'll be bullets flying everywhere. What if the governor decides to use you as a hostage to get himself out?"

Crystal looked back to the mayor.

"That's why we'll have someone in there with you. He'll be armed, and the governor likely won't."

Carla shook her head. "If you have someone that close to the governor, why can't you just assassinate him?"

Mayor Ellis sighed. "I wish it were that simple. There's a whole chain of command below the governor. If he's killed, the next person in line will simply take over. In this case, it would likely be one of his generals. To circumvent that, we need a two-pronged approach. We remove him, yes, but we don't kill him. We hide him, and at the same time, we make sure that we've thoroughly exposed his dealings with the Specs by putting up our posters all over the city." Ellis walked to a nearby chair to retrieve one of the posters. "In the chaos and confusion that follows, we'll step out of the shadows and take credit for deposing the tyrant.

"The people will be on our side at that point, but we'll further bolster public support for our coup by revealing that we have the moral high ground precisely because we *didn't* kill the governor. We'll assure everyone that we are only there to establish an interim government until a proper election can be held. No one will dare to stand against us after that."

"A lot of things could still go wrong with this plan," Adam pointed out.

"That is why we need every edge that we can get. We *need* Crystal for this. Like it or not. She's the perfect distraction, and the governor won't do anything to her."

"What makes you so sure?" Adam asked.

"Because he'll want to use her to bait *you* out of hiding. You're the one he really sees as a threat."

Adam frowned. "It's been five years. And it's not like I went there to point a finger at the bastard."

Mayor Ellis nodded slowly. "No, you didn't. And he overreacted. But after he tried to kill you, and you escaped, he'll know that you are more dangerous than ever. His attempted cover-up is proof of his guilt, and that makes you a loose end."

"I want to be a part of this," Crystal said.

Ellis looked at her with a smile.

Adam grimaced. "Christie, don't do this. It's a bad idea, and I won't be there to keep you safe."

"This was important enough for the three of you to join up and risk your lives," Crystal said. "So why am I so special that I get to stay out of it? Why do you three get to run off and play the hero but I have to stay here and hide?"

"Because if something happens to you…" Adam trailed off meaningfully, and Connor winced.

"What if something happens to *you?*" Crystal countered. "Or to you," she added, with an icy look at Connor. "None of you thought about what it would do to *me* if you died in this fight. You just assumed that the risk would be worth it, so why are you surprised that I agree? You need me for this, and I know how to look after myself. I'm not some helpless little girl. I survived the invasion, and the wastes, and the raiders who attacked Sunny Valley. I'll survive this, too."

Adam sighed, his shoulders rounding with defeat, but he wasn't giving up yet. "Maybe, but there is something that the mayor isn't telling you." He let his gaze rove around to each of them in turn, waiting until he had everyone's attention.

"And what is that?" Ellis asked.

"The fact that Governor Miller didn't have a choice about collaborating with the Specs. If he didn't have his Vultures telling them who to take, they would have abducted people anyway. Deposing him isn't going to change anything. The Specs will still be taking people, except that they'll be less discreet about it. We'll be lucky if they don't invade all over again and begin harvesting us en masse."

Ellis scowled. "That's pure assumption."

"A reasonable assumption, given what we know," Adam countered. "And what exactly are you going to do about it if that happens? Are you going to cut a deal, too?" Adam smirked and shook his head. "I guess we'll have come full circle then. One tyrant deposes another. The same crown, just a different head that wears it. But maybe that's the real objective here."

"You're out of line," Major Hunter warned, stepping between them as if to break up a fight.

Carla and Connor looked concerned by the implications of what he'd said, but neither of them said anything. Maybe like everyone else in the Nightingales, they'd been so focused on defeating their enemy and pursuing justice that they hadn't stopped to think about what they were actually going to change.

"If it comes to it, we will institute a fairer system," Ellis said.

"When," Adam replied.

"Excuse me?"

"You said *if* it comes to it, but like it or not, this will happen. The Specs are taking people for a reason. We might not know what that reason is, but we're not going to change anything just by removing their puppet from office."

Major Hunter spoke in a low, angry voice, "This is not the time or place to discuss your misgivings, Sergeant. People are listening to you, and you're damaging our morale."

Adam made a show of looking around, taking in the myriad faces that had turned his way, listening to the conversation. "With all due respect, sir, maybe people should listen to me," Adam said, raising his voice rather than lowering it. "We don't get a do-over for this, and our people should know if their cause is bankrupt before they throw their lives away for it."

Hunter muttered a curse, and his blue eyes bored icily into the mayor's. "I *told you* he's a liability. We never should have brought him into this."

Ellis held up a hand for patience. "He's precisely the kind of person we need for this. An idealist. Someone with a vision, and a low tolerance for bullshit."

Adam frowned, surprised to hear that the mayor was on his side.

"You want to know what our end game is?" Ellis asked. "Maybe it's time that we showed you."

Adam slowly shook his head, feeling more confused than ever. "There *is* an end game?"

"Of course there is. You must think I'm an idiot. Please, follow me, Sergeant." Mayor Ellis walked briskly away, heading for the far end of the football field. He waved to them over his shoulder, beckoning.

Adam hesitated, looking to Major Hunter for his reaction. He appeared even less happy than he had a moment ago. Deep lines were drawn around his mouth and the crow's feet were scrunching up around his eyes. He knew exactly what Ellis was going to show them, and he didn't like it one bit.

***

Adam followed Mayor Ellis across the football field, up through the bleachers, and then down a winding ramp to the main floor. At that point, both Major Hunter and Mayor Ellis produced flashlights to light the way. Adam reached to his belt and plucked his out for good measure. Crystal produced a flashlight of her own—but hers was the headlight of a bike.

As they went, Adam sensed a dark, ugly aura building around his wife like a storm cloud. He tried reaching for her hand—as a peace offering —but she seized his hand and shoved it away.

He did a good job of feigning innocence, but he knew what he'd done. He'd threatened to kill her son.

Fine, Adam thought. *Be mad. But if the tables were turned and it was Crystal who'd lured your son into joining a dangerous mission, you'd be pissed, too.*

Rather than lead them outside as Adam expected, Ellis ducked down a narrow hallway, and from there he chose a particular door with the faded symbol of a staircase on it. He pulled it open, revealing a long, dark stairwell.

"What's down there?" Crystal asked in a faltering voice.

"Answers," Ellis replied as he followed Major Hunter down the stairs. Adam hesitated at the top with the others.

The last time they'd been led down a dark stairwell with no idea of what they'd find at the bottom was in the Capitol. A team of Miller's Rangers had led them down a long, winding stairwell only to lock them in a bunker full of stalkers.

"Well?" Connor prompted. "Are we doing this, or not?"

Adam grimaced. "I'll go first." He stepped through the doorway just as Major Hunter and Mayor Ellis were passing out of sight. Adam caught up to them at the second landing, which turned out to be the bottom of the stairs. The way forward was barred by a big blue metal door.

"Where are you taking us?" Adam asked as Major Hunter opened the door and led them out. The sound of machinery droning filled the air. It sounded like generators. Since the floodlights had been on in the stadium, that made sense.

The major's flashlight sent shadows dancing through a vast underground loading area that looked just like any underground parking garage that Adam had ever seen, with concrete walls, pillars, and floors. A couple of trucks were still parked down there, backed up to storage units with blue metal doors, but other than that, the space was empty.

Adam began to suspect a trap. "Hey, if this is your idea of shutting us up…"

"Relax. I am not the governor," Ellis said.

"Not yet," Adam muttered under his breath.

"What about stalkers?" Connor asked, glancing about nervously.

"The stadium is secure," Major Hunter said. "All of the entrances and exits have been barricaded. Including the loading dock. And we have armed guards outside."

"If it's not a trap, what's with all the secrecy?" Crystal asked. "Just tell us what you're going to show us."

"Patience," Ellis replied.

Major Hunter rounded the front of one of the trucks in the loading dock, and Adam finally saw where they were headed. A handful of expandable green shipping containers were connected to big, matching canvas tents at the far end of the loading area. Adam recognized the setup as a TURMAKS' mobile field hospital. A handful of floodlights stood around the facility, illuminating it.

Carla glanced at Adam, her expression pinched with worry. A field hospital implied patients. But who were they, and what did that have to do with the coup that Ellis was planning?

Connor and Crystal pulled ahead of them, holding hands. Apparently, Crystal was already over the fact that Connor had tricked her into coming here and that he was secretly a Nightingale.

Adam felt like she should have been holding more of a grudge over those betrayals. Carla certainly was with him.

They reached the mobile hospital and walked down the side to a door that was guarded by a pair of Rangers. The guards stiffened with their approach but relaxed as they appeared to recognize Major Hunter and Mayor Ellis.

"As you were," Ellis said. He stepped up to a door in the side of the container and tapped a code into a numeric keypad. The door buzzed and clicked, and Ellis pulled it open, leading them into a cramped space full of medical equipment and actual, working computers. Rangers looked up from two of those stations, but Ellis offered no word of explanation as he crossed the container to another door. They followed him into an adjoining container lined with shelves full of medical and lab equipment. Reaching the end of the supply area, they came to the metal wall of another container, once again guarded by a keypad. Ellis tapped in his code again, but this time he hesitated with his hand on the door handle.

"I think, perhaps, it would be better if only Adam saw this," he said.

"What?" Crystal blinked at him. "You made us come all this way for nothing?"

Ellis smiled sheepishly. "I do apologize."

"Do you?" Carla asked.

"Major, would you please escort the others back outside?" Ellis asked.

"With pleasure," Hunter replied.

"What about me?" Connor objected.

"This is way above your pay grade, son," Hunter said.

Connor scowled, and Carla glared at Adam as she left as if it was somehow his fault that he was the only one Ellis would trust with this secret.

Ellis waited for them to vanish inside the first container before directing his attention to

Adam. "Are you sure you want to see this?" Ellis asked.

Adam smirked. "No, I'm not. I'll just take your word for it that you've got an actual plan to deal with the Specs."

"Ah yes, sarcasm, the lowest form of wit."

"But the highest form of intelligence."

Ellis fixed him with a bemused look. "Excuse me?"

"That's the full quote," Adam explained. "Oscar Wilde."

"Is it really?" Ellis mused.

"Open the door," Adam prompted.

"Very well…" Ellis pushed the door open and walked through.

Adam hurried in after him, eager to get to the bottom of whatever was going on.

What he saw on the other side of the door stopped him cold. There, lying in the center of the medical unit, strapped to a stretcher with thick, padded nylon restraints, and surrounded by beeping life signs monitors, was a young woman with two suspiciously glowing growths on either side of her head. Her eyes were shut, and she was being attended by a medical corpsman and a doctor. Each of them wore gloves and surgical masks as they picked at the blue growth, leaving the red one alone. Those alien parasites were slowly pulsing with internal radiance as they rhythmically inflated and deflated, breathing in and out like the living creatures that they were.

Adam shivered at the recollection of having those same creatures attached to his skull—however briefly. They had burrowed into his brain with thin nerve-like tendrils, subverting his will and hijacking his nervous system, making it impossible to oppose the collaborator who had captured him in the stalker den below the Capitol. That collaborator had turned out to be none other than Carla's previous husband, Harrison Cooper.

Adam was glad that Connor and Carla weren't here to see this. Neither of them needed the reminder of what had happened to Harry.

"You captured one of them," Adam said slowly.

Ellis was grinning like a fiend. "Yes."

"I'm assuming you've had some kind of a breakthrough?"

"You could say that." Ellis turned to address the medical officer in the room. "Doctor Janssen? Would you care to explain the significance of your research to my friend here?"

CHAPTER TWENTY-THREE

The doctor straightened from probing the azure growth on the side of the patient's head. He pulled off blue surgical gloves and yanked down his mask, revealing a thick white beard.

"Who is he?" the doctor asked.

"Does it matter?" Ellis countered.

"It does if he can't be trusted."

"How dangerous is it for me to know what's going on down here?" Adam asked.

"Very," the doctor replied.

"Then let's get this over with before I change my mind."

Ellis smiled cryptically and nodded to the doctor. "Janssen, would you like to explain, or shall I?"

"We have discovered a way of immobilizing the parasites that control human hosts," Doctor Janssen said.

"How?" Adam asked.

"They are a type of fungi—nothing like what

we have here on Earth, of course, since they can move around and actively breathe the air. To us they're more like animals, but what defines them as fungi is how they reproduce —through airborne spores. Fortunately, the spores themselves are not infectious. They grow in fertile soil like mushrooms, and once they reach maturity, they sprout legs and look for a host.

"Once they find a suitable host, they splice themselves into its brain and nervous systems, effectively taking control of the creature's body. Once attached, detaching them is dangerous and may result in the release of deadly toxins, but we have discovered two ways around this.

"One is with fire. If they sense smoke or the heat of a fire, then they will automatically detach themselves from their hosts and flee for safety."

Adam remembered how the parasites that had been attached to his skull had dropped off and scuttled away when he'd been trapped by burning debris at Sunny Valley Ranch. "That happened to me," he said.

Ellis did a double-take. "You were infected?"

"Briefly."

"Then you got lucky," the doctor said.

"No argument here," Adam replied. "It's like the jungles. They uproot themselves to get away from fire."

"Precisely," Doctor Janssen said. "That

is actually what made us think of it. Unfortunately, detaching fully-grown fungi does come with significant risks, even if they decide to leave their hosts voluntarily. But there is another way to deal with them, and it's even more useful than the first. We've discovered an injectable compound, derived from charcoal, of all things, that when introduced to a host's bloodstream, puts the fungi into a state of hibernation. Ordinarily, they sleep when their hosts do, but we have been able to sedate them for extended periods without also sedating their hosts."

Adam looked over at the female patient, noticing that her eyes were still firmly shut. "She doesn't look very awake to me."

"She is a particularly advanced case," Doctor Janssen replied.

"What does that mean?" Adam looked to Ellis, who shrugged. The doctor nodded to his corpsman. "Wake her up."

"But, sir—"

"Did that sound like a suggestion to you, Specialist?"

"No, sir."

Janssen went to the woman's bedside, and the corpsman pushed something into her IV. The woman's eyelids fluttered. A moment later, bright green eyes flicked open, and she stared fixedly at the ceiling. The color of her eyes, her relatively young age, and her long blonde hair reminded Adam of his daughter. But unlike Crystal, she clearly wasn't in full possession of her faculties. On waking, Adam had expected her to battle her restraints, or to see her head turn and look at one of them, but she didn't even seem to realize that anyone was there.

Doctor Janssen snapped his fingers a few times beside her ear, but she didn't even blink.

"What's wrong with her?" Adam asked.

"Left long enough to their devices, the fungi will completely replace the host's mind with their neural pathways. We've woken up what's left of her, and unfortunately, it isn't much."

Adam felt sick to his stomach, but at least this put some context around Harrison's death. When one of his parasites had died and released him, Harry had experienced a moment of lucidity in which he'd *recognized* his family. Ever since then, Adam had wondered if that meant Harry could have been saved. Maybe if they'd found some way to knock him out and take him captive rather than shooting him... but this new information told him otherwise. Too many years had passed. His parasites would have replaced almost everything inside his head. That brief spark of memory that had allowed Harry to say goodbye to his family might have been all that was left of him.

"How does this help us?" Adam asked. "If putting the parasites to sleep turns the hosts into vegetables, it's not exactly a way to bring them back."

"No," Doctor Janssen agreed. "But that's not what this is for. Imagine if we were to inject hosts before infection, or possibly just after. They would still retain their autonomy and their identities, despite seemingly being infected."

"You want to infiltrate the Specs," Adam realized.

Mayor Ellis began nodding grimly. "*That's* our end game, Adam. We're going to learn about our enemy from within, and then we're going to find a way to defeat them."

"How long does the sedative last?" Adam asked.

"As far as we can tell, it's permanent," Doctor Janssen replied. "We would have to administer an antidote to wake them, but so far we haven't discovered one."

"Won't the Specs realize that there is something wrong with the people you've inoculated?"

"Well, that depends…" Ellis began.

"On?"

"How good our operatives are," Ellis replied. He looked Adam up and down speculatively. "Something tells me that *you* would be a natural."

Adam took a quick step back with his hands raised. "Hey, I didn't agree to be your guinea pig."

"True," Ellis said, "but you wanted to know how taking the governor down will change anything with the Specs. Did I assume wrong that you might be interested in striking back against them yourself?"

Adam hesitated. "Why not share this intel with the governor and work with *him* to infiltrate the Specs? You could skip the coup entirely."

"It's too risky," Ellis replied. "The governor has been working with them for years. After all of that, do you really think we would entrust him with our secret weapon?"

"I guess not..." Adam trailed off with a frown.

"And besides, we didn't stumble upon this discovery on our own. Doctor Janssen was sent to us from the North American Coalition. They've been helping us with this project, and as you know, there's no love lost between the NAC and the Republic."

"So why would they help us?" Adam asked.

"Because we're taking out their rival for them, and because we don't subscribe to Governor Miller's warmongering policies. If we get into power, we'll ally with the NAC. It's time for us to stand together as a species. What is it the good book says? Something about a divided kingdom being doomed."

"If a kingdom is divided against itself, it

cannot stand," Adam supplied.

"That's it," Ellis agreed. "The Coalition wants us to infiltrate the Specs and steal a lander using this treatment. Supposedly they already have one of their own."

Adam's eyes widened. So the rumor was true. "Sanctum," he whispered.

Doctor Janssen stiffened. "Where did you hear that word?"

"It's a long story," Adam replied.

Janssen's eyes darkened. He looked to Ellis, but the mayor seemed oblivious. "What is Sanctum?" he asked.

"A closely guarded secret," the doctor replied. "But not closely guarded enough, it seems. No one is supposed to know about Sanctum unless they're already on their way there."

"It was a rumor that I heard from a dying man," Adam explained. "I don't think he expected me to live, but here I am—still kicking."

"Is someone going to let me in on the secret?" Ellis asked.

Doctor Janssen looked pointedly at his corpsman. "Specialist, leave us."

The man set his scalpel down and dumped his surgical gloves in a red hazardous waste bin. He went to a door opposite the one they'd entered by.

As soon as the door clicked shut behind him,

Janssen nodded to the mayor. "Sanctum is the backup plan. In case we don't find a way to beat the Specs."

Ellis frowned. "What is it?"

"It's a colony," Adam explained. "On another planet," He looked to Janssen as he said that, waiting for confirmation.

Janssen nodded. "The Coalition has been evacuating people there for years."

"Is *that* why they want us to steal a lander?" Ellis asked. "So we can speed up the evacuation? What are they not telling us?"

Doctor Janssen pursed his lips. "I'm afraid that's above my pay grade, Mr. Mayor. I've just told you everything that I know. If we are fighting a lost cause down here, then no one has thought to tell me about it."

"It doesn't matter," Adam decided. "One way or another, we'll find out. And if we do need to make a strategic withdrawal, then that's all the more reason we need to have a lander of our own. We can't depend on the NAC to evacuate all of our people as well as theirs."

Ellis didn't look satisfied. "There are millions of people in the Republic. Have you seen the size of those landers? I'd be surprised if we can evacuate more than a few dozen at a time. That's not enough to save a meaningful number of our citizens."

"No," Doctor Janssen whispered grimly. "But it *is* enough to save the species."

"Is that what it's come to?" Ellis asked.

"We already are an endangered species," Janssen said. "Our numbers are shrinking by the day. If we continue on that trend, sooner or later, humans will go extinct."

"Someone needs to teach the Specs about sustainable farming," Adam muttered. "Shouldn't they be working to preserve us as a resource?"

"They might not have reached that phase of the invasion yet," Janssen said. "Or they could already be breeding us in captivity, in which case they might not care what our numbers are in the wild, so to speak."

"We need to find out," Ellis growled. "As soon as the governor is out of office, we can begin planning our next steps. In the meantime… Doctor, would you please inoculate Sergeant Hall?"

"Yes, of course," Janssen replied.

"Say what?" Adam asked.

Ellis looked at him with his eyebrows patiently raised. "Now that you know about our secret weapon, there's no reason not to inoculate you against possible capture."

Adam frowned and watched as the doctor approached him with a syringe full of some black, tarry liquid. "Are there any side effects?"

Janssen shook his head. "Nausea, muscle pain at the injection site, dizziness… I believe that covers it."

"Dizziness and nausea, and I'm supposed to be going into combat tomorrow?"

"You'll have time to recover," Ellis said, "and not everyone experiences the side effects. I didn't."

"You took the injection?" Adam asked.

Ellis nodded.

"All right, fine." He rolled up his sleeve and watched as the needle went into his muscle. It ached sharply, and his arm went slightly numb, but the effects wore off after just a few seconds.

"You're good to go," Janssen said as he applied a small band-aid.

"Who else has been inoculated?" Adam asked.

"Who else?" Ellis asked dumbly.

"If it comes to it, I need to know who I can trust."

"All of our sergeants, a few corporals, the doctor, and of course, Major Hunter. Not everyone knows what it was, but... at least they're prepared."

Adam nodded. "I want you to give me a few extra inoculations."

Ellis's brow furrowed and he looked to the doctor. "You don't need more than one."

"It's not for me," Adam said.

"Knowledge of this program is dangerous, Adam," Ellis warned. "You can't just inoculate whoever you like. If the specs find out what we're doing here..."

He shook his head. "I'm not going to tell anyone anything. If the coup fails, the plan is to steal a lander, right?"

"Even if we don't fail," Ellis confirmed.

"Then give me the means to do it. You can trust me."

"Can I?" Ellis asked. "I've been blackmailing you since you arrived in Bexar, and now I've involved your daughter in our coup without your permission. Left to your own devices, I wonder whose side you'd really be on."

Adam scowled. "Cut the crap, Ellis. If you can't trust me, then what am I doing here? With or without those inoculations, I can still tell people what you're doing down here. I'm on humanity's side. And the last time I checked, that was your side, too."

"Very well. Doctor? Give the sergeant two more doses."

"Three," Adam said.

Ellis shook his head. "Two is all you're going to get. Use them wisely."

Adam nodded grimly, while privately thinking to himself that this operation had just gotten a whole lot more complicated. The mission had started with an ill-fated coup, but even if they succeeded in deposing the governor, it was just the start of a much larger coup against the Specs themselves.

If Adam were a betting man, he'd have given odds to anyone betting against them.

PART THREE: INSURRECTION

CHAPTER TWENTY-FOUR

Crystal was surprised to find how extensive the abandoned sewer system was. They were able to follow it almost all the way to the old supercenter where Carla worked, which was the staging point for this operation.

She glanced about nervously as Carla used her keys to open the doors of the massive cinder block building. Adam and Connor stood guard, sweeping their rifles and flashlights across the old parking lot. The others were all waiting around the back for her to open up from the inside.

Carla pushed the reinforced sheet metal doors apart with a grinding shriek from the aging mechanisms. "Let's go," she said, waving them through.

The four of them hurried into a darkened entrance full of shopping carts, and Carla shut and locked the doors behind them.

This facility supplied almost all of Bexar

with food and other basic necessities. A few smaller corner stores bought from them to stock their shelves, but price-conscious consumers all bought directly here.

Carla pocketed her keys and opened the next set of doors with just her hands. Another shriek erupted from rusty rails and rollers. "We're in," she whispered.

They followed her through the darkened building. Crystal's dad and Connor lit the way with their flashlights. Crystal fished into her pocket for the headlight she'd taken from her bike and added its beam to the others.

They hurried down aisles of sparsely stocked shelves until they came to a heavy metal door in the back with a sign on it that read *Authorized Personnel Only*. Here Carla used a security badge rather than her keys to open the door, and they passed into a spacious loading zone stacked high with pallets of dry food and other non-perishable items.

Carla crossed the storeroom to another set of metal doors at the back of the echoing chamber. Once again she flashed her badge across the scanner. The lock clicked, and she pushed the doors open.

Mayor Ellis and Major Hunter were waiting directly on the other side with the rest of the insurgents.

Crystal stepped aside as they came bustling in. Solar and battery-powered lanterns were turned on and distributed around the space to provide illumination. Carla shut and locked the back doors, and the sound of rising voices quickly filled the store room.

Crystal wanted to ask the mayor how they were supposed to infiltrate Travis without being discovered, but no one was paying attention to her, and she didn't want to interrupt their work.

Major Hunter was busy snapping orders to his men, including Connor and Adam. Rangers bustled about, raising scuffed and beaten white sectional doors along the outer wall to reveal the empty backs of the trucks that they'd be using tomorrow.

This was the supply convoy. Crystal assumed the mayor intended for them to hide in the backs of those empty trucks, but she couldn't see any way to do that safely. Rangers routinely checked vehicles entering the safe zones.

But then Crystal saw the Rangers opening hidden panels at the front end of each of the trailers. Those compartments looked big enough to fit at least five or ten people, and with nine trucks, that meant they could smuggle at least a hundred insurgents into Travis.

Crystal crowded into the back of one of the trucks with the others to watch as Mayor Ellis illustrated how the compartments worked. He directed one of the larger groups to stand inside the compartment, and then Ellis shut the door with those people standing shoulder to shoulder inside.

"It's a three-hour trip from here to Travis," Ellis explained as he opened the door again. "It won't be very comfortable, but you'll be safe from discovery as long as you stay quiet."

"I wouldn't be so sure about that," Crystal heard her dad say. "You can bet that the Rangers at the gates will have dogs. They could still sniff us out."

Ellis fixed him with a look of strained patience. "This is an *officially* sanctioned convoy, one that I will be leading personally. That will help to deflect suspicion, but we have also thoroughly sealed and insulated the compartments." The mayor pointed to the edge of the camouflaged door, and Crystal saw that it was at least six inches thick. Hopefully, that would be enough to prevent any smells or sounds from escaping.

"The compartments lock from the inside," Ellis added, so there won't be any way to open them. "Even if the Rangers in Travis suspect something, they'll have to pry our trucks apart with crowbars to prove it, and they'll need more than a hint of suspicion to justify *that*."

Nods and murmurs of appreciation spread through the group, but Crystal was far from having all of her questions answered. Ellis and the rest of the Nightingales must have been planning this operation for weeks or months, but she had only been brought in on their plans now.

Crystal thrust her hand up to ask a question, but no one seemed to notice. Apparently raising one's hand to ask questions only worked in school. She cleared her throat in the relative silence that followed the mayor's demonstration. "How will we know when it's safe to come out?"

Ellis spent a moment craning his neck to peer over the heads and shoulders of the crowd, searching for her. "That is a good question, Crystal. The drivers or their Ranger escorts will enter the vehicles and knock on the doors in a specific sequence once it's safe to come out." Ellis illustrated by rapping on the door. *Knock—knock-knock—knock.* "Are there any other questions?"

Crystal thrust her hand up again. "You mentioned the convoy is leaving at dawn…"

"That's correct," Mayor Ellis confirmed.

"That means we'll be arriving in the morning, but you said the coup starts tomorrow night. What will we be doing with all the time in between? We'll need to hide somewhere in the city."

"We have a scheduled stop planned before we get to the Supercenter in Travis," Ellis explained. "We'll head straight for the nearest fuel depot, which is being operated by our people. Our operatives will hide in the admin building until sundown."

Crystal nodded uncertainly. "And then what?"

Murmurs of disbelief filled the back of the truck. "*Why* wasn't she briefed?" someone asked.

"She shouldn't even be here!" another said. "She's not ready for this."

Ellis made a calming gesture with his hands. "There wasn't an appropriate time, until tonight, to brief Miss Hall, but I have prepared a briefing for her. Rest assured, she will play her part well. Before she leaves Bexar, she will know exactly what to say and do, and where she should go. Now, since the rest of you already know your parts, I suggest you get some rest."

Still grumbling, the crowd dispersed inside the store room.

Ellis pulled Crystal aside and handed her a dirty plastic folder with a drawstring. "You'll find everything you need in here. If you have any questions, feel free to ask Private Cooper. If he can't answer you, come and find me or Major Hunter." Crystal accepted the folder with a frown and opened it to peek inside. Mayor Ellis smiled tightly at her as he walked away.

Inside the folder were a handful of papers. One of them had her photo pinned to it with a paper clip in the top left corner. She pulled that one out and read a few paragraphs about why she was moving to Travis and where she was going to stay until she got a job and found a place to rent. She was shocked to read that she would be staying with her old friend, Emily Brooks, and her mother, Sophie.

She hadn't seen Sophie and Emily since they'd gone their separate ways after arriving in Bexar five years ago. Sometime after that, the two of them had relocated to Travis.

"Is everything okay?" Connor asked.

Crystal startled at the sound of his voice. Arms encircled her waist, and he propped his chin on the top of her head as he peered over her shoulder at the document.

Crystal gently pried one of his hands away and turned to face him. "I'm staying with Emily?"

Connor nodded, still frowning. "Yeah."

"Does *she* know that?"

"She does. We have a conclave of Nightingales in Travis, too."

"So Emily and Sophie are..."

"Members?" Connor nodded.

"I guess everyone joined up except me," Crystal muttered.

"Until now, you mean."

"What about Bowser?" Crystal asked suddenly. "He'll be all alone at home! I don't even think he has enough food and water."

Connor smiled and shook his head. "Your

dad is on his way to get him as we speak."

"He is?" Crystal looked around suddenly for her dad, realizing only now that he was missing.

Connor nodded to the folder. "Bowser is a part of your cover if you keep reading. He's going to ride up front with you in one of the trucks. The story is you caught me cheating on you, and we broke up. Determined to get a fresh start, you paid one of the drivers to let you and Bowser hitch a ride to Travis."

"Is that reasonable?" Crystal asked. "Isn't this a government convoy?"

Connor smiled slyly. "You mean because government officials can't be bribed, right?"

Crystal fixed him with a dry look. "Not what I meant. How are they going to explain me and my dog being there when they get to Travis? This isn't just any old convoy."

Connor pointed to the folder again. Crystal dug through it until she found a plastic security badge like Carla's. She spent a couple of seconds staring at the blurry picture of her on the front. "I'm a supply manager in Bexar?"

Connor nodded. "We put a lot of thought into this. You don't have to worry."

Crystal rounded on him with a look that she reserved for the troublemakers in her class. "Don't remind me. I still haven't forgiven you for tricking me into this, you know. Or hiding it."

Connor winced. "I'm sorry."

"Are you? You could have told me what was going on."

"Could I?" Connor countered. "You remember when we first learned about the Nightingales? On the boat ride, when we saw that dead body and the mask floating on the river?"

Crystal shook her head, not sure where he was going with that. "Yeah, it was our first night in Bexar."

Connor smiled wryly at that. "It was our first night *together* in Bexar."

"We slept in separate beds."

"We cuddled first," Connor said.

"What about it?" Crystal asked, getting impatient with the walk down memory lane.

"I wanted to tell our parents about what we saw, but you didn't want to say anything, because you were afraid that your dad would get himself into trouble."

"And?"

"You made it very clear, you came to Bexar to stick your head in the sand."

"That's not fair," Crystal muttered.

Connor shrugged. "But it's true, isn't it?"

"I wanted a chance to have a real life. Somewhere safe to grow up and one day settle down and have a family, but I guess I was the only one who wanted that." Crystal turned away with a bitter scowl.

"Hey," Connor whispered. He grabbed her hand and turned her gently back to face him. "I want that, too. But…"

"But?"

Connor appeared to hesitate. "When I joined the Rangers, I realized that some of them were secretly working for the governor."

"Don't you *all* work for the governor?" Crystal asked.

"No, I mean, a shadow organization inside of the Rangers."

Crystal had heard the rumors. "Vultures."

Connor looked uneasy, clearly not happy that she'd put a name to the group. "Yeah."

"Okay, so what?"

"So, I couldn't ignore it anymore. I had to do something about it. For *you*." Connor leaned in close and whispered, "They're taking people, Christie. Sneaking into their homes in the middle of the night and abducting them."

"You were afraid that would happen to me?"

Connor nodded slowly. "Or to our kid someday. Suddenly, my whole job seemed like a lie. I was supposed to be protecting people, and here there was this group of Rangers actively handing them over to the Specs."

"So you wanted to put a stop to it."

Connor hesitated, but then his chin dipped in a nod.

Crystal smiled wanly and went up on tiptoes to kiss him. He kissed her feebly back, and then curled an arm around her shoulders, guiding her away from the open trailers. He led her to a semi-private corner of the loading area where there were two sleeping bags rolled out next to each other behind a pair of half-empty shipping pallets. One of those battery-powered solar lanterns glowed brightly there, making the space look halfway cozy.

Crystal sat on one of the sleeping bags and propped her back against a pallet of flour while she sifted through the remaining documents in her folder. The setup with the lantern and the sleeping bags reminded her of warm summer nights on the ranch as a kid, when she, Connor, and Emily had pitched tents in their rooms to pretend that they were out on a camping trip, surviving against the elements with nothing but their impressive outdoorsmanship and a couple of pocket knives.

It hadn't been hard to pretend, with the window open and bringing in the sounds of crickets, owls, nighthawks, and even stalkers. Crystal smiled wistfully at the memory of three kids lying wide awake with their sleeping bags tucked up to their chins, listening to every whistle of the wind and every squeak of a mouse, pretending that they were outside and hiding from the very real threat of monsters lurking in the dark.

"What is it?" Connor asked.

Crystal just shook her head. "Nothing," She

went back to reading the flimsy back story that was supposed to help her topple a tyrannical regime.

CHAPTER TWENTY-FIVE

Crystal sat gently stroking Bowser's back as she peered nervously out her window at the dry landscape and scattered ruins between Bexar and Travis. Despite his thirteen years of age, Bowser was wide-eyed and panting eagerly as he watched the scenery roll by. They were coming up to the midpoint of their journey at the Ranger outpost in San Marcos. Old, rusty road signs kept marking down the number of miles to reach the city, which was now a ghost town filled with overgrown, decaying ruins, stalker dens, and maybe even raiders.

Crystal glanced at the shotgun and the M4 carbine sitting beside her and Bowser.

"Relax," Major Hunter soothed, catching her eye from the driver's seat of the truck. "It's broad daylight. Stalkers won't be a problem."

"And raiders?" Crystal asked. She would have felt better if Connor were riding up here with her. Instead, he was hiding in the back of the truck behind hers with her dad and a handful of other insurgents. They couldn't risk one of them being identified at the gate. Even after all these years, they were still hiding from Governor Miller and his men.

"The I-35 is well patrolled," Major Hunter said. "We have outposts all along this route."

Crystal nodded, and the major smiled, holding her gaze a second longer than he should have. Worried that he might miss something on the road, Crystal pointed out the windshield. "Eyes front, Major."

He snorted at her appropriation of military lingo, but his amusement didn't last. The brake lights of the truck ahead of theirs flickered to life and it abruptly swerved to the left. As the trailer snaked through that turn, it revealed a big, twisted piece of metal that might have come off a truck or trailer like theirs.

Major Hunter cursed under his breath and stomped on the brakes. He spun the wheel like the captain of a pirate ship in a storm, and the truck and trailer skidded noisily behind them, while the entire rig leaned ominously to the right.

Bowser went tumbling into the door and then into Crystal's lap as Major Hunter turned back the other way. Crystal lunged for the grab handle on her side to steady herself.

Holding the wheel one-handed, Major Hunter fumbled for the radio to warn the rest of the convoy.

"Supply Two to all drivers, there is debris in the road. Repeat, we have debris in the road."

Static crackled in the wake of his warning, and Crystal glanced in her mirror to see what the truck behind them was doing.

His warning came too late. She was just in time to see that truck barrel right into the twisted piece of metal. It kicked up an impressive spray of sparks from the truck's wheels. A *bang* erupted, and the truck slumped to one side as one of the front wheels gave out. Careening onward, but now favoring its damaged side, the rig skidded for the shoulder of the highway, carried on by its momentum. Crystal clutched the side door and pressed her face to the window to get a better look just as the truck went plunging over the side of the interstate and then rolled down the shoulder with a crashing roar.

"No!" Crystal screamed, remembering that both her dad and Connor were riding in the back of that truck. This was exactly how her mother had died, rolling down an embankment on the side of a highway. She slapped the window with her palms. "No!"

Bowser barked, his snout sweeping around to search for the source of her distress.

Major Hunter cursed again. The brakes squealed and then hissed as he brought the rig to a stop on the side of the road. Crystal threw her door open and Bowser jumped out, barking steadily now. She flew out after him, and then, almost as an afterthought, she turned back and grabbed the shotgun.

Major Hunter was back on his radio, calling Rangers to the scene of the crash. Not waiting for him to come, Crystal spun away and ran with Bowser leading the way.

As soon as she reached the edge of the highway, Crystal saw the smoking, twisted ruin of the truck. It had dug an impressive trench through the grass and shrubbery on the side of the highway, and there was no sign of anyone trying to get out yet. Crystal hesitated at the top of the embankment, willing the back doors of the trailer to come swinging open. But that didn't happen.

Rangers wearing combat fatigues and hefting M4 carbines went rushing down the slope to either side of her. Their sergeant led the charge, snapping orders to the others as he went.

Crystal raced after the Rangers with Bowser at her side. Rangers began attempting to pry open the back doors with their combat knives, while others were using brute force to battle the ruined locking mechanisms. None of it was working.

Crystal stood behind them with her hands flexing restlessly on the shotgun, feeling helpless and scared.

"Put your backs into it!" the sergeant roared. "Come on!"

Banging and muffled voices started up in the back of the trailer, giving Crystal hope that her dad and Connor weren't trapped or wounded. But they still had to find a way to pry the trailer open.

Thick black smoke came chugging from the front of the truck. Crystal coughed and waved the smoke away from her stinging eyes.

Bowser growled menacingly, sounding more like a lion than a dog. Crystal glanced at him to see what he was growling at—only to realize that he wasn't the one who'd growled.

"Stalkers!" someone shouted.

Adrenaline spurted like fire through Crystal's veins. Her shotgun snapped up to her shoulder. One of two Rangers running toward the cab of the truck abruptly screamed as he went skidding inexplicably away through the long grass. But then Crystal noticed the big golden-brown blur that was dragging him.

The other Ranger snapped off a ringing shot that missed its target.

"Check fire! Check fire!" the man who was being dragged shouted.

"I can't get a clear shot!" his partner shouted back.

The stalker dragging the Ranger blended almost perfectly with its surroundings. It was running toward a massive brown hill of hard-packed dirt that looked like a giant termite mound. In the center of that, Crystal knew, would be a hole big enough to swallow a car. Looming in the background behind the entrance of the den was a shadowy wall of glossy black alien trees and soaring, mushroom-shaped *protos*.

The rest of the Rangers burst into action, abandoning their attempts to pry open the truck and sprinting after their brother.

The one who was being dragged managed to squeeze off a burst from his rifle. The stalker shrieked piercingly and released him. It spun around, its long claws kicking up a spreading brown cloud of dust.

The stalker rose on its hind legs, looming over the Ranger like a grizzly bear. Its puckered mouth dilated open and four independent jaws thrust out, seeming to crack its giant skull open. The stalker shrieked again, and four pink tongues flickered out between dagger-like fangs.

Another burst of rifle fire tore into the creature's chest, but the bullets shattered harmlessly on its thick, scaly hide.

The stalker reacted swiftly. Its tail flicked through the air and stabbed straight down into its prey. The Ranger cried out again, but this time his screams faded quickly into silence.

"Light it up!" Major Hunter shouted as he ran past Crystal. He stopped and raised a carbine to his shoulder in unison with a dozen other Rangers. They fired precision bursts at the stalker. It shrieked piteously, its whole body spasming with the impacts. Armored scales shattered like glass, and finally, it fell thrashing to the ground. A few more rounds cracked the air, and the monster stopped moving altogether.

Rifles stopped their chattering and a ringing silence fell. Crystal blinked. Suddenly remembering to breathe, she sucked in a ragged breath and looked around for Bowser. But thankfully, he was still standing right by her side. At his age, he was well past the bravado of puppyhood where he'd somehow thought that he could take on whole packs of stalkers by himself.

"Sergeant Jackson!" Major Hunter called out. "Let's crack this rig open before more of those fuckers come sniffing around!"

"Yes, sir!" the sergeant replied. "You heard the man! Get Private Wilson back over here and let's get to work!"

Two soldiers ran over, dragging the wounded man back by his arms. Crystal went to see how he was doing. A medic with a red and white patch on his arm beat her there. After just a moment, he stepped away, slowly shaking his head.

Crystal slowed to a crawl, realizing that the man was dead. Stalkers typically didn't kill people with their stingers. Their venom was a paralytic, not a poison, but in this case, the sharpened tip of the stalker's tail must have done some actual physical damage.

One of the Rangers who'd dragged him ran a hand over the man's face, shutting his dead, staring eyes.

Crystal stood there for a long time, staring at the body through a blurry curtain of tears, and wondering what she would do if it had been Connor. Or her dad.

The Rangers left. One of them whispered his condolences as he went, probably thinking that she had known the deceased. Yet she didn't even know his name.

"Hey, it's okay," a familiar voice whispered and strong arms curled around her waist from behind. "It's not me."

Crystal turned and fell into those arms, burying her face in Connor's chest and inhaling his familiar scent. "Thank God," Crystal mumbled through a muffled sob. After a moment, she pulled away. "Where's my dad?" she asked, now looking for him. Connor pointed, and she saw him standing ten yards away with Carla, standing guard with his carbine while the last of their people crawled out the back of the trailer pushing heavy packs of supplies.

Crystal smiled and waved to them. Her dad nodded and waved back.

"Hustle up!" Major Hunter shouted. "Everybody back to the road! Group Three, you'll be riding in trailers four and five now."

"Come on," Connor urged, gently pulling her away from the dead Ranger.

Crystal hesitated. "We're just going to leave him here?"

Before Connor could answer, two Rangers ran over and carried him back up the embankment. "I guess not," Connor said.

"We'll put Private Wilson in the back of our truck," Major Hunter explained as he strode over to them. "The scent will distract any dogs they bring to sniff out our people."

"You say that like it's a good thing," Crystal objected.

"If we had seven more corpses to deflect suspicions from the rest of the trucks, then it might be."

Crystal scowled. "How can you be so heartless?"

"The word you're looking for is pragmatic." Major Hunter frowned and glanced around unhappily. "We should go." He gestured to the highway while keeping one hand on his carbine.

Connor led her up the slope to the interstate. Bowser struggled up the hill beside them. About halfway up, he slowed to a crawl, exhausted, and Connor had to carry him the rest of the way.

The major jumped in behind the wheel of their truck and slammed the door. Connor walked around the front to the other side and dumped Bowser in the cab. Turning to Crystal, he gave her a quick kiss on the lips, and whispered, "Be careful."

"You, too," she said and then watched with a deepening frown as he ran back to the next truck in the convoy. Being lured by her fiancé into joining these rebels made her wonder if he loved her as much as she loved him.

Would she have tricked Connor into this if the tables had been turned? She didn't think so. Ellis claimed that he hadn't given Connor a choice in the matter, but that wasn't true. They could have fled Bexar together. At the very least, she would have liked for Connor to tell her what was going on.

And it wasn't even just about her. Something could easily happen to him, or to her dad, or even to Connor's mom.

"Are you getting in, or what?" Major Hunter growled.

Crystal stepped up on the running board to climb in and slammed the door behind her. The truck's engine gave a throaty roar as it rumbled to life. Machinery ground together as Major Hunter shifted gears, and the engine revved subtly higher as they rolled into motion, quickly picking up speed.

Within seconds they were barreling along

at forty miles per hour, hurtling toward an uncertain future.

CHAPTER TWENTY-SIX

Adam stood in perfect darkness, his feet aching as he listened to the rumbling roar of the truck thundering across the interstate. It was hot and stuffy in the compartment, and his back itched with trickling rivers of sweat. To top it all off, his bad leg was blazing with fire. He wished there was enough room for him to bend down and massage the scarified ruins of his tibia and calf muscle. With each pothole and fissure in the crumbling interstate, the truck rocked to one side or the other, sending hot spikes of pain radiating up to his hip.

The truck's brakes squealed and it swerved slightly to get around some unseen obstacle. Flashbacks from the crash ricocheted through Adam's mind as Connor stumbled into him, knocking him into the woman beside him, like human dominoes. Adam apologized to her and righted himself with a wince before rounding on Connor with a glare that the boy couldn't see.

Neither of them had said more than a

handful of words to each other since this whole sorry operation had begun. Adam had known what he was getting himself into when Ellis had forced him to join the Nightingales. He'd also known the risks when he'd helped to plan this ill-fated mission to overthrow the governor. But what he *hadn't* known was that Ellis would drag his daughter into it, or that his wife, Carla, had signed up ages ago to be a Nightingale herself.

She'd probably been going to all of the same meetings as him, and somehow he'd just never seen through her mask.

Adam frowned. No, that couldn't be it. If they'd been going to the same meetings, one or both of them would have noticed that they were making excuses about work on the same nights. Carla must have gone to the meetings in the morning, while he'd attended the ones at night. Whatever the case, it didn't matter. Thanks to Ellis and Connor, Adam's entire family was standing squarely in the line of fire.

"If she doesn't give you that ring back..." Adam muttered, while slowly shaking his head.

"Keep your nose out of it," Connor replied.

"Fuck you," Adam replied.

"She won't be in any danger," Connor whispered, taking a softer tack.

"Yeah? If you think that, then either you're as dumb as rocks, or you just crawled out from under one, and I'm not sure which is worse."

Engine brakes roared to life, and everyone fell against the front of the trailer.

"I could say the same about you," Connor muttered. "What is my mom doing here?"

"You think I knew about that?" Adam demanded.

"I think you *should* have," Connor replied.

"Shut up, shut up!" someone growled. "We've reached Travis."

"Already?" another person asked.

"What part of *shut up* didn't you understand?"

This time Adam recognized the voice. It belonged to Sergeant Chase. Adam recalled the man's bald, age-spotted head, rheumy blue eyes, and deeply-lined cheeks. Like Adam, Chase had a background in the armed forces from before the invasion, but Chase had been a drill sergeant at West Point, and an E-7, which was two pay grades higher than Adam as a lowly E-5. Chase had been close to retirement age when the Specs had arrived. By now he had to be well into his sixties. "Unless you want to be standing in front of a firing squad by this time tomorrow, nobody talks again until we get the signal."

The truck stopped braking and its rumbling engine died. Silence thickened the air. Adam spent the time alone with his thoughts, wondering what Chase had done to get stuffed in the back with them.

A minute later, muffled voices approached, then walked away, heading for the back of the trailer. Dogs barked eagerly.

The sound of heavy locking bolts opening at the back put Adam's nerves on edge. He steeled himself as he heard those muffled voices arguing about something, followed by more barking, and then footsteps thumping around in the back of the trailer.

Adam found himself staring at a thin bar of sunlight bleeding in at the bottom of the door to their compartment. *So much for being well-sealed,* he thought.

If those guards got too close to the door, Adam had a bad feeling their dogs were going to lose it.

Heavy footsteps approached. Adam heard dogs breathing hoarsely, straining at the ends of their leashes.

Then the footsteps stopped and the muffled voices returned. This time it sounded like they were arguing. Adam made out a few of the words, "—*stalker got him*—" and he almost breathed a sigh of relief. That dead Ranger had stolen the show. The guards wanted to know what had happened to him.

Moments later, their voices and footsteps retreated along with the pitter-pattering of dogs' feet. There came a *boom* and *thunk* from the doors, and that was the end of the search.

The truck rumbled to life once more, and this time Adam did breathe a sigh.

"Don't get too excited," Sergeant Chase muttered. "They've got seven more trailers to search, and we're fresh out of bodies to distract those bloodhounds."

"Six more," Adam corrected.

"Excuse me?"

"Ellis is at the front of the convoy. They'll have checked his truck first," Adam explained. "That means they've got six left to check."

"Now is not a good time to be a wiseacre, Hall."

"Yes, sir," Adam replied.

***

Crystal let Major Hunter do all of the talking. He had all the same answers as she did, anyway.

"If this is a government-sanctioned convoy, then what is a civilian doing riding up front with you?" the Ranger Lieutenant from the gate asked.

Bowser smacked his lips, and Crystal smiled innocently at the lieutenant, but his scowl never wavered.

"I already told you," Major Hunter said. "She's a friend of mine. She was looking for a safe way to get to Travis, and I had room in my truck."

The lieutenant didn't look happy with that explanation. He studied her ID card in his hands. "Crystal Hall, born October 17th, 2017. Is that correct?" he asked, looking back up at her.

Crystal nodded.

"And your dog? You have his health certificate?"

"Uh…" Crystal trailed off uncertainly, blinking rapidly.

"I can't let him in without a health certificate," the lieutenant said.

Crystal imagined Bowser being forced to stay outside the walls all because of a stupid piece of paper that someone had forgotten to get. The thought of him wandering around alone out here until some stalker picked him off put a painful lump in her throat. If it came to that, she'd stay out there with him.

Major Hunter looked at her with eyebrows patiently raised and nodded to her side of the cab. "Didn't you put his certificate in your door this morning?"

Crystal blinked at him, then looked at the compartment in her door. A brown manila folder was peeking out just above the seat. She reached for it and flipped the folder open. Inside were a handful of her personal documents—a resume, a reference letter from the elementary school where she worked in Bexar, and a health certificate for Bowser, duly signed by his vet.

Crystal gaped at the sight of those documents. Who had put them there, and why hadn't they thought to tell *her* about them?

They hadn't been in the folder that Ellis had given her last night.

She yanked out the health certificate and handed it over to Major Hunter, who then passed it out his window to the lieutenant.

"Hmmm... well, everything seems to be in order." The Lieutenant passed the certificate back through the window along with both Crystal's and Hunter's ID cards. "Enjoy your stay in Travis."

Major Hunter nodded and put the truck in gear. The engine rumbled to life, and they began rolling gently toward the open gates of the safe zone.

As soon as Major Hunter put his window up, Crystal let him have it. "Why didn't you tell me you had that before we got here? I almost blew the whole thing!"

"Relax, you did fine, and I thought your husband would have told you when he put the certificate there this morning."

Crystal crossed her arms over her chest and scowled. "He's my fiancé, not my husband, and no, he didn't tell me."

"My apologies then."

Crystal leaned against her door, peering in the mirror to see what was happening with the truck behind theirs. It was busy rolling ahead as well. As far as she could tell, the one behind that one was, too.

"They're done searching the convoy?"

Crystal asked.

"You sound surprised," Major Hunter replied.

"They couldn't have searched all of the trucks in that time."

"They didn't have to search them. They just had to open the doors and see that the trailers were empty. Why would they suspect the *mayor* of Bexar to be smuggling insurgents into Travis? If he's not above suspicion, then who is?"

"I guess," Crystal said.

"Relax. All you have to do is wait for your friend to hand you over to the governor tonight, and then stick to your story when you see him. We'll do the rest."

Crystal nodded uncertainly while stroking Bowser's fur. She watched a tight knot of high rises come marching over the horizon while old chain stores, restaurants, and suburbs flashed by on either side of the highway.

Her thoughts jumped to Emily and Sophie. She hadn't seen them in five years. Would they still be holding a grudge over what had happened with Owen? Most of their anger had been directed at her dad, but Emily hadn't even come to say goodbye when they'd left Bexar.

Crystal idly scratched Bowser behind the ear, hoping that they would at least look after him if things went south tonight.

CHAPTER TWENTY-SEVEN

The truck came to a grinding halt, and Adam heard the signal: *knock—knock-knock—knock.*

"Finally," he muttered.

"Crack this can open!" Sergeant Chase ordered.

Someone turned the locking mechanism, and the false wall of the trailer went sweeping open, letting in a bright swath of daylight.

Major Hunter was waiting with a team of Rangers on the other side. Adam and the others followed them out. Fellow insurgents handed them bottles of water and granola bars as they jumped down from the trailer.

It wasn't much of a breakfast, but it would do.

Adam glanced around to get his bearings, seeing as he did so that they'd backed their trucks into the open garage of what looked like a commercial fuel depot.

Beyond the opening of the garage, a chain-link fence surrounded the compound, with trees beyond that. The garage connected to some type of admin building made of plain gray cinder blocks. Rangers and a few civilians that Adam hadn't seen before were busy waving everyone energetically up a ramp to a pair of open doors at the top. Adam assumed those civilians were the ones in charge at the depot. He hurried toward the rusty steel doors at the top of the ramp, doing his best to ignore the fiery ache in his leg as he went. Connor kept pace beside him, but as soon as they were through the doors, he broke into a sprint and beat him to where Crystal and Bowser stood with some of the other civilian operatives.

Connor folded Crystal into a big hug, while Bowser yipped and spun in happy circles around their legs. Then he spotted Adam and began tugging insistently on his leash.

"Hey, boy," Adam said, dropping to his haunches to scratch him behind the ears while Bowser showered him with kisses. Bowser hadn't seen him for a few days. That might as well have been a year in dog time.

"Are you all ready to go?" Connor asked Crystal.

Adam straightened to see Carla walking over to them. She went to stand with her son, ignoring Adam completely. Frowning at that, Adam took his place beside Crystal. "You don't have to do this, you know," he said. "What do you think they would have done if you *hadn't* followed Connor last night?"

Crystal just looked at him, her eyebrows raised with a question that she never got to ask.

"Oh, I'm afraid that she *does* have to do this," Mayor Ellis said, joining the reunion suddenly with a bland smile. "It's too late to turn back now. The wheels are already in motion, and you can bet that it won't be long before the governor learns that Crystal is here—if he hasn't already."

"Because your people are going to tell him?" Adam suggested.

Ellis smiled but said nothing.

"Excuse me," Connor said, and he began walking away from the group.

"Where are you going?" Crystal called after him.

"The restroom," he replied, shaking his empty water bottle by way of explanation, before getting lost in the crowd.

"I'd probably better go to the bathroom, too," Crystal said. "Can you hold Bowser for a minute, Dad?"

He nodded as he accepted the leash. With both their kids having departed, Adam and Carla were left to share an awkward silence in their wake.

"Look, Carla…" Adam began.

"Don't," she cut him off with an upraised finger.

He sighed. "I'm not actually going to *kill* him you know."

"Good, because if you did, then I'd have to kill *you*, and we'd find ourselves living in a Greek tragedy."

Adam reached for her hand, and this time she didn't jerk it away. "Connor lied to her and tricked her. I'm allowed to be upset about that."

"You mean like how I'm allowed to be upset about the deal that you and Ellis cut behind my back for us to stay in Bexar?"

Adam blinked at her. "What deal?"

"You joined the Rangers and the Nightingales, and we got to stay. You agreed to risk your life so that he'd grant us asylum. Isn't that how it went?"

"How did you find out?"

"Ellis admitted to it on the drive over."

Adam frowned. "You were riding with him?" He'd lost track of Carla's whereabouts after he'd been sealed in his compartment.

"He asked me to. Ellis seemed quite amused by the irony that all of us wound up joining the Nightingales."

"All of us except for Crystal, you mean," Adam replied. "She wasn't supposed to be here. You have to see how that would make me angry."

"That was the mayor's fault, not Connor's," Carla said. "Ellis admitted it. He didn't give Connor a choice, just like he didn't give you one, right? If I can forgive you for that, then you should be able to forgive Connor. Lay the blame where it belongs, not with the scapegoats."

"Fine," Adam agreed, while quietly grinding his teeth. He glanced around, looking for the mayor, but Ellis was nowhere in sight.

"I don't want to fight with you," Carla whispered. She gestured to the bustle of activity going on around them. "We've got enough to worry about without turning on each other."

Adam nodded. Carla stepped in and kissed him. He withdrew and tucked a stray lock of curly brown hair behind her left ear. "You'd better look after yourself out there," he said. "If anything were to happen to you..."

Carla smiled and shook her head. "I won't be fighting. I'll be out with the civilians on the street, papering the town with Miller's dirty laundry."

"But if Rangers catch you—"

"It'll be the middle of the night. No one will be out to see me."

"Except for the *night* patrols, you mean," Adam said.

"If they have more than two Rangers to cover every square mile, I'd be surprised," she countered.

"All the same," Adam insisted.

"You just focus on getting yourself back to

me in one piece. You're the one who's going to be in the line of fire. You'll be joining the assault on the Governor's Mansion, won't you?"

Adam nodded. "I will."

"You'll be in the thick of it with bullets flying all around you, and *I'm* the one who needs to be careful?"

"I can look after myself," Adam said.

"And I can't?" she countered.

"Not what I meant."

"You have a bad leg. If you have to run for it, you'll be dead last, won't you?"

Adam gripped his wife by her shoulders. "I'll be okay."

"You can't promise me that."

"I just did."

Carla heaved a frustrated sigh. "Cocky bastard."

Adam smiled. Pulling her into another hug, he kissed the top of her head. "That's me."

***

Crystal emerged from the unisex restroom feeling slightly better now that her bladder was empty. Somehow she hadn't run into Connor on her way over here, but maybe he'd found a different restroom than she had. She glanced around, feeling disoriented in the gloomy confines of the unfamiliar building. She was standing in a darkened hallway lined with doors on one side, and a wall of broken windows on the other. Crystal spent a moment staring out the nearest window, wondering what monsters might have crawled in here with them.

But they were in the middle of the Travis Safe Zone. There wouldn't be any stalkers in here, would there?

She was just about to head back through the facility to join her dad and the others when she heard something outside. Someone talking—no, *arguing*.

Curious, Crystal strained her ears to listen. She couldn't make out what was being said, but she could tell *who* was saying it. It was Connor.

Crystal peered through the broken panes of glass, searching the debris-strewn parking lot behind the admin building. She spotted Connor pacing back and forth behind a pair of big green dumpsters. He was speaking quickly into his radio... then waiting for a reply... then speaking again...

A few seconds later he tucked the radio into a pouch on his uniform and he began striding toward the building. Crystal belatedly realized that he was headed straight toward her. He didn't appear to have noticed her standing there yet. Crystal spun away and ran back to the restroom. Just as she reached the door, another one flew open behind her, and Connor came storming back inside.

Crystal turned from the restroom to look in his direction. "Connor?" she asked, feigning surprise.

His gait slowed as he noticed her. "Hey, what are you doing here?"

"I needed to go, too," Crystal explained.

Connor blinked. "Oh, okay."

"What were you doing outside?"

"Hmmm?" Connor asked.

"You just came in from outside," Crystal said.

"Oh, when I got here the bathroom was already occupied, so I went outside to pee."

"Must be nice," Crystal said slowly, pretending to buy his story. Except that now she knew that he'd just lied to her.

"Are you ready to go?" he asked as he wrapped an arm around her shoulders and guided her toward the distant strains of the other insurgents' conversations.

Crystal nodded. "Almost," she replied, now wondering what the hell was going on. A part of her was tempted just to ask Connor point-blank who he'd been talking to on that radio, but something told her that even if she did, he'd only tell her another lie.

She needed to ask someone else about it, but who? Her dad?

No, he was still mad at Connor for dragging her into this. He'd probably jump on any excuse to get Connor into trouble.

Major Hunter would be a better bet. He could look into it. Maybe he was even the one who'd been talking to Connor. That had to be it. She'd check in with him before she left, just in case.

Crystal chewed her lip some more as they waded through the crowd. *In case of what?* she wondered.

"Hey, is everything okay?" Connor asked. "You look like you saw a ghost."

Crystal fixed him with a shaky smile. It was her turn to lie. "Do you blame me?" she asked. "I was just thinking about the mission."

"You'll be fine," Connor said, squeezing her shoulders and leaning his head against hers.

"What about you?" Crystal asked.

"I'll be fine, too. Don't worry. After tonight, all of this will be over."

"That's exactly what I'm afraid of," Crystal muttered.

CHAPTER TWENTY-EIGHT

Adam left Bowser with Carla and went to stand in line with the other Rangers to receive his guns. Sergeant Chase directed the men and women from his squad to pass out weapons from three separate crates that had been offloaded from the trucks. When Adam got to the front of his line, he accepted an M4 carbine, four spare magazines, a pair of smoke grenades, one frag, and a sidearm.

Adam slipped the rifle's shoulder strap over his head, pocketed the mags and the grenades in his combat vest, and then holstered the sidearm. Finally, he checked the M4 carbine and noted with some dismay from the scratches that someone had carved into the side, that this weapon wasn't *his.*

Adam took meticulous care of his weapons, making sure to clean and oil them regularly. As for the owner of these firearms, he had no idea what kind of gun care routine that

Ranger kept. The last thing Adam needed was for his carbine to jam up in the middle of combat because some idiot had neglected to clean it properly. Then again, anyone who took the time to carve in notches for kills probably had the same feelings about handling someone else's hardware.

Adam flipped the carbine up to check the stock. Sure enough, he found the soldier's initials carved into it—*A.S.*

From his time with the Rangers in Bexar, he had a feeling he knew exactly who that soldier was—Corporal Amanda Stevens. He glanced around quickly, scanning the Rangers around him for a particular woman with rust-colored hair and freckles. He found her standing off to one side with her unit, muttering about her weapon.

"Looking for something, Corporal?" Adam asked as he approached.

Stevens saw him coming and promptly stood at attention.

"At ease," he said. "Corporal *Amanda* Stevens? A.S.?" he added, again reading the initials on the stock and then turning it around so she could see. Adam ducked out of the strap and held the weapon out to her. "I think I might have something that belongs to you."

She accepted the weapon with a grateful smile. "Thank you, sir."

"Don't you sir me," he growled. "I work for a

living."

Stevens nodded and smiled tightly at the oft-repeated saying.

"Copy that, Sergeant." Stevens handed him her unmarked carbine to replace the one he'd given her. He nodded his thanks and spent a moment checking it over, wishing as he did so that he'd carved initials into his own weapons.

"Looks like you've found your squad," a familiar voice said.

Adam turned to see Major Hunter approaching. It was Adam's turn to stand at attention. "My squad, sir?"

Major Hunter nodded. "Delta Squad. I'm leading Alpha, Sergeant Chase has the Bravos, and Sergeant Jackson is leading Charlie."

Adam accepted his last-minute assignment with a frown. He supposed that there hadn't been time until now to assign Rangers to their units, but this all felt too rushed to him. Ideally, unit members should know each other well and have experience working together so that they would function like a well-oiled machine.

"We'll be staging out directly from here at nineteen hundred thirty hours." Hunter brought his wrist up to check his watch. "It's ten hundred fifteen right now. Lunch is at twelve hundred sharp. Make sure you and your squad are organized before then, Sergeant. After lunch, we'll be conducting drills and reviewing our battle plan."

Adam nodded. "Yes, sir."

With that, Major Hunter walked away, leaving Adam to get to know the men and women in his squad. Just as he was turning to address them, he noticed Crystal intercepting the major and pulling him aside. The two of them spoke in hushed tones for about a minute, at which point Major Hunter walked away with a deeply furrowed brow, looking like he'd just received bad news.

Adam wondered what that was about. What could Crystal possibly have to speak to the major about? He made a note to ask her about it later.

Adam ordered his squad to fall in behind him and then he led them over to a quiet corner of the depot and took attendance. He introduced himself, and then went around with the rest of them, assigning names to numbers. Adam was Delta One, Corporal Amanda Stevens was Delta Two and the leader of Fire Team One. In her team was Private Tony Smith, "Delta Three," a powerfully-built African American man with a shaved head, followed by Private Jake Sanders, a tall, pasty-white kid with glasses and blue eyes, designated "Delta Four," and finally, Delta Five was Private Julio Morales, a short Latino man with a pair of wings tattooed on the back of his neck.

Before Adam even began designating the

members of Fire Team Two, he realized that they were one man short of nine for their squad. He was about to go speak with Major Hunter about it when Connor ran over and joined them.

"Sorry," he said breathlessly. "The major wanted to speak with me about something."

"Would you care to share it with the rest of us?" Adam asked.

Connor shook his head. "Nothing important, Sergeant."

Adam grunted his annoyance. "This is Private Connor Cooper. He'll be with Team Two, designated Delta Nine since he was the last one to the party. Corporal Stevens, would you mind making the introductions for Team One?"

Stevens did as she was asked and then they moved on to the other three Rangers who had yet to be introduced. Delta Six was Corporal Dave Martin. He looked like the oldest member of their group, with leathery, sun-damaged skin and plenty of white hair showing through his stubble and the short blonde hair on his head. Then came Delta Seven, Private Erica Ramirez, short and fit, with black hair tied in a braid. Finally, Private Alan Lee was a Chinese American with an easy grin and plenty of laugh lines that marked his age somewhere around forty.

After all the introductions were made, Adam

did his best to mentally record their names and faces, or at least, their numbers and their faces. He went around in a circle, pointing to each of them and repeating their designations, both for his own benefit and that of his squad. If he or either of his corporals wound up giving orders to the wrong person in the middle of a firefight, that could be all it took to get someone killed.

Realizing just how important that would be, Adam had each of them share a defining moment from their past so that they could get to know each other better.

Corporal Amanda Stevens told them about a beloved dog she'd had up until the invasion—a German Shepherd by the name of Hanz. He'd gotten himself killed defending her and her parents from a stalker. Adam could relate to that—Amanda was a fellow dog person. Private Tony Smith talked about his wife, Felicia, who had been taken from Bexar by the Specs during one of their nightly abductions. *No mystery why he joined the Nightingales,* Adam thought to himself.

Private Jake Sanders got all choked up talking about his best friend and childhood sweetheart who had died during the invasion. They'd been just fourteen at the time. It took a moment for Adam to realize that Sanders was gay, but no one seemed to care about it one way or the other, which Adam thought was a good sign for his squad. They had enough to worry about without being divided by their prejudices.

Julio Morales spoke of robbing a gas station when he was eighteen and then going to prison for it, which was where he had gotten his wing tattoos. Then came parole and barely making ends meet at a halfway house. He'd been living there when the Specs came. He jokingly pointed out that they'd leveled the playing field for him. Now everyone was living in a halfway house.

True enough, Adam thought.

Corporal Dave Martin told the story of how he'd graduated from MIT with a master's in computer science and a job waiting for him at Tesla, then the Specs had come and made it all worthless.

Erica Ramirez said that her defining moment came when her father got killed during a protest in the hunger riots. She'd thought that Governor Miller was a hero for forming the Republic and consolidating their food supply to make sure that everyone had enough to eat. That was until Miller's secret police, the Vultures, had tried to recruit her.

"So you just turned them down, and they were okay with that?" Connor asked.

"No, I joined them," Ramirez replied.

Shock rippled visibly through the squad, but Adam was still waiting for the punchline.

There was no way that she would admit to being a Vulture, here, to a bunch of Nightingales, on the eve of their coup.

"I've been feeding the Nightingales with intel from the inside," Ramirez explained.

Connor didn't look amused. "So that's how the Mayor knew who he could trust for this operation? Because you were there to check attendance?"

"Exactly," Ramirez confirmed.

"Makes sense," Adam replied. "Private Lee? You're next."

The Chinese American's smile faded and he shifted uncomfortably on his feet. "Can I skip it? No one will forget me. I am the only Asian man here."

"Sorry," Adam replied, shaking his head. "You heard everyone else's stories. Fair is fair."

Private Lee drew in a shaky breath. "Okay, well, I suppose my defining moment would be joining the Nightingales."

"That's *it?*" Ramirez scoffed. "Come on, you've got to have more than that, Lee."

A haunted look briefly entered Lee's eyes, and then cleared, leaving behind two dark, empty black wells. "I do not. Next please."

"Not good enough," Ramirez insisted.

Adam frowned, wondering what could be so bad that Lee didn't want to tell them. No one was forcing him to recount the most painful moment of his life, but that was obviously how he'd interpreted the assignment. "Okay, we'll come back to you, Lee. Private Cooper?"

Connor told them about his proposal to Crystal on a boat ride through Bexar that recreated their first date. Adam scowled. That proposal seemed disingenuous to him now, after Connor had lured Crystal into joining this operation.

"What a touching story, Romeo," Private Ramirez scoffed while puckering her lips and making kissing noises.

The rest of the squad chuckled.

"All right, can it," Adam said. "Now that we've all gotten to know each other, let's run a few combat drills to see how this unit operates as a team."

"Hang on, Sergeant," Corporal Stevens said. "What about you?"

"What *about* me?" Adam asked.

"You didn't share anything."

Adam sucked his teeth unhappily. "Fair enough. Let's see, I served in the US Army as a Sergeant in Afghanistan until a bullet shattered my leg and sent me home."

Private Morales whistled softly at that. "Looks like we got a member of the OG here."

Adam went on, "After that, I got a job as a high school English teacher here in Austin. I was working there right up until the invasion began, at which point I got the hell out and joined an old Army buddy on his ranch. About five years ago, we lost the ranch to raiders, and I went to Bexar with my daughter, Crystal, and her fiancé, Private Cooper"

Everyone looked to Cooper then back to Adam.

"What about the girl's mother?" Stevens asked. Adam got the sense that she was asking in a roundabout way if he was single.

"She died during the invasion," Adam said flatly. "Anything else?"

Stevens shook her head and averted her eyes.

Adam realized that he'd snapped at her without really meaning to, and he deliberately softened his tone. "Sorry. It's been a long time, but I still don't like to talk about what happened."

"It's okay," Stevens said. "I get it."

Private Lee nodded along with that. Whatever story he'd been trying not to tell them, it still haunted him, too.

"All right, let's see what Delta Squad is made of," Adam said.

Lukewarm enthusiasm rippled through the squad. Someone standing behind Adam cleared their throat, followed by the familiar whimpering of a dog. Connor perked up with a smile, and Adam turned to see Crystal and Bowser standing right behind him.

"I have to go," she explained.

Adam took her aside to speak with her in private, but Connor joined them, making it awkward with both of them vying for her attention. "Is someone taking you to Emily's?" Adam asked.

Crystal shook her head. "I hitched a ride. That's my story, remember? So I'm leaving the depot with the convoy. They'll drop me as close as they can on the way to the supply center, but I'll be walking from there. It's about twenty blocks."

"No escort?" Adam asked.

Crystal shrugged. "Ellis said it would only draw more attention to me if they gave me an escort. It might blow the operation."

Adam scowled. That wasn't what he'd wanted to hear. Connor didn't look happy about it either. The safe zones were a lot more civilized than the wastes, but that didn't stop people from preying on each other, and Crystal was a beautiful young woman which made her a target anywhere, let alone in a strange city where she didn't know to avoid the bad areas.

"Relax. I have Bowser for protection, right boy?" Bowser snapped his snout shut and fixed her with a solemn look.

"He's like ninety years old!" Connor objected. "And he's a golden, not a pit bull."

"Someone should probably tell him that," Crystal said through a smile.

Adam snorted. He was unusually aggressive for a golden retriever. Maybe the arrival of the Specs had brought it out in him. He patted

Bowser on the head. The dog responded by giving Adam a big lick.

"I also have this," Crystal fished into her jeans pocket and produced a small can of pepper spray.

Adam frowned, still not happy with the situation.

"It's okay, Dad. I'll be fine. Emily is supposed to meet me halfway there."

Carla chose that moment to join them, and Adam decided to drop it. At least, she'd be walking around in the middle of the day. There would be plenty of Rangers on patrol.

Adam and Carla took turns giving Crystal hugs and saying their goodbyes. When it was his turn, Connor kissed her and whispered that he loved her. Adam wasn't sure if he believed it.

"I have to go, too," Carla said, grabbing Adam's hands to get his attention.

He nodded and they kissed, reminding each other to be careful.

"Carla, Crystal! Wrap it up over there!" Ellis called out from the door. "The trucks are fueled up and ready to go!"

Carla began backing away with one of her hands still holding his until their arms stretched taut and finally forced her fingers to slip through his. She turned away with a fading smile.

Crystal blew a kiss to Connor and waved to Adam. He waved back to both her and Carla, feeling more troubled than ever about their involvement in this operation.

Something was wrong. He could *feel* it. What was he missing? Something about Crystal? Or about the mission in general?

"Sergeant?"

Adam turned to see Corporal Stevens standing behind him, her expression hesitant. "You mentioned conducting drills before lunch?"

Adam let out his worries with a sigh and nodded. "Right. Let's get to it, Corporal."

CHAPTER TWENTY-NINE

Crystal stopped on an underpass below the I-35, grateful for the shade that it provided. Bowser was panting noisily and looking generally exhausted. He eased himself down onto his haunches and looked up at her expectantly.

She smiled and shook her head. "No, we're not there yet." Feeling her hairline prickling with beads of sweat, she used her sleeve to dab it dry. Then she pulled out her shirt and whipped it up and down, fanning her torso.

Even in September, the midday sun was merciless. Crystal shrugged out of the backpack of basic supplies that she'd been given and placed it on the ground beside Bowser.

This bag was supposed to be all the luggage that she'd packed for this trip. She zipped it open and hunted for a cooler shirt. There were only three spare changes of clothes in the bag. Crystal smiled ruefully at that. She was a young woman relocating from Bexar to Travis and somehow she'd only packed *three* spare changes of clothes? Maybe the mission planners hadn't paid as much attention to detail as they thought. At least the bag contained *her* clothes and personal effects. Connor must have packed it for her at some point. The fact that she hadn't noticed these clothes missing from her closet was a testament to the fact that she rarely wore them, and for good reason. Crystal ultimately settled for a midriff-baring blue tank top with an old blood stain on it. Glancing around to make sure she was alone on the underpass, Crystal quickly traded her long-sleeved shirt for the figure-hugging tank top.

Better, Crystal thought as a warm breeze funneled below the interstate, drying the sweat from her arms and stomach. She stuffed her dirty shirt into the bag and then dug into the side pocket for her thermos. She folded out the rigid plastic straw and took a few sips of mercifully cool water. As she drank, Crystal thought about Connor and the mysterious radio contact that he'd made at the fuel depot. Thankfully, she'd been worried for nothing. Major Hunter had reassured her that he was the one who had called Connor on the radio. They were conducting comms checks to make sure that everyone had their handsets on the right channel.

Crystal felt better after the Major had dismissed her concerns. Connor wasn't involved in anything nefarious. He probably *had* just gone outside to pee, and he hadn't thought to mention the radio check because it wasn't worth mentioning.

Bowser licked his lips, watching Crystal intently as she lowered the water bottle from her lips.

"Oh, you must be thirsty, too, Bowie. I'm sorry. Here—" She unscrewed the top of the bottle and cupped a hand to pour water into it. Bowser lapped it up with two quick licks. She repeated the process another three times until he turned his head away.

Crystal tucked the bottle away and reached into her pocket for her map. Unfolding the dirty square of paper that she'd found in her briefing folder last night, she studied the crudely drawn map. The overpass where she stood now was marked at about one-third of the way between the fuel depot and Emily's house. Her house was marked on the map with a simple X, while the ones around it were represented with crudely drawn rectangles. Hers was white and yellow with a wraparound porch, in a suburb just a few blocks from the Colorado River. Crystal pictured quiet streets lined with cute single-family homes with white picket fences and stately trees.

She imagined it probably looked a lot like the neighborhood where she and Connor lived in Bexar.

Crystal was looking forward to seeing Emily and Mrs. Brooks again. It was just a pity that she wouldn't get to spend much time with them. She raised her wrist to check the time on her old analog watch. It was just after midday. The operation was meant to commence at sundown, which was around seven. By then she was already supposed to be at the Governor's Mansion, enduring whatever interrogation he would subject her to. Crystal estimated that gave her maybe five or six hours to catch up with Emily.

"Assuming I ever get there," she muttered to herself. She traced the path to Emily's home with her index finger. From here she was supposed to walk past the next two cross streets and then enter a hiking trail that ran along the river. She'd follow it upstream until she reached an old high school. Emily was supposed to meet her in the dugout of the school's baseball diamond.

That rendezvous wasn't halfway to her destination like she'd told her dad, since the baseball field was only about four blocks from Emily's home.

"Ready to go again, Bowie?"

His chin dipped slightly as if nodding in the affirmative. Crystal smiled and gave his leash a little tug.

He eased up from his haunches with a visible effort, and she bent to pat him on the head. He was getting too old for long walks. "Just a couple more miles to go," Crystal said. "We'll take it slow, all right?"

As she stepped out of the shadows of the overpass, she checked her jeans pocket, feeling for the cylindrical bulge that was the can of pepper spray she'd been given for self-defense. She would have felt better if she'd had a gun, but civilians weren't allowed to carry them inside the safe zones, and the last thing she needed was to get picked up by Rangers for unlawful possession of a firearm. Like that, she'd wind up sitting out the coup in a jail cell at the nearest Ranger station.

Crystal frowned, wondering hypothetically what the Nightingales would do without her to act as bait. Probably the same thing that they would have done if she hadn't followed Connor last night. Maybe her dad was right. They didn't *need* her. What would they do if she conveniently never made it to Emily's? She could go hide somewhere and lie low until it was over. Would it even make a difference if she did?

Those thoughts ran around in circles in Crystal's head, distracting her until she reached the hiking trail along the river. She crossed the street to enter it, but just as she was reaching the other side, a pair of Humvees came roaring around the corner behind her. They turned onto the street and came rumbling directly toward her. Crystal flinched at the sight of them. Were they here for her? Had the governor found out that she was here?

Bowser gave a low growl. Not wanting to look conspicuous by staring at the approaching vehicles, Crystal began dragging Bowser toward the trail, but he dug in his heels, using the excuse to take another break.

"Bowie!" Crystal hissed. "Let's go!" The vehicles slowed as they approached. Her heart began slamming in her chest, but she pretended not to notice, and turned around, walking down the trail as quickly as Bowser would let her.

Then a horn honked at her a few times.

Reluctantly, she turned back around to see the driver of the lead vehicle leaning out his window and waving to her from about fifteen feet away.

"Are you lost, Miss?" he called out.

Crystal summoned a bright smile and shook her head. "No, I'm just out taking my dog for a walk! It's a nice day for that, don't you think?"

"A young woman like you shouldn't be out walking on her own. Especially not along the river."

"I'll be all right," Crystal said, wondering what he meant by *a young woman like you*. "I know how to look after myself."

"All the same, ma'am, I would feel better knowing that you were accompanied. I can have a couple of my men escort you if you like. We're overdue to check the park for stalkers, anyway."

That gave Crystal pause. "They've tunneled into the park before?"

The Ranger nodded. "Once or twice."

Crystal summoned all of her courage and shook her head, still smiling, even though her guts had just turned to ice. "I'll take my chances, but thank you!"

"Well... all right... Take care of yourself, ma'am. Keep your head on a swivel."

"Yes, sir!"

Crystal watched the trucks roar away, wondering if she'd made the right call. She had to weigh the hypothetical threat of stalkers against the more tangible one of the Rangers themselves. They weren't all good guys like her dad and Connor, and she didn't know these men. Some of them were little better than raiders in uniform—the so-called Vultures. If she wasn't careful, Crystal could go missing on her way to Emily's and wake up on board a Spec lander, learning firsthand about the Specs' so-called *integration therapy.*

She shivered and turned away, shaking Bowser's leash like the reigns of a horse. "We'd better pick up the pace, Bowie."

***

Adam finished his meager lunch early. He left his squad sitting in their corner of the hot, dusty lobby of the fuel depot's admin building to go looking for Major Hunter. He still had at least a hundred questions about his squad's role in tonight's operation, and now that Mayor Ellis had left with the convoy, Hunter was officially the one with all of the answers.

After walking up and down the length of the lobby twice and not finding the major, Adam broadened his search to the facility's corridors, checking behind closed doors in the offices. He eventually found Major Hunter in the third office that he checked. Hunter was sitting by himself at the desk, eating one of the stale sandwiches that they'd brought with them from Bexar with one hand, and paging through an old magazine with the other.

Adam hesitated in the open doorway.

"Something on your mind, Sergeant?" Major Hunter asked without looking up from his magazine.

"Uh, yes sir."

"Come in," Hunter prompted, still not looking up from the magazine.

Adam approached the desk with a frown, wondering if maybe it wasn't a magazine that he was reading, but a battle plan, or a blueprint for the Capitol or the Governor's Mansion.

When he reached the desk, Adam was

surprised to find that he was wrong on all accounts. It was an old comic book, the pages faded and torn.

Perplexed, but not wanting to pry, Adam stood quietly at parade rest with his hands clasped behind his back and his feet apart, waiting for the major's full attention.

"We never did get to finish this one," Hunter whispered.

"I'm sorry?" Adam asked.

"My daughter and I." Hunter looked up with a smile. "Summer."

"I see..." Adam trailed off uncertainly. He craned his neck to get a look at the comic book.

"Garfield comics," Hunter explained, holding up the book so that Adam could see the cover. "She was obsessed with him. Cats in general, really. I was using the comics to teach her to read. We were reading this one when the Specs arrived. Stalkers took her that same night. They dragged her away right in front of me. I followed them for twelve blocks until I lost the trail. Six years old, and they took her. What the hell kind of monsters prey on children?"

Adam remembered Carla's husband being taken that same night, and he slowly shook his head. "Not just children, sir," he said.

Hunter sneered at that. "True enough, I suppose. But then why didn't they take me instead? I was only twenty-nine. If they were looking for able-bodied slaves or soldiers, you'd think that I'd be a better fix. So why *her?*"

"Kids don't put up as much of a struggle. They're lighter and easier to carry."

The major tossed the comic book across the desk with an angry sneer. It landed on the floor at Adam's feet. He stared numbly at the cover for a second, not knowing what to say to make the major feel better. No wonder he was hiding out in here. He didn't want the other Rangers to see him falling apart.

Adam absently read the title of the comic —*Garfield at Large...* and the subtitle at the bottom *His First Book.* He bent down and picked it up. "This is the first one? And you never finished it?"

"It's a *signed* first edition," Hunter muttered. "I went all the way to Comic-Con so I could get it signed for her by Jim Davis. Kind of a dumb gift for a six-year-old when I think about it now. I guess I just thought that maybe she'd keep it until she was older and then she'd always have it to remember me by. But that's even stupider now that she's some kind of mind-wiped slave."

Adam pinned his carbine under one arm, freeing his other hand to open the book and read the generic autograph.

TO: SUMMER AND JAMES HUNTER-
Best wishes!
Jim Davis

Adam gently flipped through the pages. The very first panel showed a man sitting on a stool in front of a drawing board with his iconic orange-striped cat beside him on a red filing cabinet.

"Hi, there... I'm Jon Arbuckle. I'm a cartoonist, and this is my cat, Garfield."

Adam smiled tightly at that.

And then realization hit him like a lightning bolt, and he froze. He blinked in shock, and read the name again.

Jon Arbuckle.

Memories trickled back to Adam, of hiding out in a dumpster behind an abandoned warehouse in Bexar where a group of Vultures were supposed to be meeting. They'd never shown, but while flicking through channels on his handset, Adam had accidentally overheard two of them talking—*"Arbuckle"* had been one of the call signs that they'd used that night. That *couldn't* be a coincidence, could it? But if it wasn't, then Major Hunter was a Vulture. And with his rank, he probably wasn't just *any* Vulture. He was probably their leader, in Bexar anyway.

Adam covered his reaction with a smile and shut the comic book. He smoothly handed it back to Major Hunter. "Maybe it wasn't for her to remember you by, sir. Maybe it was for *you* to remember *her*."

Hunter accepted the comic book with

muscles jerking in his cheeks and his eyes glittering coldly. Wordlessly, he rolled the book into a cylinder in his fist, then turned his chair and tucked it into his pack. He slung it over his shoulders as he stood up and then retrieved his carbine from a filing cabinet beside the desk.

"I assume you came to see me about the battle plan?"

Adam nodded once, working hard to contain his reactions. "Yes, sir."

"We'd better get to it then. Not a lot of time left before this shit show gets on the road."

Adam followed the major out of the office, feeling like a ton of bricks had just settled across his shoulders. This entire operation was compromised, and he was the only one who knew it.

If Major Hunter was a Vulture, then Governor Miller was *expecting* them, and that meant they were walking straight into a trap.

CHAPTER THIRTY

Crystal did her best to enjoy the walk along the river. The sun was beaming down from a clear blue sky. Birds were chirping in the trees. A warm breeze was blowing off the river, keeping her at least reasonably cool. She passed an old gym and a dock stacked high with colorful kayaks. Paddle boats were moored to one side of that, and a handful of people were out rowing kayaks on the river.

Up ahead, someone else was out walking their dog. An apartment building soared to her right. People were out on the balconies, pinning up clothes to dry.

The trail didn't seem as lonely and dangerous as those Rangers had insisted it would be, which made her more suspicious than ever that they were the real danger. Good thing she hadn't accepted that escort.

Crystal wound along the trails, passing yet more pedestrians in the park. An elderly couple sat on a bench, overlooking the water.

A while later, the trail grew more lonely

with high walls of trees on either side. In the distance, a tall man appeared, jogging toward her. He was wearing long black pants and a hoodie with the hood up. Strange attire for the middle of the day, but maybe he was trying to work up a sweat. He slowed as he reached her, jogging on the spot and smiling. "Nice dog," he said.

"Thanks."

"Male or female?"

"Male," Crystal replied.

He nodded. "My sister has a Golden, but it's a female. Maybe we can introduce them sometime?"

"Maybe," Crystal replied, smiling tightly back as she walked away.

"When?" the jogger asked, appearing alongside her again.

"Ummm..." Crystal glanced at him. "I was just being polite. My dog is thirteen. At his age, too much excitement might do him in."

"Oh, well, that's a pity."

Crystal expected him to say goodbye and go jogging back the way he'd been headed before bumping into her. Instead, he continued jogging beside her. "What's your name?" he asked.

"Crystal," she replied slowly, now actively wondering how to get rid of him.

"I'm Kent." He thrust out a hand, and Bowser growled menacingly.

"Woah, easy boy," Kent said, withdrawing his hand to hold it up with the other one. "I surrender," he added with a charming grin.

Crystal studied him speculatively, wondering what he was after. He was tall and fit, not as strong as Connor, but wiry with long arms and legs. He wasn't unattractive, with vivid blue eyes, a handsome face, and a nice smile. She guessed that he was maybe thirty-five years old if the lines on his face and the threads of white showing through his black hair were anything to go by. She had a sneaking suspicion that he was hitting on her, which was flattering, but unnerving at the same time.

"Well, it was nice meeting you, Kent."

"Likewise, Crystal. Where are you headed?"

She frowned unhappily. He wasn't taking the hint. A thread of apprehension wove into her thoughts. She was suddenly acutely aware of how lonely the park was. She hadn't seen another person since passing that old couple on the bench and the man out walking his dog. Now that she thought about it, those people had been sticking to the open areas around the apartment building, close to the dock with the kayaks. At this point along the trail the trees and other foliage were thicker, forming high walls around the path.

"I'm going to meet up with my husband," Crystal lied and then wondered why she hadn't referred to him as her fiancé. Maybe because a *husband* seemed like a stronger deterrent. "He's waiting for me up ahead. We're going to have lunch together."

"Husband, huh?" Kent frowned. "That figures. The good ones are always taken."

"Sorry." Crystal tried a sympathetic smile.

Kent smiled coldly back.

Crystal suppressed a shiver, and her smile flickered. She looked around quickly, hoping to see someone else, but this section of the trail was abandoned. Worse yet, up ahead there was a bridge across the river, and the trail passed beneath it, forming a deep well of shadows where she would be even more hidden from view.

"Well, like I said, it was nice meeting you..." Crystal trailed off, hoping that this time he would take the hint.

"You know, you really shouldn't be out here on your own," Kent said. "I'd feel better if I walked with you to see your husband."

"Thank you, but that's really not necessary."

"I insist," Kent said.

"I said no."

Kent flashed another cold smile. "Do you have any idea how much a woman like you is worth to the Syndicate?"

Crystal's body turned to ice at the mention of raiders. She switched Bowser's leash to her left hand and dropped her right to her pocket, reaching for the can of pepper spray.

One of Kent's hands flashed into his hoodie and emerged holding a taser.

She let out a strangled cry and ducked to get away. Bowser snarled and lunged for Kent's hand just as the taser came crackling toward her. Bowser's jaws closed around Kent's wrist, deflecting the weapon momentarily. He cursed viciously, and Crystal's hand came up with the pepper spray. She depressed the button, hitting Kent full in the face. He screamed and clawed at his eyes, stumbling away.

Crystal yanked hard on Bowser's leash, but he was intent on the kill, straining to the end of his leash to get at her attacker. She had to use both hands to drag him away, and she dropped the pepper spray in the process. It bounced and rolled down the trail.

Kent was already recovering. "You bitch!" he spat, his eyes red and streaming with tears. He stumbled toward them with the taser still firmly clutched in one hand.

"Bowser, run!" Crystal cried. Finally, he got the message and abandoned the attack. Crystal ran and he kept pace alongside her.

The sound of Kent's hurried footfalls was loud in her ears, and growing louder with every passing second.

"You're going to pay for that!" Kent breathed, sounding like he was just a few steps behind her.

Bowser's pace slowed as he began to limp.

His leash pulled taut, forcing her to slow down, too. Crystal realized with growing horror that she was either going to have to let Bowser go and leave him behind or turn around and face her attacker.

Bowser snarled again and his leash tugged hard, yanking straight out of her hand. "Bowie!" Crystal glanced over her shoulder just in time to see him leaping toward Kent.

The man sneered and stopped running to deliver a sharp kick to Bowser's ribs. He yelped and he went down hard, landing in the grass beside the trail. Bowser whimpered and whined, struggling to rise.

"Stay down, you dumb mutt," Kent muttered. He aimed his taser warningly in Bowser's direction and triggered a crackling burst. He needn't have bothered. Bowser gave up trying to rise and rolled onto his side, whimpering and panting hard.

Crystal's whole body was trembling with a combination of rage and fear.

"Your turn, little girl," Kent whispered darkly, looking at her with a dark smile.

She cast about quickly, searching for *something* she could use in her defense. Her gaze seized upon a fist-sized rock, lying just a few feet away at the edge of the trail.

She dove to reach it, and Kent dashed toward her at the same time. He landed on top of her just as her fingers closed around the rock. He pinned her arms above her head and slammed her hand repeatedly into the path until the rock fell from lifeless fingers.

She aimed a knee for his groin, drawing an agonized cry from his lips. And then the taser connected with her neck, and her whole body convulsed. She felt like bees were stinging her all over, and she couldn't move. He tased her a second time, and suddenly her brain felt like it was rattling around in a jar.

Then came the sharp prick of something cold sliding into a vein in her arm, and her vision quickly faded into a darkening tunnel. The last thing she saw was Kent grabbing her feet and dragging her toward the river.

CHAPTER THIRTY-ONE

Adam endured the first two sets of drills with his squad, all the while trying to work out who he could trust, and how to deal with the discovery that Major Hunter was secretly working for the governor.

Mayor Ellis was the one he needed to warn, but there was no way to reach him. Their walkies were likely too short-ranged to contact Ellis, and anyone could listen in. The next time Adam saw Ellis would be *after* the attack on the Governor's Mansion. They were supposed to meet back up at the Capitol building, where Ellis would be waiting to receive the governor in a secure room in the basement. But now Adam knew that they'd never get that far.

The governor was expecting them. They'd be lucky if his Rangers weren't already moving to surround them.

Adam led Delta squad to victory through their second drill, this one to enter and clear a room and take a dummy governor hostage while under fire from Alpha and Bravo squads.

They were using paintball guns for the drills rather than blanks since they didn't want to risk discovery with the noise.

Adam found that to be deeply ironic, considering that Hunter must have already betrayed them to the governor. But maybe Hunter was like Ramirez—a double agent who'd been feeding the Nightingales intel from the inside.

Adam sincerely hoped to learn that was the case. But how would he be able to tell the difference between a real enemy agent and a known informant? Only Ellis could answer that, and he wasn't here.

At this point, Adam's focus was on damage control. If the operation was compromised, then the coup had already failed, but maybe they could still find a way to pull the plug before the governor sprang his trap.

The problem was, Crystal wasn't here, and neither was Carla. Alerting all three prongs of the operation before tonight, and somehow doing so without forcing the governor to play his hand early, was going to be next to impossible.

Major Hunter called for a break, and all four squads returned to the lobby. Adam saw his chance and used the brief reprieve to pull Connor aside.

"What's up, Sergeant?" Connor asked.

Adam glanced around quickly to make sure

no one was standing close enough to listen in. Their squadmates were engaged in noisy banter and good-natured ribbing of the ones who were covered in bright blue paint from the last drill. Adam dropped his voice to a whisper, and said, "Major Hunter is a Vulture."

Connor blinked at him. "What?"

"Listen up. I know we've had our differences, but I need someone I can trust, and we don't have much time."

Connor's brow furrowed. "Okay..."

"We need to expose the major, but before we do that, I need to confiscate everyone's radios. We can't afford to have anyone warning the governor. We need to find out who else here is working with him before we can trust anyone."

"Are you *sure* about this, Adam?" Connor asked. "Because if there's even a chance that you're not..."

"Either he's an agent, or he's a double agent, and we need to figure out which. There's no time to explain how I know, so right now, I just need you to trust me."

Connor nodded hesitantly. "Okay, what do you need?"

"I need you to distract the major while I go to the other squads and ask them for their radios." Only the sergeants and a few of the corporals had walkies, with exactly two per squad, so Adam had to collect exactly six handsets before he went to Major Hunter to ask for his.

"How are you going to do that?" Connor asked.

"I'm going to say that Hunter picked up some enemy chatter on our operational frequency, and he needs to scan for a new one that we can use."

"And you want me to distract him so he doesn't notice what you're doing," Connor guessed.

Adam nodded.

"All right. When are we doing this?"

"Now."

Connor blew out a shaky breath. "I'm on it."

"Good." Adam waited for Connor to walk away, heading straight for the major.

Muscles bunched in Adam's jaw at the thought of the coming confrontation. Glancing around the gloomy interior of the building, Adam quickly located Corporal Stevens from his squad and crossed over to her to ask for her radio. She made a face at the request but then nodded agreeably when he gave her the reason.

"We definitely don't want the enemy listening in on our channel tonight," she said.

"No, we don't," Adam agreed. He moved on to Bravo Squad and asked Sergeant Chase for his radio first. The senior sergeant frowned unhappily at the request. "The major didn't mention anything to me about our comms being compromised."

Adam shrugged, trying to play it cool. "He

probably didn't have a chance, or he didn't think that collecting radios was a worthy errand for his second-in-command."

The sergeant's eyes narrowed, and his age-spotted cheeks tightened into a scowl. Adam held his gaze for a few tense seconds before Chase reached for his radio and handed it over.

Adam nodded and scanned the rest of Bravo Squad, looking for which of his two corporals had the other one. A young man with shaggy brown hair leaking from his helmet came forward, grumbling, "We're probably not gonna use them anyway. Too risky."

"You never know," Adam replied. Juggling three different walkies now, Adam went to Sergeant Jackson and Charlie Squad. He offered the same excuse and hefted the bundle of walkies already in his hands to add veracity to the lie.

"What's going on here?" Major Hunter suddenly asked.

Adam froze and slowly turned to face him.

Connor was standing right behind the major, looking apologetic and shaking his head. The kid mouthed *sorry* to him as if to say that he'd done his best.

"Here," Adam said, hefting the walkies and handing them to the major.

Hunter accepted them with a deepening frown and shook his head. "Is someone going to explain what's going—"

Adam's hand flashed down to his holster and he drew his sidearm. Before anyone could react, he racked the slide and flicked off the safety, aiming it squarely at Hunter's chest.

Then came the sudden rustle of fabric and a chorus of metallic clattering as the other Rangers drew and armed their own weapons. "You should be aiming at the major, not at me," Adam said.

Hunter fixed him with an incredulous look and shook his head, but there was the slightest tremor in the set of his lips. He glanced over his shoulder at Connor. "Private Cooper, do you have any idea why Sergeant Hall has suddenly lost his mind?"

"No, sir," Connor replied.

To Adam's astonishment, Connor slowly drew his own sidearm, pulled back the slide, and leveled it at Adam's chest.

Suddenly Adam realized how badly he'd miscalculated by trusting Connor. He was a Vulture, too.

PART FOUR: ASHES TO ASHES

CHAPTER THIRTY-TWO

Awareness trickled into Crystal's mind like water through a sieve. Sunlight beamed hotly through her eyelids, turning her skin bright orange and highlighting veins like crooked red snakes. The world was rocking gently back and forth, back and forth. Water swished rhythmically.

Memories came rushing back, and Crystal's heart rate spiked with dread as she remembered Bowser going down with that kick, then whimpering and struggling to rise. Something told her he wasn't here with her now. Crystal hoped he'd had the sense to stay down after Kent had knocked her out with that taser. Hopefully, Emily would find him and help him. Crystal pushed those thoughts from her head with a deliberate effort, and her focus switched to worrying about herself.

Would Emily send someone looking for her when she didn't make the rendezvous? Even if she did, what were the chances that they would find her? Crystal focused on the sounds of water and oars rowing, trying to imagine where Kent was taking her. She resisted the urge to sit up or open her eyes. As long as she was pretending to be asleep, she had the element of surprise. That might be worth something. Feeling her arms and hands numb beneath her, she wiggled her fingers to bring some of the feeling back. Pins and needles prickled like a swarm of ants biting her all over. She tried flexing her wrists, but they were bound behind her. So were her ankles.

This was bad. Not only was she *not* going to make it to the Governor's Mansion to act as the bait for the coup, but she was almost certainly about to be sold to Syndicate slavers. Kent's dire warning sent shivers down her spine as she remembered it now: *Do you have any idea how much a woman like you is worth to the Syndicate?* The thought of winding up in some brothel for raiders in the lawless South made her stomach turn.

Crystal wished now that she'd listened to that Ranger who'd stopped to question her on the street. In hindsight, he and his men probably hadn't been preying on her. They'd been legitimately worried for her safety. Unlike her, they knew well the dangers of this city.

Crystal strained quietly against her bonds, hoping irrationally for them to suddenly give way. All she managed to accomplish was to chafe her skin raw as the ropes bit painfully into her wrists and ankles.

"Good, you're awake," Kent said, having spotted her quiet struggles. "That saves me the trouble of carrying you again."

Realizing there was no point in pretending to be asleep anymore, Crystal opened her eyes and struggled to prop herself up from lying down to more or less sitting in the back of a simple rowboat. She glared at Kent for a long, icy moment. He smiled smugly back while rowing from the prow. He had his back facing the direction of their movement, while his oars were secured in metal brackets on either side of the boat. Crystal noticed a faded blue tarp partially covering her legs, and a pile of soggy brown ropes beside her like the ones that bound her ankles and probably also her wrists. The bottom of the boat was sloshing with a quarter inch of dirty water. She wondered if Kent had used the tarp to hide her from other passing boats or maybe from pedestrians along the shore. If he'd pulled it off her already, was that because they were past the point where she could be discovered and rescued? Had he somehow managed to smuggle her beyond the perimeter of the safe zone?

Crystal twisted around to look behind her and saw the distant, pillared gray wall of a bridge. A couple of tiny, human-sized black specks were standing in the middle of it. Were those Rangers?

Realizing that she wasn't gagged, Crystal thought she might have a chance to get their attention, but they were far away. Would they even hear her? Only one way to find out. "Help!" she screamed. "I'm being kidnapped!"

"Shut up! You want me to taze you again?" Kent demanded.

Crystal sneered at him. "Go ahead. Help!"

Kent released his oars and lunged across the boat to clap a hand over her mouth. His other hand came up from his belt holding the taser. It began crackling with electricity. Crystal struggled against Kent's callused hand, trying to bite it, but he had her head pinned to the back of the boat. Her eyes widened at the flickering blue arc of electricity between the contacts of the device. He brought it within an inch of her neck, and she subsided.

"Are we done?" he asked.

Crystal nodded, and he withdrew, holstering the weapon. He took up the oars again, and she resolved to save her breath for a time when someone might actually hear. She scanned both sides of the river, hoping to see signs of activity on the shore, but it was completely deserted, lined as it was with nothing but dense walls of trees.

Kent smiled smugly at her once more, as if he'd understood what she was looking for. His reaction earlier implied that screaming might accomplish something. Maybe someone had heard her?

Crystal continued scanning both sides of the river for signs of life, just in case she got lucky and saw someone. To her right was nothing but trees. To her left was a cliff, also covered in trees, but there were sprawling mansions perched atop it. Seeing that, Crystal was tempted to scream for help again, but then she noticed the state of the homes. They were falling apart. Their windows were dark and gaping open, lawns were overgrown, and roofs were sunken and collapsing.

"Something wrong, angel?" Kent asked.

Crystal ignored the unwanted endearment. "We're not in the safe zone anymore, are we?"

His smile broadened. "No. The Mopac bridge forms the Western perimeter. About a mile behind us now."

A mile. Crystal almost sobbed in frustration. The chances of someone hearing her scream a *mile* away were less than zero, and even if someone did hear her, they wouldn't risk venturing beyond the safe zone to investigate.

"I wasn't lying," Kent said. "You can scream all you like. No one is coming."

Crystal wanted to scream again, but this time from sheer abject terror. She glanced up to find the sun. Judging from the angle of it, still almost directly overhead, she estimated that it couldn't have been more than an hour or two since Kent had taken her from the trail.

Maybe by now Emily had found Bowser and she'd realized what must have happened to her. She would send people looking for her.

But would they search for her out in the wastes? Where would they even begin with such an extensive search area? Despair clutched Crystal's heart in a cold fist as she realized that anyone who came looking for her would be searching for the proverbial needle in a haystack.

***

"Major Hunter is a Vulture," Adam insisted.

The major laughed lightly at that, but his mirth quickly faded. "That's a serious accusation, Sergeant."

"Do you have any proof?" Sergeant Chase asked.

Adam licked his lips and nodded. His aim never wavered from the major's chest. "I do." He explained about his old investigation into the Vultures in Bexar, how he'd overheard their comms while hiding in a dumpster, and in the process learned the call signs of two of their operatives. "Arbuckle was one of them. I believe that was Major Hunter."

Again, the major laughed, but this time much louder than before. "That could be anyone!" Despite his bluster, Adam thought he detected a hint of nervousness. After talking about the Garfield comics he used to read to his daughter, there was no doubt that Major Hunter understood how Adam had made the connection to him. The trouble now was in convincing everyone else that they shouldn't dismiss it as a simple coincidence.

"Before we began our drills, I happened to walk in on the major while he was eating his lunch. He was reminiscing over a comic book that he used to read to his daughter. Garfield. While I was there, I read the name of one of the characters in that comic—Jon *Arbuckle.*"

"Hey, that's right!" Private Sanders, Delta Four, said. Adam risked glancing in the boy's direction and he saw the tall pasty kid nodding. His glasses inched down his nose and he pushed them back up. "I used to watch Garfield cartoons. Arbuckle was Garfield's owner."

Whispers of concern and disbelief rippled through all four squads. Major Hunter's expression flickered, his smugness fading to a more furtive look.

"Is that true, Major?" Sergeant Chase demanded.

"That I used to read Garfield to my daughter? Sure," he shrugged and sneered indignantly at Adam. "But that doesn't mean I'm a Vulture who goes by *Arbuckle.* And we only have Sergeant Hall's word for it that he even heard what he heard. Who else knows about his alleged investigation into the Vultures?"

"Mayor Ellis does," Adam said.

Hunter snorted. "How convenient then that he's not here." Hunter nodded grimly, looking indignant now. "No one here can vouch for your story, which makes me wonder, why are you going after *me?* And on the eve of our coup, no less? Could it be because *you* are the Vulture, and the best way to defeat us is to get us to abandon our attack before it even begins?"

More muttering filled the air.

At least Adam knew that Hunter wasn't a double agent. He'd be admitting to his involvement if that were the case. But proving he was a Vulture was going to be difficult.

"Ramirez?" Adam tried, reaching for the only straw that might be able to help him right now. He recalled that she'd admitted to being a Vulture, working undercover for Ellis to ensure the security of this operation.

"Yes, Sergeant?"

She stepped into his peripheral view, and his eyes darted briefly to her. "You said you were informing on the Vultures' movements and that was how Ellis knew who he could trust for this op. Did you ever hear about an *Arbuckle* during your time with them?"

Ramirez licked her lips and her brow furrowed in thought. "I don't know... how long ago was this?"

"About three years," Adam supplied.

Ramirez winced. "Sorry, Sergeant. I only

joined the Vultures last year."

Hunter smiled thinly at that, probably realizing now that he had the upper hand. "Sergeant Chase, arrest this man and lock him in one of the supply rooms."

Chase snapped an order, and a pair of Rangers advanced on Adam with their carbines raised. "Drop your weapon, Sergeant," Major Hunter intoned. "You don't want to make this any worse for you than it already is."

Adam's aim wavered. His gaze darted to the left, then the right, studying the advancing soldiers and wondering if there was any way out of this. He didn't see one.

"Wait. I can vouch for him," Connor suddenly said.

All eyes turned to him, and the soldiers stopped advancing on Adam.

Sergeant Chase frowned, and Major Hunter rounded on Connor with an angry sneer. "Well, it's no surprise that Sergeant Hall's own family would side with him, is it? Arrest Private Cooper, too!"

Connor's aim drifted to Hunter's chest, and he slowly shook his head. "I can prove that the major is a Vulture."

"That's absurd!" Hunter scoffed.

Sergeant Chase ignored him. "How can you prove it, son?"

"Because I'm also a Vulture, and I've been working with the major to undermine this operation for weeks."

Exclamations of shock and outrage spread quickly through the crowd, but Adam's reaction was more subdued. It was like hearing the punch line of a joke that he'd already heard. He glared silently at the boy, and Connor studiously avoided his gaze.

"Do you have any proof of your collaboration?" Sergeant Chase demanded.

Connor nodded. "My radio is proof. I'm not even supposed to have one."

"You could have stolen it," Sergeant Chase pointed out.

"But I didn't," Connor replied. He slowly raised his sidearm, now aiming it at the ceiling. "May I?" he asked, reaching toward his vest with his other hand.

Sergeant Chase nodded. "Slowly."

Major Hunter scoffed and shook his head. "This is a witch hunt! If he's a Vulture, then that's all the more reason that we shouldn't trust a word he says!"

Sergeant Chase regarded Hunter with a bemused frown, but this time he didn't say anything. Adam wondered if Hunter realized that his repeated denials were only making him look guiltier.

Connor produced the radio from his vest, and Adam noticed that it wasn't the same make or model as the others they were using. "The major has one just like it," Connor explained, holding his handset out. One of the Rangers took it and carried it to Sergeant Chase, who turned it over in his hands a few times, studying the device.

Connor went on, "Hunter contacted me on it just before lunch. I had to excuse myself to the restroom so that no one would see me using it."

All eyes were on Major Hunter now. His incredulous expression flickered, his composure slowly cracking.

"Sir, I'm afraid we're going to have to search you," Sergeant Chase said. He gestured to the Rangers who'd been moving to arrest Adam a moment ago. They approached the major, who glared at them.

"Sergeant, are you certain you want to go down this road?" Hunter intoned darkly.

"This operation is far too important for us to ignore the accusations that have been made. If you're innocent, you'll have my apologies, but I'm sure you understand the necessity."

"Of course," Hunter purred. "Just so long as *you* understand that I'm going to have you court-martialed when this is over."

One of the two Rangers began patting him down and checking all of the compartments in his vest, belt, and pants. For a moment, it didn't look like he would find anything. But then he pulled out a small black handset, hidden in one of the pouches in Hunter's vest. It was identical to the one that Connor had surrendered as evidence.

"Bring it here, Corporal," Sergeant Chase ordered. He took a second to compare it to Connor's handset, then held both of them up so that everyone could see. "They're set to the same channel. It would seem that Private Cooper is telling the truth. Corporal Allan, arrest Major Hunter and Private Cooper and lock them in separate rooms for questioning."

"Yes, sir," the corporal replied, already gesturing to the others in his fire team for backup.

Major Hunter's eyes glittered darkly at Adam as Rangers bound his hands behind his back with handcuffs. Now that he'd been caught, he was considerably less vocal about his innocence.

Once both Connor's and Major Hunter's weapons had been confiscated, Adam slowly lowered his gun and holstered it. He walked over to Connor with outrage simmering hotly in his veins.

"You involved Crystal in this, *knowing* that she would be walking into a trap? What kind of spineless worm are you?"

Connor's expression twisted miserably. "It's *because* of her that I got involved in this. My mom, too. Vultures threatened to hand them over to the Specs if I didn't join."

Adam pursed his lips. "You could have told me. I could have done something."

Connor shook his head. "I was being watched. So were you. They promised that if I helped them, they'd grant Crystal and my mom immunity."

Sergeant Chase and Adam's squad mates gathered around. "What made you change your mind, son?" Chase asked.

Connor grimaced. "I didn't know that my mom was a part of the coup. Or you, Adam. And Crystal was supposed to be arrested by Rangers at the gate. Hunter promised she wouldn't actually be used as bait. But he broke that promise. That's what he was talking to me about on the radio. He said that he didn't want to spook Ellis into thinking that the governor was expecting them."

Sergeant Chase frowned, looking to Adam, then back to Major Hunter who was being dragged away to one of the back rooms.

"You'd better tell us everything, son. We need to know exactly how and when the governor is planning to spring his trap."

Connor drew in a shaky breath and nodded. He winced as one of the Rangers bound his hands with zip ties, and Adam listened with growing apprehension as Connor told them everything he knew.

The governor was going to pretend to be oblivious right up until the last moment, giving them the chance to surround his mansion. Then, just before the attack began, he was going to retreat with his guards and Crystal to a secret underground passage between the mansion and the Capitol. A platoon of Rangers would stay behind to defend the mansion from within while at the same time, a whole battalion would boil out of hiding from a building across the street, completely surrounding and overwhelming the insurgents.

"They'll be caught in the converging lines of fire," Connor finished. "If you don't surrender, you'll be slaughtered."

"You're assuming that the governor would even accept our surrender," Sergeant Chase pointed out. "It might be more expedient for him to simply gun us down."

Connor shook his head. "The governor wants to take you alive so that he can hand you over to the Specs. He'll pretend to exile you, but you'll be captured soon after you enter the wastes. Apparently, he has quotas to meet."

Adam let out a ragged sigh. "Either way, this is a disaster."

"That's putting it mildly," Sergeant Chase agreed. "You have any ideas about how we can turn this around?"

Adam regarded him with eyebrows raised and slowly shook his head. "We have to call off the coup and find a way out of the city before the governor realizes that we know it's a trap."

Sergeant inclined his head. "We need to warn

Mayor Ellis."

"Someone needs to warn my daughter as well."

"Yes." Sergeant Chase smacked his lips. "Take a fire team from your squad. I'll take one to warn Ellis, and we'll meet back here to regroup when we're done."

Adam nodded curtly, already turning to leave.

"Wait, take me with you," Connor said. "I can help."

Adam scowled at him. "You've done enough. I'll take it from here."

"You might need my help if we run into trouble. If we get captured or run into other Vultures, I might be able to get you out of it. There's a code phrase we use to identify each other—*jeepers, it's hot today.*"

"Jeepers?" Adam asked. "I don't think I've heard you say that in your life."

"Which is why it makes a good code phrase," Connor replied.

"Well, now that I know how to mark myself as friendly, I don't need you."

"He's right," Sergeant Chase interrupted. "With his fiancée in the middle of this, he's got as much riding on the outcome as you do, so he won't try anything. If he doesn't warn her, there's no telling what Governor Miller will do to her when he learns that Connor betrayed him. Take him with you, but make sure his guns are either empty or loaded with blanks."

Adam frowned unhappily but acknowledged the order. "Understood. Is there a vehicle we can use?"

Sergeant Chase slowly shook his head. "I'm afraid Ellis took them all. We weren't supposed to need transport."

Adam grimaced. "Then I'd better hurry."

Chase's chin dipped in acknowledgment of the fact. "Good luck, Sergeant."

"Likewise," Adam replied. He spun away, scanning the men and women of his squad and mentally putting together a team before rattling off their names. "Hustle up Deltas," he said, moving quickly to one side of the depot with his squad. A pair of Rangers from Sergeant Chase's squad jerked Connor over to them, leaving his hands bound with zip ties. They departed quickly, eyeing Connor darkly as they went. Adam ignored him for the moment.

"Private Erica Ramirez, Corporal Amanda Stevens, and Private Tony Smith." The three of them gathered around, looking eager despite the demoralizing shift in the mission objectives. In the span of the last fifteen minutes they'd gone from running combat drills for a coup to looking for a way to execute a strategic withdrawal. "Gear up. We move out in two minutes," Adam said.

"Copy that." Corporal Stevens said. She turned to address the other two. "You heard the sergeant!"

Clipped acknowledgments came from Ramirez and Smith.

Adam turned to Connor and drew a hunting knife from his belt. "Turn around," he growled.

Connor did so. "Adam, you have to believe I would never do anything to hurt Crystal."

"I don't have to believe anything, Cooper," Adam said as he flicked the blade through the zip tie, cutting him free.

"What would you have done?" Connor demanded, his eyes glittering with unshed tears.

Adam sucked his teeth angrily. "Not this."

"Crystal is my whole world."

"That doesn't mean much, Cooper. People have been shitting all over the world since the very first asshole was born."

Tears trembled on Connor's lashes, and he wiped them angrily off on his sleeve. "Takes one to know one."

Corporal Stevens interrupted them before Adam could wring Connor's neck. "We're good to go, Sergeant."

Privates Ramirez and Smith handed Connor a carbine and a sidearm.

"Loaded with blanks as per the Sergeant's orders," Corporal Stevens explained before Adam could ask. Looking at Connor she added, "You get in trouble out there, you're better off running for it, Cooper."

"Let's move out," Adam said. He recovered his carbine and his pack on the way out of the depot, noting as they headed for the exit that the other members of the fire team were keeping Connor ahead of them.

Sergeant Chase intercepted Adam just before they left the depot. "Switch your radio to channel nine and maintain comms silence unless I break it first," Chase said.

"Copy that, Sergeant," Adam replied, reaching into his vest for his handset and switching it to the indicated frequency.

"Here." Chase handed Adam a folded square of paper. He unfolded it to see a crudely drawn map that described the route Crystal was taking to get to Sophie and Emily's home.

"Thanks," Adam said as he pocketed the paper.

"Hurry back," Chase replied.

"You too, Sergeant." Adam ran down the ramp from the admin building and through the garage where their trucks had been parked this morning. Now the garage was empty. Adam burst into the sunlit parking lot outside and quickly identified the gate in the chain link fence around the depot.

By the time they left the compound, Adam's bad leg was already blazing with fire. Adam grimaced, limping, and wishing for the millionth time since his injury that he hadn't taken that bullet in Afghanistan.

He distracted himself from the pain by pulling out his map to study the route. According to the scale at the bottom, it was just under four miles to Sophie's place. In his youth, he could have made that in forty-five minutes or less, but now he'd be lucky to make it in an hour.

"You okay, Sergeant?" Corporal Stevens asked, walking effortlessly alongside him and nodding to his bad leg. Her concern seemed genuine enough, but somehow Adam felt like she was mocking him with her two perfectly functioning legs.

"Pain is like any other message, Corporal. Hearing is a given, but listening is optional."

"If you say so, Sergeant."

With that, Adam kicked himself in the proverbial pants and pulled ahead of her. He held his carbine loosely across his chest, keeping his head on a swivel as they followed the road from the depot to the main road.

To any onlookers, they would look just like any other foot patrol. No one would think to question them. But if they ran into other *Rangers*, they'd come up against a whole different level of scrutiny. Some might even wonder why they didn't recognize anyone on Adam's team, and at that point, things could take a much darker turn.

If that happened, Adam would be ready for it. His hand tightened into a fist on the grip of his carbine. No one would stop him from getting to Crystal and warning her.

Hang on, baby, I'm coming, he thought at her.

CHAPTER THIRTY-THREE

The boat passed beneath a bridge and drifted out into sunlit green water on the other side. Up ahead, a big sloping wall of concrete loomed. The dam at the end of the river. Kent had to row harder as they drew near, even though the spillways were dry.

"Now what?" Crystal asked.

Kent smiled. "Now, you get to meet your buyers."

Crystal's stomach turned with the way he referred to her like she was a thing rather than a person, but she swallowed her disgust and tried on a beguiling smile. "You know, you don't have to sell me to them. You could just keep me for yourself…" Crystal did her best to suppress an involuntary gag reflex.

Kent arched an eyebrow and momentarily stopped rowing. He straightened and rolled his shoulders, cracking the joints. "I have to admit that is an interesting proposition."

"It must be lonely work, doing what you do," Crystal added.

It was all she could do to keep up with the act. But she knew that her chances were better against Kent than they would be against an entire gang of raiders. If she could convince him to cut her free, she might be able to incapacitate him somehow and escape.

"You'd be surprised," Kent replied. "Money will buy just about anything, and these days, it takes less than it used to."

Crystal's smile flickered at the implication. "Maybe, but you can't buy love."

Kent smiled sarcastically. "Is that what you're offering?"

Crystal shrugged. "Among other things…"

"Nice try, sweetheart. I'm a solo act, and I'm not an idiot. You'd say anything to get me to cut you free, but given the chance you'd happily gut me like a fish." Kent dipped his oars back down and continued rowing, sending them speeding for the shore.

Crystal scowled and peered over his shoulder, checking the shore for signs of whoever was supposed to receive her. But there was no sign of anyone yet. Just a dense wall of trees leading to bare concrete walls and broken windows of the hydroelectric power plant.

They came to a jutting peninsula that crossed two-thirds of the river, lined with yet more trees. Kent rowed past it, seeming to be headed straight for a long concrete pier that sloped down to the water line at the end. A big white and black sign hung on the wall above the water, warning that automatic turbines could produce *swift water any time without warning.*

Crystal's thoughts turned to the facility behind the sign. She wondered if it still provided power to Travis, and if so, if there would be Rangers or maintenance staff inside to keep things running. Surely they weren't *all* in on the slave trade?

Hope swelled in Crystal's chest as they approached the concrete dock and the facility with the broken windows. Maybe if she screamed again now, someone inside would hear her. But as they drew near, the churning roar of the water grew loud. She imagined that the rhythmic droning of machinery inside the facility would be even louder still. It was too soon. She decided to save her breath, at least until Kent pulled alongside that pier and helped her out of the boat. Maybe she could throw her weight against him and push him into that churning water.

"I wonder, what's going on in that pretty little head of yours?" Kent asked.

"None of your business, asshole."

Kent laughed. "Feisty. That will make things harder for you."

Once again, Crystal's stomach turned at the

thought of what awaited her, but she refused to give Kent the satisfaction of seeing her cringe. She looked away to hide her face, focusing on where they were going instead of his ugly face.

The boat began veering away from the pier, aiming for the left bank of the river instead. Kent retreated from the hydro facility, now rowing parallel to the dam itself, and Crystal's hopes of a last-minute rescue from staff at the dam plunged straight off a cliff.

"Where are we going?" she demanded.

Kent looked confused. "We're going to meet your new fam—"

"No, I mean, where." Crystal frowned as she studied the opposite shore. It was completely wild and overgrown with trees with no sign of any buildings, abandoned or otherwise.

The shore sloped up gently from the river, eventually reaching the height of the dam itself. She didn't see anyone waiting to receive them, but it would be easy for them to hide among all those trees.

Crystal's heart fluttered in her chest. "Help!" she screamed at the top of her lungs. She whirled back to face the other shore with the power plant. "Help!" she tried again, but there was no sign of any movement behind the dark gaping windows in the upper story windows of the dam.

"I thought we talked about this?" Kent chided, clucking his tongue.

The fact that this time he didn't lunge across the boat to shut her up implied that the dam was either abandoned or that he knew they'd never hear her scream. Or... maybe those people were on the raiders' payroll. According to Kent, the slave trade was a profitable business. There were probably plenty of credits to go around.

Crystal heaved a stifled sob.

"Oh, cheer up, angel. It's not all bad. You'll get three square meals, and it's easy work. Truth be told, I'm a little jealous."

"Fuck you," Crystal spat, aiming for his face, but the gob of spittle landed short.

"See now, that's the kind of thing I was saying would make this harder on you. Don't be stupid, angel."

"That's not my name."

"It's Crystal, right?" Kent nodded appreciatively. "They might even let you keep it. Sounds like it could be a stage name already."

"My dad will find me. He'll find you, too, and when he does, you're going to wish you'd never been born." Crystal wondered absently why her thoughts jumped straight to her dad rather than to Connor as her avenger. What did that say about her relationship?

"Your daddy's here, in Travis?" Kent asked.

Crystal thrust out her chin. "Yes."

"I thought you were going to meet your husband."

"I was."

"But he's not the one I should be worried about?" Kent asked patiently. He was digging, trying to figure out how many people would be looking for her, and why they were supposedly dangerous.

Crystal smiled smugly at him. "He's former US Army. He used to track down terrorists in Afghanistan, and then he'd interrogate them in black sites to make them give up their associates."

"Oh, I see. So he'll probably pull out all my fingernails and cut off my balls. Maybe even water board for good measure?"

"If you're lucky," Crystal replied.

"Hmmm." Kent took another break from rowing and reached into a familiar-looking backpack. Crystal realized that it was hers. He pulled out an ID card with her photo on it. "Crystal Hope Hall," he read. "I suppose your husband is Mr. Hall? Or is that your maiden name?"

Crystal swallowed thickly, but said nothing, not wanting to give him anything he could use to find her dad or Connor before they found him.

"I'll have to do some digging in the Republic's registries. Thanks for the warning, angel."

Crystal wondered what kind of connections Kent had to be able to do that. She reflected bitterly that he was right about money buying anything.

They reached a rocky shore, and Kent ran the boat aground. He used the oars to guide them in until he'd beached them side-on, then rose to his feet and hopped out onto the rocks. He tied one of the ropes around a flanged metal cleat in the rim of the boat and then went hopping across the rocks to the nearest tree where he tied the other end of the rope. When he was done, he ambled over and climbed back into the boat. Crouching over her feet, he used one hand to pin her legs while the other untied her ankles.

"Don't try anything stupid," he warned.

Crystal smiled sweetly at him, waiting until her legs were free…

And then she twisted her right leg free and kicked up as hard as she could, using her left leg to brace the movement.

Kent was a split second quicker than she and her foot sailed through empty air in front of his nose.

"That was a mistake," he growled.

He stood up, grabbing her backpack in one hand, and a smaller, lighter bag in his other. Slinging them both over opposite shoulders, he stepped over the side of the boat again.

Crystal watched him carefully, wondering what kind of revenge he was planning.

"Come on," Kent intoned, waving to her from the shore.

"What?" She blinked stupidly at him. "Aren't you going to help me get out?" She wriggled around, flopping her body like a fish. "I can't stand up like this, with my hands tied behind my back!"

"I *was* going to help you out until you tried to kick me. Now, I think you can manage on your own. Come on. We're burning daylight. And trust me when I say, being a slave in the Syndicate is still a lot better than filling the same role for the Specs."

Crystal rocked her body toward her legs in an attempt to use her momentum to stand, but she fell back down with a splash in the half-inch of slimy green water at the bottom of the boat. She tried a few more times, finally getting to her feet on the third attempt.

"See? That wasn't so hard," Kent said.

Crystal eyed the side of the boat and the rocks on the shore. The submerged parts were covered in green slime, while the dry, jagged tops of those boulders didn't look easy to balance on. Hopping from rock to rock without her hands free for balance was going to be next to impossible.

Crystal looked pointedly at Kent. "Does your payday go down if I show up with a busted face?"

He sighed and stepped toward her. He reached for one of her arms and seized her biceps in a painfully tight grip.

"Let's go," he prompted.

Crystal stepped over the side of the boat to a more-or-less flat-topped rock. She balanced there with Kent's help. From there, she plotted a course to the shore, stepping from rock to rock, with Kent holding her arm to steady her. She was quietly looking for an opportunity to turn the tables on him by landing a kick to his groin, but Kent kept her at arm's length the whole way, being careful to avoid exactly that.

Once they were standing on dry land together, Kent stepped away from her and nodded to the trees at the highest point of the peninsula. "Through there. See the path?" Kent unslung his pack, zipped it open, and pulled out a 9mm pistol like the one the Rangers used. He flicked his wrist, waving the barrel at her. "Let's go. Pick up those feet."

Now facing a gun, Crystal realized there was no point in trying to run or fight back. She'd only get herself killed. So she did as he asked, struggling up the rocky, root-infested riverbank to the trees, doing her best not to fall on her face.

Beneath the shade of the scraggly foliage she found the path that Kent had mentioned. It was cracked and overgrown with weeds and even a few small trees. On the other side of it, another rocky bank led down to mossy black water, and she realized that this little spit of land wasn't a peninsula after all, but an island.

Kent marched her up the path, being careful to keep her ahead of him at all times. Periodic gusts of warm wind sent shadows and a mixture of brown and gold leaves fluttering across the crumbling path.

After a few minutes, they came to a bridge that led from the island to a proper road, with a bridge on either side that crossed the two forks of the river. Kent indicated that she turn right. Then he reached into the side pocket of his bag and pulled out a walkie-talkie. It chirped twice as he depressed the button a couple of times, but he never raised it to his lips to say anything.

Crystal realized he must be signaling to someone nearby. She started across the bridge to the actual shore of the river. Like the road and the path, the bridge was in a bad state. Monstrous cracks showed through the asphalt to the rusty metal I-beams below.

Crystal skirted the larger gaps, not wanting to accidentally fall through one of them. She briefly considered the possibility of doing so on purpose, or of diving over the side. The river wasn't that far down, maybe only ten or twelve feet, but it also didn't look very deep— she could see all of the rocks and fallen trees that lay submerged beneath its forest-green surface. She could easily break a leg or twist an ankle on the debris. And if she was wrong about the depth and it was actually over her head, she'd have a hard time swimming to shore without the use of her hands. Kent would definitely beat her there.

Crystal gave up on those ideas and focused on the road. She eyed the overgrown walls of trees and foliage, wondering if there might be any stalker dens around here. If she screamed loud enough, maybe she could lure one of them out into daylight. A stalker would make short work of Kent with his puny pistol. Then she'd just have to figure out how to escape the monster herself...

Kent made his radio chirp again, and this time it chirped back.

Crystal realized that it was now or never. She sucked in a deep breath.

Just as she was about to let it out with a blood-curdling scream, she heard the distant rumble of a truck's engine.

"You can save your breath, sweetheart," Kent said. "Your buyers are already here."

Crystal was going to scream anyway, but then a big white Ford came barreling around the corner, and she hesitated. Her eyes narrowed on the cracked windshield and the familiar pattern of dents in the rusty bull bar around the tow winch in the front. That, plus the ramshackle metal topper peeking over the back made it hard to mistake the vehicle for anything other than Rick's old F350. It came to a squealing stop just a dozen feet away. There could be no doubt about it. This was the same truck they'd driven out of Sunny Valley Ranch five years ago. The same one that they'd lost at that Walmart in Hondo.

"No…" Crystal muttered.

Kent regarded her curiously while keeping her covered with his gun. The front doors of the truck flew open, and two people hopped out. The driver was a familiar-looking African-American woman with long dreadlocks. She reached into the cab and pulled out a pump-action shotgun, while the man who'd been riding beside her came sauntering over with a ranger's automatic rifle. He was dark-skinned like her, with his head shaved. Crystal's heart hammered in her chest as she struggled to remember the woman's name.

She stopped a few feet away from Crystal and her dark, sunken eyes widened gradually. "Well, well, isn't this a twisted turn of fate."

"How's that?" Kent asked, his gaze snapping back and forth between the driver and Crystal. "You two know each other?"

The woman smiled. "Oh yes. She's an *old* friend of mine, isn't that right, girl?"

"I am?" Crystal asked, feigning ignorance.

"You don't remember me," the woman purred, still smiling. "I guess we all look the same to you, huh? Here, let me give you another clue." She removed one hand from the shotgun, letting it drop to her side, and then she smoothly drew a gleaming silver revolver from a holster on her hip. Both the gun's wooden grip and its metal barrel were crowded with elaborate engravings.

Crystal's mind flashed back five years ago to walking across the parking lot of a restaurant in Hondo with this woman. She'd been asking where Crystal had found that revolver.

"Kasey..." Crystal muttered, finally remembering her name.

She nodded. "That's right. Kasey Nelson. We never did get to finish that conversation about how you found this gun."

Crystal slowly shook her head as she struggled to remember whatever lies she'd told Kasey back then.

"Where's your dad?" Kasey asked.

"In Travis," Kent supplied.

The woman's eyes widened, then promptly collapsed into slits. "You met him?"

"No, but she mentioned that he'd come looking for her."

Kasey nodded. "Oh, I hope he does. Something tells me that he's the man I really need to talk to about this gun."

Kent licked his lips. "You got my money?"

Kasey jerked her chin to the other raider. He reached for a leather bag dangling from his belt, then tossed it over.

Kent almost fell on his face in his hurry to recover it. He opened the bag and poured a series of gleaming copper and silver credits into one hand.

"It's all there," Kasey said. "Count it on your own time."

"This is only fifty credits," Kent said, licking his lips again. There was no mistaking the greedy gleam in his eyes.

"That's the price we agreed on," Kasey said.

"Yeah, but look at her! She's worth a lot more than the others. You'll sell her for at least a thousand. And this is obviously personal, so you got a bonus. I want a hundred and fifty, not a credit less."

Kasey smiled thinly at him. "We didn't bring that kind of coin."

"No problem. I can wait here while you go back and get it."

"I don't think so," Kasey replied. The barrel of her revolver drifted subtly to him, as did her associate's rifle.

But Kent wasn't aiming his gun at either of them. He was aiming it at *her*. "She's no good to you dead," he warned.

"You're no good to yourself dead, either," Kasey replied. "So what's it going to be, K-man?" she asked, looking and sounding as cool as ice. "Are we doing this?"

Crystal held her breath, preparing to drop to the ground if they started shooting. This situation could still go her way. Maybe. If these three somehow managed to kill each other and none of them shot her in the process.

CHAPTER THIRTY-FOUR

Adam raced down the trail along Lady Bird Lake. He'd been here many times with his late wife, Kimberly, and even with Crystal and Bowser, although Crystal probably didn't remember it now. He followed the map that Sergeant Chase had drawn for him as closely as he could, watching the old high rises flashing by to his right, and the reservoir sparkling in the sun to his left.

Adam was about halfway to the baseball diamond where Crystal was supposed to meet Emily when he saw something that chilled him to his core: a familiar scrap of golden brown fur, lying in the shade of a big oak tree.

He immediately broke into a sprint, calling out, "Bowser!"

"Sergeant?" Corporal Stevens asked, pulling alongside him with her carbine raised and searching for targets.

"That's Crystal's dog!" Adam explained. He

wanted to add that Bowser was *his* dog, too, but there was no time to get into it right now.

Connor dashed by them both, beating them there and falling on his knees beside Bowser. Adam loomed over them, leaning on his knees and gasping for breath.

Connor held Bowser's head in his lap, gently stroking his fur. Bowie was panting hard and whimpering softly.

"Hey boy, what are you doing here all on your own?" Connor asked.

Adam noticed that Bowser whimpered more sharply each time that Connor's hand grazed his side. Adam placed his hand on the spot, probing gently with his fingers. Something gave way that shouldn't have, and Bowser yelped. His head snapped up as if to bite Adam's hand, but he wound up licking him instead.

"It's okay boy," Adam whispered. "He's got a couple of broken ribs."

Connor looked at him, his eyes wide with horror as realization dawned. Up until now, they could have assumed that Bowser simply got too tired to go on, or at worst that maybe he'd had a heart attack and Crystal had been forced to leave him. He was thirteen years old, after all. But this meant that there had been foul play.

Adam scowled and glanced around for any sign of Crystal, but the park was empty.

Corporal Stevens and Privates Smith and

Ramirez crowded in. Stevens spoke first, "Is it possible that Crystal went ahead to the rendezvous so she could come back with help?"

He pointed to the end of Bowser's leash. It was still attached to his harness, but not tied around the tree. "She would have tied him up."

"Not if she was running from someone," Connor said, and Adam winced.

"Let's say that happened, and she got away," Corporal Stevens said, nodding along. "If we continue to the Brooks' residence, we'll find out one way or the other."

Adam shook his head. "She wouldn't have left Bowser like this. How long has it been since she left the depot?" He checked his watch for the answer. "It's thirteen thirty-two. She left at about ten thirty. Walking at a regular pace, she would have been here by about eleven, maybe eleven fifteen. That's more than two hours ago."

Connor nodded gravely.

"There's no way it would have taken her that long to reach the rendezvous and come back with help."

"What about Emily?" Connor asked. "Why didn't she find Bowser before we did? She would have been closer than us. By twelve-thirty or thirteen hundred at the latest, she'd have known that Crystal missed the rendezvous."

Adam studied him quietly. "You're

suggesting that they ran into trouble together?"

Connor shrugged. "Maybe."

"Heads-up!" Private Ramirez warned. "We've got incoming. Female jogger..." Ramirez hesitated while sighting down her scope. Adam straightened and turned to look, his hand flexing on the grip of his carbine.

"Early twenties," Ramirez concluded. "Shoulder-length, curly black hair in a ponytail."

"I think we just answered our question," Adam muttered. "That's Emily."

Connor jumped up, looking ready to run out and greet her.

"Stand down, Private Cooper," Adam said. "Let her come to us. We don't need her spooking and pulling a gun before she knows who we are."

Connor visibly restrained himself, the muscles in his jaw bunching.

Adam strolled lazily back to the path, waving to Emily as she approached. Her pace slowed at the sight of him, obviously not recognizing him from a distance.

Adam walked toward her to narrow the gap faster. "Hey there!" Adam called out in his friendliest voice. He wanted to use her name, but he wasn't sure what identity she was using here in Travis, and he didn't want to blow her cover if someone was watching them.

One of the many explanations for Crystal's disappearance was that Governor Miller had picked her up early.

Emily appeared to recognize his voice and she sprinted the rest of the way. She stopped in front of them with her hands on her knees, breathing hard. "Mr. Hall," she whispered between gasping breaths. "It's good to see you."

Adam nodded. "Did Crystal make the rendezvous?"

Emily straightened, shaking her head. "No. That's why I came down the trail…" Her gaze drifted away from him as Bowser's strained, whistling whimpers approached. "Is that Bowie?" she asked, her voice cracking.

Adam turned to see Connor approaching with Bowser in his arms. Emily ran over to them and gently stroked Bowser's head, receiving a few lackluster licks on her cheeks.

"What happened to him?" Emily asked.

"Someone took Crystal," Adam explained. "Bowie tried to defend her, and they broke his ribs."

"Oh no, Bowie, you poor thing." Tears ran freely down Emily's cheeks.

"Em, do you have *any* idea who could have taken her?" Adam asked.

She shook her head while probing gently at Bowser's side. Bowie gave a sharp yelp and bared his teeth, struggling weakly in Connor's arms.

"Maybe the governor's men?" Emily suggested, still probing Bowser's side. He yelped again and she withdrew her hand. "His twelfth and thirteenth ribs are both broken. He might need surgery. I have to get him to my clinic. Hold him as still as you can," she said, speaking to Connor. "We don't want any of the fragments to puncture a lung."

Connor nodded.

"Your clinic?" Adam interrupted.

"I'm a vet—or a vet's assistant, anyway."

Adam nodded, relieved to know that Bowser was going to get the treatment he needed. "You said the governor might have taken Crystal?"

"Who else?" Emily asked. "Maybe he learned she was here and sent Rangers to pick her up." She shrugged. "If so, it shouldn't be hard to find out from our contact on the inside."

Adam pursed his lips, realizing now that it didn't make any sense for the governor to be involved, but Emily didn't know that Miller was expecting the coup, so it probably seemed like a reasonable suggestion to her.

Adam glanced around quickly to make sure they were alone before explaining that Connor and Major Hunter had betrayed the operation to the governor.

Emily's brow furrowed. She glared briefly at Connor, then her expression grew slack and she looked confused. "But if that's true, then…"

"He wouldn't have taken Crystal," Adam

concluded for her. "He wouldn't want to risk alerting us to his trap until he has us surrounded at his mansion tonight."

"Then who took her?" Connor asked miserably.

"Raiders," Ramirez whispered.

Everyone looked at her. The Latina woman looked uncomfortable under their combined scrutiny. Probably because her ethnicity made it seem like she might have first-hand experience with the Syndicate. They'd originated in Mexico, after all.

"Explain," Adam prompted.

Ramirez adjusted her patrol cap and tucked stray locks of black hair under it. "I never ran with any of their gangs, but I can tell you that the Vultures actually kind of liked it when raiders took people from Bexar because then they could blame the ones that they gave to the Specs on the raiders, too. It took the heat off of them."

"A convenient scapegoat," Stevens muttered.

"Exactly," Ramirez agreed.

Having lived in Bexar and worked as a Ranger for the past five years, Adam knew all about it, but they'd never found any raiders operating inside the safe zone. Of course, Travis was an unknown quantity. "If it was raiders," he began, "they'd want to get her out of the safe zone, and they'd want to do it before nightfall when they'd have stalkers to worry about."

"How would they smuggle her past the gates?" Connor asked. Vehicles are searched both coming and going."

"More coming than going," Adam said, but he saw Connor's point. Slavers working inside the zones would want a reliable way to smuggle people out. They could potentially bribe guards and time their exits to coincide with specific shifts, but it would be hard. Rangers rarely worked the same gates two days in a row, and schedules weren't always known in advance. Not to mention, there was always more than one guard. They'd need at least two on their payroll to make it work.

Adam found himself staring absently over Lady Bird Lake. That was when he realized what must have happened.

"They took her out on a boat," he whispered.

"What?" Connor asked, looking confused. "How do you know that?"

Private Ramirez and Corporal Stevens were both nodding.

"Because there won't be a gate across the lake," Adam explained.

"They must have some kind of perimeter guards," Connor objected.

"On the expressway bridge," Emily supplied, nodding quickly. "But they don't search boats *leaving* the zone. They search them when they come in."

"And by then, there won't be anyone to find," Adam said. "Whoever took her will have already made the drop."

"Shit," Connor muttered. "She could already be halfway up the river by now!"

"No, there's a dam," Emily said, pointing upstream.

"Right," Adam remembered it well. "The Tom Miller Dam. But that can't be more than a few miles from here."

Emily nodded.

"If they used a motorboat, they could have crossed it in minutes," Connor said.

"They wouldn't have," Emily replied. "Those get more scrutiny from Rangers. They'll have used a small recreational vessel to avoid drawing attention to themselves."

Adam grimaced.

"It doesn't matter if they were rowing," Connor decided. "It's been at least an hour since they took her."

"But how fast can a man row?" Stevens asked.

"Not *that* fast if they've got a boat big enough to hide an unconscious passenger," Adam replied. He tried to estimate, but it was hard without even knowing what kind of boat it was. "It would take about an hour to reach the dam. Maybe an hour and a half if they weren't in a rush."

"So they'd just be arriving there now,"

Connor concluded.

"Assuming that was their destination," Adam pointed out. He looked to Emily for the answer.

She appeared to think about it. "The guards on the expressway can see clear up the lake, but not all the way to the dam."

"Why not?" Adam asked.

"Because it goes around a bend at Red Bud Isle, right before you reach the dam."

Adam remembered the island. It was an off-leash dog park. He'd gone there with Bowser a couple of times to throw a Frisbee. "So if raiders wanted to hand over captives somewhere that's out of sight of the perimeter guards, then they'd have to do it there."

Emily nodded.

"They've got a decent lead on us. We're going to need a ride," Adam said next.

"We can use my mom's car," Emily suggested.

Adam was surprised that Sophie had a vehicle. That implied she must have an important job in Travis, but there was no time to ask about it now. "All right, let's haul ass. Deltas, fall in!" Adam broke into a sprint, not waiting for the others to acknowledge the order.

"Copy that!" Corporal Stevens replied. "You heard the sergeant! We're double-timing it to the Brooks' residence!"

Bowser yelped as Connor ran to catch up.

"Slow down!" Emily snapped at him. "You want to puncture his lung?"

"We have to hurry!" Connor objected.

Adam slowed and turned to address the situation. "Private Smith, take over for Private Cooper."

Smith's brow furrowed deeply above his tinted orange sunglasses. "Sergeant, you're going to need armed Rangers with you when you catch up with those raiders. Private Cooper is firing blanks."

"I'm not sitting this one out," Connor growled. "She's *my* fiancé!"

"All the more reason to have armed operatives rescue her," Smith insisted.

"After what he pulled, we can't leave Cooper alone," Corporal Stevens said.

Adam gritted out a sigh. "Smith, Connor, and Emily you bring up the rear at whatever pace you need to for Bowser's sake. Ramirez, Stevens, and myself will run ahead, get the car, and find Crystal."

"You have a bad leg," Connor argued. "You'll only slow them down. Send me with Ramirez and Stevens."

"I was doing ruck marches before you were born," Adam growled. "You have your orders— all of you! Fall in Deltas!"

"Yes, Sergeant!" everyone except for Connor shouted.

CHAPTER THIRTY-FIVE

"One hundred credits," Kent insisted. "She's easily worth that."

Kasey scowled. "Like I said, we don't have it on us."

Crystal felt nauseated listening to these raiders bartering over her.

Kent scowled. "Fine. Fifty now, fifty on credit to be paid with my next delivery."

Kasey appeared to consider that. She glanced at her partner, who shrugged but said nothing. "I think we can arrange that," Kasey agreed. She tucked the revolver back into its holster.

Crystal let out the breath she'd been holding, but she wasn't entirely relieved. The fact that they'd settled their differences wasn't good for her.

Kent smiled. "A pleasure doing business with you." He gave Crystal a shove, and she stumbled toward the raiders.

"Yeah, likewise," Kasey muttered. "Come on, girl. Hurry up."

Crystal shuffled toward them, her eyes

darting to the trees on either side of the road as she went. If she made a run for it, maybe she could lose them in the foliage.

But the odds of her outrunning any of them with her arms tied behind her back were abysmal. She'd probably trip and fall on her face, having gained nothing but a few scratches or a concussion for her trouble.

Kasey's partner crossed the gap between them and grabbed her arm, jerking her toward the truck. Something landed behind her with a quiet thump, and Crystal glanced back to see Kasey bending down to pick up the bag with her clothes and personal effects in it.

Kent backed away slowly, keeping the raiders covered with his gun until he passed around the corner and out of sight.

The man holding Crystal yanked open one of the back doors of the truck and shoved her inside. She fell inside, taking up the whole back seat.

Doors slammed, and the engine revved. Crystal craned her neck to watch as Kasey performed a three-point turn to get them facing back the other way.

"You escaped the Walmart when the Rangers came," Crystal said, watching the woman in the driver's seat.

"What was your first clue?" Kasey replied.

"Where is your son?" she asked.

"None of your fucking business," Kasey

snapped.

Crystal wondered if that meant he was dead, or if this was just more of the raiders' trademark hostility. Kasey hit the gas, spitting gravel and sending Crystal rolling into the back of the seats. She lay there on her side, watching sunlight flicker brightly through the trees, refracting on the cracked and dirty windshield.

The side windows were all broken except for one of the back two, leaving the wind to thunder through. She tasted the coarse grit of dust on her tongue, nearly choking as it paved her throat. Potholes made the suspension rattle and rocked the cab violently from side to side, but Kasey showed no signs of slowing down. She skidded through a sharp left turn, and Crystal rocked and wriggled around in the back, working herself up into a sitting position so that she could see where they were going. Thick foliage parted to reveal moss-covered stone walls and overgrown lawns leading to stately mansions.

The homes looked abandoned now, but Crystal could only imagine how opulent they must have been before the invasion. The further they went, the bigger and more impressive the homes became. Kasey blew through a stop street. A few seconds after that, she hit the brakes, and turned left across the oncoming lane toward a pair of old wrought-iron gates across two separate roads, one coming, one going. Crystal read the dirty signs on the pillars to either side of the gates.

Stratford P ace.

Place? she thought, filling in the missing letter.

A pair of armed raiders stepped out from behind those columns, and one of them pushed the gate on the right side open. Kasey rumbled through the opening, waving to the guard on her way through. He tossed a sloppy salute back. Crystal poked her head out the back window to watch as he pushed the gate shut behind them.

From the familiar way they'd greeted each other, Crystal realized that this band of raiders had probably been camped out here for a while. She wondered how many people they'd abducted and smuggled out of Travis right under the governor's nose. They couldn't be more than a few miles from the safe zone's perimeter. How was it possible that Rangers hadn't found them yet? That implied a deep level of corruption.

On the other side of the gates, the road immediately forked into two. Kasey went left again, rolling slowly by an old, cracked stone fountain. Kasey turned right immediately after the fountain, rolling through an open gate and up a long, wide cobblestone driveway that was big enough to park about thirty cars.

Like the roads, the driveway was overgrown

with weeds. The home it led to was in a similar state of disrepair, with peeling paint and broken windows that had been subsequently boarded up or covered from the inside with steel bars.

The mansion was better described as a hotel than a home, with a large detached three-car garage and guest house facing an attached three-car garage on the other side of the driveway. The home itself sprawled out from there, reaching three stories in height, with the third nestled in the attic.

Kasey drove straight into the furthest space in the attached garage, where one of the doors was already gaping open. As soon as she'd parked, the garage door went rumbling down behind them, plunging the garage into darkness. A bobbing lantern approached the vehicle, blinding Crystal as it drew near. Someone opened her door from the outside just as both Kasey and her partner opened their doors and climbed out.

The raider holding the lantern reached in and dragged Crystal out.

"*Jefa,* you want me to put her with the others?" he asked in thickly accented English.

Crystal caught a glimpse of the man's features—tanned cheeks and a scruffy black beard. He was short, but wearing a big cowboy hat that added to his height.

"Not yet, Eduardo," Kasey said. "Bring her

into the main house. I want her to meet Cory."

"Cory?" the man asked. "Why Cory?"

"Just bring her into the house."

"Yes, boss…" Eduardo replied.

She's in charge? Crystal wondered as the man with the lantern led her through the garage to a door at the back. He pushed her toward a short flight of steps behind Kasey and her accomplice. She opened the door and they breezed through into a cozy sitting room with old, dusty furniture that was bleeding yellow stuffing from punctures that looked like bullet holes.

A wall of shattered lattice windows looked out on the grounds behind the home, revealing a broad, paved mezzanine around a dormant fountain that overlooked a pool below. The windows had been crudely reinforced from the inside with rusty metal bars that were anchored to the floor and ceiling at regular intervals. The old window frame was splintered in the middle, leaving a gaping hole big enough for a stalker to creep in, were it not for the metal bars.

From the sitting room they progressed to a big, open living area with high, double-story ceilings. A couple of raiders were lounging on the couches in the living room, playing a game of poker with gleaming stacks of credits. One of them was skinny and pasty-white with long, stringy black hair and angry red sunburns on his arms, nose, and the back of his neck. The other was big and muscular with darkly tanned skin and cutaway sleeves revealing thick arms covered in faded tattoos. He wore a black leather vest with bright yellow patches all over it, and a red bandanna tied around his head. A thick crop of salt and pepper stubble shadowed his cheeks. Crystal realized that she'd seen him before—back in Hondo where she'd met Kasey.

Kasey cleared her throat, and both men looked at her. The skinny raider frowned unhappily, but the bigger man nodded to her as if to say *'sup*. He leaned back and draped his arms over the back of the couch. Then he appeared to notice Crystal and his dark eyes narrowed as they slithered appraisingly over her from head to toe.

Crystal wanted to vomit from the way he was looking at her. He didn't appear to recognize her, but Crystal wasn't sure yet if that was a good or a bad thing.

"Where is Cory?" Kasey asked.

"In his room," the big man answered in a deep, throaty voice. He jerked his chin to Crystal. "Why does she look familiar?"

Crystal grimaced, realizing that she'd read him wrong.

"Go get him," Kasey snapped at the skinny one.

"I ain't your errand boy!" he replied.

"Just do it, John," the big man growled. "I don't need you two measuring dicks today."

The skinny raider stood up with a scowl and stormed away, disappearing quickly into the shadowy recesses of the mansion.

"So, Kase, are you gonna answer me, or are you waiting for me to guess? Where do I know this girl from?"

She sighed, looking annoyed. "You remember those people we took in just before Rangers descended on us in Hondo?"

"Ahhhh…" the man's voice creaked like rusty hinges. "The ones with the gunshot victim who needed a transfusion."

"Yeah." Kasey nodded. "Them."

Crystal pretended to ignore the fact that they were talking about her as if she wasn't there. She took a moment to study the view from the big, curving wall of lattice windows at the far end of the living room. Like the windows in the sitting room, these were also broken and reinforced with metal bars. Due to the sheer height of the room, there were also several cross beams bolted to opposing walls.

"Small world," the big guy in the biker vest said.

Crystal stared out over overgrown grounds. The pool was in full view below the mezzanine. It was missing big patches of tiles and was only half-full of dirty, mossy green water. Beyond that, dense walls of trees went marching abruptly down a steep cliff to the river below. On the other side, Crystal saw the sprawling wastes, and far in the distance behind that, a shadowy wall of alien jungle that soared as a stark reminder that humans weren't the only thing to worry about in this world. Crystal belatedly realized that this mansion and the others in the neighborhood were the decrepit mansions that she'd seen perched on that cliff overlooking the river.

"What's your name, girl?" the big man finally asked.

"Crystal," she managed, risking a brief glance at him as she said it.

"Pretty name," he replied. "You'll do all right."

She shivered, and he smiled. "Hey, don't worry, cupcake. It's not as bad as you think."

"Oh?" Crystal challenged, cocking an eyebrow at him. Her whole body was shaking with dread, but she managed to thrust out her chin defiantly and scowl at the raider. "What would *you* know about it? Have you been traded like a commodity to the scum of the earth and then sent to work in a brothel full of ugly disease-ridden pigs?"

The man's smile flickered, and his expression became confused. He looked at Kasey and shook his head. "Damn, Kase, is that what you told her we do?"

"I didn't tell her shit," Kasey growled,

looking annoyed. She glanced back in the direction that the other raider had gone, looking impatient.

The other two who'd come with them from the garage were still there, but hanging back in the shadows and chatting in low tones around a massive kitchen island. So far, Crystal counted five raiders, plus the two guards at the gates. If her dad found her here, he'd probably have at least a couple of others with him— Connor, at the very least. That made two or three against seven. Those odds weren't too bad, but how long would the raiders keep her here? Would her dad even find her before they moved her somewhere else?

The one with the Mexican accent had mentioned taking her to *the others. Other captives?* she wondered. If there were more captives here, then the odds were that they had at least a couple more guards watching them. *That makes nine,* Crystal decided.

"Let me put your mind at ease," the man in the biker jacket said. He removed his arms from the couch and leaned forward, propping his elbows on his knees. "You're not going to be sold to a brothel."

Crystal frowned, doing her best to look bored as she waited for him to describe her fate. A cautious thread of hope wove into her thoughts. Maybe she was going to be a different kind of slave.

"You'll be sold on the open market to the highest bidder," the raider explained. "The ones with the deepest pockets are the *directors,* and you'd make a worthy addition to any of their harems. That's a lot better than a brothel. You'll be treated well. Even pampered."

Crystal shivered again as that cautious thread of hope burst into flames. Joining a harem full of women that belonged to some vicious kingpin wasn't much better than working in a brothel. But maybe her owner would get bored, and she'd wind up lounging around his mansion with nothing better to do than keep up her appearance.

Crystal's thoughts were interrupted by the repeated squeaking of a rusty wheel. She turned to see what was causing it—

And saw another vaguely familiar face. It belonged to a Caucasian man with shaggy blonde hair, hollow cheeks lurking below a thick beard, and dead, staring eyes. He was sitting in an old wheelchair being pushed by the skinny raider that Kasey had ordered to go and get *Cory.*

"Do you recognize him?" Kasey asked.

Crystal slowly shook her head, unsure of what she'd be admitting to if she said that she did.

"Are you positive?" Kasey drew the engraved revolver from her hip and held it up. "This was his. Cory used it to shoot the man that you brought to us."

Crystal's eyes flared as her mind flashed back to a memory of him stepping into a sunlit clearing in a trailer park outside Bandera. That had been just after he'd shot Owen. She remembered watching it happen from the back of the truck with Connor, Emily, and Sophie. Owen had his hands raised. He wasn't even a threat, but this man had shot him anyway.

She was glad that he was paralyzed. He deserved every bit of suffering that he had endured, but she didn't dare to let that reaction show.

Kasey went on, "According to Cory, a tall man with buzz-cut blonde hair and a limp was the one who shot him in the back and killed my husband. That sounds kind of like your father, doesn't it?"

Crystal refused to acknowledge the woman's guess, but Kasey smiled thinly and nodded as if she had.

Cory spoke in a thready whisper that made it sound like he hadn't used his voice in a while. His lips barely moved, but Crystal heard him loud and clear. "I want her," he said.

Crystal felt the blood draining from her face. What did he mean by that? He was in a wheelchair, obviously paralyzed from the waist down, so it couldn't mean what she thought it meant, could it? But somehow, the other possibilities were even worse.

Crystal realized that this wasn't just about selling her to the Syndicate for credits anymore. It was about revenge.

CHAPTER THIRTY-SIX

Adam arrived at Emily's house exhausted and out of breath, with a deep, fiery ache running from his calf to his hip. He did his best not to show it, but by this point, he was limp-running no matter how much he ignored the pain.

Adam hurried up the walkway of a large two-story home with a wraparound porch with peeling yellow siding and white trim.

He stepped quickly across the slumping wooden boards and hammered his fist on the door. He was in such a hurry that he completely forgot to use the Nightingales' signature knock. He tried again.

Knock—knock-knock—knock.

The door swung open before he even finished the last knock. Sophie appeared at the entrance, looking older and more world-weary than he remembered, with plenty of gray showing through her frizzy brown hair.

She blinked at the sight of him, then took a step back and crossed her arms over her chest. "Hello, Adam…" she said slowly. Her eyes flicked past him to the other two Rangers behind him. "What's this about?" she asked.

"We need your car," he managed between ragged breaths. He winced from the pain in his leg and leaned heavily on the door jamb.

"My car?" Sophie arched an eyebrow at him. "I don't think so."

"They took Crystal."

Shock transformed Sophie's face. "What? Who did?"

"Raiders."

Her eyes darted past him. "Where is Emily?"

"She's fine," Adam said, "bringing up the rear with Connor and Bowser. Whoever took her broke his ribs." Adam straightened from the door jamb. "Sophie, we're short on time. We need that vehicle."

She nodded. "Come in and catch your breath while I get the keys."

"Thank you."

Adam entered the home, nearly tripping over the threshold. *Pull yourself together, Adam,* he chided himself.

Corporal Stevens and Private Ramirez came in behind him and shut the door. They stood around in the entryway, waiting for Sophie to return.

"Water's in the kitchen in case you need some!" she called from the recesses of the home.

Adam frowned and reached for the canteen in his pack. "We've got our own, ma'am," Corporal Steven answered for him.

Adam looked around disinterestedly. A staircase rose to his right, a coat closet on the left. An office or maybe a dining room came after that, followed by what he supposed was the kitchen and living area.

The house was relatively well-maintained. The walls looked recently painted, and the wooden floors were clean. Adam tried a light switch next to the door and found that the light bulbs in the chandelier all worked, which was unusual. Adam was trying to understand what kind of position Sophie had that she'd been given a car. Given her pre-invasion occupation as a nurse, maybe she worked at a hospital. Since he didn't have a medic on his team, she might be a valuable addition.

Sophie appeared a moment later, striding quickly down the hall with a set of keys jingling in her hand. "It's an old beater, but it'll get you where you need to go."

Adam spared a hand from his carbine to reach for the keys. Just before he could take them, they were interrupted by the sound of wheels skidding on asphalt and heavy doors slamming.

Adam withdrew sharply, silently indicating for Ramirez and Stevens to check the curtained windows to either side of the front door. They each peeked through the curtains.

"We've got Rangers incoming. Two Humvees full," Stevens warned.

Adam grimaced. Maybe raiders hadn't taken Crystal, after all. "Is there another exit?" he whispered to Sophie.

She nodded. "Out the back. You might have to jump a fence or two, but the neighbors aren't home."

"All right, let's go," Adam ordered, already limp-running down the hall.

"Wait—" Ramirez interrupted from her place by the front door. "Does that look like Mayor Ellis to you, Corporal?"

"He's wearing a hoodie, how can you tell?" she countered.

"His walk. He waddles."

"Shit, it *is* him."

Adam spun back around. "Get them inside, quickly," he ordered.

Sophie ran to the door and yanked it open. Sergeant Chase came bustling in with a pair of Rangers on his heels, followed by Mayor Ellis—and Carla!

She ran to Adam and they collided in a hug. "I heard about Crystal," she whispered. "I'm so sorry, Adam."

"Who told you?"

"Connor. We ran into him along the way. He's almost here."

Adam nodded.

The hallway quickly became overcrowded. The door clicked shut, and hazy shadows swept over them. Sophie suggested they speak in the living room and turned to lead the way.

"I need to go after Crystal," Adam objected as he trailed behind them.

"You need a plan to do that," Ellis said. "What are you going to do when you get to the gate and the soldiers check your names against their logs only to find that there's no record of you legally entering Travis?"

Adam grimaced. Dammit, Ellis was right. He couldn't just blast out of the safe zone with no questions asked. He needed someone to smuggle him out.

Carla's hand touched his arm in a calming gesture. "It's okay," she said. "We'll figure this out."

They reached the living room and Ellis went to stand in front of the fireplace, raising his hands to get everyone's attention. "I understand that there are competing interests at play here, but the mission is still our first priority. We've managed to get Major Hunter tentatively back on our side. He has assured us that he hasn't told the enemy everything and that he was only going through the motions with this betrayal. The Vultures have been letting him see his daughter who was taken by the Specs at the start of the invasion. They promised to get her released, but that never happened, so he's a grudging traitor at best. Hunter will remain in radio contact with the enemy from a controlled setting so that Miller doesn't realize we're onto him. That should buy us time to come up with an alternate plan."

Hearing that Hunter had flipped back to their side put a frown on Adam's face. After everything the major had done, how did they know that they could trust him? They probably had him at gunpoint whenever he had to use the radio, but even so, it was risky. But at least it sounded like he hadn't betrayed Ellis's project to inoculate people against the invaders' parasites.

The mayor went on, "We need to either commit to a new plan or get out of Travis before nightfall. I need ideas… anyone?" he asked with his eyes roving through the room.

Adam scowled. "You can do whatever you want, but I'm going to find my daughter and get the hell out of here."

Ellis fixed him with a disappointed look. "Then you'll be placing your daughter's life above all of ours, and above the cause itself. Sympathetic as I might be, she's just one person, and this operation can and will go on without her."

"Good," Adam replied. "Then it can also go on without *two* people because I'm leaving."

"I'm afraid I can't allow that," Ellis replied. He gestured vaguely to someone, and hands seized Adam's arms, holding him in place.

"What the fuck, Ellis!" Adam roared.

"Keep your voice down. We're conspicuous enough as it is with two Humvees parked outside. Listen, I didn't say we have to sacrifice your daughter or forget about her, only that I need you to stay on task. Give me a solution. You need a ride out of the city. We might be able to help with that, but I need a good reason to send my men out there and take that risk."

"How about the fact that a girl who traveled with your convoy this morning went missing by Lady Bird Lake, and you suspect that raiders smuggled her out on a boat?"

Ellis frowned. "That might work. But what about our mission? How does committing assets to get her back advance our cause?"

Adam licked his lips, his mind racing at light speed. There had to be a way to convince Ellis to stick his neck out for this. Something. Anything...

An all-but-forgotten memory trickled to the forefront of Adam's mind, and suddenly he had it. "The bunker below the Capitol."

"Excuse me?" Ellis asked.

All eyes were on Adam now. "There's a bunker beneath the Capitol. You can get into it through a crack in the ceiling just outside the east wall of the city. If you can blow the door to the stairwell that leads back up to the Capitol building, then you'll be able to get in there without being seen. That puts you just a block away from the Governor's Mansion. He might not expect us to pop up there."

Ellis's eyes lit up. "How do you know about this?"

"My daughter and son-in-law and—" Adam cut himself off, glancing around for Sophie. "—and her husband," he added, pointing to her. "—crawled out through there when the governor locked us in his bunker to die."

Ellis was grinning now. "This is brilliant! If I'd only known about it earlier... but then I suppose this plan would also be compromised thanks to Major Hunter."

"How does this help us?" Sergeant Chase asked.

"That bunker is connected to the Governor's Mansion by a tunnel," Ellis explained.

Adam blinked in shock at that revelation.

Ellis continued, "If we threaten the governor at his mansion, he will almost certainly use the tunnel to escape. We could be waiting there for him when he does." Ellis looked to Carla, and then to Sophie. "It looks like we'll need to distribute those fliers we printed, after all. We're going to start a riot, and march on his mansion, not with soldiers, but with civilians. Miller won't have Rangers mow down his own people. He'll just remove himself from the premises when things get too hot."

Adam frowned. "The governor's bunker was

overrun with stalkers. He won't evacuate there."

Ellis shook his head. "The tunnel leads to the bunker and the Capitol. There are separate entrances for each. If he knows the bunker isn't safe, he won't go there, but he'll still use his tunnel to escape the rioters. And when he does, we'll be waiting on the other side. Ironically, Adam, your daughter's abduction has given us exactly the excuse we need to go poking around outside the walls with our troops."

"Well, I'm glad she could be of service, after all," Adam replied.

"Go find her," Ellis said. "You can join us when you're done—or don't. You've already handed us everything we need to win this fight."

The front door flew open behind them, and everyone spun around to see Connor, Emily, and Private Smith come in, the latter carrying Bowser.

Emily and Connor ran down the hall, exchanging hugs and greetings with Sophie and Carla respectively. Adam went straight to Ellis. "Time is not on our side. If I'm going to find my daughter, then we need to move now."

"I understand," Ellis said. "Sergeant Chase?"

"Sir?"

"I need to know which of these Rangers entered the safe zone as official escorts for our convoy."

Chase nodded. "Yes, sir." He directed the Rangers to divide themselves into two groups —the ones who were smuggled in like himself, Adam, and Connor on the left, and the ones who'd registered at the gate on the right. Adam spotted both Corporal Stevens and Private Ramirez among the officially registered escorts, as well as Private Lee. Adam indicated that he wanted Stevens and Ramirez with him to look for Crystal, and Ellis made the remaining selections, including Private Lee in his group.

"I'm going with you," Connor said. "I'm not taking no for an answer."

"You absolutely are," Ellis agreed as he crossed the living room to join the eight Rangers that they'd chosen to leave the city. "But you're going to lead me to where you escaped the governor's bunker. Adam is perfectly capable of finding your fiancée on his own."

"I won't help you until I know that she's safe," Connor insisted.

Ellis sighed theatrically. "I'm afraid you don't have a choice, Private. If you don't do this, I won't smuggle anyone out to look for Crystal, and we'll find the entrance of the bunker for ourselves."

"You'll never find it before tonight," Connor said.

"I'll take my chances," Ellis replied.

"We're wasting time," Adam growled. "Connor, go with the mayor. I don't need a soldier that I can't trust."

"That's not fair," Connor objected.

Carla scowled at Adam, crossing her arms over her chest. Did she even know how Connor had betrayed them? If she did, then she was taking the wrong side in this argument, and Adam didn't appreciate it.

"I did this for Crystal, and you know it," Connor said. "Let me help you find her."

"Lead them to the bunker," Adam replied. "I'll find Crystal. Mayor?"

"Yes, Sergeant?"

"We need to move out before this operation gets any more complicated."

"I agree," Ellis said. "I'll hide you and Connor in the back of my vehicle. We should be able to avoid a search with the urgency of our mission to find Crystal. Sergeant Chase, Mrs. Hall, Mrs. Brooks—"

"Sir?" Chase asked, and Carla and Sophie both looked at him.

"I need the three of you to get everyone else organized. Spread the word, as quietly as you can, about the governor's dealings with the Specs. Stoke the outrage and organize a demonstration tonight at his mansion."

"Yes, sir," Chase said.

Sophie nodded. "I'll call the local conclave together for an emergency meeting."

"Good," Ellis replied. "We're counting on a big turnout. It needs to be enough to spook the governor into evacuating."

"Understood, sir. We'll take care of it," Chase said.

"I know you will." Ellis turned and led the way to the front door. Adam hesitated, hanging back for a second to look for Carla. His eyes met hers. She still looked angry, but her expression softened somewhat. "Be careful, Adam," she said.

He nodded. "You, too."

And then he went running down the hall after Corporal Stevens and Private Ramirez. Connor came rushing up beside him. "If you don't find her, I'll never forgive you."

"Yeah, likewise," Adam replied. "Don't forget whose fault it is that she's here. If you want to blame someone, you can start with yourself."

"Trust me, I already am," Connor said, his voice cracking. "Just find her and bring her back to me. Please."

Adam nodded stiffly. "I will. But if she's smart, she'll dump your ass after this."

Connor said nothing to that. Maybe he'd finally realized he wasn't good enough for her.

CHAPTER THIRTY-SEVEN

"Hold your horses, Cory," the big raider said. "I know you've got an ax to grind, but we don't mess with product." He amended that with a shrug. "At least, not with grade A product like her. We need to deliver her in *pristine* condition."

"Bobby," Kasey intoned darkly, giving Crystal a name for the big raider in the biker vest. "We can use her to lure her father here."

Crystal's eyes widened sharply at that. *No...* she thought. *Say no. Say no...*

The big man frowned and leaned back against the couch while stroking his darkly-stubbled chin. "Seems like a whole lot of trouble to go to just for you to get your jollies, Kase."

"It's not just for me. Cory, too. And you owe me," Kasey growled.

"Do I now? How's that?"

"Do I need to spell it out for you? You know

what they did. What you *let* them do!" She shook the revolver at him, her eyes wild and feral as spittle sprayed from her lips. "Caleb would still be here if you hadn't been such a fucking *coward*."

Bobby drew himself up and slowly stood. "What did you just call me?"

Kasey licked her lips, her chest heaving. She looked completely unhinged like she could murder everyone in the room without even blinking, but her finger never entered the trigger guard of the revolver.

"Listen up, Kase, the Specs took your boy, not me. That I didn't go runnin' after them guns blazin' sure as hell ain't cowardice. That's just plain old common sense. Now, I'm gonna give you a free pass on this because you're still grieving, and I know what it's like to lose somebody, but you need to pack that shit in and remember who the enemy is."

Crystal studied the raiders, her gaze flicking back and forth from Bobby to Kasey, wondering how much bad blood there was between them, and how she might be able to exploit it.

"Her father took Jaden from me," Kasey said. "Maybe you couldn't go after the Specs, but you *can* do something about the bastard who killed one of your *falcons*."

Bobby sighed. "All right, fine. I'll give you this. Probably best to tie off all the loose ends anyway."

"How are we gonna do it?" the skinny man standing behind Cory's wheelchair asked. "I mean, are we just gonna go lookin' for him and lead him here, or..."

Bobby glanced at him. "John, take the girl upstairs and lock her in one of the guest rooms. There's no sense discussing our business in front of her. Especially seein' as how it's got to do with her daddy."

The skinny raider nodded and abandoned Cory's wheelchair in the middle of the room. He crossed swiftly over to Crystal, grabbed her arm, and began dragging her away.

She jerked free and turned to sneer at Bobby. "My dad is going to kill all of you when he gets here."

"Oh, will he now?" Bobby seemed genuinely amused by the threat. "I sincerely doubt that, but it might be nice to have some action. We've been stuck in a bit of a rut lately." He waved dismissively to her, and the skinny raider grabbed her arm again.

"Move it!" he shouted in her ear as she struggled to break free once more, but this time his dirty fingernails dug in to the point of bruising and drew a stifled cry from her lips.

"Music to my ears," he said. "I like 'em better when they scream."

Crystal gave him a horrified look, and he gave a *sissing* laugh, sounding just like the snake that he was. The others laughed with him, all except for Kasey, who glared hatefully at her instead.

Crystal thought about all of the other women that these people must have taken and sold across the border to the Syndicate, some of them probably just children. Bile stung the back of her throat, and suddenly she found herself rooting for the Specs. *Let them kill us all. Good riddance,* she thought bitterly. *We don't deserve to make it if this is how we pull together at the end of the world.*

They came to the end of a long, opulent hallway cloaked in shadows, and the skinny raider slowed and fixed her with a hungry look. Crystal pretended not to notice, focusing instead on the echoing foyer with its sweeping staircases on either side of the entry hall. She noticed a balcony overlooking the entrance from the second floor.

"You know," the man whispered close beside her ear. "This don't have to be so hard," he purred. "Maybe you'd like to make a friend around here?"

Crystal's upper lip curled involuntarily at what he was implying.

"Oh, don't be shy, darling," he said, blasting her with foul breath and flashing a grin full of crooked teeth. He nudged her toward the foot of the nearest stairwell. John's teeth perfectly matched his stringy, sweat-matted hair. Apparently, he had something against basic hygiene. He let go of her arm and brushed her cheek with a trembling hand. "I can be gentle, too," he added.

Crystal drew herself up and nodded pointedly in the direction they'd come from. "Bobby said that I need to be delivered in *pristine* condition, remember?"

"He sure did," John agreed. "But there's a whole lot that a boy and a girl can do together that don't leave a mark. It'd be our little secret."

Crystal couldn't contain her revulsion this time. She swallowed thickly, her lips trembling and guts churning. "I'll scream," she said.

"Oh, darling, don't tease me like that. I told you I can't resist a good screamer." He wrapped a cold hand around her throat and squeezed until the fuzzy darkness of the foyer thickened to a soup. "Go ahead," he whispered with his lips mere inches away from hers. Foul, alcohol-soured breath invaded her nostrils. "Let's see what you've got."

"That's enough!" Kasey interrupted.

John turned to look, and his hand quickly fell away from Crystal's throat. She took full advantage of his inattention and brought her knee up as hard as she could between his legs. John doubled over with a strangled squeak, and stumbled back a few steps, struggling to breathe through the pain. With his hands planted on his knees and his head bowed, he fumbled for a knife on his belt and drew it with a gleaming flash of steel.

"You're gonna pay for that!"

Crystal's heart beat like thunder in her ears as she eyed the knife.

Kasey stepped swiftly between them. "I'm taking her upstairs."

"Bobby told *me* to do that."

"He changed his mind."

"Bull*shit*!" John gasped, still struggling with the pain.

"He's not an idiot, he knows what you are," Kasey sneered, and then she spat on the floor at his feet.

John finally straightened and fixed her with flashing eyes, his knife held in a tight fist. "And what is that?" he hissed.

"A sadist, a rapist, a murderer... should I go on?"

"That sounds like a basic resume for what we do, sister."

"I'm not your sister," Kasey hissed.

John flashed another grin. "That's right, sweetheart. You ain't. Best you remember that next time you cross me."

Crystal noticed that Kasey's hand was resting on the engraved handle of her revolver. "Was that a threat?" she asked quietly.

"No, darling. Just a simple statement of fact." He re-sheathed his knife. Looking past her, he smiled and nodded to Crystal. "I'll be seein' *you* later." With that, he turned and strode away.

"Fucking lunatic," Kasey muttered.

The tension left Crystal's body like an elastic snapping.

"Up the stairs," Kasey ordered.

This time Crystal went without complaint, climbing the steps on violently shaking legs. As she went, she wondered if Kasey might ironically turn out to be her only ally in this hell hole. "Thank you," Crystal managed.

"Don't thank me. I'm not your friend."

"I know," Crystal said, but she was grateful all the same.

They reached the top of the stairs in silence, passing the balcony that overlooked the entry hall, and then continued down a broad, door-lined corridor with creaky wooden floors. Kasey stopped beside the third door on the right and turned the knob, revealing a massive bedroom with a messy four-post bed and very little else.

"Make yourself comfortable," Kasey suggested, giving her a helpful shove from behind.

Crystal stumbled forward, only narrowly avoiding falling on her face. The door banged shut behind her, and then she heard the handle jiggle and a metallic click as the lock turned. Crystal turned to look, noting the old, antique door handle with a keyhole beneath it. Short of breaking the door down, she wasn't getting out without that key.

She switched to studying her surroundings for some other avenue of escape. The room's only window was just like the ones below, reinforced with steel bars that were bolted to the floor and ceiling.

But they'd left her in here unattended, and that was something. If she could get her hands free, then maybe she could remove one of those bars and climb out the window.

Crystal studied the old four-post bed, the night tables, and then the wardrobe, wondering if there was anything in here sharp enough to cut the ropes that bound her hands. The wooden floors were buckling and warped beneath crumbling, moldy patches of plaster where rain had been leaking in. A door stood open to an en suite bathroom. She headed in there, struggling to open the cabinet beneath the sink, and then using her teeth to open the one over the toilet. Both were empty, except for half of an old toilet roll. The raiders had already screened the room for anything that could be used against them.

But Crystal wasn't ready to give up. Her gaze settled on the toilet, and she remembered something. Years ago, back at the ranch, her Dad had been fixing a toilet that wouldn't flush. She'd walked in on him to show him a drawing that she'd made of him, her, and Bowser. He'd turned to look and accidentally knocked the toilet tank cover off the bathroom sink. It had shattered into a million pieces. He'd gotten mad and yelled at her, and she'd bent down to help him pick up the pieces. In the process, she'd accidentally cut her palm. Those pieces of ceramic were a lot sharper than she'd expected.

Crystal chewed her bottom lip, considering how much noise it would make if she tried to break the tank cover now. Would those raiders come running up to see what had made the sound? Probably. But it *was* a very big house. Maybe the sound wouldn't carry that far? Crystal moved to the toilet and turned around to work her fingertips under the edge of the tank cover.

She managed to wiggle it off and began nudging it gently toward the tiled floor on the other side. After a few seconds, she had it teetering precariously above the tiles. Flexing her fingers sharply, she tipped it over. The lid fell with a crash.

But it didn't break.

Crystal stood staring at it with her heart hammering in her chest, wondering if the raiders were already on their way up to see what had happened. If Bobby sent John instead of Kasey, she could be in for more trouble than she'd bargained for.

Crystal waited a handful of seconds, listening to the silence for signs of a reaction from downstairs. When she didn't hear anything, she let out a shaky breath and glanced around the bathroom for inspiration. She needed a bigger drop or a harder surface to shatter the tank cover.

Seeing the shower gave her an idea. The threshold of the shower was a low tiled rim designed to keep water in. Above that was a glass door. She moved to the shower and pushed the door open. It banged softly against the far wall, leaving the tiled rim exposed. Going back to the toilet cover, she bent awkwardly with her knees until her fingertips curled around the tank lid. She lifted with her legs and walked awkwardly to the shower, lining up the ceramic lid with the tiled edge of the threshold. As soon as it was in position, she stood up on tiptoes and shrugged her shoulders to get a little extra height and momentum. Then she dropped it and stepped quickly away.

It fell with another booming crash. Crystal flinched at the noise and spun around to look. This time the tank cover had broken, but not into a million convenient pieces like it had with her dad all those years ago. Instead, it had simply cracked in half, leaving two big chunks with exposed edges and a handful of tiny fragments that wouldn't be good for anything. The edges looked sharp enough to be useful, but Crystal was worried that someone might be coming up to check on her, so she ran out of the bathroom and shut the bathroom door behind her—which was no easy task with her hands tied behind her back.

That done, she stood staring at the door, her pulse pounding like a drumbeat in her ears, and a cold sweat prickling along her spine. For a moment it seemed that no one had heard anything.

But then the door handle began to jiggle. Crystal bolted for the four-post bed and dropped to the floor beside it. She leaned precariously against the night table and arranged her legs and body facing the door in a way that looked haphazard. The door flew open. To Crystal's relief, it was Kasey, not John.

"What the hell are you doing in here?"

Crystal managed a wincing smile. "I was trying to get comfortable on the bed, but with my hands tied behind me, I rolled off…"

Kasey glared at her suspiciously for another second while glancing around to make sure there wasn't another explanation for the noise. She gave up with a scowl and looked back to Crystal. "If I were you, I'd *stay* on the floor. If you give John another excuse to come up here, I won't be able to stop him."

Crystal nodded quickly, doing her best to look terrified. It wasn't hard.

Kasey withdrew, shutting and locking the door behind her. Crystal clambered off the floor. She half-waddled and half-ran back to the bathroom, opened the door, and dropped down beside the shattered halves of the tank lid. Carefully maneuvering her wrists and hands, she positioned them so that the rope around her wrists was positioned beside one of the sharp edges. And then Crystal began sawing the ropes back and forth.

She continued maniacally at that for the next ten minutes before taking a break to catch her breath and rest. Pins and needles were shooting up and down both arms, making it hard to feel her fingers, and her wrists felt like they'd been sliced open from all the chafing, but she couldn't afford to be weak right now.

Her one desperate hope was suddenly her worst fear—that her dad or Connor would come here to rescue her. Those raiders downstairs were actively planning for it, plotting to lure them in with her as bait. She *couldn't* allow that to happen.

Crystal went at it again for a few more minutes. Sweat trickled maddeningly from her brow, dripping into her eyes and making them sting. Growing tired, she accidentally ran one of her wrists along the sharpened edge, slicing it open with a hot flash of blood. She took a break to get a look at the injury and saw blood running between her wrists, seeping into the coarse brown ropes and dripping from her fingertips. It was pretty bad, but not bad enough to stop her.

Crystal started sawing the ropes again, being more careful this time. After another five minutes, something gave way, loosening to the point that she could roll her wrists. She strained her arms and shoulders against the ropes, putting all of her strength into it.

Suddenly, her arms flew away from her sides, and she caught a glimpse of the torn, bloody flesh of the gash in her wrist. Crystal gently probed at the injury with her fingertips, noting that the gash was running along the outside edge of her right wrist. She'd missed all of the major arteries, but it still needed stitches. Crystal settled for mopping up the blood and putting pressure on it with the hem of her tank top. As she did so, she noticed something else—

Her engagement ring was missing.

Kent must have taken it after he'd knocked her out.

Crystal blinked stupidly at the sight of her naked finger, remembering how Connor had proposed to her on that sunset boat ride around the Riverwalk in Bexar. After she'd said yes, he'd taken her to dinner at the Drury and then they spent the night together in one of its finest rooms. He'd aptly recreated their first night together in the city, but this time, they weren't kids anymore, and they'd shared the same bed.

Crystal smiled fondly at the memory, and

her eyes blurred with tears that swiftly fell and made muddy puddles on the floor. Somehow, she was going to get out of this. They'd overthrow the governor, and then they'd get married, have kids, and build the life that they'd always dreamed about together.

Crystal's lips trembled and more tears fell. Even accomplishing *one* of those things sounded impossible now, let alone all of them. No wonder Connor had changed his mind about having kids with her. The odds were not in their favor.

Maybe they never had been.

CHAPTER THIRTY-EIGHT

Brakes squealed softly and one of the Rangers in the back of the Humvee whispered, "We're at the gate."

Adam lay still in the darkness of the trunk, working hard to slow and control his breathing. Connor was busy doing the same, lying just inches from Adam's nose. The two of them were concealed in the back by a heavy-duty canvas tarp that the other Rangers had thrown over them. They'd also stacked cases of supplies and ammo between them and the cabin of the vehicle, making sure that the only way anyone would see them was to crack open the armored trunk.

Moments later, Adam heard Ellis speaking with one of the guards, explaining where they were going and why. But the Ranger wasn't convinced that a missing person was a good enough excuse to skip the usual procedures.

"I still need to search your vehicle, Mr.

Mayor," the man said.

"As I said, we're in a hurry," Ellis growled.

"I can't break protocol, sir. It's my job. We'll be quick. I promise."

"This is absurd! I am the mayor of Bexar, and when I tell you that a close personal friend of mine was abducted from your city by raiders, you should be tripping over your own feet to get out of my way. Damn, son, have you no shame? This happened in your city, on your watch! What's your name?"

"Uh… Lieutenant Johnson, sir."

"Okay, Lieutenant Johnson, I'm going to bust your ass back to private and stick you on the night watch for the next six months. Does that sound like a fair trade for your idiotic protocols?"

"Sir, I really can't let you go without searching—"

"The hell you can't! Now raise that boom before I drive through it and leave you to pay for the damages out of your pathetic salary."

"Y-yes, sir!"

Adam let out a shaky breath as he heard footsteps retreating from their vehicle. The engine roared sharply, and the Humvee jerked into motion, rumbling away.

Connor looked about as relieved as Adam felt.

"Don't get too excited," Adam whispered. "That was the easy part."

He waited a minute before he risked peeking out from under the tarp. He was just in time to see Ellis turning off the main road, headed for the lake.

Old abandoned apartment buildings flashed by to their right. Ellis drove straight to the edge of the water and hit the brakes. "This is your stop, Sergeant!" Ellis said.

"I'm ready," Adam replied.

Doors flew open, and Rangers piled out. The armored trunk rose, and Adam threw off the tarp and scooted out. Cooper began to follow him, but the Ranger who'd opened the trunk held up a hand and slowly shook his head.

"Private Cooper, you're staying with us. Mayor's orders."

Connor gritted his teeth but said nothing. They'd already had this conversation back at Sophie's house.

Adam reached back in for his carbine. He peered over the tops of the supplies and ammo boxes to meet Ellis's gaze. "I'll need the other vehicle, sir." He jerked a thumb to the second Humvee.

Ellis regarded him steadily. "Take it."

"Thank you, sir."

"Good luck, Sergeant. I hope that you find your daughter. I mean that."

Adam nodded, not wanting to waste any more time. He ran to the other truck and yanked open the driver's side door. Corporal

Stevens regarded him with one eyebrow raised, her coppery hair leaking out from under her patrol cap. "Sergeant?" she asked.

"I'm driving," Adam explained.

"Copy that," Stevens replied, jumping out in a hurry. Adam took her place behind the wheel and stowed his carbine in the door. He twisted around to regard the two Rangers in the back. Ramirez was already seated beside him, so he said, "You two, get out. You're with the mayor."

"Yes, Sergeant," one of them answered, and then they both smoothly exited the vehicle.

Corporal Stevens yanked open the passenger's side door. "Get in the back, Private," she said.

Ramirez exited without comment. As soon as they'd finished swapping seats, Adam hit the gas. Ellis had parked in a traffic circle beside an old jetty and a boat launch. Adam was planning to drive straight up to the Tom Miller Dam and Red Bud Isle where they assumed that Crystal had been handed over to whatever band of raiders was trafficking people out of Travis.

Mayor Ellis's Humvee went roaring by them, obviously in a hurry to find the entrance to Miller's bunker.

Adam hesitated, checking his mirrors and his surroundings. His gaze wandered briefly over the lake—

And he slammed on the brakes. Corporal Stevens nearly cracked her head on the dash, while Ramirez actually *did* collide with the back of Adam's seat. None of them were wearing their seatbelts, but Adam had his hands on the wheel to brace himself. Stevens muttered a curse and looked to him for an explanation. He pointed over the lake. "Does that look like a boat to you, Stevens?"

"Well it sure as hell isn't a fish," she replied.

A man in a black jacket was sitting in the front, rowing away. That could have been anyone—a fisherman, an undercover Ranger on patrol, or just some idiot civilian out getting their exercise. But something told Adam that the real explanation wasn't so innocent.

"That's our guy," he said.

"How do you know?" Stevens asked.

"Timing, for one," Adam said. He turned off the engine, then threw his door open and jumped out, grabbing his carbine and racing toward the water and the old jetty. He didn't even bother to shut the door behind him. Stevens pulled alongside him.

"How are we going to get out there, Sergeant?"

Adam pointed. Lucky for him, there was a pair of old fiberglass canoes lying overturned on the shore. If the thick layer of dirt and moss that caked the bottom of them meant anything, they hadn't been used in years. Adam just hoped that they came with oars and that one of them was in good enough shape to make it across the lake.

CHAPTER THIRTY-NINE

Crystal sat on the bathroom floor staring with bleary eyes at her bloody, swollen wrists.

Pull yourself together, Christie, she thought to herself, swiping angrily at her tears. She jumped to her feet and spent a moment studying the broken toilet tank cover, trying to decide if she could break it further to make a shiv that she could use against the raiders.

Maybe she could, but the noise would definitely bring them back up here, and something told Crystal that Kasey wasn't joking about John being the one to check on her next time.

Crystal hurried out of the bathroom and carefully shut the door behind her to hide the evidence of what she'd done. If someone did come up to check on her, she could easily flop down beside the bed with her arms behind her back to pretend like she was still tied up.

Now that her hands were free, she went

straight over to the rusty metal bars anchored in front of the window. She grabbed each of them, one after another, checking to see if any of them were loose.

One of them gave a little more than the others, wiggling just enough to indicate that the screws were loose. Crystal studied it more closely and found that two out of three screws were missing from the base plate. Crystal wondered if maybe some other captive had been quietly working on an escape plan up here. A flash of guilt and dismay shot through her with the realization that they obviously hadn't had enough time to escape themselves. Crystal quietly thanked them and wrapped both of her hands around the bar, close to the bottom anchor point. She began throwing her weight against that one remaining screw.

After just a few attempts, the bottom of the security bar broke free. Using it as a lever against the anchor point in the top, Crystal tore it free. She carefully set the bar aside and reached through the bars to fiddle with the old, rusty locking mechanism of the window itself. She undid the clasp and swung the window open. By this point, Crystal's legs were shaking, and her heart was beating so fast that she felt dizzy. If one of those raiders came in now, this would all be for nothing. She had to hurry!

Squeezing sideways between the remaining bars, she peered out the open window and saw the paved mezzanine and fountain far below. There didn't appear to be any way to climb down safely, and it was too high to jump. In the distance, the river sparkled tauntingly in the late afternoon sun. If she could get there, she could swim across it and then hike back to the perimeter of Travis.

All she had to do was find a way down from this room without those raiders seeing her. Her gaze settled on the rotting window sill outside. She could shimmy down it to the back corner of the house. From there, she noticed a sloping black roof that led straight to the paved driveway between the attached and detached garages. It was still a good twelve-foot drop, even from the lowest point of the roof, but that was manageable.

Crystal drew in a deep breath and gripped the bars tightly for support as she climbed out onto the window sill. The rotting edge of it was soft and spongy beneath her feet, but it seemed to be holding. Of more concern was the fact that now she could clearly see the big bay window in the living room where Bobby and John had been playing poker. It was hard to see more than vague shadows past the glare of sunlight reflecting off the broken panes of glass, but she had a bad feeling that anyone looking up here would have a much easier time seeing her.

Crystal looked away and focused on

shimmying down the window sill to the back corner of the home. Her entire body was electrified with adrenaline, sweat prickled, and the hairs on the back of her neck rose in anticipation of a raider seeing her and calling the alarm.

Please, God, don't let them see me… she thought.

***

"Shit," Adam muttered as he turned over the second canoe, only to find a hole the size of his fist in the old fiberglass body.

He looked up, scanning the shore for any other likely prospects. In the process, he spotted a nearby warehouse with a sign on it that read *Rowing Center.* And beneath that, in a much smaller font, *The Uni ersity of Te as at Austin.*

"Over there!" Adam pointed. He ran for the building with Stevens and Ramirez right behind him. One of two dirty white garage doors was cracked open at the bottom. "Cover me," he ordered as he shrugged out of his pack and dropped to his belly to shimmy under the door. On the other side, he flicked on the tac light of his carbine and swept it around inside of the building.

The big, glossy hulls of multi-person boats that the university had used for its rowing club were stacked on either side of the warehouse and on racks in the ceiling.

In all this time, no one had thought to steal them—probably because they weren't useful for much besides recreational rowing. There wasn't any space inside them to store cargo or fishing equipment. The boats would be speedy with the right crews, but also unwieldy for their length and the fact that they needed multiple people rowing in unison to get anywhere. Fortunately, Adam had just the right team to make that work.

"Stevens, Ramirez, get in here!" he called to them.

Seconds later, the two women came shimmying under the doors.

Stevens whistled appreciatively at the sight of the boats. "You struck gold, Sergeant."

Adam nodded absently as he swept his tac light over the racks, studying the various types of boats. Some of them were longer than others, but none of them were exactly small. Adam picked one of the four-person boats and patted the keel. "Help me get this one down."

"Ramirez," Stevens gestured vaguely to her.

"On it," the shorter woman replied as she shouldered her carbine. Adam did the same, and then each of them took one end of the boat.

Adam grunted with the weight of it, his shoulder rounding as the boat pulled him down. He noticed that Ramirez was using both hands to carry her end. They walked quickly with it to the entrance and carefully set it on the floor in front of the partially open door. Stevens scooted back outside to cover them while Adam forced the door up a few extra feet. The rusty rails shrieked in protest, but he got it up to shoulder height.

"On three..." Adam said.

They both lifted again, and Adam speed-walked with Ramirez to the water's edge. As they went, he noted that the rower he'd spotted earlier was already halfway back to the old expressway bridge that formed the perimeter of the safe zone.

If they didn't get to him soon, it would be too late to intercept him without the guards on that bridge taking notice and getting involved. And for all Adam knew they might be involved with the slave trade.

They reached the edge of the water and promptly flipped the boat over and set it down. There were four separate rowing positions inside, each of them flanked by sweptback metal arms that were meant to hold the oars.

"Where are the oars?" Ramirez asked.

Adam frowned. The inside of the boat was empty. "Must be in the boathouse," he said. He turned and ran back up there, provoking a white-hot spike of pain from his leg that drew a gasp from his lips. It felt like someone was driving nails into his leg with every step.

He ducked back inside the boathouse with Ramirez and Stevens. He found three pairs of long oars and carried two sets himself, insisting that Ramirez keep her hands free to cover them.

"We're lucky we found a *quad*," Stevens said as they reached the water's edge. She held the boat steady while Ramirez and Adam climbed in. Adam was about to take the bow position, but Stevens stopped him. "Do you know how to toe steer?"

Adam's brow furrowed. "*Toe* steer?"

"I do," Stevens explained. "Better let me take the bow."

Adam nodded and kicked through the shallow water to the back of the boat instead. Climbing in, he balanced the oars in his lap along with his carbine. He dipped the ends in and out of the water experimentally, pretending to row by passing the oars just above the surface. They slid around hopelessly on the metal arms that he was using for fulcrums. That was when he noticed the open brackets at the ends.

Stevens hurried over. "You have to attach them to the *riggers* with the oarlocks," she explained, giving him the terminology to understand what he was missing.

"Right," Adam said.

Stevens shouldered her carbine and took one of the oars from him, then illustrated by unscrewing one of the mechanisms at the end of the metal arms that Adam supposed were what she had called *riggers.* Stevens slotted the oar in and then secured a metal bar over it by tightening a plastic nut.

"You have experience with this," he realized.

She nodded. "I used to be big into rowing before the Specs came and University stopped being a thing. Never did get to finish."

Adam nodded absently. They still had schools, but these days they focused less on teaching book smarts and more on teaching practical survival skills like marksmanship, fishing, hunting, and farming.

Adam swung his aching left leg over the side and into the water to secure his other oar.

Stevens helped Ramirez secure her own oars. "Have either of you *sculled* before?" she asked.

"What the hell does that mean?" Ramirez asked.

"I'll take that as a no," Steven replied. "It just means rowing with two oars instead of one, while facing in the opposite direction to the movement of the vessel."

"I've rowed a kayak," Adam said, "but never with two oars at the same time."

"Me too," Ramirez said.

"Great," Stevens muttered. "All right, Adam, since you're in the stern, you'll have to set the pace. We'll watch you to time our strokes."

Adam nodded and glanced impatiently over his shoulder to check on the progress of the rowboat that they were trying to intercept.

Having now *passed* their position, the man was *facing* them. Adam realized that was because he was also using two oars.

"We've got a problem," Adam muttered. "The target's going to be watching us as we come up on him, so if he's armed…"

"Then he'll get the first shot," Stevens finished for him.

Adam nodded. "And you're in the bow, so you'll be first in line to get hit."

Stevens licked her lips. "I can cover us and steer at the same time, but I won't be able to row."

"And you're the one with all the rowing experience," Adam said.

She nodded, and he grimaced.

"How does the steering system work?" Adam asked.

"It attaches to your foot. You pivot your shoe, twisting a metal plate that's attached to cables that turn the rudder. You point your toes in the direction you want to steer."

"Steering sounds easier than rowing," Adam decided. "Let's switch places." He clambered out of the boat and splashed over to the bow position. Stevens tossed the final two oars back on the shore, then helped him fit his shoe to the steering mechanism.

"All set," she said before hurrying over to the stern.

Adam tested the toe steering by pivoting his

boot. It seemed easy enough.

"Ramirez, watch me," Stevens said. "Long, smooth strokes." With that, she grabbed her oars with one hand over the other and made a fake rowing motion above the water. "You twist your wrists at the end of your stroke to pull out the oars without them catching in the water. Got it?"

"Affirmative," Ramirez replied.

Adam tried aiming over his shoulder, realizing as he did so that it was going to be awkward at best, and he needed to be careful not to throw his weight, or he'd make them capsize.

"Ready?" Stevens asked.

"Ready," Ramirez confirmed.

"Sergeant, I need you to steer to starboard," Stevens instructed. "Toes pointing to the right," she added.

"Done," Adam confirmed as he twisted his foot."

"On my signal, Ramirez... and stroke!" Stevens said. Ramirez joined her, but her timing was off and she was completely out of sync, causing her to knock oars with Stevens. "Careful!" Stevens growled.

"Sorry, Corporal."

Even with their poor timing, they raced past the jetty at an impressive speed. After a few more strokes, they found their rhythm and got up to a blinding speed.

Adam aimed cautiously down his sights at the man in a black hoodie sitting in the back of a gleaming white boat with a square back end.

Between the fact that they had twice as many rowers and a boat that was much more streamlined than his, they were gaining on him quickly.

The target reacted almost immediately to their trajectory by increasing his pace. To Adam, that only served to confirm his guilt.

But they were getting uncomfortably close to the expressway bridge and the Rangers guarding it. By the time they reached the target, they'd be within spitting distance of those guards. And they were already well within the effective firing range of a standard-issue M4 carbine.

Adam grimaced. "Let's pick up the pace, Stevens!"

"Copy that, Sergeant!" Stevens replied. "And stroke…! Stroke…! Stroke!"

Adam called out to the target as they drew near. "Freeze! Hands in the air!"

The man pulled in his oars and did as Adam had asked. "Is there something wrong, Ranger?" he asked.

CHAPTER FORTY

Crystal reached the edge of the roof and braced herself on the window sill as she stepped across to the edge of the roof above the garage. That left her straddling the window sill and the roof. She made the mistake of looking down to see the cobblestone mezzanine some twenty feet below, and her head spun in dizzy circles. She hugged the corner of the house for dear life, unsure if she could throw her weight to get both feet securely on the garage roof. There were no handholds to speak of, nothing but the rotten siding to cling to.

Steeling herself for a deadly fall, Crystal pushed off with her leg and her arm at the same time, lunging for the roof. She got both feet planted squarely on the shingles but teetered dangerously on the edge. Just as she was about to find her balance, one of the shingles slipped, and she went careening down.

Crystal felt her weight pulling her backward toward the pavement below, but somehow she managed to throw herself forward instead, and she went rolling down toward the low end where the driveway was.

The sky and moldy shingles traded places in a rapid blur. Crystal threw out her arms to stop herself, but she only managed to slow down.

The slumping, leaf-filled gutter caught her eye, and she reached for it with both hands just as she sailed over the edge. Her fingers curled around the gutter—

It tore away from the roof and bent in the middle with a roar of metallic thunder. Then the gutter caught on its remaining screws. Her fingers held for a split second, redirecting her from a deadly sideways roll to a feet-first drop. Her fingers gave way, and the ground rushed up to greet her, driving her knees into her chest and knocking the wind out of her. She fell over backward and landed *hard* on her coccyx. The impact ricocheted up her spine, leaving her dazed and lying there in breathless agony. She stared blankly at the sky for precious seconds.

Adrenaline surging anew, she recovered with a thready gasp and sat up. Fortunately, there weren't any guards standing around outside the garage, and the door was still firmly shut.

She jumped back to her feet, grateful to find that her legs were uninjured. She spun in a quick circle, looking for signs of trouble. She didn't see any raiders, but she did identify the nearest cover position—a wall of mature trees and hedges to her left, just below the edge of the driveway.

She aimed for the deepest pool of shadows and sprinted for cover. On reaching the end of the driveway, she leaped over the curb and sailed through a short drop to the overgrown grass on the other side. Her feet plowed into the ground, and the sharp slope sent her pitching forward. This time the grass cushioned her fall, and she sprang back up again almost immediately. Breathing hard, her heart slamming in her chest, she leaned on the trunk of the nearest tree and glanced around for signs of pursuit.

Nothing.

She let out a shaky sigh—

And then she heard a familiar shriek of rusty rails as someone forced the garage door back up. Muffled voices sounded from within. Crystal's eyes flew wide, her skin prickling with dread. They were going to see the broken gutter hanging above the entrance! Someone must have heard her tumble down the roof.

Not waiting to see who emerged from the garage, Crystal turned and ran. Wind whipped past her face as she flew down the sloping lawn beside the mezzanine and the pool.

Another shriek sounded from the garage door.

"What the hell?" someone muttered.

It sounded like John.

Crystal glanced over her shoulder in time to see him peering up at the roof, then dropping into a crouch and sweeping the area with an automatic rifle.

He froze as his gaze locked with hers. "It's the girl! She escaped!"

"*Deténla!*" someone else said, stepping out of the shadows of the garage. It was the short Mexican man with the cowboy hat.

John's rifle snapped up to his shoulder, and Crystal dove for a nearby tree, thinking to put the trunk between her and his line of fire. A bullet *crunched* into it and bark exploded in her face, stinging her eyes with debris.

Crystal gasped and nearly fell. She fumbled blindly with her palms against the tree trunk, blinking furiously to clear her eyes.

She pushed off the tree, not daring to slow down for even a second.

Another crack split the air and this time she heard the bullet whistling past her ear. She realized with a jolt of horror that the Raiders weren't even trying to capture her alive.

"¡*Oye! No la dispares, ¡idiota! ¡Búscala!*"

"Go get her yourself!" John snapped.

Crystal struggled to summon what little Spanish she'd learned from Connor and Carla over the years. She wasn't sure, but she thought the Mexican guy had just ordered John not to shoot her.

Further confirmation came in the fact that

no more bullets flew through the air as she stumbled down the sloping grounds toward the river. Swiping at her eyes, she struggled to clear them of debris. She threw a quick look over her shoulder to see John running after her.

He was only about thirty feet away. She looked back to the fore just in time to see the trees at the bottom of the grassy slope marching off a cliff. She skidded to a stop and narrowly caught herself on a low rock wall at the edge of it.

"There's nowhere to run, darling!" John taunted.

But he was wrong. Crystal spotted the break in the wall that formed the entrance of a long winding pathway that all but vanished in the trees and shrubbery below. She turned and ran along the wall, diving through the gap and down a short set of stairs with a wiggly iron railing.

Hope soared in her chest as she raced along the path. If this led down to a boat on the river, she might still be able to escape.

Unless John started shooting at her again...

CHAPTER FORTY-ONE

"Keep your hands up," Adam insisted with his carbine trained on the suspect as their boat drifted alongside his.

"Have I done something wrong, Sergeant?" the man asked.

Adam realized that the suspect had seen the insignia on his uniform, a tiny Velcro patch that most people wouldn't know to look for, much less recognize. Whoever this was, he was familiar with the Rangers or maybe the US Army before them.

"What are you doing out here?" Adam asked as Stevens used her oar to stabilize their boat against his. As soon as she'd done that, Ramirez brought her own carbine into line with the suspect.

The man smiled blandly at them. "Oh, I was just out getting some exercise."

"Beyond the perimeter?" Adam challenged. "There's plenty of lake to row inside the walls."

"The same old scenery gets dull after a while. Easy to go stir crazy inside the zones."

"What's your name?" Adam asked.

"Kent Mitchell. And you, sir?"

Adam bit his tongue, not wanting to offer any information that could tie him to Crystal. He ground his teeth for a moment, silently contemplating the man before him. He had vibrant blue eyes and a ruggedly handsome face. He looked to be in his thirties. Black hair with a shock of premature white running through from his left temple.

Adam looked away, studying the contents of his boat, hoping to find something incriminating. He spotted an old faded blue tarp and piles of soggy brown ropes in the back.

"What are those ropes for?" Adam asked.

Kent's expression grew puzzled. "You need ropes to tie a boat to a dock."

"Hey, watch your tone," Stevens warned.

"I meant no disrespect. Is there something I can help you Rangers with?"

Adam realized that if there was anything in the boat to incriminate Kent, he would have already hidden it, having seen them approaching from afar.

"I'm going to have to come aboard and search your vessel," Adam said.

Kent stiffened with the suggestion, then visibly forced himself to relax, making Adam more certain than ever that he was Crystal's abductor.

Kent smiled and jerked his chin to indicate

their racing scull with its broad silver riggers that kept them separated from Kent's boat by a clear margin of two or three feet.

"Are you sure about that, Sergeant? You might just flip your boat trying to get over here. I can stand up and turn my pockets inside out. Maybe that would save you the trouble?"

"I'll hold us steady, Sergeant," Stevens said. She shouldered her rifle and used both oars to balance them.

Adam nodded and slowly rose to a crouch on his seat. The boat began rocking from side to side, indicating just how unsteady it was, and Ramirez quickly joined Stevens' efforts to stabilize them.

"Guys, I don't know what you're looking for," Kent said, "I can row to shore if you want. It'd be easier to search me there."

"I appreciate your concern," Adam grunted while waiting for the boat to stop shaking. He slowly rose, trying to decide how best to enter Kent's boat. At just three feet away, it would be easy enough to step across, but that simple movement could easily capsize their boat, or even Kent's.

"I've got you, Sergeant," Stevens assured.

With Adam's full attention on Kent's vessel and both women working to stabilize them with their oars, no one was keeping Kent covered. Adam caught a flash of movement out of the corner of his eye and pivoted to bring his carbine to bear. Kent had his hand on one of the riggers. His face contorted with exertion as he heaved, pulling up with all of his strength. Adam felt himself going over—

And lunged for Kent's boat.

Stevens and Ramirez went overboard, shouting warnings to each other a split second before their tandem splash erupted behind Adam.

He was lying on his side in Kent's boat atop the tarp and the pile of soggy ropes, but his carbine was still effectively aimed. "Drop it!" he snapped before he'd even properly registered that Kent was reaching beneath his seat for a weapon.

Stevens and Ramirez breached the surface spluttering and cursing, and Adam worked himself up into a crouch.

Kent reluctantly released his weapon— a Glock—and slowly raised his hands again. "This is a mistake," he said. "I'm innocent."

Stevens pulled herself up into Kent's boat, followed by Ramirez. Both women leveled their carbines at Kent.

"Innocent?" Adam scoffed. "Then why'd you capsize our boat when we insisted on searching yours?" He stepped forward and retrieved the Glock from below Kent's seat, his eyes and aim never leaving the man as he did so. Tucking the extra sidearm into his vest, Adam glanced pointedly around inside the boat. It was pretty crowded with the four of them on board. Stevens looked pissed as hell. Ramirez was already feeling around in the back with the ropes and the tarp, looking for incriminating evidence.

She appeared to be coming up empty, but having a firearm was incriminating enough all by itself.

"Where did you take her?" Adam asked.

"Excuse me?" Kent asked. His head tilted curiously to one side. "Take who?" But there was a flicker of something in his ice-blue eyes that gave him away.

Was that amusement? Adam wondered. Adam handed his carbine to Stevens. "Keep him covered while I search him."

"With pleasure," Stevens replied, now juggling two carbines and aiming both of them at Kent's chest.

Adam removed the Glock and then his own sidearm and tossed them both in the pile of ropes at Stevens' feet so that Kent wouldn't be able to turn the weapons on him.

Taking a slow, crouching step toward Kent, he kneeled in the dirty water at the bottom of the boat and promptly began a pat-down search. The suspect wore a black hoodie and baggy black joggers. Adam checked his pants pockets and immediately found something. "A *taser?*" he asked while shaking it in front of Kent's nose. He depressed the switch and a crackling beam of electricity appeared between the contacts, making Kent flinch.

"For self-defense," he explained.

"Sure," Adam growled. The taser was even more incriminating than the gun. He continued his search, finding a backpack behind Kent. Inside of it were thinner versions of the ropes in the front of the boat, a pair of hypodermic needles, one of them empty, the other full, a pouch full of Republic credits, and finally... a familiar-looking diamond solitaire ring set in white gold. Adam's guts clenched up. There was no doubt about it. The ring belonged to Crystal.

"Is that..." Stevens trailed off uncertainly.

Adam held it up in front of Kent's eyes and grabbed a fistful of his hoodie to yank him in for an even closer look. "Where the fuck is she?" he demanded.

Kent smiled. "Take it easy, old man, I'll take you to her."

Adam released him with a shove and stepped back. "If there's even one hair out of place on her head..." He trailed off warningly as he pocketed the ring.

"There won't be," Kent replied. "They need her in prime condition if they want to get their money's worth."

Adam felt sick with the implications of that statement. He retrieved the two sidearms from the bottom of the boat, holstered his, and then aimed Kent's own Glock at his chest. "Start rowing," he snapped.

Kent took up the oars and began turning the boat around to head back up the lake. As he did so, Adam caught a glimpse of Rangers on the Mopac bridge, aiming their carbines down over the side, but if they hadn't opened fire yet, then they weren't about to. If any of those Rangers were involved with Kent's operation, they obviously weren't going to stick their necks out for him. They'd probably seen through their scopes that Adam, Stevens, and Ramirez were wearing Ranger uniforms. Adam raised his left hand to wave, and one of the Rangers waved back.

Kent snorted at the exchange. "Must be nice. Brothers in arms—right up until one of you sees an opportunity to make some extra credits, that is."

"Shut up and keep rowing," Adam said.

CHAPTER FORTY-TWO

Crystal reached the bottom of the path, only to find that it led to a small, land-locked pond surrounded by trees. There was a private dock on the lake and a pair of old, swan-shaped paddle boats on the shore, but she was still at least fifty feet *above* the river.

"There's nowhere to go!" John gloated from the top of the path.

Despair clutched Crystal's heart, making her chest ache and her head swim. She realized that she was holding her breath and let it out in a rush. Just because there wasn't a way down to the river didn't mean she couldn't get there. She sprinted off the dock and ran around the spongy shore for the far end.

"Come on back, darling! I won't bite!" John's laughter followed her.

It took only a few seconds to reach the other side of the glorified puddle. It had been formed by building a small dam across the mouth of a dry creek bed. Right now the water level was low, and both the spillways and creek bed below the dam were dry. The crevasse formed a debris-strewn path down to the river. Crystal clambered down from the lowest side of the dam just as John reached the dock with the paddle boats.

He muttered a curse and started running around the edges of the pond to reach her. Crystal jumped the last few feet to the bottom of the crevasse. Her ankle twisted between hidden rocks and she cried out as she fell. Her foot still stuck, she stifled a sob as she tugged at her leg to free it. *Come on...* she whispered while periodically glancing up at the dam to see if John had caught up to her yet.

It only took a few seconds to free her foot, but somehow it felt like an eternity. Crystal struggled to her feet and tested her weight on her twisted ankle. It hurt, but she could manage the pain. She hurried down the dry river bed as quickly as she dared, being careful this time to test her footing as she went. Now and then her feet still sank into hidden gaps between the rocks, but she managed to avoid getting stuck or injuring herself further.

The river came sparkling into view between the trees, and Crystal glimpsed mossy green rocks submerged at the edges of the river. Not far now. She looked back over her shoulder to see John clambering after her, hopping from rock to rock. She tried to do the same thing, but almost took a bad fall as her wounded ankle gave way.

Come on, Crystal, she urged herself while blinking past stinging rivulets of sweat. *You're almost there!*

Moments later she reached the bottom of the cliffs. There weren't any boats or docks in sight, leaving nowhere for her to go except to wade out into the water and swim. It couldn't have been more than a few hundred yards across, and there didn't seem to be any dangerous currents to worry about.

"End of the line, sweetheart," John said. "There's nowhere left to run."

Crystal glanced back up the cliffs to see John stepping down sideways, moving slower now, and no longer hopping from rock to rock. Maybe he was hoping that she didn't know how to swim, or that she wouldn't dare to try.

Crystal went kicking out into the water, being careful to avoid the more slippery rocks.

A muffled curse sounded from John, and she heard pebbles skittering down as he picked up the pace. She didn't waste any time turning back. As soon as she was up to her waist, she raised her arms above her head to dive in.

"I wouldn't do that if I were you!" John shouted.

Crystal hesitated, thinking that he was threatening to shoot her.

"Look!" John added.

And then she saw it—a long, snaking black

thing in the water with a line of fins rippling along its back and jutting from the water. It was far too big to be a fish.

"Come on back now," John said.

Crystal stood frozen where she was, unable to tear her eyes away from the approaching creature. Its fins slipped languidly beneath the surface, and it vanished, leaving Crystal to wonder if she'd imagined it.

Moments later, it breached the surface again, now fifty feet farther away, having traveled the distance in a heartbeat. The water began churning into a frothy white funnel as it spun in circles. Its fins flashed around and around in a blur like the spokes of a wheel. And then all of a sudden, it vanished again, and the water grew calm.

"What *is* that?" Crystal asked, suddenly less afraid of the raider behind her than of the monster in front.

"We call 'em river drakes! Bigger than Loch Ness, if it ever existed, and with more teeth than a shark! Funny, I only ever seen 'em up above the dam, where the river butts against one of the Specs' landscaping projects. I guess one must have snuck over the dam. Maybe they're runnin' out of fish to eat upstream, gettin' desperate for food just like the rest of us."

Crystal stared unblinkingly at the spot where the drake had been churning up the water a second ago. She'd heard rumors about sightings of other dangerous creatures besides the stalkers, but this was the first time she'd seen one of them with her own eyes. A series of low waves rolled past her waist, peeling her sweaty shirt away from her body and gently rocking her on her heels.

"What a stroke of luck, huh?" John asked. "It got here just in time to stop you from making your great escape." He laughed gratingly at that. "Looks like fate has it out for you, sweetheart!" He laughed again, and Crystal's whole body began to tremble with rage. That gave her the courage to stay right where she was.

What if he's lying? she wondered. *Maybe river drakes aren't even dangerous.*

Crystal raised her arms again, and this time she dove in and swam out as fast as she could.

John shouted for her to come back before she got herself eaten. Adrenaline and fear pushed her to swim faster than she ever had in her life, but soon she was completely out of breath, and only a third of the way across the river. She slowed down, treading water to catch her breath. She glanced around for any sign of the drake.

Not seeing fins snaking toward her, she peered into the water in front of her nose, worried that it might be slithering around beneath her feet, but the water was too murky to see anything.

"Here it comes!" John screamed. "I warned you!"

Crystal flinched as she noticed a snaking line of gleaming black fins speeding straight toward her from a hundred feet away. She let out a strangled cry and turned around, kicking and clawing for the shore.

John opened fired, not aiming for her this time, but for the drake. Bullets kicked up spikes of water beside the monster's fins, and it dove, taking cover below the surface once more.

Crystal couldn't tell if John had hit the drake or discouraged its attack, but if not she knew it wouldn't take more than a couple of seconds to reach her.

Crystal stubbed her knee on a rock, and she stumbled to her feet, struggling to the shore. It was exactly like one of those nightmares where she could never run fast enough to get away.

A loud *whoosh* erupted behind her as something big burst out of the water, followed by the whistling shriek of an alien creature. John cursed and opened fire again, this time on full auto.

Crystal dove back into the water, hoping to evade the creature's gaping maw. Warm, fish-smelling breath washed over her, and Crystal screamed in terror.

Swimming again, she kicked as hard as she could, hoping to catch the drake in the teeth.

Something sharp grazed her leg, slicing it open, and she swallowed a mouthful of water as another scream tore past her lips.

CHAPTER FORTY-THREE

The deafening roar of gunfire drew shrieking cries from the drake. It slapped the water repeatedly, sending waves of murky water lapping over Crystal as she swam feebly to the shore. Her fingernails scraped the slime off rocks, and she pushed off the bottom, running the rest of the way to the shore. John continued firing, but more sporadically now. Crystal reached his side and spun around to get a better look at the monster.

It was already slithering away, but now that it was swimming in the shallows, she finally got a sense of its size. It appeared cylindrical like a snake, easily as thick around as a sewer pipe and as long as two school buses. She was lucky it hadn't swallowed her whole.

John took one final parting shot at the creature. The bullet drew a spurt of clear white blood from one of its fins, and then the creature vanished beneath the water once more, leaving nothing but spreading ripples in its wake.

Crystal let out a shaky breath, and with it the adrenaline faded from her system, leaving her cold and shaking. The pain from her wounded leg came throbbing to life and she dropped to the pebbled shore and turned her leg to check the back of her calf. Her jeans were torn, and a bloody chunk the size of a chicken thigh was missing from her leg. The wound was bubbling with blood that ran in diluted rivers off her wet skin.

"Oh, he got you good," John said. "Coulda been worse, though. Let's go get you patched up." He grabbed her arm and jerked her to her feet.

Crystal didn't have the strength to resist, but walking up the hill made her mutilated muscle seize up a few times, and the blood loss left her feeling weak and sick to her stomach.

After just a minute of walking, she had to stop for a break.

John regarded her disdainfully as she collapsed on the ground. "You should've listened to me."

Crystal glared up at him, then shook her head as she attempted to put pressure on the wound with her hands. She cried out as touching the injury made it sting sharply. Blood ran steadily between her shaking fingers. "I'm never going to make it all the way back up. I'm too weak."

"You will," John insisted.

"If I go into shock, it will be your fault. You need to do something to stop the bleeding."

John's dark eyes cinched into angry slits. "Stop exaggerating and get up." He thrust out a hand to help her, and Crystal pushed weakly off the ground to grab it, but as she did so, her head swam and dark spots crowded her vision. Her ears rang sharply and she fell over backward, rolling down the hill. Rotting leaves and sky traded places repeatedly until she landed in a muddy puddle on the shore of the river. She struggled to rise, but there was no strength left in her body. And then a deep blanket of shadows swept over her and smothered her thoughts.

***

"Did you hear that?" Adam asked, his ears straining against the silence as the boat drifted with its momentum.

Corporal Stevens nodded where she sat beside Ramirez in the back. "It sounded like a girl screaming."

"It sounded like *Crystal* screaming," Adam replied. "Followed by gunshots." He stared pointedly at Kent. "Row, damn you!" he roared, rattling his carbine in the other man's face.

Kent grimaced and put his back into rowing again. They were riding low in the water, with the aft end of the boat barely an inch above the water. Now and then the lake came sloshing in with a swell or the rocking of the boat as someone shifted their weight.

Adam noticed that the slimy green water in the bottom of the canoe was growing steadily deeper. He sat on the middle bench of three, keeping Kent covered and searching both sides of the lake for any hint of where Crystal was.

He tried not to think about what those gunshots might mean, or why Crystal had been screaming. He wasn't even completely sure that it was her, but as her father, he gave himself better than even odds of recognizing her voice.

How far would a scream carry across the water? he wondered, trying to gauge the distance. He was pretty sure it was less than a mile, and from how loud she'd sounded, he estimated that she had to be closer than the dam. Adam scanned the sides of the lake, noting the thick walls of trees and foliage that should have muffled the sound. Yet he'd heard her clearly, so either she'd been screaming from somewhere close to the shore, or else...

Adam's eyes tracked up the cliffs on the left bank, which also happened to be the direction the screams and gunshots had come from. Opulent mansions stood atop that cliff. Maybe Crystal had been screaming from up there? Adam couldn't remember the name of the area anymore, but it had been well-known back before the invasion.

"Ah, Sergeant... do you see what I'm seeing?" Stevens asked.

"See what?" Adam's gaze tracked swiftly down from the cliffs to see what had caught her eye. It only took a second for him to spot it— a dark line of fins, snaking rapidly through the water toward them.

Adam's brow furrowed at the strange sight.

Kent stopped rowing and glanced over his shoulder to see what they were looking at. Then his whole body stiffened, and he screamed, "River drake!"

***

Connor crouched at the bottom of the crevasse that led into the governor's bunker. Ellis was breathing hard, gasping in the dank, dusty air.

Clambering down the walls to the bottom of this chasm had been almost more than he could manage, even though there had been plenty of handholds and footholds in the craggy concrete walls.

The mayor's poor physical condition made him a dubious choice for this mission. Connor walked to the edge of a vast cylindrical chamber with a ramp that spiraled down past five different landings with heavy metal doors. The slanting rays of the evening sun filtered in weakly from above, narrowly illuminating the dark well of emerald shadows below. That green color, Connor recalled, was from the alien growths that garnished the debris inside the bunker.

Memories flooded back from five years ago of escaping the bunker with Crystal, Owen, and that Ranger Sergeant from Kerr. He remembered racing up those ramps while Adam held the door at the bottom against several stalkers. Connor shivered with the memory and gripped his carbine tighter, only to remember that it was still loaded with blanks.

"Well?" Mayor Ellis whispered from just behind him. "What are you waiting for?"

Connor glanced down at the crumbling ledge that led around the curving wall of the chamber to the railing at the top of the ramp. He turned to regard Ellis dubiously, realizing that the mayor's stout frame was not going to do him any favors while balancing on that ledge. His belly would push him away from the wall, making it impossible not to fall.

"What's wrong?" Ellis demanded.

Connor pointed to the ledge, and Mayor Ellis leaned around him for a better look.

"I knew I shouldn't have eaten all those pastries," he muttered, shaking his head. "I'll never make it."

"Let me see," Corporal Williams said, pushing between them. He was a big man, fit, with white stubble frosting a jutting lower jaw. Dark eyes hardened and he lifted his patrol cap to scratch his scalp through short, thinning gray hair.

"The mayor's right," Williams agreed. "We'll have to push on without him. Private Cooper?" He gestured to the ledge. "After you."

Connor frowned. "What if a stalker comes creeping up that ramp? You really want me taking point with blank rounds?"

Williams clenched his jaw and looked at Ellis. "He's right, sir. With your permission, I suggest we provide him with live rounds."

The mayor appeared to hesitate.

Connor added, "You trusted me to take you this far. I could have easily led you into a trap or alerted the guards on the east wall, but I didn't."

Ellis conceded that with a sigh and gestured offhandedly to Williams, who then reached into his vest and produced one of his spare magazines.

Connor ejected the useless blanks and tucked them into his vest before slapping the live ammo in and hauling back on the charging handle to chamber the first round.

"Here I go," he muttered, shouldering the weapon and starting onto the ledge. He gripped the corner of the crevasse until the last possible second, then crab-walked around the ledge with both palms planted firmly against the wall. It only took him a few steps to reach the railing at the top of the ramp. He seized it in both hands and quickly vaulted over to the other side.

Corporal Williams leaned his head out, and Connor signaled for him to come. He crept out along the ledge next, followed by two of the privates in their unit, Privates Lee from Delta Squad, and Hanson from the Bravos—the latter being a petite young woman with long brown hair tied up in a bun.

Connor kept them covered as they inched along the ledge, watching for signs of stalkers creeping up from below. Ellis popped his head out and waved. Connor frowned, wondering what use he was if he couldn't even lead them to the governor's tunnel.

Once all four Rangers were standing at the top of the ramp, Corporal Williams stepped over to the rusty metal door on their landing and reached into his pocket for a folded square of paper. He pinned his carbine beneath his armpit to free his hands, then unfolded the paper and flicked on a small silver flashlight. He placed the flashlight between his teeth and studied the paper.

"What is that?" Connor whispered as he crowded in beside Williams.

"Door codes," he mumbled around the flashlight.

Connor stared dubiously at the old analog keypad beside the door. The bunker was obviously abandoned. What if the door controls were no longer powered?

Williams began tapping in a sequence of numbers. When he was done, a red light blinked in the lower left corner, and the control pad emitted a tinny beep.

"Not that one," Williams muttered while shining his light on the paper to study the next code.

At least the panel has power, Connor thought.

Williams tapped in the next code, and again the control panel beeped and the light flashed red.

Connor frowned. What if the codes had been changed? Or maybe they'd been given the wrong ones. What if their undercover operative in Travis wasn't really on their side after all? Connor glanced around quickly.

This could easily be a trap. If it was, would the governor wait for the stalkers that inhabited the bunker to find them like he had the last time, or would he send Rangers to deal with them instead?

Williams tapped in a third code, only to receive yet another error beep.

Connor stared fixedly at the door, half-expecting it to fly open and a blinding barrage of bullets to cut them down where they stood.

"Guys..." Hanson whispered. "I've got contact below... one stalker. Scratch that, two stalkers."

Connor and Lee both joined her at the

railing, peering through their scopes to the bottom of the chamber.

"Are they inbound?" Williams asked from the door.

"Negative, Corporal," Hanson said. "We're clear for now."

Another error beep erupted from the control panel, and someone gave a stifled cry. Connor spun toward the sound just in time to see Ellis leaping from the crumbling end of the ledge to the railing. Ellis collided with the railing, drawing reverberating metallic thunder from the barrier. Bits of concrete shattered on the ramp below and then an answering shriek erupted from one of the stalkers below.

"Incoming!" Hanson warned.

Ellis clung fast to the railing, but he obviously couldn't pull himself up. "Help!" he whispered.

Connor lunged for the railing, reaching over it for one of Ellis's arms.

"What are you doing?" he hissed at the mayor.

"He's using the wrong door codes," Ellis explained as Lee came and grabbed the mayor's other arm. Together they pulled him over and then left him lying on the concrete landing. Connor and Lee dashed back to Hanson's side to see two blurry gray shadows that blended against the bare concrete walls and floor loping languidly up the ramp.

The stalkers were already passing the first landing. Connor estimated that they had maybe ten or fifteen seconds to get the door open before the stalkers reached them. "Mr. Mayor," Connor warned. "If you don't get that door open right now, this coup is over!"

Ellis pushed Corporal Williams out of the way and pulled a piece of paper from one of his own pockets. He unfolded it with shaking hands while Williams shone his light on it. Ellis quickly tapped in the code.

And yet another error beep erupted from the panel.

"That's impossible!" Mayor Ellis cried, no longer bothering to whisper.

Another shriek erupted from the stalkers below, and Connor heard them snorting as they increased their pace.

"Firing positions!" Corporal Williams ordered.

All four of them rushed to the top of the ramp. Connor dropped to a kneeling position with Lee, balancing his left elbow on his knee for greater stability.

Lee glanced at him, his eyes wide with horror. "I never shared," he said.

Connor blinked incredulously at him. "What?"

"When the sergeant asked, I didn't share. The day they arrived, stalkers took my family, and I ran." Tears sliced quickly down his cheeks, and Private Lee shook his head. "Whatever happens, I want you to know, I am not running today."

Connor nodded and settled his cheek against the stock of his carbine to peer down the scope. Why was Lee telling *him?* Maybe he thought a confession would ease the burden of his guilt. Whatever the case, he'd picked a hell of a time for a confession.

Shrieking snorts mingled with thundering footfalls as the stalkers drew near. *Any second now...* Connor thought, with his finger tightening on the trigger.

CHAPTER FORTY-FOUR

There was no time to ask what a drake was, or how Kent knew about it. Adam's carbine snapped up to his shoulder. "Light it up!" he roared, even as he squeezed off his first few shots. The stock kicked into his shoulder, and water sprayed from the points of impact. Two more shots joined his from Corporal Stevens and Private Ramirez. The creature slipped below the surface just before it reached them, vanishing smoothly and leaving nothing but spreading ripples to indicate that it was ever there.

Ramirez and Stevens rocked the boat as they swept their weapons around. Water lapped the sides, sloshing in. Adam peered over the port side into the inky-black depths of the lake.

"I've lost contact," Stevens said.

"Likewise," Ramirez added.

Adam grimaced, checking the starboard side, and then aft for signs of movement. The boat continued rocking gently in the wake of the creature's passing.

"What the hell was that?" Adam demanded.

"Quiet," Kent whispered, his eyes wide. "It'll hear you!"

Seeing his apprehension, Adam came to a snap decision. "Row us to shore." He pointed to the tree-lined cliffs. They couldn't be far from where he'd heard Crystal screaming. "We'll walk the rest of the way."

Kent nodded and picked up his oars, slowly dipping them into the water and hauling them back for his first stroke. On his second, one of his oars got stuck on something, and he muttered a curse. When the oar emerged from the water, the end of it was missing, and Adam saw that the aluminum pole was crimped and dented.

Kent's eyes widened at the sight of it.

"Shit," Stevens hissed.

Something knocked violently into the bottom of the boat, sending it surging a foot out of the water, only to *slap* back down a second later. Adam nearly tumbled into Kent but managed to recover his balance at the last second.

Silence fell once more. The water stirred on the port side in a snaking pattern, and Adam glimpsed an immense black shadow drifting by. Then it switchbacked and grew suddenly larger as it came racing for the surface.

"Brace!" Adam shouted, releasing his carbine to steady himself on the sides of the boat.

The vessel *thumped* with another impact, but this time the force was distributed sideways and they went keeling over. Dark water rushed up to greet them. Kent screamed, and Stevens cursed.

Adam's head plunged into the water, and cottony silence filled his ears. Dark water swallowed every ounce of the light, making it impossible to see more than blurry smears of light and shadow. He kicked back up to the surface, fighting the sodden weight of his gear. His head burst into blinding light between Stevens and Ramirez, but Kent was nowhere to be seen. Both women were clutching the sides of the overturned boat. Stevens was struggling to right it on her own. "Help me flip it over!" she shouted. Ramirez joined her, pulling down while Stevens pushed up, but all Stevens managed to do was submerge herself again.

"Forget it, Corporal!" Adam said while whirling around to look for signs of the sea monster. "Just swim!"

"Copy that!" she replied.

They abandoned the boat and swam as fast as they could. As soon as he rounded the other side of the boat, Adam saw where Kent had gone. He was already halfway to the shore, having wasted no time abandoning ship.

Adam felt something solid slap his bad leg

with bruising force. "Contact!" he spluttered through an agonized gasp.

And then Ramirez let out an abbreviated scream as something yanked her under. She vanished in an instant, leaving nothing but a foaming stream of bubbles in her wake.

"Where is she?" Stevens shouted, whirling in frantic circles.

Adam stopped swimming to tread water above the spot where she'd disappeared. He reached for his belt and drew his combat knife.

"I'm going to look for her!" he said, and then sucked in a deep breath and ducked below the surface. The murky depths clarified slightly below the refractive surface, but visibility was still only four or five feet, and it dropped sharply the deeper he went.

Yet those depths were illuminated by a fuzzy blue glow. Adam saw a churning shadow beneath him, roiling in circles around a blurry human shape that was streaming a trail of white bubbles.

Ramirez.

Adam swam harder. He reached the roiling monster and plunged his knife in blindly. The creature slapped him with its tail and sent him tumbling away. Adam managed to take the knife with him, raking it down the length of the monster's tail as he went. A muffled squeal of pain erupted from the creature, sounding something like a cross between a whale and a burst of electronic interference.

The shadow came flashing back around, growing taller and bigger with its approach. Jagged edges hinted at a massive maw ringed with teeth. Adam swam to get away, even though he knew that he couldn't hope to outswim the creature.

Another dark shadow swelled before him, that of a submerged log jutting up at an angle like the Leaning Tower of Pisa. Adam dove over it for cover and twisted around just in time to see it shatter as the monster clamped its jaws around the log.

His lungs burned for air, sucking against the walls of his chest. Adam ignored the pain, knowing that if he surfaced now, the monster would swallow him whole. It rushed at him once more, its jaws no longer gaping wide. Another shadow flitted down from the surface and latched on. It was Stevens. The creature bucked and shrieked again, knocking her loose. It darted away just as it reached Adam, and he plunged his knife into its side once more. This time he grabbed one of its fins, using it to hang on tight as it tried to throw him off. He stabbed down over and over again, drawing fluttering white streams of blood. Alien shrieks filled his ears, making it impossible to think. There came a gleaming flash of jagged teeth as the monster's head twisted around. Adam saw a bright, glowing blue eye the size of his head.

Remembering that the eyes were a weak spot on the stalkers, he lunged to reach it. Teeth flashed down, intending to cut him in two, but he brought his legs up and kicked off the creature's snout, buying precious seconds as he stabbed the knife straight into that glowing blue orb.

Another shriek tore through the water, deafening from its proximity. Feeling his lungs about to burst, Adam kicked off the monster's thrashing body to reach the surface. A gushing white stream of alien blood followed him up, and he emerged treading water between Ramirez and Stevens. Ramirez looked battered, but she was alive.

"Swim!" Adam spluttered.

And then three of them sprinted for the shore.

**

Connor listened to the rhythmic thunder of the stalkers' snorts and padded footfalls, their claws skittering on concrete as they followed the curve of the ramp.

"Brace for contact!" Corporal Williams warned.

Connor flexed sweating palms on his carbine, knowing that he wouldn't have time for more than one or two shots.

And then the door opened beside them with a thunk and a groan from its hinges. A Ranger appeared on the other side, waving urgently to them.

Ellis launched himself through the door, and Corporal Williams dove for the opening. Connor jumped up and ran with a sparking burst of adrenaline.

Skittering claws and snorting breaths reached a crescendo. Connor spun around as he flew through the entrance, sweeping his carbine into line—

Just in time to see two massive gray stalkers leaping into the air. Private Hanson was just an arm's length away, and he couldn't get a clear shot. He spared a hand from his carbine to pull her through, seeing as he did so that Lee was still crouched in a shooter's stance at the top of the ramp. He opened fire with a stuttering roar.

And then one of the stalkers fell on him, its claws raking down his chest. He cried out in agony as blood sprayed the air. Everyone opened up on the stalkers, riddling them with bullets. Both monsters shrieked. One of them looked up with an angry snort while the other continued mauling Private Lee.

Someone shoved Connor aside and dragged the heavy metal door shut. The stalker collided with a *boom,* and shrieked in outrage, raking its claws furiously across the barrier.

Connor rounded on the one who'd shoved him out of the way. "Lee is still out there!"

He was surprised to find that he recognized the man, but he was older than the last time they'd met. This was Captain Fields, the one who'd escorted them from the south gate of Travis to their meeting with Governor Miller five years ago.

"Hello, Connor," Fields said, proving that his memory was just as sharp.

"You left him to die," Connor growled. He jabbed a finger at the now-shut door for emphasis.

Captain Fields grimaced. "That man was already dead."

Mayor Ellis released a heavy sigh. "We're lucky they didn't get us, too."

Fields nodded gravely and turned to walk down a dark concrete corridor lined with exposed pipes and flickering lights in the ceiling. "This way. Quickly," Fields said.

Connor fell in behind Corporal Williams and Hanson. The latter was crying, her cheeks stained with tears.

"The codes you gave me didn't work," Ellis accused.

"I know," Captain Fields replied. "That's why I came to get you."

"*He's* our man on the inside?" Connor interrupted.

Ellis glanced back at him. "Is there a problem with that?"

Connor quickly shook his head. "No, sir."

"Good," Ellis replied.

It made sense in retrospect that Fields

was the one helping them. He had been sympathetic to them from the start, and he'd been conspicuously absent from the team of Rangers that had locked them in this stalker-infested bunker five years ago. When he found out about it later, he'd probably realized that the governor had to go. Or maybe he'd reached that point later when he learned about the Vultures.

"How did you know where to find us?" Ellis asked.

"Sophie Brooks called me. She told me what happened with Crystal, and that you'd left by the north gate, allegedly to look for her. She also mentioned that you were planning to sneak in here, and why. I came as quickly as I could."

"We're lucky you had such good timing," Ellis said.

"*Good* timing?" Connor scoffed, thinking of Lee getting his guts ripped out by that stalker.

Captain Fields turned to regard him with a heavy frown, and Corporal Williams shot him a reproving look. Connor shouldn't have been questioning a ranking officer like Fields, much less Mayor Ellis, but he couldn't help it. They were acting like Private Lee's death had meant nothing.

They came to another metal door with a keypad and the captain tapped in a code. This time the light flashed green and the panel made a pleasant chime. "Here, before I forget," Fields reached into his pocket as locking mechanisms in the door *thunked.* He handed a piece of paper to Mayor Ellis. "These are the new codes."

Ellis nodded. "Thank you, Captain."

Fields pulled the door open, revealing a hexagonal chamber with three more doors at right angles to each other. Grates in the floor and ceiling concealed two slowly spinning industrial-sized fans that sent flickering shadows racing around the chamber. Fields pointed to the door directly across from them. "That leads to the Governor's Mansion. I have to leave you now to avoid raising suspicion, but I'll look to help you from up there in any way that I can." Fields appeared to hesitate. "I should ask, now that I know Major Hunter was a traitor, have I been compromised?"

Connor winced, grateful that he hadn't also been named in that breath.

Mayor Ellis shook his head. "You were never named in any of our mission planning."

"Good. Then there's still a chance that this might work."

Ellis nodded. "Watch your back out there tonight, Captain."

"You too, Mr. Mayor." Fields turned and ran for the door on the left. Connor waited for it to shut behind the captain before turning to address the others. "So we're just going to wait here until the riot forces the governor to evacuate?"

"You have a better idea?" Mayor Ellis asked.

"I need to go look for my fiancée," he said. "If I find her and Sergeant Hall's team, I'll lead them back here for reinforcements."

Ellis blinked at him. "You must be joking. He pointed to the door they'd come in by a moment ago. "There are two stalkers out there in case you forgot."

"I'll wait until they're gone," Connor insisted. "You could use the reinforcements, sir."

Mayor Ellis scowled. "Have you forgotten that you and Major Hunter betrayed us? Why the hell should I trust you on a solo mission after that?"

"I turned against the major," Connor said. "If not for my confession, this operation would still be compromised."

"Where would you even look for her?" Ellis demanded.

"I know where Sergeant Hall was going. To the dam at the top of the lake. *Please,*" Connor insisted. "You have to let me try."

"You don't even have a vehicle," Ellis said. "And you can't take ours. We'll need it to make our escape later."

"I can go on foot. It's not that far to the dam from here. A few miles."

"At least three," Ellis corrected.

"Thirty minutes," Connor replied.

Ellis pursed his lips.

"You can't seriously be considering this!" Corporal Williams hissed.

"Call me an old romantic, or maybe a fool, but I am," Ellis said. "I'll let you go, Private, but if and when you find her, I want you and Sergeant Hall back here to cover our retreat. Is that understood?"

Connor blinked and quickly nodded. He hadn't expected his desperate appeal to work. "Count on it, Mr. Mayor."

"Check the dock where we stopped earlier before you run all the way to the dam. I saw Sergeant Hall exiting his vehicle and running down to the lake as we drove away. I'm guessing he decided to row up the lake instead of driving to the dam."

Connor nodded quickly, remembering the traffic circle with the boathouse and the docks just outside the wall. "I'll find it."

"Good. One more thing." Ellis reached into his pocket for the folded paper that Captain Fields had given him. He unfolded it and pointed to the second of six different door codes that had been hastily scribbled on the paper. "Memorize that one," Ellis said.

Connor quietly committed the sequence of eight numbers to memory. "Got it," he said. "You won't regret this, sir."

"I'd better not. Just remember what's on the line here, son, and for God's sake, don't throw it all away for a girl."

Connor frowned at the mixed messages. "I won't, sir."

With that, he turned and ran for the door to the bunker.

CHAPTER FORTY-FIVE

The lake bed came swirling up beneath Adam's feet and he went stumbling and tripping across the slimy rocks with Stevens and Ramirez. All three of them collapsed on the shore below the cliff, gasping for air.

"Report!" Adam managed to croak out between ragged breaths.

"Got knocked around pretty bad, but I'll live," Ramirez said, checking herself over. Her cheek was swollen and bleeding from a gash, but otherwise, she looked fine.

"Good to go," Stevens added.

Adam nodded against the bed of rocks and rotting leaves where he lay. He sat up and fumbled with his carbine to cover them as they caught their breath. He scanned the shore and water for signs of trouble. There was no sign of Kent, or of any raiders that he might have been trying to link up with, and the water was curiously still.

"Did you kill it?" Stevens asked.

"I don't know," Adam whispered.

With the immediate threat now safely past, he pushed to his feet and searched the rocky, moss-covered cliffs for a way up. About thirty feet upstream, the cliffs parted to reveal a steep, debris-covered slope. Adam pointed to it. "On me," he said, already moving swiftly in that direction.

Stevens and Ramirez fell in quietly behind him. After just a few steps, they found the spot where Kent must have left the water, marked by wet leaves and rocks. That trail of moisture led in the same direction that they were moving. Encouraged by that sign, Adam picked up the pace.

They reached the break in the cliffs, and Adam discovered that it was a dry creek bed. It looked like they could follow it up to the homes he'd seen from the boat.

Kent's dribbling trail of water had almost dried up entirely by this point, but somehow the rocks and leaves along the shore were soaking wet. Adam frowned at that. Had Kent waded back in for some reason? After narrowly escaping that sea monster, Adam doubted it. A handful of familiar, gleaming specks of brass caught his eyes. He bent to retrieve one of them and held it up to the light.

"Is that what I think it is?" Stevens whispered.

Adam nodded. "A spent round. Looks like five fifty-six cal."

"Same as ours," Ramirez said.

"There's dozens of them…" Stevens added.

Adam dropped to his haunches to look for any other signs of what might have happened here. There was no sign of blood, thank God. He almost breathed a sigh with that.

But then he saw a flat gray rock that was smeared with a partial bloody handprint. He measured that partial print against his hand to get a sense of its size. The fingers were long and skinny, the palm small.

Ice slid into Adam's veins, and his heart began to pound. There was no way to know if it belonged to Crystal, or to whoever had been firing the gun. Wet rocks glistened along the shore, but there was no sign of a boat.

"She escaped and tried to swim across," he realized.

"What?" Stevens asked. "With that thing in the water?"

"She turned back," Adam replied. "And she was bleeding when she reached the shore."

Stevens winced. "From a gunshot?"

"Maybe," Adam conceded. "But either way, she wasn't alone." He straightened and nodded to the river bed. "We're going up. Stay alert."

Adam yanked his carbine up to his shoulder and went rushing up the slope, moving as quickly and quietly as he could.

Here and there he spotted signs of blood spatter on the rocks. That only spurred him to run faster.

They came to a short concrete wall that formed a dam below a small pond. A pathway led up from a dock on the other side where a pair of swan-shaped paddle boats sat on the shore.

Adam signaled to the other side and pushed up, moving quickly around the pond and watching for signs of hostiles lurking in the trees or the winding path above the pond.

There were no signs of anyone yet, but Adam knew better than to trust that. He reached the dock and saw a few more freckles of blood. He went racing up the path and emerged at the bottom of the grounds of a sprawling mansion. To the left of the home, he saw what looked like a detached garage or maybe a guest house.

Adam went slinking along a low wall to stay out of sight. A neighboring home appeared through the trees, almost equally as large and ostentatious as this one. The dry river bed they'd followed up from the lake formed a natural division between the two properties. Adam ducked down into it, using the craggy depression for cover to continue his approach. Adam saw that the river bed snaked around behind the guest house. An attached three-car garage faced it. One of the doors was open, and a big white truck was nestled in the shadows within.

Adam ducked behind the guest house and

leaned around the corner with his carbine's scope to get a better look at the open garage.

There were at least two people inside. One of them vanished into the deepening shadows, while the other reached up and rolled the garage door down with a piercing metallic shriek that set his teeth on edge.

Before the door had fully shut, Adam realized that he recognized the vehicle inside. It was *his* truck—or Rick's, anyway. The same vehicle that they'd driven out of Sunny Valley Ranch and later lost in Hondo. It was unmistakable from the ramshackle metal topper welded to the back.

Had some of those raiders from Hondo escaped and used his truck to get away? It seemed unlikely at best, coincidental at worst. Whoever they were, he needed to find out if they had Crystal and neutralize them.

Adam pulled back from the corner of the guest house, contemplating the situation. Stevens and Ramirez regarded him expectantly, waiting for orders. Adam wanted nothing more than to bust in there, guns blazing, but he had no idea how many raiders were camped out inside. On top of that, that mansion gave them a defensible position, and if Kent had already come up this way, which seemed likely given the evidence he'd found below—then he had probably warned them to expect company.

Adam needed a plan. And a good one. He ground his teeth and glanced around, contemplating the grounds of the mansion. At the very least, they needed a blind approach that wouldn't expose them to enemy fire.

But then Adam spotted something that he hadn't been counting on, and a grim smile curved his lips. He jerked his chin to indicate the spot. Stevens began nodding to herself, having understood his intentions without the need for a verbal explanation.

Adam peeled away from the guest house, using the trees and foliage for cover as he advanced on a shadowy mound of dirt, dug up at the edge of a flat, grassy portion of the neighboring yard. It was easy to miss thanks to the sheer height of the grass in the overgrown, weed-infested lawn, but there was no mistaking that mound of dirt for anything other than what it was—

The entrance of a stalker den.

CHAPTER FORTY-SIX

When Crystal came to, she found herself staring at a gleaming pile of credits on an old coffee table. Her hands were tied again behind her back, but this time she was gagged, too.

Her leg was throbbing sharply, but the pain was more subdued than it had been before she'd passed out. She blinked bleary, tear-crusted eyes to see that her leg was bound with a blood-soaked beige compression wrap.

She struggled to sit up, straining against her bonds to find that she was lying on one of the couches in the living room of the raiders' decrepit mansion.

"Had a nice nap?" John asked, glaring icily at her from where he stood by the living room window, aiming his rifle out a broken pane of glass. Crystal noticed that John's right cheek was swollen and there was a bloody gash taped shut just below his eye, right over the cheekbone. It looked like someone had punched him in the face. Or maybe he'd fallen as he'd struggled to carry her back up the cliff.

The short Mexican raider stood on the opposite side of the window, covering the house with a scoped hunting rifle. Crystal struggled to remember his name. *Eduardo?* she thought. That sounded right. But why were they guarding the house?

Hearing fierce whispers, she twisted around to see the rest of the raiders standing around the kitchen island. Bobby and Kasey and her dark-skinned accomplice were arguing with another man who hadn't been with them earlier. He was tall and skinny and wearing dark clothes. He seemed familiar somehow, even though his back was turned. Then he pointed vigorously at her and she caught a glimpse of his face. Recognition hit her like a slap in the face. It was Kent, the man who'd abducted her from Travis. But what was he doing here? Hadn't he taken his money and left?

Suddenly the tone of the conversation shifted. Bobby drew a silenced pistol from his hip and aimed it at Kent.

He threw up his hands and took a quick step back. "What the hell, Bobby?! I didn't have to come here and warn you, you know!"

"We were supposed to *lure* them here!" Bobby said, his voice rising angrily. "But you *led* them straight to us!"

Crystal's spirits soared as she realized what that meant. Somehow, her dad and Connor had found her!

"What's the difference? You wanted them here, right?" Kent asked.

"If you don't know the difference between plotting an ambush and *being* ambushed, then you're an even bigger idiot than I thought!"

"Bobby… listen to me," Kent said. "There's only three of them, and the drake must have taken at least one. You've got them outnumbered, and now you know that they're coming. We still have the advantage."

"We?" Bobby echoed. "There's no *we* here. I'm done with you."

"Bobby, wait!"

PLIP.

Kent toppled like a tree and hit the floor with a thud.

"Fucking traitor," Bobby spat as he holstered his gun. "Grady—"

"Yeah?" Kasey's dark-skinned accomplice asked.

"Go check the perimeter. Take Eduardo with you. We need to know if they've found us and how many of them made it to shore."

"Copy that," Grady replied. He retrieved his carbine from the kitchen counter and ducked under the strap. "Eduardo!" he whispered sharply.

The short Mexican man turned from the window. "Yes, Mr. Grady?"

"Let's go. We're on recon."

"Yes, boss," Eduardo said as he peeled away from the window with his hunting rifle.

He and Grady strode quickly down the hall, heading for the garage.

"Kent said it was just the three of them," Kasey soothed.

"He'd have said anything to save his ass," Bobby muttered. "For all we know, they have a whole platoon on the way. Get the trucks packed and everyone loaded up. We're leaving."

"Now?" Kasey asked. "It's almost dark! Stalkers will be coming out to hunt. At least wait for Grady to report back," Kasey urged. "Kent said that he wasn't followed. If that's true, there are a lot of houses up on this ridge. If they have to search all of them, stalkers will find them before they find us."

"Just get the trucks ready," Bobby growled.

Kasey sighed. "Fine." She snatched up a shotgun that was leaning against the island and pumped the action before following the other two raiders out.

Crystal hoped she was wrong. If her Dad and Connor had to search the whole neighborhood for her, stalkers probably *would* find them before they found her.

***

Carla sat on the bleachers of the basketball court at the old YMCA they were using for their new staging point. She was surrounded by all of the Nightingales from Bexar as well as a couple of dozen new ones from Travis. Sophie stood in the middle of the court below beside a tall man with buzz-cut black hair and a round face. He introduced himself as Captain Sean Fields, the *proctor* of Travis's conclave.

Carla listened attentively with the others while he laid out their revised plan for the night. The Nightingales from Travis were going to go out on foot, distributing their fliers with the proof of the governor's collaboration, along with instructions to rendezvous at dusk in Wooldridge Square, a city park just a few blocks from the Governor's Mansion. From there they would march together on the Governor's Mansion.

Carla was right with him until the part where he explained that they weren't going to be carrying any weapons.

Mutterings of shock and discontent spread quickly through the stands.

"How are we supposed to face Rangers if we're unarmed?" someone asked.

"This is going to be a peaceful protest!" Captain Fields replied. "The governor has an entire battalion of Rangers waiting in a building across the street from his mansion. And for those of you who don't know what a battalion is, that's almost one thousand soldiers."

The crowd grew louder with that until Captain Fields had to shout to be heard.

Beside him, Sophie whistled sharply. "Quiet!" she shouted into the restless silence that followed.

"Thank you," Fields grated out. "Miller won't use lethal force on his own people. So long as none of the protesters are carrying weapons, he won't have an excuse to open fire on you. Doing so would only further erode public support for his government, so he'll try to take the high road."

"I hope you're right," Carla muttered under her breath.

The rioters' only mission was to spook Miller into using his secret tunnel to escape. Carla wondered idly how they were supposed to accomplish that without any weapons, but she decided to give the captain some credit and wait to see how it all unfolded.

Her thoughts turned to Connor, hoping that he'd found a way into the bunker with Mayor Ellis. And that they hadn't run into any stalkers. And that Adam had found Crystal. Carla caught herself biting her nails and forced herself to stop.

It was going to take a miracle for this plan to succeed, and another one for all of them to survive it.

***

Adam crept as close as he dared to the entrance of the stalker den, and then he produced one of the two smoke grenades from a pouch on his vest.

Corporal Stevens' eyes widened as she appeared to realize what he was planning. "You're going to throw that in?"

Adam nodded. "Should flush at least one of them out," he said.

"So that it can rip us apart?" Ramirez asked.

"Not *us*," Adam explained.

Ramirez looked skeptical. "It'll be closer to us than the raiders. How are you going to lead it to them?"

Adam patted the frag grenade in one of his other pouches and pointed up to the garage of the mansion where they were camped. "I'll lob it over. The sound will draw the stalker to them, and if we're lucky, it will also draw the raiders out." Adam mimed the two groups clashing by knocking his fists together.

"What if it sees us first?" Stevens asked.

Adam shook his head. "The smoke will take a while to filter through the tunnels."

"It's risky," Stevens said.

"You have a better idea, Corporal?" Adam asked.

"I wish I did," she replied.

Taking that as encouragement, Adam nodded and turned back to the entrance of the stalker den. "Get ready to run," he whispered. Then he waded out into the overgrown grass, aiming for the hard-packed mound of dirt that formed the entrance of the stalker den. As soon as he came within clear sight of the gaping hole in the side of the mound, he pulled the safety pin and tossed the grenade down the hole. Almost immediately, thick white clouds of smoke began gushing from the entrance.

Adam ran back over to Stevens and Ramirez, and they fled the scene, racing across the dry river bed and up to the guest house where they'd been hiding a few minutes ago.

An overgrown hedge lay between them and the stalker den. Adam peeked over it to watch the smoking entrance for signs of activity.

"Anything?" Stevens whispered, interrupting the perpetually buzzing cicadas.

Adam shook his head.

A tortured shriek split the silence, and Adam flinched. For a moment he thought it was a stalker, but then he belatedly recognized the sound as coming from the rusty rails of the garage door the raiders had shut earlier.

Adam risked peeking around the corner of the guest house. Two men came creeping out of the garage, one tall and dark-skinned, armed with a carbine like his, the other short, with a scoped hunting rifle. They stepped out into the sunlit driveway and swept the area.

One of them signaled to the other, and they both moved to the edge of the driveway and jumped down. Adam ducked into cover so they wouldn't see him.

Stevens regarded him curiously.

He held up two fingers and pointed in the raiders' direction.

She nodded.

One of the raiders called out in alarm, saying something about smoke in Spanish. Adam smiled tightly to himself. Maybe he didn't need a stalker for a distraction after all.

Yet even as he was thinking that a piercing wail split the air, and the cicadas took a breath.

Adam peeked back over the hedge to see a stalker emerge in the grassy clearing below. It tossed its massive head, sneezing violently and stumbling in circles.

One of the raiders muttered a curse, and Adam heard them whispering fiercely, then warning each other to shut up.

It was time to kick things up a notch. He drew the frag grenade from his vest. Both Stevens and Ramirez visibly tensed at the sight of it. He pulled the pin and held down the spoon. Leaning around the corner, he lobbed the grenade straight for the two raiders.

"Grenade!" the dark-skinned raider cried, and then he dove for cover, deliberately rolling down the hill.

"*Que?*" the shorter man asked, looking around stupidly.

The grenade exploded with a *boom*, and the man screamed as shrapnel ripped into him.

The stalker shrieked and went bounding toward the commotion. The Mexican man was still screaming. The grenade hadn't killed him, but it had blown off an arm, and he was bleeding from a hundred different places.

The dark-skinned raider scrambled to his feet, cursing steadily. He turned and ran back up the hill, glancing frantically over his shoulder at the stalker bounding toward him. He raced straight past his partner, not even hesitating to lend a hand.

The stalker didn't slow down either, all of its instincts now firing at the sight of its prey running away.

The raider jumped back up onto the driveway and spun around to fire at the stalker. Two rounds clipped the beast in its shoulders just as it reached the short raider. The bullets shattered uselessly on its scaly armor. It darted sideways and leaped on top of the Mexican man, biting off his head and silencing his screams. The dark-skinned raider cursed again and ran for the open garage.

The stalker bounded after him, smacking its jaws and crunching noisily. The monster caught up to the second man just as he skidded through the open door. Claws raked down his back, ripping him open with a blood-curdling scream. Then the monster fell on top of him with claws and teeth flashing, and the man's screams faded to grim silence.

Stevens and Ramirez exchanged wide-eyed looks. Adam signaled for them to advance, indicating the direction of the stalker.

"Are you *crazy?*" Stevens whispered.

Adam smiled tightly, choosing not to call her out on the insubordinate remark. "The stalker's got point," he whispered back. "Let's go."

Sounds of gunfire erupted from the open garage, followed closely by the shrieking cries of the stalker taking fire.

Adam crept carefully around the corner of the guest house with his carbine tucked tightly to his shoulder. The gunfire faded to silence, but the stalker went on shrieking, enraged by the assault.

Adam reached the edge of the driveway and aimed down his scope, scanning the shadows inside the garage and hoping to find that the monster had killed the raiders that had shot at it.

But the stalker was raging around blindly inside the garage, knocking down shelves and raking its claws across the sides of Adam's old truck. The raiders had driven it to a frenzy with their attack, but Adam didn't see any sign of extra bodies, so they must have retreated inside the house.

After a moment, the stalker appeared to calm itself, shrieking more softly now. It began sniffing around, searching for its attackers. With a sudden snort, it stared at the inside door.

"Good boy," Adam whispered.

It bounded up the steps and slammed into the wooden door, splintering it with the impact. Gunfire exploded once more, and the stalker shrieked again.

Adam cringed, realizing that he might have gotten more than he'd bargained for by unleashing that monster on them. At this rate, it could kill Crystal, too.

He hoped she was locked safely in one of the rooms.

Muffled shouts sounded as two more raiders came racing in from the far end of the driveway where the street was.

Adam aimed at the nearest one and pulled the trigger. The raider's chest exploded with a puff of pink mist and he collapsed, dead before he hit the ground.

The second one fled for the cover of the guest house, but he was cut down by two more bullets from Stevens and Ramirez.

"Clear," Adam whispered, and then he signaled for them to advance, and he ran for the open garage, following the stalker's shrieks and the chattering roar of the raiders' weapons.

CHAPTER FORTY-SEVEN

Crystal heard the telltale shrieking of a stalker, followed by a blood-curdling human scream that cut off sharply into silence. Bobby cursed and then he, John, and Kasey all ran for the garage, leaving her to her own devices. She jumped up from the couch and ran, grateful that her ankles weren't bound. She sprinted down the corridor on the other side of the kitchen. Stopping at the first door she found, she turned and awkwardly grasped it with her hands tied. She turned the knob and the door creaked open to reveal a messy bedroom. The raider who'd shot Owen was lying in the bed with his empty wheelchair beside it.

He struggled to sit up as she came in, and they stared hatefully at each other for several breathless seconds.

Crystal wondered if shutting herself in with this monster was any better than facing the one outside. Then again, Cory was paralyzed.

How dangerous could he be? And she was tied up. They were both incapacitated in their own ways.

Gunfire came rattling to Crystal's ears from the direction of the garage, followed by shouts of alarm.

"Shut the door!" Cory screamed.

Crystal flinched. Coming to a decision about him, she used her shoulder to close the door. It clicked shut, and Cory's eyes darted to his wheelchair.

Crystal sensed his intentions even before she noticed the shotgun leaning against the wheel. He lunged for it, falling out of bed with his fingers splayed and reaching for the gun.

Crystal screamed in outrage, but the sound was muffled by her gag. She half-waddled and half-ran to beat Cory to the shotgun, unable to believe how stupid she'd been to trust him. Cory was going to kill her long before that stalker could!

She dove for the floor just as Cory's hands closed around the shotgun. She landed on top of him, pinning the weapon between them, and the shotgun went off with a deafening *boom!*

***

Adam burst into a formal sitting room with a hallway leading away into the rest of the house. At the end of that passage, the stalker was rearing up on its hind legs with a long kitchen island between it and a tall, skinny raider standing on the other side. It narrowly missed him. He screamed in terror and opened fire. More bullets plinked and shattered against the stalker's hide.

Undeterred, the monster leaped straight over the island. The raider yelped with fright and scrambled away.

The stalker narrowly missed with another swipe of its claws, then snorted and skittered after its fleeing prey.

The man screamed again, now firing blindly over his shoulder and forcing Adam and Stevens to plaster themselves to the walls. Adam saw that the man was running for an open door at the end of another corridor where a second man was waving frantically to him.

Adam darted to the entrance of the hall that led out of the sitting room. Using the door jamb for cover, he sighted down his scope for the second raider. That man was wearing a familiar-looking *Bandidos* biker's jacket. Adam snapped off a hasty shot, narrowly missing his shoulder.

The Bandido ducked into the room, then peeked around the corner and fired back, splintering the door frame in front of Adam's nose. He plastered himself to the wall again, and then Stevens ran over to lay down covering fire from the other side of the door, while Ramirez kept them covered from the splintered door to the garage.

Adam risked peeking around the corner again. He was just in time to see the fleeing raider dive past the one in the biker vest. The stalker went crashing after him, but the passage was too narrow for the creature's broad shoulders, and it got stuck in the opening. It thrashed around angrily, splintering the walls and floors with its claws.

The door to the room where the raiders had fled promptly slammed, and Adam heard heavy furniture being dragged in front of it to block the entrance, but it didn't look like the stalker could reach them. Now that beast was Adam's problem.

He spent a moment watching it wriggle and writhe around, looking like a square peg trying to force itself into a round hole. Its tail lashed the floor and claws raked both walls, making the corridor subtly wider in the process. The stalker snorted furiously, making inching progress. Maybe it *would* be able to reach them.

Adam signaled for Stevens and Ramirez to follow him as he crept swiftly down the corridor behind the stalker. They emerged between the living room and the kitchen, about thirty feet behind the beast.

Adam scanned the other entrances and exits for more hostiles, but the rest of the mansion seemed to be deserted, and so far, the stalker hadn't noticed them. But wedged as it was in that narrow passage, it had a bad case of tunnel vision. Literally.

Adam was of half a mind to let it reach the raiders and simply deal with whoever was left when the dust finally settled.

But then he heard a girl scream. It was Crystal, and she was in that room where the raiders were hiding.

***

Connor hauled back on both oars, rowing as hard as he could. He was glad to have found a single-seater boat in the warehouse beside the docks, but it wasn't like any boat that he was used to. He'd rowed kayaks and canoes before, but he'd never sat *backward* while rowing with *two* oars. At least he was making good time up the river.

The only problem was, he had no idea where he was supposed to be going. He'd found Adam's Humvee still parked exactly where Ellis had said it would be, but no sign of Adam, or of the other two Rangers who'd gone with him.

Connor twisted around in his seat, scanning upstream for other boats on the water.

Nothing.

He grimaced and went back to rowing. The sun was sinking fast, shining orange on the water with a fiery sunset already blooming in the west. He had maybe another hour before dark. If he didn't find Adam before that, stalkers were going to find him.

Connor gritted his teeth, heaving harder and

faster with each stroke. Maybe Adam had gone all the way to the dam, after all?

While he was still thinking about that, he passed the upturned hull of an aluminum rowboat, glinting in the sun. Connor dropped his oars and snatched up his carbine, twisting around frantically to look for signs of trouble.

Despair seized him as he realized that there was another possibility—that Adam had run into trouble on the river long before he'd found Crystal. Maybe whoever had taken her had also ambushed him.

Then something *thunked* into the bottom of Connor's boat.

"What the…?" he muttered, leaning over the side to see what it was.

A giant shadow passed close below the water. *Submerged debris?* he wondered. *A log, maybe?*

Connor released his carbine and went cautiously back to rowing, keeping wary eyes on the cliffs above him.

He hadn't taken more than a handful of strokes before his boat surged impossibly out of the water, rocketing straight into the air. Connor cried out and reflexively clutched the sides of the boat, only to find jagged rows of teeth puncturing the hull mere inches from his fingertips. Those teeth belonged to a glistening black monster that looked like a giant snake, with glowing blue eyes protruding slightly from the sides of its head. One of those eyes winked at him as a milky white membrane swept over it.

Connor screamed and recoiled from the monster, reaching again for his gun.

He hit the top of his arc above the water, suspended fully a dozen feet above the shimmering surface, and then his stomach leaped into his throat as the monster that held him went crashing back down, dragging him along with it.

CHAPTER FORTY-EIGHT

Crystal bit back another scream as Bobby slapped her for the second time. Her gag had slipped free with the first slap, but this one left her ears ringing.

"You killed him!" Bobby roared, looming over Crystal. She stumbled backward and tripped over Cory's lifeless body. This time Bobby drew his pistol and aimed it at her head, just like he'd done with Kent.

Crystal froze, her whole body growing cold.

Kasey and John swept in quickly and pulled his arm down. "We need her," Kasey hissed at him.

"Fuck that," Bobby growled.

The sound of the stalker shrieking grew abruptly louder as gunfire erupted outside. Everyone turned to look.

"They're going to get in here," Kasey said. "Look around!" she added. "The windows are barred. The only way we're getting out is *through* those Rangers. We *need* the girl for that."

All eyes slid back to Crystal, and she cringed, wishing she could melt away and seep through the floor. "Need me for what?" she asked quietly.

Bobby sneered. "A hostage. Your daddy's not gonna shoot through you."

Crystal gaped at them as she listened to the dying screams of the stalker outside and the sporadic gunfire that was eliciting those tortured shrieks.

She couldn't believe it. Her dad and Connor were here! They'd come all this way, beating impossible odds just to find her, and now... they were going to fail. Because of her. Because someone was holding a gun to her head.

"Don't worry, sweetheart," Bobby said, smiling grimly at her. "I'll dispatch them quickly. Just like you did with Cory. RIP, buddy," he added, nodding to his dead friend.

Crystal glanced down at the body, lying limp beside the wheelchair with a gaping hole in his chest. She wanted to deny it, to explain that Cory had been reaching for the shotgun that John was now holding and that he'd accidentally shot himself instead of her. But she doubted the raiders would care about that petty distinction between an accident and cold-blooded intentions.

"Get up," John snapped at her. He swooped

down and grabbed her by the arm, wrenching her to her feet.

Bobby took over, turning her to face the door. Crystal saw that an old wardrobe had been shoved in front of it, but now John and Kasey pushed it aside and went to stand on either side of the door. Bobby jammed the barrel of his pistol against the side of her head. "Get ready, girlie," he whispered as the gunfire faded with one final crack of a rifle going off. "How about you call your daddy over here for us?"

Crystal shook her head, refusing to be used as bait. But then Bobby grabbed a fistful of her hair, and she screamed again as he forced her head back sharply, exposing her throat.

"Go on!" Bobby growled. "Call him!"

Still, she refused.

"We need her alive, not in one piece," John said. "Cut off a finger and toss it out the door. That should be proof that we have her."

"Good idea," Bobby replied. "You wanna come over and do the honors?"

"Happily," John replied.

Crystal's eyes bulged as he approached.

"Wait!" she hissed. Sucking in a deep breath, she cried, "Dad! Don't come! It's a tr—" The air whooshed out of her lungs as Bobby elbowed her in the stomach.

"He already knows it's a trap thanks to that idiot, Kent. Lucky for you, it doesn't change anything." Bobby jerked his chin to the door. "Open her up, Kase."

She regarded him dubiously.

"You said it," he explained. "Only one way out, and daylight's burning. We need to beat it before nightfall."

Kasey carefully unlocked the door, and John hurried back to his position on the other side, holding his shotgun high with the barrel aimed up at the ceiling.

***

Adam stood frozen over the lifeless body of the stalker with the smoking barrel of his carbine still aimed at the ruined yellow eye of the beast. Crystal's screams echoed painfully in his ears. It took every ounce of his will not to charge in and kill whoever was making her scream like that.

Adam blinked past stinging drops of sweat, wondering if killing the stalker had been a mistake. Hearing the muffled strains of the raiders' conversation, but no gunshots or further screams, he glanced back at Stevens and Ramirez. Stevens was right behind him, standing on the stalker's back, while Ramirez was at the mouth of the corridor, watching their six.

Adam gestured to the door, then drew a circle with his finger, miming what he wanted Stevens to do. She nodded once, quickly, and clambered away. Ramirez looked to him expectantly as Stevens ran past her, but he shook his head.

This wouldn't be believable if both of them were missing. Seeing Kent's body in the living room confirmed what he'd already suspected— that these Raiders had been warned to expect them, so they knew that three Rangers were coming. But they didn't know that all three Rangers had made it.

Adam heard another scream, followed by, "Dad! Don't come! It's a—"

Adam's heart slammed inside his chest. His hands flexed angrily on his carbine. Moments later, he heard something heavy being dragged away from the door.

Ramirez clambered over the dead stalker and dropped to a crouch beside him to cover the door. It clicked open, the hinges groaning as it swung wide.

"We have your daughter!" a woman said.

"I know," Adam growled, his carbine flashing up to the door. "And you think you're going to use her to get through me, but I don't give two shits about you. Send Crystal out, and I'll leave."

"Bullshit," a vaguely familiar baritone answered. "You're a bleeding heart if ever I met one. You dragged your buddy into a rat's nest to save him."

Ramirez shot Adam a questioning look. He licked his lips and grimaced, realizing now where he remembered the man from. The

Walmart in Hondo where Owen had died.

"We can all still walk out of this," Adam insisted. "Send my daughter out."

The gleaming silver barrel of a revolver peeked around the corner, along with one dark eye. Adam hit the floor a split second before a bullet cracked out and *crunched* into the wall behind him.

Ramirez returned fire, forcing the raider back into cover.

"That was a mistake!" Adam roared, picking himself off the floor. "Last chance!" he gestured to Ramirez, indicating that she should sneak along the wall to the open doorway. She nodded and began creeping forward.

"All right, you win!" the Bandido said. "We're sending her out!"

Adam braced himself. Crystal came shuffling into the passage, and his heart leaped into his throat. Her left eye was swollen, and her cheeks were streaked with tears, but otherwise, she looked okay. Right behind her, holding a silenced pistol to the back of her head, was the big raider in the Bandidos jacket. He was wearing a red bandana around his head, and a smug grin that showed clearly despite the dim light filtering in from the curtained window at the far end of the corridor. "Long time," the Bandido said.

Ramirez froze, keeping him covered.

Adam was also covering him, but he knew

how delicate the situation was. He had to keep the man there, standing in the doorway to buy time for Stevens to get into position.

"Drop your guns," the raider said.

"If I do that, you'll kill us, and then you'll kill my daughter."

"Hah!" the man snorted. "You think I'm gonna *kill* her? She's my payday, man. We're gonna be eating for months thanks to her."

A muscle jerked in Adam's cheek, but he said nothing to that.

"I'm sorry," Crystal sobbed.

"Not your fault," Adam replied.

"It is," she insisted.

"Awww, what a touching reunion. Drop the guns."

Another couple of raiders slipped out behind the big man holding Crystal hostage, using them for cover and aiming two shotguns at them from point-blank range.

Adam was surprised to note that he recognized them as well. A dark-skinned woman and a gaunt-looking Caucasian man with stringy black hair. They'd answered the gate at the Walmart five years ago, right alongside this guy in the biker vest.

"Just shoot them, Bobby," the woman said. "We don't have time for this."

Ramirez shifted her aim to the woman.

"Listen to me," Adam tried again. "We don't care about you. We're just here for my daughter. Send her over, and we'll go."

"Really," the big man nodded. "And what happens when she tells you that there are others here? You still gonna be able to walk away?"

Adam's guts clenched up at the thought of more abducted girls waiting to be sold into slavery. "That's none of my concern," he lied.

"Oh, that's a ripe old pile of bullshit," Bobby replied. "You might leave, but you'll call in a whole platoon to come after us and rescue the other hostages. We'll have to relocate our whole operation, all because we spared one little girl. And what happens to my payday? Who's gonna compensate me for—"

A cracking report sent the skinny raider to his knees with blood gushing from his throat. He pulled the trigger reflexively, but the shot kicked up into the ceiling. The female raider opened fire, too, thinking it was Ramirez. The shell hit her square in the chest, and Ramirez fired back as she fell. Bobby ducked away from the doorway, screaming, "Fall back!"

Adam struggled to find an opening to shoot him, but he kept Crystal between them as he retreated. She struggled and fought him every step of the way, but he was far too strong for her.

Adam popped off a hasty shot at the woman who'd hit Ramirez, and she cried out as her lower leg exploded with a fountain of gore.

The woman limped away, clutching her leg and firing one-handed over her shoulder at him.

Unable to brace against the recoil, her shot went wide, but it still forced Adam to flatten himself to the wall. The big raider yanked open another door on the opposite side of the hallway from where Stevens was set up outside.

Adam squeezed off another shot just before both raiders vanished into the room. Adam cursed under his breath, keeping the entrance covered as he stepped sideways to check on Ramirez. A quick glance told him everything he needed to know—dead eyes staring, but he spared a hand from his carbine to check for a pulse just in case.

Nothing.

"That was real *fucking* stupid!" the man in the biker jacket screamed.

The tall skinny raider that Stevens had shot through the window was still clutching his throat with bloody hands, and gurgling softly. Adam crept over to him, pulling even with the doorway and catching a glimpse of Stevens crouched in the bushes outside. He pointed to the door on the opposite side of the hall, and she nodded, already moving to circle around.

Adam saw the man creeping up behind her a second too late. "Stevens! Six o'clock!"

She whirled around—

And a shotgun boomed at point-blank range.

Her chest exploded, and she hit the ground with a muffled *thud.*

Adam fired back, twice in quick succession. Her attacker went down next as one of those shots hit him in the side of the head. Feeling watched, Adam swept his carbine back to the open door where the raiders had taken Crystal.

He was just in time to lay down suppressive fire for himself. The barrel of a shotgun vanished from the open doorway, and he heard the female raider cursing on the other side. He didn't think he'd hit her, but at least he'd forced her back.

"You know what? I think I changed my mind!" Bobby roared. "This shit ain't worth it! Either you drop your weapon now, or I'm gonna shoot your daughter in the head. I'm going to count to three. One!"

Adam clenched his teeth, hesitating. Was it a bluff?

"Two!"

If he dropped his weapon now, he was as good as dead. But Crystal would probably live. She'd be sold down south, but she'd live.

"Three!"

"Wait!" Adam shouted. "I'm throwing it over." He ducked out of the strap and tossed his carbine toward the open door. It landed with a noisy clatter.

"Sidearm!" Bobby added.

Adam grimaced and reached down for his

pistol. As he did so, a final gurgle drew his gaze to the shotgun-wielding raider that Stevens had shot. He reached cautiously for the man's gun, inching it around so that the barrel was facing the open doorway, and then he kneeled beside the weapon to hide it from view.

"Hurry up!" Bobby snapped.

Adam tossed the pistol, and it landed with a clatter beside his carbine.

"Good," Bobby growled. The raider peeked around the door jamb and scowled as his eyes flicked to the dead raider beside Adam.

"Hands up and stand up," Bobby said.

"I want your word that you won't hurt my daughter," Adam said, stalling for time as his finger tightened on the trigger of the shotgun.

"She's inventory. You think I'm gonna devalue my own stock? It's bad enough that drake bit her leg!"

"Is she okay?" Adam asked.

"She's just peachy! Now stand—"

BOOM!

The shotgun pellets sprayed the raider's leg, and he sagged abruptly to that side, howling in pain. But that movement only brought him into clearer view.

Adam snatched the weapon up and pulled the trigger again. This time the shell hit him squarely in the chest and opened him up like a blooming tulip.

The raider screamed as he fell. His silenced

pistol went off and the bullet crunched through the wall behind Adam. He surged to his feet, racing to recover the weapons he'd thrown. Snatching up his carbine, he was just in time to see Bobby's pistol swinging into line with him for a final, dying shot.

Adam beat him to it and pumped a round from his carbine into the raider's forehead. His skull cracked into the floor, and he lay still.

"You stupid fuck! Your daughter's dead!" the female raider screamed.

Adam's whole body grew cold, and he sprinted for the door, feeling time slow to a crawl.

Crystal screamed, and another shotgun blast *boomed* just before he reached the opening.

CHAPTER FORTY-NINE

"Crystal!" Adam roared as he raced around the corner, skidding on the blood-slicked floors. He saw that Crystal was miraculously still standing, mere inches away from the female raider with a pattern of shotgun pellets in the wall beside them.

The female raider shoved Crystal away and swept her gun around for a killing blow.

Adam fired repeatedly, hitting her twice in the torso before she could bring the shotgun into line, but she was still standing, still sweeping her gun around.

Crystal dove for the ground. The shotgun boomed, and Adam shot the raider in the face. Her cheek exploded, and she spun around as she fell, dead before she even hit the ground. Adam rushed to Crystal's side, his heart hammering, thoughts racing.

She was lying flat on her face, not moving.

He reached her side and fell on his knees beside her. He flipped her over, fearing the worst—

Crystal blinked up at him and smiled. "You found me," she whispered.

Adam's whole body sagged with relief. He scooped Crystal into his arms, hugging her to his chest and burying his face beside her ear.

"You're okay," he whispered, then quickly withdrew to an arm's length, checking her over again just to make sure.

Hurried footfalls hammered down the hall, approaching fast.

Adam leaped back to his feet, swaying dizzily and blinking spots from his eyes as he aimed at the open door.

A man in Ranger's fatigues skidded into view, aiming a matching carbine right back at him. Adam's finger spasmed reflexively on the trigger, but he managed to stop himself just before he pulled it.

"Connor!" Crystal cried a split-second before Adam registered who it was.

She went racing by him, her shoulders wiggling with her hands still bound behind her back.

Connor enfolded her in a breathless hug, kissing her cheeks and then her lips.

"I thought I'd lost you," he sobbed.

"Did you see anyone else outside?" Adam demanded, already running to the door and aiming down the corridor to check.

Connor shook his head. "Just a lot of dead bodies. I'm guessing that was your work?"

Adam nodded grimly and pulled back from his scope. Now that he had a chance to catch his breath, his thoughts went to Stevens and Ramirez. Both of them had died to save Crystal. One life had cost two.

Adam looked out the window, noting how dark it was getting. The sun was fading fast. "We need to get out of here before more stalkers come sniffing around," he said.

Connor nodded absently while using the knife from his belt to cut the ropes around Crystal's wrists.

"They have our truck," she said.

"I know," Adam grunted. "Any idea who has the keys?"

Crystal appeared to think about it while wincing and massaging her swollen, bloodied wrists. Connor took her hands in his and shook his head in dismay. "Those bastards. What have they done to you?"

"Nothing that won't heal," she replied.

"Christie," Adam prompted. "The keys."

"I think it was her." Crystal pointed to the woman lying on the floor in a spreading pool of blood with one half of her face missing.

Adam ran over and bent down to search her pockets. He found a familiar set of keys in her left jeans pocket. "Got them."

"I need a gun," Crystal said.

Adam turned and snatched the giant engraved revolver from the dead woman's hip.

"Here. Colt Python," he said.

Crystal grimaced as she took the weapon.

"Cooper, take point," Adam said, realizing how exhausted he was. His whole body was shaking and cold from spent adrenaline.

"Copy," Connor said, leaning out the door. "Clear," he said and then stepped out into the hall.

Adam went with Crystal next. He glanced down at the raider in the Bandidos jacket as he went, but the man was clearly dead. Adam scooped up his silenced pistol and tucked it into his holster, thinking that it might come in handy later.

On their way out, they pulled alongside Ramirez once more. Adam grimaced again at the sight of her lifeless eyes. He wanted to go check on Stevens, too, but he knew she was gone after taking that shotgun blast to the chest at point-blank range. And if by some miracle she wasn't dead, she'd be screaming from the pain.

They went clambering back over the dead stalker.

"Clear," Connor said again as he swept the living room and kitchen on the other side.

Adam noticed that Crystal was limping badly.

"You okay?" he asked.

"No, but I'll live," she replied. "Something in the river took a bite out of my leg."

Connor cursed and glanced sharply back at her.

"Eyes front," Adam snapped at him.

Connor tore his gaze away with a visible effort, once again sweeping for targets as he led them back to the garage. "It almost got me, too," he muttered.

Adam blinked. "It's alive?"

"Capsized my boat," Connor said.

They reached the splintered door to the garage and Connor poked his carbine through. "Clear," he whispered and then stepped through.

Adam and Crystal followed him to the truck. Thankfully, none of the tires had been slashed or punctured from that stalker's furious tantrum.

Adam yanked open the rear door for Crystal, but she hesitated. "What about the others?" she asked.

"Where?" Adam asked as he remembered Bobby alluding to them.

"In there, I think." Crystal pointed across the shadowy driveway to another three-car garage. Adam noticed a faded black door at the top of a short flight of steps between three different garage doors.

He looked to Connor. "We'd better make it quick."

Connor nodded.

Adam handed Crystal the keys to the truck.

"Get the engine running. At the first sign of trouble, you get the hell out of here."

"I'm not leaving without you," Crystal replied.

Adam frowned, but there was no time to argue. "We'll be quick," he said.

Crystal nodded and shut the back door, moving for the driver's side instead.

Adam signaled to Connor, and they exited the garage together with their carbines up and tracking.

No sign of hostiles. "Clear," Adam whispered. Long shadows from the trees skittered over them with a light gust of wind.

They reached the door. Adam tried the knob, but it was locked. "Cover me," he said. Stepping back, he braced himself on the railings at the top of the steps and hammered the entrance with his foot.

The old wooden frame splintered and the door flew open. Adam dropped to one knee, his carbine flashing back up.

The shadowy hall on the other side was empty, just a small foyer with a door to the garage and a staircase leading up. Adam flicked on his tac light and started up with Connor close behind him. At the top of the stairs, the space opened up into a small living room and kitchen, both of them empty. Adam pointed to a pair of doors on the other end of the building. Moving quickly, they reached the first door.

Adam tested the door handle. Also locked.

He heard muffled voices on the other side and pressed his ear to the door, listening.

All of them were women. Maybe three or four, but it sounded like they were gagged. Adam looked back to Connor and curled his thumb and forefinger around his throat—the hand signal for hostage—and then he held up four fingers.

Connor nodded. Not hearing any raiders among them, Adam took a few steps away from the door—

And then he charged it with his shoulder. The door splintered and burst open. The hostages screamed, but Adam ignored them as he swept the room for hostiles.

"Clear," he said a second later.

Connor let out a gritty sigh.

"Watch the door," Adam ordered.

"Copy," Connor replied.

Adam studied the hostages. Two women and two teenage girls sitting on the floor with their hands and feet bound and gags tied around their mouths. Adam's upper lip curled, wishing that he could go back and kill the raiders all over again.

He lowered his carbine and quickly went around the room removing gags and cutting ropes with his knife. He asked about the raiders as he did so, trying to find out how many there were in case he'd missed any of them.

The girls were both sobbing and incoherent, so Adam left them alone and focused on the adults instead. One of them, a woman with long, straight black hair and freckled cheeks was able to confirm the same number of raiders as he had killed.

"Was that a stalker we heard?" she asked shakily.

"Yes."

"Is it…"

"Dead?" Adam nodded. "But more will come if we don't get out of here soon. What's your name?" He asked.

"Charlotte," she replied.

"I'm Adam. Are any of you injured? Can you walk?"

Charlotte hesitated, looking at the other three while massaging her ankles. "I think so."

"Good." The other woman was busy consoling the two girls, and they sounded like they were calming down now.

"We need to go, Sergeant," Connor whispered from the door.

"Follow us," Adam said. "Stay quiet and stay close."

Charlotte nodded.

They hurried back down the stairs and Adam peeked out the front door, checking for signs of trouble. The sun had all but fully fallen now, leaving nothing but a fading pink glow above the trees.

Stars freckled the deepening blue sky, and a deep well of shadows now covered the driveway—to say nothing of the tree-covered grounds below.

Adam kept a wary eye in that direction as he signaled the all-clear and then led the way across the driveway. He half expected to see a stalker come bounding out of the shadows just as they reached the open door of the garage.

But that didn't happen.

The one working headlight of the truck flicked on, indicating that Crystal had seen them.

The light was landing strangely on the pavement, the beam falling inexplicably short. It was blocked by a shimmering gray mound. Adam almost barreled straight into it before he realized what it was.

"Stalker!" Crystal cried.

Adam skidded to a stop just as it drew itself up in front of him. Two giant yellow eyes flicked open, and it hissed as massive jaws thrust out, revealing four separate sets of razor-sharp teeth, and a fang-lined throat.

Adam fired repeatedly into its throat, and silvery gouts of alien blood jetted out like party streamers.

The stalker shrieked and lunged, knocking him over. Its tail flashed up, the venomous tip glinting in the fading light.

CHAPTER FIFTY

Carla marched swiftly up the street, being jostled roughly from side to side and shoved along from behind. She felt like a cork bobbing on a sea of angry faces. The turnout at Wooldridge Square had been much bigger than she'd expected, with easily a thousand people meeting there for the demonstration. Now, as they left the park behind, someone started chanting, "Gov-er-nor Mil-ler is a trait-or!" More voices joined in, and soon their chanting became a thunderous roar.

A sweaty flash of apprehension and claustrophobia came over Carla as she realized that she couldn't get out of this crowd even if she wanted to. She cast about frantically, looking for Sophie, but the other woman was nowhere to be seen. That only served to amplify her anxiety. Sophie had been standing right in front of her a minute ago, addressing the crowd from the top of the steps to an old gazebo with a pergola roof.

Where had she gone after that? Somehow,

Carla had lost track of her. She scanned the sea of faces around her, but their features all blurred together in the dark.

There was no sign of any Rangers yet, but Carla remembered Captain Fields had warned them that there was a whole battalion camped out in a building across the street.

Even as she thought about that, the sound of horses' hooves came *clip-clop-clipping* into hearing, and someone shouted over a megaphone, "You are in illegal violation of the established curfew! Disperse immediately and return to your homes!"

Carla twisted around to see Rangers on horseback trotting swiftly up both sides of the street, threatening to out-flank the protesters and block the street.

But there were only about a dozen of them, not nearly enough to stop a crowd of this size. And the protesters knew it. They roared and chanted louder, "Gov-er-nor Mil-ler is a trait-or!"

The illuminated red and blue facade of the mansion came sweeping into view at the end of the street, peeking through the trees. Someone shouted, "There it is! Follow me!"

With that, the crowd surged ahead, and Carla was forced to match their pace or else be trampled.

The Rangers' horses whinnied and snorted in alarm, with several of them bucking and threatening to throw their riders. A few of them fell back to deal with their spooked horses, while others surged ahead of the crowd. Eight Rangers on horseback peeled away from the sides of the street and lined abreast to block the way.

"Disperse!" the one with the megaphone shouted. "This is your final warning!"

The crowd screamed and charged.

Horses whinnied.

"Hold position!" megaphone man screamed, followed by, "Ready weapons!"

Rifles snapped up to shoulders, and Carla's pace faltered. They wouldn't open fire. It was a bluff.

"Fucking Vultures!" someone screamed.

A flaming projectile went arcing high above the crowd, whipping end over end.

Carla realized what it was a second before it smashed into a wave of spreading fire in front of the Rangers. A Molotov cocktail. That was the last straw for the frightened horses. They squealed and reared up on their hind legs.

Two riders cried out as they fell from their saddles. Another one went galloping away, clinging on for dear life. The remaining five shuffled their feet and turned in anxious circles, making it impossible for the Rangers to aim their guns.

One of them went off anyway with a *cracking* report, and someone in the crowd screamed as that shot found a target.

"Hold your fire and dismount!" megaphone man screamed as he abandoned his bucking horse.

So it was *a bluff,* Carla realized.

But it was too late.

Two more Molotovs went whipping through the air, followed by the *pop* of another gunshot, softer, but just as lethal. A Ranger fell out of his saddle, and lay still, revealing that someone in the crowd had fired that last shot.

The Molotovs hit the street in tandem, and one of them lit the megaphone man on fire. He ran away screaming, and then all hell broke loose.

The remaining Rangers opened up on the crowd, spraying their rifles on full auto. Protesters fell by the dozen. Carla ducked, keeping her head down to avoid stray bullets.

The crowd surged ahead and crashed into the Rangers, washing over them and sucking them under like a tidal wave. The gunfire abruptly ceased as protesters stole the Rangers' weapons and executed them. The remaining horses fled, snorting and tossing their heads as they galloped away.

A rifle thrust up above the seething multitude and sprayed the night with a roar of bullets. "Onward!" the man holding it screamed, and the crowd roared with him.

The Ranger with the megaphone was still on

fire, thrashing around on a narrow spit of grass beside the road as he struggled to put himself out.

The rioter with the stolen rifle sprayed him with bullets, and the Ranger lay still with flames licking hungrily over his corpse.

"Gov-er-nor Mil-ler is a trait-or!" the crowd roared anew.

A chill swept over Carla. She felt sick to her stomach from the sudden spark of violence. It wasn't supposed to be like this. They were supposed to have the moral high ground, but killing those Rangers felt *wrong*. Maybe it was because both her husband and son were Rangers. Under different circumstances, they might have found themselves on the wrong side of this coup, cut down by an angry mob.

As it was, Carla couldn't be sure that wouldn't still happen—except instead of a mob, it might be a firing squad. Carla gritted her teeth, suddenly wishing that she had a weapon so that she could mete out some violence of her own. She cast about, checking the ground for discarded guns that the other protesters had missed.

"Here!" someone shouted behind her.

Carla turned to see Sophie. Flickering orange fires were dancing in her eyes. She thrust out a sidearm, grip-first.

"Take it!" Sophie insisted.

Carla didn't need to be asked twice. She

seized the weapon and promptly pulled back on the slide to check the chamber. A gleaming brass round was already seated there.

So much for a peaceful protest, she thought as she let the slide snap back into place. She threw her head back and shouted, "Gov-er-nor Mil-ler is a trait-or!"

CHAPTER FIFTY-ONE

The hostages screamed as Adam dove for the pavement, narrowly evading a stab of the stalker's tail. He rolled and came up on one knee, aiming for the monster's eyes. He pulled the trigger steadily, missing as the monster tossed its head. Bullets were shattering indiscriminately on the stalker's armored hide as Connor laid down suppressive fire. The creature roared, and all four of its tongues fluttered as it reared up on its hind legs and swiped blindly at the air, trying to swat away the bullets like they were bugs. Each impact did little more than chip its scaly hide. But then Adam scored a direct hit on the stalker's left eye. It burst open like an overripe melon, and the monster screamed, now blinded on that side.

"Run!" Adam yelled. "Get them in the truck!" He rounded the monster's blinded flank, still firing and aiming for the gory mess of its ruined eye.

Connor went racing by, covering all four

hostages as they streaked toward the open garage.

A sweeping flash of the stalker's tail caught Adam across the chest, and he went flying onto his back, struggling to suck in a breath.

The stalker reared up in front of him, glaring with one giant yellow eye canted in his direction. It hissed, jaws thrusting out and gaping for the kill.

A throaty roar erupted from the garage followed by wheels squealing on the pavement. The stalker whirled toward the sound—

And a familiar F350 with a dented bull bar slammed into it. The stalker went skidding along the pavement, and Crystal leaned out the window, shouting, "Get in!"

Adam jumped up and ran for the passenger's side, seeing as he did so that Connor already had the back open and was helping the hostages in. Adam ripped open the door and dove into the passenger's seat.

The wounded stalker stumbled to its feet, hissing and shaking its giant head.

"Connor get in!" Crystal shouted. "We have to go!"

"I'm in!" he replied just as the doors at the back slammed.

Crystal hit the gas, roaring down the driveway and swerving just in time to avoid a swipe from the stalker's claws. Adam peered into the cracked side-view mirror, watching as the creature came bounding after them.

"Here it comes!" he warned.

Crystal spun the wheel and sent them skidding through a high-speed turn at the end of the driveway.

"I'll deal with it!" Adam said. "Just focus on your driving!"

He twisted around in his seat and leaned out the window, aiming the carbine out the back. With the truck rocking and rolling through potholes, it was almost impossible to get a clear shot. He fired anyway, missing twice before his trigger clicked sullenly. Adam ejected the spent magazine and reached for a fresh one in his vest.

Several more shots cracked out from the back as Connor opened fire. Shattered scales exploded from the beast's back and shoulders, but it showed no signs of stopping. It came within reach of their rear bumper and lunged, claws raking violently through the doors at the back. The truck sagged with the monster's weight and the engine whined sharply in protest. The stalker was clinging to the back, its hindquarters dragging on the pavement and kicking up sparkling clouds of dust.

Crystal sent them through another skidding turn. "Brace!" she screamed.

Adam withdrew sharply from the window to thrust his hands against the dash. They slammed into a wrought iron gate, and it burst open, kicking up a brilliant wave of sparks as it dragged across the asphalt. The stalker lost its grip on their bumper and went tumbling away. Crystal turned again to the right on the other side of the gates, and then roared away, flooring it down the street.

Seeing that the stalker had finally given up the chase, Adam let out a ragged breath. "Nice driving."

Crystal flicked a wan smile at him.

"We need to find somewhere safe to hole up for the night," Connor said.

Adam twisted around to see him poking his head through the back window. He frowned, considering the matter. Technically the truck was its own shelter, but they wouldn't all fit in the back. As it was, with Connor and those four hostages crammed in there, it had to be standing room only. "Where is Ellis?" Adam asked.

"In the bunker," Connor said. "Waiting for the governor... why?"

"A bunker seems like a pretty safe place to hide from stalkers."

Connor grimaced. "Not when it's already overrun with them."

"Then what's Ellis doing down there? Playing fetch? The governor's evacuation route has to be secure, or else he wouldn't even think about using it."

"It *is* secure," Connor sighed. "Getting to it is

the problem."

"You made it," Adam pointed out.

"We lost a man in the process. Private Lee."

Adam grimaced as he recognized the name of the Chinese American from Delta Squad. Crystal glanced sharply at Adam, then back at Connor, looking scared, but determined. "We have to join the fight."

Adam nodded, surprised by her answer. "Carla's in there, along with Sophie and Emily. By now they've already stirred up a riot to flush the governor out. The faster we can capture him and spread the word that he's been deposed, the sooner the coup will be over."

Crystal nodded, but Adam caught a glimpse of Connor frowning unhappily in the rear-view mirror as he withdrew from the back window. He was probably afraid that Crystal could get hurt in the fighting. Adam could relate. The thought of something happening to her struck terror into every fiber of his being. After she'd been abducted by raiders, he was somehow irrationally convinced that she'd be safe as long as he kept her close. But he couldn't shield her from bullets, or stalkers, and much less from the governor's wrath if this coup failed.

She really would be safer if she stayed out of it, but how was he going to convince her to do that? The last time he'd insisted that she sit on the sidelines, she'd turned his argument around, saying that it wasn't fair for everyone she loved to risk their lives for a cause, and yet somehow she couldn't risk hers.

The only problem with that logic was that she'd assumed they were all fighting for the same cause. Adam hadn't joined the Nightingales or their coup to save the Republic. He'd joined them to save her. And after seeing the lengths that Connor had gone to for Crystal, he suspected he wasn't the only one.

The only sure way to keep her safe was to keep her out of it. If the coup failed, the governor wouldn't simply drop it. He'd hunt the instigators to the ends of the Earth.

Planning for that possibility was the safest option of all, Adam realized. If nothing else, at least he could give Crystal a head start.

CHAPTER FIFTY-TWO

The Rangers at the gates of the mansion were swept under by the same wave that had dismantled the mounted unit, and the crowd surged through the gates with a collective roar. Carla was caught up in the moment, shaking her pistol in the air, and screaming right along with them before she even realized what she was saying.

"Burn it to the ground!" they shouted.

"Kill them all!" someone else cried.

Carla bit her tongue.

The two Rangers standing watch outside the main entrance of the mansion saw the rushing crowd and they quickly ran inside and locked the doors. Rioters crashed into the entrance, attempting to batter their way in.

More flaming bottles of moonshine went whipping through the night. One of them smashed into a magnificent oak tree beside the mansion, and flames went racing up the trunk, turning it into a giant torch that silhouetted the crowd with long, flickering shadows.

Another bottle smashed through an upper-story window, setting curtains ablaze. Two more followed, crashing through a window on the first floor. A whooshing roar of fire burst out, sprinkling the mob with glittering debris.

If that doesn't flush the governor out, nothing will, Carla thought grimly as she watched the fires burn.

"We need to get out of here!" Sophie screamed in Carla's ear, already tugging her away. Carla spun to face the other woman and saw that Emily was there, too, their features flickering with reflected firelight. Emily looked frightened.

"We just arrived!" Carla shouted back, tugging in the opposite direction.

Sophie gritted her teeth. "This was supposed to be a peaceful protest! That battalion of Rangers is going to surround us! It'll be a massacre!"

Those words hit Carla like a slap to the face. Sophie was right. Carla spun in a dizzy circle, searching for a path through the seething crowd.

"This way!" Sophie said.

Carla let her lead, and they waded through milling masses of elbows and shoulders, taking dozens of accidental blows to the stomach and ribs. After about a minute of that, the crowd seemed to part for them, and they broke into a sprint, aiming for the simple iron fence around the compound.

They crashed into it and hastily clambered over. Carla landed hard on the crumbling sidewalk and stumbled into the street. Sophie raced for the mouth of a dark alley on the other side. Emily was right on her heels.

As Carla hurried after them, a man bellowed into a megaphone, "This is Colonel Rollins, lay down your weapons and surrender immediately!"

Carla reached the alley and spun around to search for the speaker. She was just in time to see floodlights snapping on from upper story windows of an office building across from the mansion—and then in a sequence from several other buildings on all sides of the compound. "We have you surrounded!" the colonel added.

"Get in here!" Sophie hissed and yanked her into the cover of the alley. "Are you trying to get yourself shot?" she demanded.

Carla blinked stupidly at her and slowly shook her head. Sophie and Emily were already striding quickly away from the developing confrontation. "What about everyone else?" Carla asked, pointing vaguely in the direction of the riot and wondering if she was about to become complicit in the mass murder of more than a thousand people.

"If they're smart, they'll listen to the colonel," Sophie said.

Carla said nothing to that, her ears straining

for the telltale rattle and pop of gunfire that would signal the start of the massacre.

But that didn't happen.

Maybe the rioters had given up? Governor Miller had sprung his trap, and it was over, but by now, he was probably fleeing his burning residence for the basement of the Capitol, and that meant that Mayor Ellis's plan had worked.

Sophie turned down another alley, and then another, running from block to block in a zigzag, seemingly at random.

"Where are we going?" Carla asked.

"To my house," Sophie said. "Our part in this is over. It's up to Ellis and Captain Fields now."

Carla nodded, relief spreading quickly through her system with that assertion. They flashed by an old, smelly dumpster and a rotting pile of garbage. A hollow *boom* erupted from the dumpster, and a four-legged creature leaped out in front of them, hissing sharply. Carla skidded to a stop, thinking that it was a stray cat.

But it was far too big to be a cat. Yet, somehow, it was also too small to be a stalker. About the size of a tiger. A familiar set of four jaws came thrusting out of the monster's head, razor-sharp teeth glistening in contradiction to Carla's assessment.

"Stalker!" Sophie cried. Her gun flashed up, and she fired repeatedly at the creature.

Bullets shattered on its armor, and it

screamed, darting into cover behind the dumpster.

They stood blinking stupidly at the spot where it had been a moment ago. Carla's mind raced to catch up. This was a *baby* stalker, not an adult. But then where was its mother?

A soft hiss erupted behind them, answering her unspoken question. Carla whirled around to see a massive shadow oozing into the alley behind them.

And then the baby peeked around the dumpster.

"We're trapped," Emily whispered.

"Up there!" Sophie whispered, pointing to the dangling ladder of a fire escape beside them.

Hope soared in Carla's chest—then quickly fell as she realized that the ladder was out of reach.

CHAPTER FIFTY-THREE

Crystal skidded to a stop in front of the boathouse, looking even more perplexed by the detour than she had when Adam had explained it to her.

"Dad, what are we doing here?" she asked.

"I told you," he said. "I need another vehicle. Besides, we can't take our hostages into combat, can we?"

Crystal appeared to be satisfied by that.

The back of the truck opened up, and Connor clambered out. Adam heard him helping the women and children out. He opened his door and warily swept the shadows with his carbine. Seeing no sign of stalkers, he walked around to Crystal's side and yanked her door open.

She looked at him with eyebrows raised. He leaned in without comment and promptly twisted the keys and yanked them out, killing the engine.

"What are you *doing?*" Crystal demanded. Adam withdrew sharply and folded the keys securely into his fist. He strode around the back of the truck and handed them to Connor.

He looked almost as confused as Crystal had. "Sergeant?" he asked.

"You got your wish," he said. "You and Crystal are holing up here for the night."

Connor's eyes widened, but he accepted that with a quick nod.

"The hell we are!" Crystal roared.

"Quiet!" Adam snapped in a fierce whisper. "You want to bring stalkers down on us?"

Her eyes glittered angrily in the moonlight. "You said we were going to join the fight."

"I am," Adam clarified, "but *you're* not."

Connor scuttled under the garage door to check the inside of the boathouse.

Crystal's hand flexed restlessly on the over-sized revolver that Adam had given to her.

"What are you going to do, shoot me?" he asked sarcastically.

"If you get yourself killed, I'm never going to forgive you," she whispered.

"Likewise, kiddo," he replied.

Connor came crawling back out. "It's clear," he whispered and waved urgently to the four hostages. The women raced over and began slipping under the door. Adam grabbed Crystal's arm and half-dragged her over to join them. There was no time to stand around arguing about this.

"Let me go," Crystal said, jerking her arm away.

Adam did and bit his tongue to forestall an angry retort. Let her be mad. Better that than bleeding out in the governor's bunker.

Connor guided Crystal gently under the door.

When it was Connor's turn to follow, Adam stopped him with an upraised hand. "Stay here until dawn. If I'm not back by then, you get the hell out. Drive north and join the Coalition. If this coup fails, nowhere in the Republic will be safe for you."

Connor nodded. "Understood, Sergeant."

"Get to Chicago. Find a way to take her to Sanctum."

Connor smiled sarcastically. "If it's real, you mean." Now that he was older, he'd had some time to reflect on their misguided mission from five years ago. Sometimes rumors are just that—rumors. But Connor hadn't met Doctor Janssen from the Coalition, or seen Ellis's vaccine in action.

"It's real," Adam insisted. He felt around in his vest for the pair of syringes that he'd sealed in a padded pouch the night before, hoping that they'd survived everything he'd been through since then. He drew one of the syringes out and held it up in the moonlight.

The tarry black contents were still safely locked in the bulb of the syringe.

"What is that?" Connor asked.

"If one of you gets captured by Specs, inject

this. The parasites won't take. They'll think that you're under their control, but you won't be. Just play along until you see a chance to get away. When you do, remember you can remove those growths with fire and smoke."

Connor nodded quickly and pocketed the syringe. "You're going to the bunker?" he asked.

"I am. And after that, to find your mother."

Connor nodded. "Do you know the way?"

"I'm good with landmarks. How about you give me a few?"

Connor described in detail how to reach the crack in the ceiling of the bunker.

"You'll need the door code when you get there," Connor added, and then he recited an eight-digit code.

"Got it," Adam said, quietly repeating the sequence a few times inside his head.

"Good luck," Connor said.

"It's going to take a whole lot more than luck for this one, Connor."

"I know."

Adam turned and started to leave. He'd barely taken two steps before he found himself turning back. "Hey, kid—"

"Sir?" Connor asked.

"I was wrong about you," Adam said. "For what it's worth, you've got my blessing. Look after her."

"Thank you, sir. I will."

With that, Adam ran for the Humvee that

he'd left parked beside the boathouse earlier. He dove through the driver's side door, tossed his carbine on the passenger's seat, and drew a throaty roar from the engine as he hit the ignition.

He flicked on the headlights and roared away, remembering the route that Connor had described.

It wasn't five minutes before he was killing the lights and slowing to a crawl so that he could cruise undetected around the north end of the safe zone.

At last, he came to Connor's final landmark, the *Moody Amphitheater at Waterloo Park.* He parked on the street, right behind Mayor Ellis's Humvee, and quickly checked his mirrors for signs of trouble.

Nothing yet. He shut off the rumbling engine and reached for his carbine. Easing out the door, he closed it softly behind him and ran down the street and then across a short bridge to the crumbling amphitheater. In the distance, the domed spire of the Capitol shone brightly, lit up in red and blue. Cool evening air whipped by Adam as he ran.

He reached the end of the bridge and spied the grassy, tree-covered spot that Connor had described. Somewhere in that overgrown grass, he'd find a ragged fissure leading down to the top level of the governor's bunker.

Adam slowed as he drew near, seeing the

spotlights that were sweeping atop the east wall of Travis on the other side of the amphitheater. It was barely a hundred feet away. If Adam shouted, the guards up there would hear him. And if he ran into a stalker, he'd be forced to defend himself and the gunfire would draw the spotlights to him in seconds.

Adam shouldered his carbine and drew the silenced pistol that he'd stolen from that raider. He couldn't afford to use his carbine this close to the wall.

A couple of Rangers were pacing around up there, waltzing stick-figures painted against the midnight blue of the sky.

Adam ducked behind a bush just as one of the spotlights from the wall swept over his location. His heart hammered painfully hard in his chest, his ears straining through the sound of frogs croaking and crickets chirping to listen for some sign that he'd been spotted.

Not hearing anything, Adam peeked over the bushes to the wall. The sweeping spotlight roved on, moving slowly enough that he could move in its wake without getting caught.

Adam eased up from his haunches and ran into the field that Connor had described. The sweeping beam of that spotlight stopped and started coming back around.

Shit. Adam searched frantically for some sign of the fissure that Connor had described, but he couldn't see anything.

Was this the wrong field? Waterloo Park was fairly big, with plenty of open fields of grass to choose from.

The spotlight inched progressively closer, threatening to sweep over him. None of the trees were big enough to hide him, and it was too late to run for better cover. If any Rangers were looking his way when that spotlight swept over him, he wasn't just going to get himself captured, he'd wind up blowing the whole operation.

CHAPTER FIFTY-FOUR

Sophie heaved, and Carla's fingers curled around the lower rung of the ladder. Her shoulder popped painfully, but she managed to swing her other hand up and reach the next rung.

"Hurry!" Emily whispered, waving urgently from the first landing.

Carla's arms ached sharply as she pulled herself up, one rung at a time. Scarcely ten feet below, both Stalkers were padding steadily toward Sophie, hissing softly and clicking their jaws in anticipation of the kill.

Carla kneeled painfully on the bottom rung and leaned back down, reaching for Sophie's hand. The other woman jumped, and their fingertips brushed.

"Higher!" Carla urged.

"Mom! Hurry!" Emily sobbed. "They're almost there!"

Carla leaned down farther, reaching as far as she dared without compromising her own grip.

Sophie gritted her teeth and jumped again.

This time her hand caught Carla's just above her wrist. Carla nearly lost her grip on the ladder as Sophie's weight yanked her down, wrenching her injured shoulder and popping the joint once more.

Sophie dangled there for a moment, swinging gently back and forth with her grip slowly slipping down Carla's sweaty skin. "Pull me up!" Sophie screamed. She swept her other hand up and wrapped it above the first.

Carla bit back a scream as she heaved her shoulder to get Sophie within reach of the ladder, but she couldn't get her up more than half an inch.

"I can't!" Carla cried.

"Mom! Look out!" Emily warned just as a muttering alien sigh erupted from below. The adult stalker stepped into view, and giant yellow eyes turned up to look at them. The monster's jaws were already within easy reach of Sophie's dangling feet, but it snapped them shut and snorted loudly.

The baby stalker came creeping forward, its legs bent at the elbows as it crouched.

Sophie pulled her feet up just as it sprang into the air. It swiped at her leg in passing, and Sophie cried out in pain.

"Mom," Emily sobbed. "Please!"

Carla was nauseated from the pain of her slowly dislocating shoulder, but she couldn't let go. Sophie would die if she didn't find some way to do this. "Pull when I tell you to," Carla managed.

Sophie nodded.

"Now!" Carla heaved with all of her strength, wrenching her entire body and twisting her torso to aid the movement.

Sophie pulled herself up at the same time, and then suddenly, she let go.

This time she made it.

Carla sagged with relief, screaming silently from the pain. But it wasn't over yet. The adult stalker was beginning to get impatient.

"Climb!" Carla urged, and they both battled their way up the ladder, grunting from the effort of reaching each successive rung.

The baby stalker made another leap, but this time it missed Sophie's dangling legs by a wide margin.

Carla climbed awkwardly on the other side with one arm, keeping the dislocated one curled protectively against her chest.

Emily pulled them over the railing into the landing, and they collapsed on the grated metal floor, gasping raggedly from the exertion and pain. Emily crushed her mother into a hug but quickly withdrew to check on her wounded leg. It was bleeding steadily from two deep, parallel gashes. Emily tried to staunch the blood by wrapping her hands around it.

"It's okay," Sophie said. "I'll be fine."

Carla struggled to her feet, peering over the

railing to the stalkers below. The baby was mewling petulantly, while the adult paced in angry circles, peering curiously up at them.

"Can it reach us?" Carla wondered aloud.

Even as she asked, the adult stalker stood up on its hind legs and wrapped its fingers and dagger-like claws around the rungs of the ladder. It heaved with powerful forelegs, and something metallic *plinked* as it gave way.

The ladder went telescoping down with a thunderous crash, and both stalkers leaped away, hissing and snapping their jaws.

"Now it can!" Sophie cried, lurching to her feet.

Carla watched, frozen in disbelief as the baby stalker crept back over and began sniffing around at the bottom of the ladder. Its mother nudged it from behind, placing one of its paws on the rungs, and then nudged it once more.

"What are you waiting for?" Sophie said. "Climb!"

***

Adam backpedaled quickly, moving away from the light. His foot caught in something, and he felt himself pitching over backward. He twisted around to catch himself as he fell—

And that was when he saw the fissure in the ceiling of the bunker. It gaped darkly before him, vanishing into shadows below. He caught himself in a plank position on the other side, straddling the crevasse. Realizing the spotlight would still see him if he didn't hurry, Adam pulled his legs down to hasty footholds in the walls below and then ducked into the gap. The spotlight swept harmlessly overhead, and Adam let out a ragged sigh.

He clambered down quickly, landing on the floor of the cleft in the old concrete structure, then flicked on his carbine's tac light and quickly swept the shadows.

One end of the fissure narrowed down to nothing, while the other widened into fuzzy darkness. Adam hurried in that direction, reaching the edge and peering down seventy or eighty feet into a familiar, circular chamber with a winding ramp running around its circumference.

Five years ago, he'd been stuck holding the door at the bottom while Crystal, Connor, and Owen got away. Stalkers had broken through and stung him, knocking him out, and then they'd dragged him into their den, which was connected somewhere to the bowels of this bunker.

At least there was no sign of those stalkers now, but he knew they were here. Connor had mentioned that they'd lost a man along the way.

Adam swept his tac light back up and scanned the upper level of the chamber for the door he was supposed to reach. It was about twenty feet away at the top of the ramp, with a gap of maybe fifteen feet for him to traverse along a narrow ledge that ran along the wall. There were no handholds, and just that one foothold, with a thirty-foot drop if he didn't make it.

Adam grimaced and shouldered his rifle. The chamber plunged back into shadows with that movement, and he stepped out onto the ledge feeling blindly for it with the toe of one boot. Feeling solid concrete below his boot, he began shimmying down to the end.

When he was just five feet from the railing at the top of the ramp, his leading foot plunged through empty space. He caught himself at the last possible moment by lunging for the railing. It thundered with a metallic boom.

Clambering over quickly, Adam hurried to the upper-level door that Connor had indicated. There was a giant bloodstain in front of the door, but no sign of the body.

Adam grimaced, stepping around the blood. He tapped in the eight-digit door code. The panel chimed and winked green, and the door *thunked* open. He yanked it open just as the distant shriek of a stalker drifted into hearing.

He slammed the door behind him and hurried down the corridor. Reaching another door, he tapped in the same code as before and opened it into a large hexagonal room lined with doors and two slowly spinning fans. A group of three people was clustered around the far door. Two Rangers and their cherubic mayor. The Rangers stiffened with his approach, aiming their carbines at him.

"Sergeant," Ellis whispered as he drew near. "You're just in time. Did you find your daughter?"

Adam nodded.

"And Private Cooper?"

"He's in a secure location with her and the other hostages that we rescued," Adam replied.

"Good." Ellis smiled.

Adam turned off his tac light to save the battery, leaving the whooshing fans in the floor and ceiling to send shadows pinwheeling through the room.

One of the two Rangers placed his ear to the door that they were guarding. He was a big man with a jutting chin.

Corporal Williams, Adam read from the name tape and insignia on his uniform.

Ellis regarded the man with eyebrows raised. Williams stepped back and his weapon flashed up. The four of them fanned out with two on either side of the door. Adam took Ellis's side and waited with his weapon aimed at the door as the sound of approaching footsteps drifted through from the other side.

CHAPTER FIFTY-FIVE

Carla flew up flight after flight of stairs, after Sophie and Emily. They stopped at each of the landings along the way to check the windows, only to find that they were barred from the inside.

A rattling sound issued from below, and Carla glanced back down through the grated stairwell to see the baby stalker clambering from the ladder to the first-floor landing.

"Here it comes!" she warned, reaching for her pistol, where she'd tucked it into the waistband of her jeans. Her sweaty palm gripped the weapon and she planted her feet to make her stand.

"Not yet!" Sophie said. "There should be a door on the roof!"

Carla nodded and hurried up the stairs. They reached the roof on the fifth floor and raced by old, rusting air conditioners to a boxy concrete structure that rose above the roof. A plain metal door shone like a beacon in the moonlight.

Emily reached it first, turning the knob and yanking on it.

"It's locked!" she cried.

Carla's spirits plunged. She spun back around and raised her pistol in a two-handed grip just as the baby stalker crept over the low wall around the roof.

Its hide was black, the same color as the shadows in the alley below, but as it stepped into the moonlight, its skin shimmered and lightened until it blended almost perfectly with the matte grays of the roof. The only part of it that still stood out was its two gleaming yellow eyes.

A low hiss bubbled from the creature's puckered black lips, and long claws clicked softly on the roof as it approached.

***

The door swung open with a shuddering groan, and four people came rushing through.

Adam reacted instantly. "Hands in the air!" he shouted. Carbines and sidearms swept toward him.

The other two Rangers rounded the open door, adding their aim from the front. "Drop your weapons!" Corporal Williams bellowed.

One of the men with Governor Miller raised a sidearm and planted it against the side of the governor's head. It was Captain Fields.

"Do it," the governor gritted out as he slowly raised both his hands.

The other two released their weapons and raised their hands as well.

Miller regarded them with a thin smile. "Very clever," he said.

He was wearing the same expensive blue suit and red tie that he'd been wearing when they met five years ago. With his thick brown hair, ice-blue eyes, and rugged good looks, he was impossible to mistake for anyone else. He scanned the faces of his captors, nodding to himself. "I know you," he said as his eyes locked with Adam's.

"You bet," Adam replied. "I spent the night at your mansion, remember?"

"You mean the one that your people are busy burning to the ground?"

Adam smiled sweetly. "Couldn't happen to a nicer fellow."

Miller snorted. "I'll build it back twice the size, and then I'll hang you all from the rafters." Miller glanced sideways at Captain Fields, who was still holding a sidearm to his head. "And you. I expected to find a traitor in my inner circle, but I never imagined it would be *you.* You were like a son to me, Sean. I took you in and raised you, and this is how you repay me? You'd be lying dead in a gutter if it weren't for me! Or maybe not. Maybe the Specs would have found you by now, and you'd have died on some benighted world, fighting an alien war you don't understand."

A muscle jerked in Captain Fields' cheek, but he said nothing to that.

"Is that what they're doing with us?" Ellis demanded. "Making us fight their wars for them?"

Governor Miller looked at him, and his smile only broadened. "What other use could we possibly have to them?"

From the way the governor framed that question, Adam suspected that not even he knew what the Specs were doing with the people they took. He nodded sideways to indicate the other two Rangers who'd come through with the governor. He was surprised to find that he recognized one of them—a woman with a hard face, short black hair, and ice-blue eyes like the governor's—Lieutenant Jameson. She was the one who'd locked them in this bunker to die five years ago.

Corporal Williams quickly disarmed the lieutenant and the other ranger while Adam and an unnamed private kept them covered with her carbine.

Williams patted down both enemy Rangers, removing their radios and knives as well. That done, he searched the governor and removed another radio from an inside pocket in his jacket, a switchblade from his right ankle, and a small, compact pistol from a concealed body holster.

"Tie them up, Private Hanson," Mayor Ellis

ordered.

"Yes, sir," she replied.

They herded the governor and his men to the middle of the room, while Ellis shut and locked the door to Miller's escape tunnel.

"Let me guess, Ellis," Miller began while Private Hanson zip-tied his hands behind his back. "You're here to depose me because of Valentina Flores?"

"Keep her name out of your mouth," Ellis snapped at the governor as he crossed the room.

Corporal Williams zip-tied Jameson and the other Ranger, and then Ellis opened the door and gestured for Adam to go first. Ellis shut the door behind them with a softly echoing *boom* and the others hurried to catch up with Adam.

They stopped halfway down the corridor and Ellis nodded to an exposed pipe running down the wall from the ceiling. "Tie the Rangers to that," he said.

"What are you afraid of?" Lieutenant Jameson demanded. "We're already tied up."

Ellis glared at her. "You know the door codes. You might have to peck at the keypads with your nose, but I'm sure that won't stop you."

Jameson scowled while Corporal Williams and Private Hanson zip-tied their wrists to the pipe.

"Much better," Ellis declared. "Let's go, Governor," he said, giving Miller a shove.

"This won't work," he warned as they hurried down the corridor. "Colonel Rollins will take command in my absence, and he has more than enough manpower to put down your pathetic riot."

"Let him try," Ellis said. "Tomorrow, instead of a thousand peaceful protesters, you'll have an armed rebellion."

"Peaceful?" Miller scoffed.

They reached the second door, and Ellis tapped in the code. The lock thunked, and Adam gently pushed the mayor aside. "Let me clear the way, sir."

Ellis nodded and stepped back.

Adam pushed the door open gently, peeking out with his rifle to make sure stalkers weren't waiting for them on the other side. Not seeing anything, he pushed the door all the way open. "Clear," he whispered.

Corporal Williams and Private Hanson came out next, followed by Captain Fields and Ellis, both of them prodding the governor with the barrels of their guns.

They reached the upper-level landing, and Adam led them back to the railing.

"I'll go first," Adam said, already climbing over.

Seeing where he was going, the governor snorted. "I can't crawl along that ledge with my hands tied behind my back!"

"Quiet!" Captain Fields hissed.

Adam stood frozen on the other side of the railing, listening to the silence that followed.

Not a second later the distant shriek of a stalker split the air. When no subsequent shrieks or frantic skittering of claws rose from the well of shadows below, they let out a collective sigh.

Miller grinned. "Oops," he whispered now. "Were we trying to be quiet?"

"Idiot," Fields muttered. "We should have gagged him."

"Do it," Ellis snapped.

Fields patted himself down, checking his pockets. "With what?"

Ellis yanked a white pocket square out of the governor's jacket. He balled it up and stuffed it down Miller's throat, and Corporal Williams used zip ties to secure it.

"Much better," Ellis said.

"What about his hands?" Adam asked. "He's right. He can't walk the ledge like that. He'll fall."

"Good riddance if he does," Fields muttered.

"Unfortunately, we still need him," Ellis replied. "The only way we're going to get his Rangers to surrender is if he gives the order."

The governor raised his eyebrows at that and mumbled something that didn't make it past his gag.

"Cut his ties," Ellis ordered. "If he tries anything stupid, shoot him in the foot."

Adam shouldered his rifle once more and slipped out onto the ledge, this time being careful to mind the gap. Moments later he was waving to the others from the crack in the wall on the other side. Ellis came next. He was slow and awkward, his balance questionable at best, and there were a couple of times where Adam almost had to look away, but somehow Ellis made it to Adam's reaching hand, and he yanked the portly mayor into the gap.

"Remind me when all of this is over to go on a diet," he muttered. He poked his head out, and whispered, "Miller goes next."

Good idea, Adam thought. This whole operation would be for nothing if a stalker came bounding up that ramp and ripped him to pieces now.

The governor came creeping along the ledge, twice narrowly avoiding a deadly fall himself. As soon as he came within reach, Adam yanked him inside and jammed the barrel of his carbine into his back. Miller mumbled something against his gag and began fiddling with his jacket. Adam stopped him with another warning jab of his carbine. He double-checked the governor's pockets, reaching into the inner ones, and finding them empty.

Miller raised his eyebrows patiently as if to say, *are you satisfied?* Adam frowned and backed away, keeping the governor covered. As soon as the rest of their team finished crossing the ledge, Ellis ordered everyone to climb up. They still couldn't bind the governor's hands, since he needed them to climb, but just in case, Adam tightened the zip ties around his gag to the point of cutting into the creases in the governor's cheeks.

With Miller gagged, Adam smiled as he stepped away, gesturing to the ragged concrete walls with the barrel of his weapon.

As they climbed up, Adam saw the blinding glare of the spotlight sweep by, and he warned the others to keep their heads down. They'd probably climbed down here when it was still light out, relying on inattention from the guards rather than the cover of darkness to conceal them.

They reached the top of the fissure, waited for another sweep of the light, and then scrambled out. Adam pulled Miller up and dragged him roughly across the clearing, running for the bridge to the street where they'd parked the Humvees.

About halfway there, Miller tripped and fell. Corporal Williams reached down to help him back up, but Miller grabbed his carbine instead and pulled the trigger. The weapon went off with a cracking report. The round slammed uselessly into the ground, and Williams leaped out of reach before the weapon could be turned on him.

But it was too late.

Muffled shouts rose from the wall. Spotlights blinded them.

"Cover!" Adam screamed just as bullets went zipping through the field. Private Hanson screamed as she crumpled to her knees. Adam grabbed Miller's arm and dragged him to the nearest shelter that he could find—an old food truck halfway between them and the bridge.

Ellis and Captain Fields came skidding in after him.

"Tie him up!" Ellis growled, and Fields zip-tied the governor's hands again.

"Where's Williams and Hanson?" Adam asked, remembering now that the private had been hit.

He glanced back into the field to see Corporal Williams lying prone beside Hanson, hiding in the grass. Adam peeked around the corner of the food truck and fired off a couple of shots to distract the guards on the wall.

"Williams! Fall back!" Adam called.

The corporal struggled to his feet, dragging Hanson one-handed and firing as he went. Adam continued his own assault on the wall, scoring a lucky hit on one of the guards.

Incredibly, Williams and Hanson both made it, but Hanson was clutching a bloody wound on the right side of her chest and grimacing from the pain.

"Damn it," Adam muttered as he saw how much blood she was losing.

"Keep pressure on it," Williams said.

"Leave me," Hanson managed between shallow, wheezing breaths.

"And go where?" Ellis asked. His gaze was locked on the bridge, barely a dozen yards away, but there was no cover between them and their escape route. "We're trapped," he muttered.

A shot from one of the Rangers exploded on the pavement beside them as if to emphasize his point.

Governor Miller stared at them, his eyes dancing with amusement as he somehow managed to smile around his gag.

CHAPTER FIFTY-SIX

Carla screamed, firing repeatedly at the stalker as it approached. Sophie and Emily drew matching pistols and joined their streams of fire to hers. The creature shuddered and shrieked in time to each impact. Glittering shards of scaly armor exploded into the air.

Carla's pistol clicked, the magazine spent. "I'm out!" she shouted.

Then one of them scored a lucky hit. A gleaming yellow eye burst and the stalker collapsed and lay still.

The three of them stood there, frozen in shock. They waited breathlessly for the mother to come climbing up, but she never came. She probably couldn't fit her much larger frame into the narrow confines of the fire escape.

They gradually lowered their weapons, and Carla's body sagged with relief. Emily and Sophie hugged each other and traded grim smiles.

The three of them stood gazing over the rooftops of surrounding buildings, watching the governor's mansion burn in the distance. The grounds were still flooded with chanting protesters, even as Rangers encircled them on all sides. Would it be a massacre as Sophie had warned? Maybe not. Maybe they had laid down their weapons as the colonel had instructed.

"We should stay up here for a while," Sophie whispered. "That other stalker is probably down there still."

Carla nodded grimly and they went to sit with their backs to the rusty metal door.

"How's Bowser?" Carla asked, suddenly remembering the family dog.

"About as well as can be expected," Emily said. "I managed to remove the broken pieces of rib and stitch him up. He's sleeping it off at our place with Tony."

"Tony?" Carla asked.

"Private Smith," Emily explained.

Carla nodded as if she remembered who that was, content at least to know that he was being looked after. Carla's thoughts turned to Adam and Connor, hoping that they had found Crystal and that all of them were okay. She felt guilty to be sitting up here, safely removed from the conflict, while they could be out there fighting for their lives.

Her guilt was short-lived.

A low hiss was her only warning before a slinking gray shadow crept alongside her, and a giant yellow eye flicked open, the milky membrane sweeping aside, and the creature's jaws thrust open as they swept toward her.

"Stalker!" Emily screamed. Two bullets crunched ineffectually into its armor, showering Carla with sharp, glittering fragments.

Then the stalker hissed, and its lashing tail came whipping through the air. It stabbed Carla in the stomach, and she fell over backward with the force of the blow.

Her body went blissfully numb from the venom. More gunshots sounded, along with muffled shouts. Carla lay staring up at the starry sky with heavy lids, watching the stalker's tail stab repeatedly through the air.

Then silence and darkness fell as her eyelids dropped a curtain over her eyes.

***

The familiar roar of a V8 caught Adam's attention. Headlights swept into view at the far end of the bridge, and the sound grew progressively louder with its approach. Adam recognized the old Ford. The Rangers on the wall switched to firing at the truck, their bullets crunching into it.

"Who is that?" Ellis demanded.

"It's Connor!" Adam all-but shouted, even as he hoped that Crystal wasn't with him. He jumped to his feet, waving his arms high to get the driver's attention. The truck swerved toward them and stopped with the bull bar lightly tapping the back bumper of the food truck.

The driver ducked out and gestured hurriedly to them as a rain of fire from the wall pelted the truck. Adam was grateful to see that it really was Connor.

"Get in!" he cried.

"Let's go!" Adam shouted to the others. But then he hesitated as his gaze fell on Hanson.

"Go," she said, shoving Corporal Williams weakly away from her.

"I'm not leaving you," he insisted.

Adam grimaced, realizing that they didn't have time for this. "Surrender once we're gone. They'll have a medic at the wall."

Williams nodded and Adam spun away, leading the others around to the armored back of the truck. The doors swung open before he could reach for them, and Crystal's head popped out.

Adam's guts clenched with dread and she waved to them from the inside. "Hurry up!"

He didn't need to be told twice. Adam jumped in and Captain Fields shoved Governor Miller in next. The captain hopped in after him, Ellis came last, and then Crystal and Adam swung the doors shut.

Moments later the engine roared again, and the sound pitched up sharply as wheels spun on the pavement. Bullets continued raining into the truck, crunching through metal. A sharp hiss erupted from the engine, and Adam stumbled to the back window to see what was happening.

Reams of thick white smoke were gushing over the hood and through the open windows. Connor was hacking into his sleeve.

Those Rangers must have hit the radiator. Somehow, Connor was still driving despite the curtains of smoke clouding his view, but it wouldn't be long before the engine seized up on him. Fortunately, they had another two vehicles waiting.

"Just get us to the Humvees!" Adam said.

"What do you think I'm doing?" Connor shouted back.

The truck went thundering through a massive pothole, and Adam almost lost his footing. Moments later the engine choked and rattled, giving a final gasp before they came to a rolling stop on the other side of the bridge.

Adam stood listening to the silence that followed. *Silence.* That meant that the Rangers weren't shooting at them anymore.

"Everybody out!" Ellis ordered.

Crystal threw the doors open, and they clambered down in the cover of an old container truck that was parked along the side of the road.

Connor met them around the back, keeping wary guard as they exited the vehicle.

Adam cast about for the Humvees and saw

that they were parked on the other side of the street, about twenty yards away. Close enough. He pointed to them.

"Follow me!" he said, and then he sprinted across the street. He reached the side of the Humvee he'd driven, pulled open the door, and waved to the others. Crystal ducked inside, followed by Connor. Captain Fields shoved the governor in next, forcing Connor to clamber into the passenger's seat to make room.

"Keep him covered!" Ellis said, even though Connor and Crystal were both already aiming their pistols at the governor.

"We'll take the next one!" Captain Fields said as he withdrew, slamming the door behind the governor. Adam hopped in the driver's seat and hit the ignition just a second before he saw the brake lights of the other Humvee wink on in front of him.

Bullets went crunching into that vehicle as the Rangers on the wall found them again. Ellis spun the wheels and rocketed down the street. Adam grimaced and gunned the engine to give chase. A few scattered shots clipped them as they went, but didn't make it through the truck's armor.

Adam smiled grimly to himself, unable to believe that they'd pulled this off. But it was probably too soon to declare victory. They still had to elude pursuit. He glanced in his side mirror, half-expecting to see the sweeping headlights of enemy vehicles approaching.

But the road behind them was dark and empty.

Adam followed Mayor Ellis through a skidding right turn, then down a street that was clogged with rusting relics. Adam followed the mayor through swerving turns to avoid colliding with any of them. At the next intersection, they hooked a left and drove up onto the curb to get around the snarl of parked cars.

Adam began to fear they'd have to get out on foot, but Ellis seemed to know where he was going as he expertly negotiated the cluttered streets of the wastes. They flew through another intersection, whipping by a shadowy high rise, and then Ellis's destination became clear: the interstate.

Up ahead a bridge across it led to the ramp on the other side. They roared over it, driving up onto the sidewalk to squeak past more frozen lines of traffic. And then they went roaring down to the mercifully clear lanes of the I-35. Governor Miller had made it a priority years ago to clear all the main arteries between the safe zones, and this was one of them. Ironic, that he'd paved the way for his own demise. Adam smiled smugly at that.

Until he heard the familiar *thump-thump-thumping* of a chopper. He blinked in shock. There weren't a lot of working aircraft left, much less fuel to fly them, but somehow Travis still had one.

Adam glanced over his shoulder and caught a glimpse of the governor once again smiling around his gag as if he'd somehow known that it would come to this.

"What do we do now?" Connor whispered.

Adam slowly shook his head. "We keep driving. They can't shoot us without risking they hit the governor."

"And what happens when we run out of fuel?" Crystal asked.

Adam grimaced and ducked down behind the wheel as the chopper pulled alongside them and shone a floodlight over them. Someone shouted into a megaphone. "This is Colonel Rollins! Pull over and surrender the governor now, or we will open fire!"

Adam's radio chirped, and he answered, "Go for Sergeant Hall."

"Adam," Ellis said breathlessly. "Don't stop."

"I wasn't planning on it," he replied.

"Good. We've got this covered," he replied.

"You do?" Adam asked.

Silence answered his question, but then Adam saw Captain Fields leaning out the window with a stinger missile launcher. There came a loud *skrish* as a bright orange tongue of flame erupted from the barrel of the launcher.

A missile jetted out and slammed into the chopper with a blinding flash, followed by a cracking *boom.* Flaming debris rained over the interstate, and the shock-wave slammed into them like a giant hand, making Adam swerve to compensate.

"Nice shot," Adam muttered over the radio.

His radio chirped back in acknowledgment.

Adam glanced back at the governor.

He wasn't smiling anymore.

They drove on in silence for several minutes. Adam began to wonder where they were taking the governor. He glanced periodically in his side mirror, checking for signs of pursuit, but this time none came. Maybe they had too much of a head start. At this point, the real threat was running into stalkers, but they were going sixty on the interstate. At that speed, they wouldn't be a problem. At least, not until they ran out of fuel.

"Ummm, Dad?" Crystal whispered. "What is that?"

Adam turned to see what she was looking at. She was peering out her window into the pitch-blackness of the wastes.

"What is what?" he asked.

And then he saw it—a familiar, bulky black shadow keeping pace beside them as it flew low above the wastes. After a second of that, it rocketed ahead of them, flying out over the interstate. There it stopped and hovered, turning on the spot to present its longest side as it drifted down for a landing, completely blocking both sides of the interstate.

Mayor Ellis's brake lights blazed crimson, and Adam reluctantly brought them to a squealing stop.

Adam reached for his radio. "Sergeant Hall, standing by for tasking," he said.

His radio crackled with static, and Ellis's garbled voice came through indistinct.

"Say again?"

More static...

And then a new voice joined the conversation, flat and emotionless, "Exit your vehicles immediately. Attempt to resist and you will be eliminated."

CHAPTER FIFTY-SEVEN

Adam waited for Mayor Ellis and Captain Fields to exit their vehicle, and then slowly followed suit. Crystal and Connor came next, followed by a smug-looking governor. Apparently supplying the Specs with slaves had earned him a certain amount of goodwill.

"So that's it?" Crystal asked as all of them gathered beside Ellis's truck, waiting for whoever was inside that lander to emerge. A ramp dropped from the back, angling down with a hissing sigh of pneumatic pistons or whatever alien equivalent powered the platform.

"And what would you have us do?" Ellis asked calmly.

"Shoot it with another one of those rockets!" Crystal replied.

Ellis frowned, but this time he said nothing.

Adam explained, "The night the Specs invaded, we fought back. Our air force gave them everything we had. F-35s were shot down like confetti." He chose not to add that one of them crashing into the interstate was what had caused the accident that had taken her mother's life.

Captain Fields nodded. "If air-to-air missiles didn't cut it, a Stinger isn't going to do more than tickle them."

A pair of humanoid figures in glossy black suits came striding down the ramp with long-barreled sidearms drawn. Adam stiffened with their approach. *Collaborators.* He turned to see Connor deftly stab Crystal's arm with a familiar syringe full of ink-black liquid. She flinched, but he leaned in and whispered something in her ear, and she subsided.

Adam caught Connor's eye, and the boy nodded.

Governor Miller had missed the exchange.

Adam felt for the second syringe inside his vest. Still there. He was tempted to inoculate Connor, but he couldn't afford to risk revealing their secret weapon.

The two collaborators marched steadily across the moonlit river of asphalt between them. The headlights of Ellis's Humvee reflected brightly off their armor. Adam noticed that one of them was carrying a big silver case.

They stopped a dozen feet away. "Cut the governor free," the one not carrying the case intoned. It was the same one who'd spoken over the radio.

Captain Fields produced a knife from his belt and used it to cut the governor's bonds, as well as the zip ties that held his gag in place. Miller promptly spat his pocket square out. He spat a few more times for good measure and then walked over to his allies while massaging his wrists and bloodied cheeks.

"Kneel," the collaborator said.

Adam ground his teeth, but now wasn't the time to resist. Governor Miller regarded them with a thin smile as they kneeled on the pavement.

"I guess it really does pay to have friends in high places," he said with his eyes flicking up to the sky.

The collaborator with the case holstered their weapon and set the container gently on the ground. Then they dropped to their haunches beside it. The case hissed open, revealing a dimly illuminated interior lined with craggy rocks, like some kind of a portable habitat for a pet reptile. The collaborator reached in and withdrew a pair of golf-ball-sized red and blue growths, plucking them from the rocky walls of the case and revealing a forest of writhing white tendrils on the underside of each. The enemy soldier regained their feet and stalked over to them with those parasites raised.

"Him first," Governor Miller indicated, pointing to Mayor Ellis.

The collaborator stopped in front of Ellis and placed one of the creatures on either side of his head. The mayor winced as they latched on. Moments later, his eyes appeared to glaze over.

Adam frowned, wondering if that meant the inoculations hadn't worked. He remembered acutely what it had felt like to be under the influence of those creatures. He'd been unable to fight his captor, a prisoner trapped in his own body.

"Now, show him your face," Governor Miller said, smiling gleefully.

Adam didn't get it.

The collaborator's glossy black visor cleared, revealing the face of a beautiful young woman who couldn't have been more than thirty years old.

Mayor Ellis paled, and some of the life returned to his eyes as they filled with tears. He quickly covered his reaction, but Adam took comfort from it.

Governor Miller missed the significance of those unshed tears. He was too busy gloating.

"Who is she?" Crystal asked.

The governor looked at her. "His long-lost love, and my one-time rival, Valentina Flores. The grand proctor of the Nightingales herself."

Adam gaped at that.

"Ellis never had the chance to tell her how he

felt about her," Miller explained. "Not that she would have reciprocated his feelings. After all, look at him. He's a lump! And look at her... It's almost a shame that I had to hand her over to the Specs."

Ice slid into Adam's veins with the significance of that revelation. Somehow, this meeting was no accident. Miller had these two collaborators on call, waiting for this moment. Beside him, Captain Fields' shoulders rounded as he seemed to realize the same thing.

"You figured it out, didn't you?" Miller said, nodding to Adam and grinning once more. "I was never your captive. You were always mine." He reached for the hem of his suit jacket, fiddling with it for a second, then withdrew a small, button-sized silver device and held it up in the glare of the Humvee's headlights. "The Spec equivalent of a GPS tracker," he explained. "Also a two-way comms. They've been listening to every word you said since you captured me."

Adam remembered seeing the Governor fiddling with his suit once they reached the bottom of the crack in the ceiling of the bunker, and he realized that must have been when Miller had activated it. He'd searched the governor, but not knowing how tiny the tracker was, or that it had been sewn *into* Miller's jacket, Adam couldn't have possibly known to look for it. No wonder he was wearing the same blue suit today that he had been five years ago. He probably only had the one tracker, so he always had to wear the same suit. And tonight of all nights, he'd want to have his panic button close.

"Why her?" Mayor Ellis managed, still struggling with the revelation. "You could have called anyone to pick me up. Why did it have to be *her*?"

"I actually didn't call her because of you," Miller replied. "She's been working with me for years. The irony of turning my nemesis into my ally was simply too tempting to pass up. She's been operating out of my bunker for years, so she was simply the closest asset the Specs could send."

Adam grimaced, watching as Valentina slowly turned and walked back to the open case. She reached in again, and returned carrying two more sets of the glowing blue and red parasites. She affixed one to Captain Fields, and the next set to Adam. He winced as those questing white tendrils pricked through his skin like dozens of needles. The pain quickly faded to a warm, tingling numbness that reminded him of stalker venom, but he could still *feel* those tendrils writhing around inside of his head, questing for purchase in his brain. He reached up to claw them off, then quickly dropped his hands back to his sides as he realized that he actually *could* pry them away if he wanted to. He was supposed to pretend to be under their influence. Now wasn't the time to play the only remaining card in his hand.

So Adam watched numbly as they attached parasites to his daughter and then to Connor. Crystal also tried to pry them free, but then she subsided, too, seeming to understand the value of discretion.

And then all of them were marched up the ramp of the lander and into a shadowy airlock that glowed dimly with misshapen green and blue growths like the ones that decorated the stalkers' dens.

CHAPTER FIFTY-EIGHT

Adam crowded into the cockpit of the lander with the others. The male collaborator took the pilot's seat, and Valentina sat beside him. The vessel jumped into the air and slowly turned to face the forbidding glow of Travis with the sweeping floodlights atop its walls, and its sparsely illuminated streets.

Governor Miller spoke into his alien comms as they went. "This is Miller. I am en-route to the Capitol. What is your status, Jameson?"

Adam blinked in shock at the familiar name. *Lieutenant* Jameson? he wondered. Hadn't they left her zip-tied to a pipe in the bunker? But of course, if Miller had known that they were going to abduct him, he must have had Rangers standing by to rescue her.

The comms erupted with the lieutenant's voice, sounding much louder and clearer than it should have from such a tiny device. "We're rounding up the last of the protesters now. I'm afraid Colonel Rollins is dead, however."

"I know," Miller replied. "His sacrifice will be

remembered."

"Yes, sir. Meet you in the Capitol. We're herding the protesters there now for your speech."

"Excellent. It's time that the people knew the score."

Adam frowned, wondering what *that* meant. Was the governor really going to *admit* to working with the Specs? Surely he didn't believe that the people would just accept that revelation and move on.

"The rebellion isn't over," Adam growled.

"Perhaps not," Miller agreed, nodding sagely as he stared over the rolling black shadows of the wastes. He glanced over his shoulder at Adam and smiled. "But it's over for *you*. Our petty Earthly squabbles are no longer any of your concern. You're going up to space, Sergeant! Don't forget to send me a postcard when you get to wherever the Specs send you." He snickered at that.

It took a supreme force of will for Adam not to give himself away by reaching out and crushing the governor's throat.

They flew on toward the walls and the sweeping floodlights. The illuminated red and blue dome of the Capitol building loomed hatefully on the horizon.

But the pilot banked sharply before they ever reached the wall, dropping quickly down and then zipping into a long, angled tunnel with furrowed dirt walls.

The pilot landed in a big, circular chamber with polished, reflective black floors and more of the same dirt-brown walls. Adam remembered the chamber clearly. This was where he'd met Harry five years ago after waking up in that stalker den below the Capitol.

The lander slowly turned on the spot to face the exit. A group of dirty, battered-looking people swept into view, and another armored figure promptly began herding them across the gleaming floor as the lander settled gently onto its struts.

There had to be at least twenty captives of all different ages—men, women, and even a few adolescent children.

"It looks like we have a new shipment all ready to go!" Miller declared brightly. "Your little coup certainly made that easy. Well, at least you won't be lonely up there," he added. "Maybe you'll even find a nice woman to make you forget all about your wife, hey Adam? I hear the Specs don't mind us breeding. You might even say that they encourage it! Good news for you, Connor. You and Crystal might just get to start a family after all."

Connor didn't reply to that, and Adam scowled inwardly at the governor's words, incensed to learn just how much he knew about their personal lives.

"Let's go meet them, shall we?" Miller went on, already striding out of the cockpit. "Come! Misery loves company, as they say."

They followed him down a long, dimly-lit corridor with rounded walls and glowing blue and green patches of light that simulated the illumination inside the stalkers' dens.

At the far end of the corridor, the governor waved a broad door open, revealing an echoing chamber with a high, curving ceiling that made it look somewhat like an artificial cave.

Broad doors rumbled open at the far end of the chamber. Beyond that opening was a much wider ramp than the one they'd been led up earlier. The battered and broken captives came shuffling up the ramp, not even attempting to resist the one herding them. They'd probably already tried, only to learn that there wasn't much that they could do against those armored collaborators. That, and they were likely terrified within an inch of their lives, having been dragged down here by stalkers only to awaken in an underground warren full of half-eaten corpses.

"Adam?"

No... He whirled around, searching for the source of the voice. Carla pushed through the shuffling crowd. She collided with him in a fierce hug, and began sobbing against his shoulder. He clung numbly to her.

"How?" he mumbled.

She withdrew to an arm's length and her eyes widened at the sight of the glowing creatures on his head. She reached up with shaking, bloodied hands, as if to remove them.

"Uh uh uh," Governor Miller chided. "They're still fresh."

Carla saw him standing there, and her eyes flashed darkly.

"Oh, that's right, I don't believe we've been introduced," he said, stepping quickly toward her. "I'm James Miller, Governor of the Republic." He thrust out a hand. "You must be Carla Hall. Adam's wife? I've been rooting for you two, you know. So few marriages make it, but yours still seems to be going strong. Good for you."

Adam's skin was crawling. If Miller knew this much about them, what were the odds that he didn't also know about Ellis's inoculations?

But he hadn't said anything yet to warn the collaborators. So they still had a chance. It was a good thing that Ellis had been so cautious about revealing his secret project. In hindsight he probably shouldn't have even trusted Adam with it. What if he had told Connor, and Connor had told another Vulture?

One of the collaborators came over with a pair of parasites upturned and ready for a host. Adam eyed the forest of writhing white tendrils on their undersides as the collaborator reached for Carla.

She recoiled, but the enemy soldier was much too fast, slapping them against her skull and leaving her to stumble around, batting weakly at her head until the parasites themselves convinced her to stop. Adam struggled not to react, but his eyes burned with angry tears.

"Well," Governor Miller said brightly. "At least you're both on the same team again. See you on the other side, Adam. Here's hoping the next life's better than this one. Sure would suck to die and go to hell when we're already there."

On that note, the governor left them, striding quickly for the open end of the cargo bay. One of the collaborators escorted him out, protecting him from the glaring captives still waiting to be fitted with parasites.

Adam wondered at the governor's words. For someone who'd just admitted this was hell, he'd sure embraced the Devil's role. But maybe that was just what evil people did, better to victimize others than be a victim oneself.

Ellis shuffled over to him. "There's a special place in hell, am I right?" the mayor whispered.

"The throne, apparently," Adam replied. Carla stared blankly at them, and his tears trickled swiftly down. He quickly wiped them off on his sleeves, just in case real converts weren't supposed to cry.

A special place, indeed, he thought.

CHAPTER FIFTY-NINE

The ramp came folding back up and the cargo bay doors rumbled shut. To his dismay, Adam saw that Carla wasn't the only one in the crowd that he recognized. Somehow, Sophie and Emily were also there. Adam grimaced and looked back to Carla. He noted how dramatically her face had changed, her expression slack and eyes vacant. He felt around inside his vest for the remaining syringe, thinking that if he inoculated her now, maybe he could protect her from whatever horrors were to come. Maybe if he and Carla and Crystal could keep their wits about them, then somehow they'd find a way to escape together.

Ellis caught his eye and gave his head a slight shake, as if he knew what Adam was thinking. His hand fell back to his side, and his thoughts turned to what else he could do with the last remaining dose of their secret weapon. Did Ellis have any extra inoculations with him?

Maybe not. He probably hadn't imagined it

would come to this.

Adam thought back to the test subject in that mobile hospital below the stadium. They'd been completely immobilized by the compound, so what would happen if he injected one of those two collaborators now? The pilot, maybe? They might not be able to fly away if he did that. Or maybe Valentina could also fly the ship.

Then Adam remembered Harry. Somehow, even under the influence of the Specs, he had still been obsessed with finding his wife and daughter. Those parts of him had been the last to go. Maybe Valentina would be the same. She'd been the *grand proctor* of the Nightingales. If he injected her, she might remember something about who she used to be and find some way to help them.

Adam's gaze tracked over to the pair of collaborators as they pushed through the crowd to finish fitting the last few captives with parasites. He studied Valentina's glossy black armor and helmet, wondering how he could inject her through that suit. Maybe he could stick the needle through the seams around her neck? Assuming the material wasn't too thick.

There was only one way to find out. Adam strode quickly toward the two collaborators.

"Where are you going?" Crystal asked, pulling alongside him, her eyes darting furtively as they went. She didn't have the same glazed look that the others did, thanks to her inoculation.

"Stay with the others," Adam whispered. "Act dumb. Blend in."

Crystal fell back with a nod.

Adam made sure to keep the collaborators' backs to him so they didn't see him coming. He reached into his vest and withdrew the syringe. Stepping behind the smaller of the two enemy soldiers, he jabbed the needle straight into the seam below her helmet and quickly depressed the plunger. Valentina reacted a split second later, spinning around and raising a hand to the injection site.

Adam dropped the empty syringe and hid it under his boot.

"What did you..." Before Valentina could finish that thought, she collapsed on the floor, convulsing.

Her partner noticed what was happening and dropped to his knees beside her. He quickly twisted off her helmet, revealing the same beautiful face that Adam had seen earlier when Governor Miller had asked her to reveal herself, but this time her complexion was blotchy, and her eyes were rolling in her head. Her lips were turning blue, and the growths on either side of her head were pulsing erratically.

The male collaborator jumped off the deck and ran to one side of the cargo area.

Ellis skidded into view and fell to the deck. He cradled the woman's head in his lap, caressing her honey-brown hair. "Val, can you hear me?" he asked. "Fight it. Don't let them win."

Adam retreated a step, wishing now that he'd saved the last inoculation for Carla. Clearly injecting someone who had been integrating with those parasites for years was a lot more dangerous and unpredictable than injecting someone who had yet to have any of their brain replaced by alien tissue.

"Move," the male collaborator intoned, shoving Ellis out of the way as he returned. He had a silver case like the one they'd carried across the interstate. He opened it, revealing illuminated compartments with various kinds of creatures inside, as well as vials of fluid and gleaming alien instruments.

The enemy soldier reached in and produced something that looked like a glowing blue blowfish. It was slowly hissing and sighing as it rhythmically inflated and deflated through tiny holes that pocked its surface.

The collaborator pried open an orifice beneath the creature, flattening it into a disc, and then he fitted it over Val's mouth. The blowfish quickly formed a seal and inflated, puffing up into a globe the size of a grapefruit, but blue. It remained inflated for a second, then deflated.

The blotchy appearance of Valentina's face cleared and her eyes stopped rolling in her head. They flicked around suspiciously, now wide and blinking. Her gaze fixed on Ellis, lingering for a moment.

"You went into toxic shock," the male collaborator explained in a flat, emotionless voice. "I have stabilized you for the moment, but the toxins are still in your system. We need to get you to a medical pod immediately."

Val nodded, and her partner pulled her to her feet. The male collaborator glared at Adam. "I do not know what you did to her, but we will address the state of your integration when I come back."

Having said that, he turned and walked away, helping Val stumble toward the door to the rest of the ship. Adam's hands balled into fists as he warred with himself over the only remaining option—attack the male collaborator and overwhelm him while he was still burdened with Val. Adam studied the sidearm on the man's hip, and his glossy armor, wondering if that plan had any chance of success. Maybe if he, Ellis, and Crystal all worked together they could overpower him.

Ellis stood up beside Adam and released a thready sigh. "You injected her," he whispered. "That's good. All we can do now is wait."

"Wait?" Adam asked. "He's taking her to some kind of pod to filter out the compound."

Ellis smiled. "He can purge the toxins, but the damage has already been done. They'll need to replace her parasites."

Adam frowned. "What makes you think they won't?"

Ellis shook his head. "They will, but first they'll want to learn what you did to her. They'll run tests. And here, on board this lander, they won't do anything other than put her in a pod to keep her stable. I don't know how much of Val is still there, but this gives us a chance for her to—" A cracking zap interrupted Ellis, followed by a clattering *thud*. "—do that," he finished smugly.

The male collaborator lay sprawled out on the deck, unmoving, with a smoking hole in his chest.

Val stood over him, swaying lightly on her feet. That strange blowfish was still attached over her mouth, slowly inflating and deflating.

Ellis ran to her. "Val!" he shouted. "It's me, Thomas!"

Adam hurried after him, unable to believe what had just happened. The inoculation had worked!

Ellis skidded to a stop, reaching for Val's arm to steady her. She looked at him, keeping her head angled slightly away so that she could see past the creature that was helping her breathe. Reaching up, she pried it away from her lips.

"You saved me," she gasped, now looking

squarely at the mayor.

Ellis appeared to hesitate, then nodded to Adam. "Actually, he was the one who injected you, but yes, it's something I've been working on for a while." Ellis smiled fondly at her and reached for one of her hands.

"Where are we?" she asked, glancing quickly around to take in her surroundings, as if only now realizing where she was.

"Below the Capitol, in Travis," Ellis explained. "We're landed in a hangar where the governor gathers his captives before sending them to the Specs."

Val's attention drifted to the crowd of captives in the cargo bay.

Adam turned to see Crystal walking over to join them, looking confused but hopeful. Connor trailed stiffly after her, along with a few others. With the exception of Crystal, they all looked like they were in a daze, as if sleepwalking, but still conscious enough to be curious about this new development. Adam saw that Sophie and Emily were among the ones who approached.

Ellis gently jerked Val's arm to get her attention. "We need your help."

She nodded, her gaze slowly drifting back to him. "Of course... we need to escape. Regroup."

"Not yet," Ellis replied. "We staged a coup, and we almost deposed the governor. We need you to help us finish the job."

Val blinked at him, looking exhausted. "What do you need me to do?"

"He's giving a speech from the Capitol right now. Fly us up there. We're going to crash the party."

Val nodded, smiling faintly. "It would be my pleasure."

CHAPTER SIXTY

Adam crowded into the cockpit with the others as Val dropped into the pilot's seat and flew the lander back up the long, angled dirt tunnel to the surface.

Crystal had insisted that they remove everyone's implants before they do anything else. Val had used a wand-shaped device that looked vaguely like a cattle prod to do so. The heat and arcs of electricity that it generated made the creatures squeal like lobsters in a pot before falling lifelessly from their hosts.

Once they'd freed Connor, Sophie, and Captain Fields, Ellis had left the captain to finish up with the remainder of the captives.

Adam noted that Val hadn't tried to remove her implants, nor did Ellis suggest it. He had a bad feeling that meant there was no way to safely remove them anymore. Maybe they couldn't control her, but excising them completely was obviously not a simple procedure.

The lander emerged just outside the walls of

Travis.

"There it is!" Emily pointed to the illuminated dome of the Capitol building. It was lit up with red and blue floodlights, and by a series of spotlights shining down from the balcony at the back.

"Can the Specs track us somehow?" Adam asked, suddenly worried that their little mutiny might lead to reprisals.

Val shook her head. "No, not with our cloaking shield engaged."

"Good," Adam replied, feeling slightly better.

In the distance behind the Capitol, a small, flickering orange fire shone bright amidst the patchy lights of the city. Adam realized that was the Governor's Mansion, busy burning to the ground.

Val slowly banked toward the Capitol building. She raced over the walls of Travis. The guards didn't even look up as they passed overhead.

"They can't hear us?" Crystal asked.

"Spec ships are quieter than anything we ever built, especially while they're cloaked."

Connor and Carla nodded along with that, but Sophie looked uneasy, her eyes angled up and searching the sky for signs of enemy aircraft.

So far they seemed to be in the clear.

Val flew over the Capitol. The grounds were flooded with light from spotlights on the balcony, revealing a dark, shadowy carpet of people gathered below. A cordon of armed Rangers with vehicles and more spotlights completely encircled them.

Val banked back around and cruised toward the balcony. Adam saw a group of people gathered there, along with a familiar figure in a blue suit standing on a podium with his hands raised. Val fiddled with the controls, and the upper left corner of the forward screen zoomed in, revealing Miller's smiling face. He was standing behind a protective wall of plexiglass.

"Can we hear what he's saying?" Ellis asked.

Val hit a switch, and a booming voice thundered into the cockpit.

"...insurrection has been crushed! Its perpetrators have been captured and exiled to the Wastes! Justice has been served, but all of you share the burden of their guilt. Yet I am not without mercy.

"Were I the monster that your ringleaders have portrayed me to be with their propaganda, then I would surely be rounding all of you up right now and shipping you off to the Specters. But mark my words, I am *not* a collaborator! Whatever proof you think you have, I urge you to question its validity. Even before the invasion, we could fake images and videos. It would have been a simple thing to create an image like this one." Governor Miller held up one of the fliers that showed him kneeling before the open ramp of an alien lander, with a group of civilians bound and gagged behind him, and Rangers guarding them at gunpoint.

"Just because advanced technology is hard to come by, does not mean that all of it is gone! Just think to yourselves, how else could they have printed this propaganda in the first place?

"With a computer and a printer, that's how!" Governor Miller laughed gratingly at the obviousness of his own conclusion. "But, I understand how easy it is to believe a lie when it comes packaged with a fragment of the truth. And that truth is, that we have been losing people mysteriously from the safe zones. This very night, a crack team of my operatives busted a ring of raiders and Nightingales that have been operating in Travis to abduct our people and sell them as slaves to the Syndicate!"

A roar of outrage erupted from the crowd, and Adam rocked back on his heels. The governor was taking credit for his work! How did he even know about the raiders that Adam had killed? Crystal looked to him, her mouth agape. He slowly shook his head, still not getting it.

"Miller was involved," Ellis whispered. "He must have sent that man to abduct Crystal."

Adam's blood turned to ice as he realized that was true. The governor's betrayal went far beyond simply working with the Specs. He was also working directly with his scapegoats and selling citizens to *human* slavers. No wonder the Republic's population was shrinking!

"I sincerely doubt that this is the only slavery ring operating in the Republic," Miller said. "In fact, I have reason to believe that there are slavers operating in nearly all of our safe zones. These are the real culprits behind the missing people that you have been blaming me for.

"But rest assured, we will work around the clock to root out and prosecute these criminals! We will not stop until we have made our cities safe again! Furthermore, I consider the Syndicate preying on our people to be a declaration of war. I have mobilized three whole divisions of Rangers from the front line with the Coalition. We will invade every settlement and every city in the Syndicate if we have to, until we find our people and bring them home!"

At that, a cheer actually erupted from the crowd. Val zoomed in further on the governor's face, displaying an enlarged image of him grinning like a fiend. Behind him, a handful of Rangers stood guard. Adam counted six, one of whom was Lieutenant Jameson.

"This is unbelievable," Val whispered, shaking her head. She stabbed a button, and the governor's droning voice cut off into silence.

"They're buying it," Adam growled. "Every word."

"Can you find some way to get us down there without those Rangers on the balcony shooting us?" Ellis asked.

"I can take them out with the lander's weapons," she suggested.

Adam frowned at that. If they came in raining hellfire from an alien ship, the crowd would be a lot less sympathetic to what they had to say. "Is there some way to stun them or incapacitate them instead?" he asked.

Val glanced at him. "My sidearm, but there are too many Rangers, and I can barely stand, let alone fight."

"What about your armor?" he asked. "I've seen what it can do. It stops bullets, and it can cloak like this ship, so we can take them by surprise."

Val nodded. "I can try."

"Not you," Adam explained. "Do you have any spare suits on board?"

"In the armory, but you don't know how to use them."

"How hard is it?"

Val licked her lips, considering the question.

"We need to hurry," Ellis added. "When that speech is over, Miller goes back inside, and the crowd will disperse. We'll have lost our audience."

"He's right," Sophie said. "The Rangers down there are the enemy. Killing them is unfortunate, but a necessary evil."

"I can teach you to use the armor in a minute or two," Val said. "At least, the cloaking functions, and the weapons."

"That's all we need," Adam said.

"I only have two spare suits," Val added.

Adam looked to Connor, and he nodded.

"We're ready," Adam said.

Val eased out of her chair and started toward the back of the cockpit.

"Be careful," Carla said, looking at each of them as she said it.

"Always," Adam replied.

Crystal chewed her bottom lip, but said nothing.

And then they ran after Val.

CHAPTER SIXTY-ONE

Adam stood in the airlock with Connor, watching him through a glowing haze of readouts and displays with icons and notations that he didn't understand.

The most important one was in the top right corner, a miniature 3D representation of his suit. It was grayed-out to indicate that the cloaking shield was active, a timer was busy counting down below it with alien symbols that Adam didn't understand, but he saw bright green shading gradually bleeding into the gray icon of his suit, inching down from the helmet to his boots.

And Val had warned them that the cloaking shield would run out of power in about ten minutes. Hopefully, that would be long enough to incapacitate everyone on the balcony. Adam raised his sidearm to check the virtual display at the back. Val had already set the weapon to stun for him, and the display showed that he only had twelve shots. He'd have to make each of them count—and hope that there weren't any more Rangers waiting inside the Capitol.

"Ready?" Val's voice reverberated inside Adam's helmet.

He went to stand on one side of the outer airlock door, while Connor took the other.

"We're in position," Adam replied.

"The airlock is opening now." A blueish light snapped on above the outer door, and it slid open. Adam and Connor both leaned out and fired dazzling white beams of energy at the Rangers on the balcony. All five of them fell before they could even figure out what was happening.

Five. Adam remembered counting six. Where was the other one? A door slowly swinging shut was his only clue. Someone had gotten away!

A squeal of interference from the mic on the podium signaled the Governor's belated reaction. He pivoted on his heel and drew a small pistol, firing repeatedly at them. Miller couldn't see them or the lander through their cloaking shields, but he could certainly see the square of dim green light radiating out of the airlock. But the bullets shattered harmlessly on their armor.

Adam jumped out and raced for the podium. Connor beat him there, knocking the governor down and smashing the gun out of his hand. Adam saw him reaching for the hem of his jacket where that alien comm unit had been sewn in. He snatched Miller's hands away and retrieved the device, grinding it under his heel until all that remained were tiny fragments. He jerked the governor to his feet.

The doors to the balcony burst open and more Rangers came flooding through. They glanced around stupidly, searching for targets, while some of them aimed their carbines up at the open airlock of the lander. Adam invisibly held the barrel of his pistol to Miller's head and deftly flicked his weapon from stun to kill.

"They're standing right next to me, you idiots!" Miller roared. The Rangers responded by aiming vaguely in his direction, but they didn't dare open fire for fear of hitting the governor.

Adam toggled his suit's comms from internal to external by using a chin switch inside his helmet. It was almost as though the Specs had studied and adapted human tech when they'd created these suits.

"Tell them to surrender, or you're dead," Adam said.

"Put down your guns!" Miller shouted.

The Rangers glanced about, as if wondering whether or not they should obey the command.

"Do it!" Lieutenant Jameson snapped, stepping out of the shadows inside the Capitol with her hands raised. The rest of the Rangers put down their guns and raised their hands, and then Lieutenant Jameson nodded to the podium. "Go on. Show yourselves," she said.

Adam used another chin switch to disable his cloak. Beside him, Connor did the same, followed by the lander itself. It slowly rotated, bringing the cargo bay at the aft end into line with the edge of the balcony, and then the ramp opened up and the crowd of captives came bustling out, flooding the balcony with dirty, angry faces.

"Keep me covered," Adam said.

"I've got you," Val replied over the comms.

He turned to the mic and the crowd below. "My name is Sergeant Adam Hall, and I am witness that what you see here is Governor Miller's doing! He rounded up all of the people on this balcony to send them to the Specs. I am one of those captives, a Ranger Sergeant, and a member of the Nightingales from Bexar. We came here to capture the governor and overthrow his government, and *this* is why! Were it not for the efforts of the Nightingales and their leader, Mayor Thomas Ellis of Bexar, we would be in orbit right now, meeting the invaders face to face!"

A megaphone squealed to life somewhere far below, and Adam heard someone say, "How do we know that you and the Nightingales aren't the real collaborators! You're wearing their armor and flying one of their ships!"

A roar of agreement erupted from the crowd.

Adam grimaced and glanced over at Governor Miller, who was smiling smugly at him.

A familiar face crowded in beside Adam. It was Ellis, looking flushed and out of breath. Captain Fields was with him, holding one of the alien sidearms and using it to keep the mayor covered. "I'll take it from here, Adam," Ellis said, while nudging him gently away from the microphone.

Ellis cleared his throat. "I am Mayor Ellis of Bexar. Everything Sergeant Hall just told you is true. We were able to commandeer this lander by turning one of the collaborators back to our side. She is none other than the Grand Proctor of the Nightingales and the legitimate, democratically elected leader of the Republic, Valentina Flores."

At that, the crowd murmured collectively. Everyone knew who Valentina was.

Whoever was manning the megaphone said, "Prove it! Bring her out to speak to us!"

Ellis hesitated, probably wondering who would be manning the lander's weapon systems if she wasn't in the cockpit.

But before he could call for her to come out, Valentina did something even better: she projected a hologram of her face in the air above the courtyard below.

The crowd gasped at the sight of her. No doubt they'd noticed the glowing parasites still attached to her skull. Adam frowned, wondering if they would discount whatever she had to say because of it. How could they trust the word of a collaborator?

Val spoke quickly, "I do not know how long I will have to speak with you before the Specters realize what is happening, and that I am no longer under their influence, but please listen carefully—everything the governor has told you is a lie, and I can prove it."

With that, the hologram switched from Val's face, to that of a recording of the hangar below the Capitol and the huddled group of captives being herded into the waiting lander. Governor Miller stood at the top of the ramp, his back turned to the camera, waving to the captives.

That scene drew a roar of outrage from the crowd, but Val wasn't done. The hologram quickly switched to another recording—this one of Adam, Connor, Crystal, Captain Fields, and Mayor Ellis all kneeling on the interstate in front of Governor Miller while he and a pair of collaborators fitted them with luminous alien parasites.

Valentina Flores' face returned moments later, looking grim. "This is what your governor does. He and his Vultures work with the Specs to abduct and enslave our people, and they have been doing it for years."

CHAPTER SIXTY-TWO

"How do we know this isn't a trick? The Specs could have faked those recordings!" the man with the megaphone said.

Val looked suddenly very tired as she shook her head. "The Specs don't care who governs us. They don't care if it's Governor Miller, or if it's me, or you, or anyone else. They only care about turning our planet into a suitable home for them and their kind, and about making us useful while they wait. On their ships in orbit and their factories on the moon and other parts of the solar system, we serve as everything from cooks and janitors to soldiers and entertainment. And when we grow too old or sick to be of use, they simply eat us, just like the Stalkers do, because that is what they are. They're all the *same* species, but with two different castes. One of them is like animals, and they live underground in dens, hunting us at night. We call them *nightstalkers*. The other is the ruling caste. We call them Specters, or Specs. They're chalk-white albinos, bipedal, and incredibly intelligent.

"The Specs cannot breed without the stalkers, who bear their young for them. Once they are born, the stalkers give their albino cubs to the Specs, and keep the rest. This strange dynamic has played among their species for countless ages, and right now, they are using the Earth as a giant harem to house their mates, feeding them with *us*.

"And for the lucky few that they see as useful for more than just animal feed, they fit us with parasites—" Val brushed the glowing, pulsing growths on either side of her head. "These creatures integrate directly with our brains, making us more docile and trainable."

The crowd rustled softly in the wake of Val's revelations.

"Prove it!" the man on the megaphone shouted.

"Are you sure you want me to do that?" Val asked. "You won't be able to unsee this. If you are squeamish, look away now."

With that, the holographic projection swirled, and Adam saw what looked like a massive cave. Within it were illuminated circles on the walls, floor, and ceiling. All of them were shining blue. Within moments, one after another, they turned red, and human figures came crawling out, completely naked, and coated in sticky, translucent goop.

The naked throng gathered, shivering in the

center of the chamber, and then bipedal *white* stalkers crept toward them on their hind legs, muttering and hissing amongst themselves in discrete patterns that were much more organized than the sounds the stalkers made.

They poked and prodded at the shivering humans. One or two were dragged out of the group and immediately beset upon by the albinos. Those people screamed hideously as the Specs literally ripped them apart. The remaining captives tried to flee, but a circle of human figures in glossy black armor fanned out around them with weapons raised. Several people tried to run anyway, only to be cut down by blinding white stun beams.

The crowd below reacted with collective horror and shock.

"Shut it off!" the man on the megaphone shouted.

The scene switched back to Val's face. "That was Governor Miller's doing," she explained. "Those were people that *he* sent to the Specs. I am not your enemy. Not anymore, at least, thanks to Mayor Ellis's intervention, but whole chunks of my life are missing. I remember only fragments, and even now, it feels like I am dreaming. I cannot competently lead you. But Mayor Ellis can. For now, I must leave you. I hope to one day return and find you have thrown off not only the shackles of this illegitimate tyrant, but also, the more abiding ones of the invaders themselves. Long live the Republic, long live the Earth, and long live humanity!"

The crowd echoed her with a collective shout of, "Long live Humanity!"

Val's hologram vanished, and Adam studied the Rangers on the balcony, trying to decide if they were still a threat.

One of them was struggling through the bedraggled crowd of civilian captives. She elbowed her way up toward the podium. It was Lieutenant Jameson. Adam tensed, ready for a fight, but Connor was already tracking her approach with his sidearm.

"That's far enough!" Adam said, pressing his gun harder into the side of Miller's head.

Jameson stopped a few feet away from Mayor Ellis, her hands raised, showing that she was unarmed. "Mr. Mayor," she said. "I would like to testify against the governor."

"Is that so?" Ellis asked, while covering the mic with one hand. "And what exactly are you a witness to?"

"Everything," she replied. "I'm the Chief Director of the Vultures."

Adam gaped at that revelation, and Governor Miller glared at her. "Are you insane? There's a lynch mob waiting down there, Jameson! There won't be a trial. They'll just wait until your feet stop twitching and then cheer and call it justice!"

Jameson glanced at him, then back to Ellis. "I understand that I can't expect amnesty after everything that I've done and been a part of, but I would like to at least try to make amends."

Ellis nodded slowly and stepped aside from the mic. "Very well, Director... here's your chance. The podium is yours."

Lieutenant Jameson drew in a shaky breath as she stepped up to the mic. She introduced herself, and the crowd gasped.

Ellis nodded sideways, indicating for Adam to join him below the podium. Adam jerked the governor down from the stage.

"You—Corporal," Ellis pointed to one of the Rangers who'd surrendered earlier. "Cuff the governor."

The man hurried forward and twisted Miller's hands up behind his back, binding them with old police handcuffs.

Miller sneered at the man. "You're a fool! They'll execute you, too!"

The corporal hesitated, as if it was only now dawning on him that he might be implicated in the governor's crimes.

"I promise you, son, that will not happen," Mayor Ellis said. "There will be a trial, and an amnesty program. I can't promise that everyone will be forgiven," he added with a glance in Miller's direction, "but every effort will be made to focus on the real enemy. The Specs. We're going to take back our planet.

Maybe not today. Maybe not tomorrow, or even ten years from now, but we *will* take it back. Do you understand me, son?"

"Yes, sir," the corporal nodded. "Thank you, sir."

Adam nodded along with Ellis's words, not sure if he bought into the mayor's optimism, but he hoped that it was true.

"Watch him," Ellis said, while pointing to Connor.

Connor's helmet dipped. "Yes, sir."

Ellis pulled Adam further away, finding a relatively empty corner of the balcony by the open ramp of the lander. "I need you to take Val and get out of here," he said.

Adam blinked at him. "And go where?"

Mayor Ellis pursed his lips and leaned in closer. "Sanctum."

Adam slowly shook his head. "We don't know where that is, or how to get there."

"Now's your chance to find out, isn't it? You have a ship. Take your family and go. We need an escape hatch. Somewhere to run to if this doesn't work."

"What do you mean?" Adam asked.

"I mean, if the Specs react poorly to the fact that we're no longer willingly feeding them with a steady supply of slaves. Things could get ugly down here, and fast. We need to ensure the survival of the species. No matter what."

Adam grimaced. "What if we're followed?

Then the Specs find us on a new world and conquer that one, too."

"One problem at a time," Ellis growled. "Find it first, and report back to me as soon as you've verified its viability. Are we clear?"

Adam nodded. "Yes, sir."

"Good. Now get your family together and get out of here before the Specs realize that they have a rogue lander down here and they call in an orbital strike to deal with it."

Adam stepped away from Ellis and jumped up on the ramp of the lander to search for familiar faces among those gathered on the balcony. He was glad to see that Carla, Crystal, Sophie, and Emily weren't there. They were still safe on board the lander. Adam waved to Connor, who hesitated and looked to Mayor Ellis.

"Go, Corporal," he said as he retrieved a discarded carbine from the surrendered Rangers and aimed it at Governor Miller. Meanwhile, Captain Fields' aim had never wavered. "We've got this covered, son," Ellis added.

Connor hurried across the balcony to the open ramp. Adam reached down and pulled him up, and then they retreated inside.

Adam flicked the chin switch to set his comms back to *internal*. "Val, Ellis wants us to —"

"I know," she said. "I heard him." The ramp

came telescoping back up, and the outer door of the airlock slammed with a reverberating *boom.*

Adam felt the ship turn and go whirring away, quickly picking up speed. The inner door of the airlock sprang open, and Adam ran through into the main access corridor, heading for the cockpit.

When he got there, he twisted off his helmet and sucked in a gulp of fresh air. It had a sharp, alien tang to it.

Carla kissed him deeply, filling his lungs with a more pleasant scent.

"Wow, that's a nice welcome," he said, smiling as he withdrew.

He noticed out of the corner of his eye that Crystal and Connor were locked in a similar embrace, his helmet now lying on the deck beside him.

"We actually did it," Carla breathed.

"Yeah, I guess we did..." Adam replied. His brow furrowed as he thought about it.

Somehow, defeating Governor Miller didn't feel as good as he'd thought it would.

The Specs were the real enemy, and they were still just as terrifying as ever.

CHAPTER SIXTY-THREE

Adam stood in the cockpit watching as the small, sparsely-lit patch of lights that defined the Travis safe zone rolled swiftly away beneath them. Finding a safe refuge away from Earth, and now having the means to actually do it, was almost too good to be true. They'd come full circle to five years ago when they'd been planning a dangerous trip to Chicago to learn about Sanctum and the stolen lander that the Coalition was using to take people there. Now they had their own lander, and getting to Chicago would be easy. But they still had to find out where Sanctum was.

The gleaming, moonlit band of Lady Bird Lake loomed on the horizon, and Adam remembered the frantic battle to rescue Crystal and those other four captives from the Raiders. "Hey, Connor…" he began.

"Yeah?"

"What did you do with those four women we

rescued?"

"Oh." He blinked. "They're still at the boathouse."

"We'd better stop and pick them up."

Val glanced back at them from the pilot's seat. "Who?"

Adam explained and gave her directions to get there.

"They're not the only ones we need to pick up," Crystal added.

Adam looked at her with his eyebrows raised.

"What about Bowser?" she asked.

Adam smiled. "Of course. Him, too. How could I forget?"

Val shook her head. "Bowser?"

"The family dog."

"Hmmm," Val replied.

They landed by the boathouse and Adam and Connor ran out in their armor to get the two women and teenagers that they'd rescued. As they went, Adam realized there was one other stop they needed to make before they left for Chicago.

The stadium outside Bexar. Doctor Janssen was from the Coalition. He could probably save them a lot of time by leading them to whoever was in charge.

Inside the boathouse they were greeted to gunshots and oars being swung like bats. Between them, Connor and Adam managed to talk the women down and explain. It took more convincing than Adam would have liked, but eventually they got all four of them to board the lander. Adam ushered the women through the ship as it took off again, heading for Sophie's house, where Bowser was recovering with Private Smith.

After another brief stop there, they had both Bowser and Private Smith in the cargo hold. Val treated Bowser with a quick injection of something, and moments later he was back on his feet and looking like a young dog again, bouncing around in happy circles and showering everyone with kisses.

Adam left that happy reunion to pull Val aside and explain about their last stop.

"This doctor recognized the name of the colony?" Val interrupted him.

Adam nodded. "He said I wasn't supposed to know about it, that no one should know unless they're already on their way there."

"He obviously knows more about it than he claimed," Val agreed. "If we're lucky, he might even be able to save us the trip to Chicago by telling us where it is."

Adam inclined his head to that. "Maybe." And then he switched to a new topic that was bothering him. "Do you know how to…" he gestured vaguely to the ceiling. "Fly to other stars?"

Val hesitated. "In principle. I know what

buttons to push, and how to lay in a course, but I've never done it myself."

"Do you know how long it could take to get there? Should we stock up on supplies first?"

"I think that's a given if we're leaving for another planet," Val replied. "But no, I'm afraid I have no idea how long the trip could take. It could be just a few weeks. Or maybe months. Or even years."

Adam pursed his lips. "How do the specs do it? Do they freeze themselves or something?"

"There are pods on board. We call them medical pods. They can stabilize injuries and speed wound healing. But they can also hibernate a patient."

"*Human* patients?" Adam pressed.

"On this ship, yes. Everything has been adapted for our anatomy."

Adam blew out a shaky breath. "Then maybe that's the answer. We'll have to hibernate until we get there."

Val nodded.

"How many?" Adam asked.

"I'm sorry?" Val replied.

"How many pods are there?"

"Oh…" Val appeared to think about it, and then she winced. "I think there's only six."

"You *think*?" Adam repeated.

"There is," Val confirmed. "Just six."

Adam did the math—Connor, Crystal, Carla, Emily, Sophie, Val… and then he was out of space.

No room for the four women that they'd picked up from the boathouse. Which was fine, because they hadn't signed on for this. But there was also no room for *him,* or for Bowser, assuming he could even be hibernated in one of those pods. And then what about Doctor Janssen? What if he wanted to tag along?

Val nodded slowly as if she were reading his mind. "We can make two trips if it comes to that," she said.

"We could," Adam agreed. "But we don't even know how long the first trip will take. What if it *is* a few years?"

Val frowned. "I don't know what to say. There's no easy solution here. I'd offer to stay, but…"

"We need a pilot," Adam finished for her.

She nodded.

Adam blew out a ragged breath. "We'll discuss it when the time comes. First, let's see what Janssen knows. Maybe he can give us more info."

"Maybe," Val agreed.

"What's going on?" Crystal asked, walking over with Connor. Bowser was prancing along beside them with a goofy grin, oblivious that he was about to be left behind.

Adam smiled tightly at them and shook his head. "I was just explaining to Val how to get to the stadium."

"Oh, okay," Crystal replied.

"We should go," Val said, striding quickly away.

Adam hurried after her, his mind churning with dread over the hard choices to come.

CHAPTER SIXTY-FOUR

Adam, Connor, and Val exited the lander in their suits with the cloaking systems engaged. They hurried into the dark, gaping maw of the underground loading zone below the Alamodome.

The sound of generators rattling in the distance grew loud with their approach. Then they rounded a group of old, rusting container trucks and saw the sterile white glow of floodlights shining on the sides of the army-green shipping containers that made up the Nightingales' mobile hospital.

They reached the door in the side of the hospital. Adam started up the steps and stared at the lifeless black eye of a security camera mounted above the entrance. He glanced at the keypad and intercom, steeling himself for what would likely be a tense exchange with whatever guards had been left behind. How were they going to convince those guards that they were allies and not actual collaborators? None of them had seen Adam's face more than once. He'd be lucky if they even remembered him from the night before.

"Allow me," Val said over their shared comms. She laid a hand on his arm to stop him from triggering the intercom. "Some of these people might remember who I am," she explained.

Adam nodded and stepped down.

Val's suit shimmered, becoming visible as she disengaged the cloak. She depressed the intercom button and looked up into the camera with her helmet visor clearing as she spoke, "This is Valentina Flores, recently freed from captivity. I am here on a critical mission from Mayor Ellis. The coup succeeded, and we have commandeered a Spec lander. We urgently need to speak with Dr. Janssen."

Val stood there for several long seconds, waiting for a reply, but nothing happened. "Maybe you'd better reveal yourselves, too," she suggested.

Adam hit the chin switch to disengage his cloaking shield and peripherally noticed Connor doing the same.

Now there were three of them standing in front of the camera. Val spoke into the intercom again, "These two are Nightingales from the coup. One of them, Sergeant Hall, was brought here by Mayor Ellis. He spoke with Dr. Janssen and witnessed tests involving a compound that we can use to fight the Specs."

This time the door buzzed and clicked as someone unlocked it remotely. Val hesitated with her hand on the door.

"Be ready," she said. "This could be a trap."

Adam nodded.

Val pulled open the door—

And a pair of armed Rangers shoved their carbines in her face.

"Keep your hands up," one of them said.

Val was blocking the entryway, but one of the Rangers was aiming over her shoulder at Adam and Connor.

Adam slowly raised his hands, hoping as he did so, that these weren't Vultures and that the hospital hadn't been raided by Miller's men.

But then Doctor Janssen stepped out from behind them, his thick white beard looking scraggly, and his gray eyes bloodshot, as though he hadn't slept a wink since they'd seen him last.

"What is it you need to speak with me about?" he asked.

Adam switched his comms to external. "May I remove my helmet?" he asked.

Janssen hesitated, then nodded. "Please do."

Adam twisted it off to reveal his face and stepped into view behind Val. She turned her profile to the entrance so Janssen could see that it was him.

"Your mission was successful, I trust?"

"Yes," Adam confirmed.

"Good."

"We need a word with you."

"I'm listening," Janssen replied.

"In private…" Adam added.

"Sir, I don't think that would be—"

"It's okay, Corporal. If these three are traitors who've come to arrest me, then it's safe to say that the jig is up whether I grant them an audience or not. Let's hope that's not the case."

The Rangers parted, allowing them into the cramped confines of the field hospital. The door promptly slid shut behind them.

"This way…" Janssen indicated, waving over his shoulder. He tapped a code into a keypad, and another door swept open.

They walked through a storage area that Adam remembered from last night, and then into the clinic where Adam remembered that a female test subject had been lying on a bed surrounded by beeping equipment. Now she was conspicuously absent and all was silent.

The doctor shut the door behind them and turned to regard them with his unruly white eyebrows raised. "Well?" he prompted.

Val looked to Adam, and he briefly explained everything that had happened with the coup, and about Mayor Ellis's mission to find Sanctum. When he was done, Adam finished by saying, "We came here to ask what you know about Sanctum."

Dr. Janssen grimaced. "I see." He drew in

a deep breath and let it out slowly. "That is unfortunate."

Adam shook his head. "Why?"

"Because Sanctum no longer exists. It was compromised years ago when the location was leaked to the enemy. The Specs found it, destroyed our lander, and enslaved the colonists. The Coalition has been working to commandeer a new lander ever since. They sent me here, hoping that this project would bear fruit and that you might succeed in stealing a vessel of your own. If you did, they planned to trick you into a rendezvous, and take it from you."

Adam muttered a curse, while Connor and Val slowly shook their heads.

Janssen regarded them plainly. "The Coalition and the Republic are not allies, what did you expect?"

"Why are you telling us this?" Adam asked. "Shouldn't you be luring us into their trap so they can steal our ship?"

"Because I had my own selfish reasons for getting involved in this operation. My family and I were on the waiting list to go to Sanctum. Flights were leaving every other week, taking just a few dozen people at a time. But then the entire operation was compromised, and we never got to go. Myself, my wife, and our son were among the lucky souls who escaped an even more certain fate than the one that awaited us here on Earth."

Adam shook his head, not getting it. "That doesn't explain why you are…" And then he got it.

"He wants us to take him and his family with us," Val explained. "He's defecting."

"Exactly," Doctor Janssen replied. "But I'm not defecting to the Republic. I'd like to propose that we represent a third faction, one that represents the interests of humanity as a whole. We must ensure the survival of the species, but to do that, we need to learn from the mistakes that led to the discovery of Sanctum."

"What mistakes?" Connor asked.

"Return trips," Janssen replied. "This time, when we leave Earth, it needs to be a one-way trip. We cannot risk that our comings and goings lead the Specters to our new home."

"Hang on." Adam held up a hand to stop him. "We haven't agreed to this yet. We can't just forget about everyone else on Earth. They'll be eaten by stalkers or enslaved by the Specs. We're talking about the fate of millions of people."

"Yes," Janssen replied, nodding gravely. "But what about the millions of people who have yet to be born in our new colony? Billions, even. What about their lives?"

"Well, they haven't been born yet," Connor said.

"Exactly," Janssen agreed. "And they never will be if we don't make the hard choices *now.* The way things are going, we'll be lucky if anyone is left on Earth in a hundred years. Although the Specs will no doubt breed us in captivity, so I'm sure we will continue to exist in paddocks of some kind. They'll weed through the herd, picking the ones they want to clean their toilets, the ones they want for dinner, and the ones they want to breed. In the latter group, they'll undoubtedly select for characteristics that *they* find agreeable. We do it all the time with our livestock and our pets, so shouldn't they? In just a few hundred years, the human race will already be vastly different from anything we remember, and that's assuming that they don't find ways to accelerate the process through genetic engineering."

Adam frowned unhappily at the picture the doctor painted.

"What I'm trying to say, is that the battle you're hoping to win has already been lost. You want to maintain ties with Earth so that you can somehow save everyone with a ship that can only carry a few dozen people at a time. It's absurd, and nothing but a salve for your survivors' guilt. The real decision here, is do we accept our fate, or do we escape now with however many we can while we still have the chance?"

Adam and Connor traded glances with one another. Val studied the doctor with a deepening frown. Adam half expected her to reject Janssen's arguments as a cover for cowardice.

"He's right," she whispered, surprising everyone. "We need to load up as many people and supplies as we can, and then leave and never come back."

"But leave for where?" Connor demanded. "And how? Do we even know how long it will take to reach another planet, let alone to find one that's suitable?"

"A few weeks was the turnaround between here and Sanctum, right?" Adam asked, having picked up on that detail during Dr. Janssen's revelations.

Janssen nodded, and Adam smiled grimly as he realized that they wouldn't need to freeze anyone in those medical pods. Even Bowser would be able to join them on this trip.

"Then hopefully we won't need much more than that to find a new home."

"What about supplies?" Connor asked. "We'll be starting over from scratch. We'll need food, shelter, equipment... training!"

"That *is* a problem," Adam conceded.

"I know where we can get all of that," Janssen replied. "There's an old survival shelter that some wealthy prepper built in the wastes outside Kansas City. It's where my family is hiding now. It has enough supplies to last a small group of people years, as well as some of the things that we'll need for a colony—seeds and fertilizer, basic farming equipment..." He shrugged. "It won't be easy, but we'll have a chance."

"You planned for this," Adam realized.

"Nothing escapes your notice, Mr. Hall," Janssen replied. "The Coalition doesn't share my concerns about promoting the survival of the species above all else, and even if they did, I'm sure that my family wouldn't make the cut. So yes, I've been rehearsing for this moment for some time already."

"This isn't just about the survival of the species for you," Connor said. "It's about *your* survival. And your family's."

Janssen cocked a bushy white eyebrow at him. "Can't it be about both?"

"We're wasting time," Val said. "We need to be in agreement on this. What's the verdict?"

Adam answered first, "I hate to admit it, but I think he's right. And even if he isn't, we'll stand a better chance of defeating the Specs someday if we can rebuild somewhere that isn't already under their thumb."

"So we're doing this?" Connor asked. "Abandoning Earth?"

"Either we abandon ship, or we go down with it," Janssen said.

Val nodded her agreement and Adam

winced. "When you put it that way, there isn't really a choice."

"I'll go get my things," Janssen said.

CHAPTER SIXTY-FIVE

One month later...

Adam stood in the cockpit of the lander, holding Carla's hand as he gazed down on a brilliant green world stippled with fluffy white clouds and pocked with bright blue lakes that might have been formed by filling in old impact craters.

"It's beautiful," Carla whispered.

"It is," Adam agreed.

A single ocean surrounded the planet's solitary landmass, while frosty glaciers domed the uppermost pole. The planet had some of the same characteristics as Earth, which Val had been able to confirm with the lander's sensors long before they reached orbit.

Gravity: 93% of Earth's at 9.1 m/s2.

Air pressure: 81% of atmosphere at sea level on Earth.

Oxygen was 26%, which was better than Earth's 21%, meaning that it would be easy enough to breathe despite the lower air pressure.

And the temperature along the equator was a balmy seventy-two degrees.

"It looks like paradise from up here," Crystal added.

"Let's hope it looks just as good when we're standing on the surface," Val said.

Everyone nodded along with that.

Val's implants were still attached, but thanks to her inoculation, those alien parasites were comatose and no longer controlling her. She had trouble sleeping and sometimes she couldn't remember simple things from one day to the next. She'd even had a few seizures that Dr. Janssen had been forced to treat with pills and injections from their precious cache of medical supplies, but so far, Val was getting through it. Which was good, because without her, they'd never have gotten this far.

She'd helped them to explore five different star systems to date. They'd even landed on two other worlds that had looked promising at first, only to learn that they had some crucial flaw—intense solar radiation on one, which had meant that they would never be able to leave shelter without wearing some type of full body suit. And on the other, the surface water and soil had been contaminated with heavy metals.

This planet was by far the most promising in terms of habitability. It was also the farthest from Earth at nearly one hundred light years away. Given how habitable it seemed, Adam couldn't help wondering why the Specs hadn't already found and colonized it for themselves.

He still remembered seeing their fleet orbiting over Earth—hundreds of darkly gleaming warships, scattered and drifting among the stars, with trickling streams of landers and much larger terraformers flitting to and fro. After seeing that, any lingering reservations that Adam had about abandoning Earth had swiftly evaporated. Dr. Janssen was right. They'd already lost the war.

With Val's inside knowledge of the Specs' technology, she'd managed to stay out of range of their sensors as they left, using their own stealth technology against them. Of course, like that, it was almost equally hard to know if they had been followed.

But the proof that they'd gotten away clean had come over the subsequent weeks of exploring. If Specs *were* silently shadowing them, then what were they waiting for to reveal themselves?

Adam re-focused his attention on the verdant green world below, wondering again, why the Specs hadn't colonized it. But he supposed that one species' paradise could be another's hell. They'd come to Earth and promptly begun terraforming it into something they liked better. They'd been at it for thirteen years already, with at least another fifty or a hundred to go. That was a big commitment of time and resources, so maybe it wasn't that surprising that they hadn't already colonized every other planet in the galaxy.

Bowser came padding in, panting noisily. "You want to see, boy?" Connor asked. He bent down and scooped the aging Golden Retriever into his arms. "Look," he said. "That's our new home."

Bowser grinned and looked over at Adam. He smiled and patted the dog on the head.

"Let's not get ahead of ourselves," Dr. Janssen warned. "Remember what happened the last two times? We could be looking at another poisoned well."

Crystal frowned. "No." She shook her head. "This is it," she insisted. "I know it is."

Adam smiled. "I like your optimism."

"You should go strap in with the others," Val said. "We'll be entering the atmosphere soon."

Adam nodded and ducked out of the cockpit, remembering from the bitter experience of their first landing that the ship's artificial gravity system could only do so much.

Carla and the kids followed him out, and soon they were strapping themselves to the walls of the cargo bay with the rest of the colonists.

Carla took Adam's hand in her lap, squeezing it hard in anticipation. Within minutes, a building roar filled the air, and the whole ship began to rattle and shake with turbulence as it entered the atmosphere.

"I hate this part," Carla whispered.

Adam smiled tightly and leaned his head against hers. "It'll be over soon."

***

"Well?" Crystal asked impatiently over the comms. "What's it look like out there?"

"Amazing," Connor whispered back.

Adam couldn't have agreed more. They'd landed by a lake in one of the crater basins, surrounded by a snowy ridge of high mountains. Now they stood by that lake on a thick, spongy green carpet that reminded Adam of moss.

Alien trees soared sporadically through the clearing. They had translucent, glassy trunks and branches with big, cup-shaped green leaves that seemed to be designed to capture both sunlight and pools of water.

The sky was a brilliant blue with a handful of scudding clouds, while the water was a stunning teal that gleamed invitingly in the sun. Schools of fish were skipping out of the water. Colorful bugs buzzed above the field, and strange, mournful cries echoed from a flock of multiple-winged creatures circling slowly overhead. They made Adam think of vultures, but these creatures had twice as many wings, and they were as brightly-colored as Toucans.

One of them flashed down from the circling flock and landed on a jutting gray rock beside them. Its wings were iridescent, and its small, round body was covered in blue and green fur. A broad, flat, white-furred head lazily lifted to regard him. Hair-like projections ran around the edge, and little black balls roved at the ends of each, making Adam think of eyes.

Farther off, some twenty yards away, grazing ruminants that looked like giant, furry white slugs slowly oozed across the spongy green field, oblivious to the arrival of the lander and its occupants with their glossy black suits of armor. To these creatures, *they* were the aliens.

Adam swept around in a slow circle, simultaneously taking in the sights and keeping Val covered with his Spec-issue sidearm set to stun.

He didn't think any of the creatures down here could hurt them through their armor, but he wasn't taking any chances. If something happened to Val, they'd be hard-pressed to fly the ship without her. Adam had been taking a crash course with her over the last few weeks, but there was still a lot that he had to learn.

Val was busy collecting water samples at the edge of the lake. She held up a clear vial of water in one hand, and a wand-shaped device in the other. She aimed it at the sample, and a holographic display full of alien symbols flashed above it. Thankfully, Val could read the Specs' language, but that was just another reminder of how lost they'd be without her.

"So?" Adam prompted. "What's the verdict?"

Making no attempt to answer, Val set the vial down and aimed the scanner at a small tray full of soil samples beside her. The holographic display flickered as it refreshed, and Val quietly studied the results.

Adam frowned, fearing the worst from her silence. He walked over to join her on a black pebble beach.

"Well?" he prompted while doing his best to ignore the spiky blue balls that were busy rolling around on the shore.

"The suspense is killing us, Val," Sophie put in over the comms.

"It's… perfect…" Val finally answered in an awed whisper.

Adam's brow furrowed inside his helmet. "Uh, maybe you can elaborate on that?"

Val looked up at him with a broad smile. "The air, water, and soil. There's literally nothing here that we would consider dangerous."

"Are you sure?" Adam pressed. "I mean… what are the odds of that?"

"We got lucky," Val agreed.

"What about alien microbes?" Adam asked.

Val smiled and shook her head. "According to the scans I've run so far, there's nothing to worry about."

"We need to run more tests to be sure," Adam concluded.

"Maybe," Val said. "But this is very promising. Far better than either of the other two worlds that we landed on."

A new voice came crackling over the comms. It was Dr. Janssen. "If I may, you won't find any alien bacteria or viruses that can affect us," he said. "Pathogenesis requires organisms to have evolved together. They learn how to prey on one another through close contact over millions of years of evolution. Microbial infection requires binding to the surface of our cells through common proteins and carbohydrates. The odds that alien bacteria will have accidentally hit upon just the right formulas for this are practically zero. And even if they *could* find a way to latch onto our cells, they'd still have to find a way to feed on us. Chances are, our cells and theirs will use entirely different formulations of energy.

"It's like trying to decode an alien language at random. It will take thousands or even millions of years for the local microbes to adapt to us to the point where we become useful hosts, and by adapting to us, they'll be maladapting to the local populations, which are arguably a far more abundant stimulus."

"Thanks for the microbiology lesson, Doc," Adam replied.

"You're welcome," Janssen replied.

"If that's so, then how do you explain the Specs' parasites being able to latch on to us?" Connor asked.

"They were almost certainly engineered to do so," Dr. Janssen explained.

"Does this mean we can come outside?" Crystal asked, sounding eager.

"Val?" Dr. Janssen prompted. "What's the surface radiation look like?"

"Well within tolerable limits," she replied. "Even lower than what we are used to on Earth. You won't need any sunscreen down here."

"Sounds safe to me," Janssen replied.

"Hang on," Adam said. He glanced up at the alien birds circling in the sky. "What about more complex organisms? Animals could still be dangerous, right? The stalkers were."

"Yes," Janssen agreed. "Although, the Specs might have also tweaked them before they landed so that we would make a better food source. But you're right, we do still need to be careful. Alien predators won't know whether or not we're food, they'll simply take a bite. If they get a stomach ache, it won't be any consolation to us."

"We've got guns," Sophie said. "I think we can handle it."

"Let's slow down for a minute," Adam said. "We should at least establish a perimeter first."

The rumbling groan of the cargo bay doors opening interrupted Adam's bid for caution.

Beside him, Connor twisted off his helmet and drew in a deep breath. "Wow! It smells amazing!"

Val took off her helmet next. "What *is* that?" she asked.

Connor bent down to smell the carpet beneath their feet. "It's the moss!"

"Is that… vanilla? Or cinnamon?" Val asked.

Adam frowned, stubbornly deciding to keep his helmet on. He glanced back at the glossy black bulk of the lander. The ramp was down and people were already surging out, muttering awed exclamations as they went. Most of them were carrying guns, just in case.

Adam hurried across the field to greet them, struggling to pick out Carla's and Crystal's faces from the crowd.

They'd picked up exactly forty people before leaving, being careful to choose them wisely, selecting for useful knowledge like agriculture, carpentry, and chemistry, while also making sure to have an even balance of men and women. Most of the people they'd chosen were already coupled up, either with children, or planning to have them soon, but a few were young singles that they'd made exceptions for because of their particular knowledge.

Mayor Ellis and Sophie had helped them with the selection process, using their experience with the Nightingales to offer personal recommendations.

Ellis hadn't been happy to learn that they weren't coming back to Earth, but once he'd heard what Janssen had to say about the fate of Sanctum, he'd understood their reasoning perfectly, and he'd simply wished them the best.

"We'll do our part, and you do yours," he'd said. *"Maybe one day our two peoples will meet again, and we'll join forces to defeat the Specs."*

Val had been so surprised by his magnanimous attitude that she'd actually kissed him goodbye.

A familiar golden streak went racing out ahead of the colonists, interrupting Adam's thoughts. Bowser barked and darted through the mossy field, sniffing excitedly at the first tree he found and lifting his leg high.

Adam snorted. That was a hell of a lot better than mopping his urine off the deck with a bucket. They'd been smelling it for weeks. No wonder Connor and Val thought this planet smelled so good.

A furry white and black streak went boiling past Bowser. He stopped peeing in mid-stream with a startled bark and gave chase.

That was Lola. Bowser's much younger female partner. Ellis had suggested that they take her off his hands to give Bowser some much-needed company. She was already pregnant.

Adam smiled at the thought of puppies

running around down here.

Connor ran past Adam and crashed into Crystal, picking her up and spinning her in circles. Adam went limping by them, having spotted Carla now. She greeted him with a smile and waved. They stopped in front of each other. "Are you going to take that helmet off so that I can kiss you, or what?" she asked.

Adam holstered his weapon and did as she'd asked. Connor and Val were right about the smell. He sucked in a deep breath of the honeyed air and smiled blissfully.

"We don't need any perfume down here," Carla said. Then she leaned up on tiptoes and kissed him, and suddenly he had other things to think about—like how it had been over a month since they'd had any privacy.

Adam withdrew with his head spinning as other parts of him hijacked his circulation. He cleared his throat and cocked an eyebrow at Carla to cover the effect she'd had on him. He flashed a lopsided grin and deliberately wrinkled his nose. "Are you sure you don't need any perfume?" he asked.

She laughed and gave him a playful shove. "Look who's talking, stinky!"

Crystal and Connor walked over, interrupting their banter. "Mom—" Connor said.

"Dad…" Crystal added. "Now that the future is looking a little more certain, we have something to tell you."

They each looked to their kids, and Adam noted the way that Crystal's hands were resting on her stomach, and how Connor had laid his over hers, hugging her from behind.

"You're pregnant!" Carla burst out before Adam could say anything.

Crystal smiled and nodded. "Yes."

Carla practically leaped on top of them both, pulling them into a hug and hopping up and down. Tears flowed freely, and laughter bubbled.

Adam joined them. "Congratulations," he said as he pulled Crystal into a hug. "Really," he added while nodding and smiling at Connor over her shoulder.

He nodded back, accepting Adam's grudging approval.

Dr. Janssen strolled over with his wife and their young nine-year-old son, all three of them looking smug. "I see that Crystal's told you!" Janssen said as he approached. "It wasn't easy keeping that a secret in close quarters for the past month, let me tell you."

Adam snorted. "It's a conspiracy."

"You didn't have to keep it a secret," Carla chided.

Crystal shook her head, wiping tears on the backs of her hands. "We didn't want to worry you."

"We wouldn't have worried..." Carla trailed

off uncertainly.

"I would have," Adam said.

"See?" Crystal countered.

"This calls for a celebration," Janssen put in. "For more reasons than one, yes?" he added while glancing around the valley. "Looks like we've found our new home."

Captain Fields could be heard in the background, snapping orders at the handful of Rangers that they'd brought with them, getting them to set up a perimeter. Adam was about to join them when Val returned from the beach. Her sample bag was dangling from the shoulder strap and knocking against her hip, and she had her helmet tucked under one arm. She smiled and waved to them as she approached.

"All good?" Janssen asked.

"I double and triple-checked," Val said. "This is it. This is where we start over."

"We should name it," Crystal said.

"The baby, or the planet?" Adam asked.

Everyone laughed at that, a dam of emotions breaking.

"How about Haven?" Crystal suggested.

"Haven…" Janssen mused. "It's a bit similar to Sanctum, isn't it? Maybe bad luck?"

"We'll make our own luck down here," Adam replied as he turned to look out over the lake. Bowser and Lola had stopped chasing each other around the field and now they were lapping up water from the shore.

"We'll put it to a vote," Val suggested. "Brainstorm a few different ideas, and put them on a ballot."

"Sounds fair to me," Janssen replied. "Personally, I like New Earth, or maybe… Eden."

"Too cliché," Connor objected. "What about Elysia? Or Valhalla?"

Adam reached for Carla's hand and tugged her lightly away from the crowd.

"What is it?" she whispered to him as they went.

"Oh, nothing bad, I just wanted a moment alone with you."

She smiled and nodded as they walked down to the lake. Bowser and Lola went racing by them again, sniffing energetically around the field and marking every stump, rock, and tree that they could find.

Adam located a big, flat-topped rock that jutted over the water and sat down with Carla there, their feet dangling above the water. He drew his sidearm again and placed it in his lap, just in case.

"I guess we can't go skinny dipping yet," Carla lamented while peering into the inviting depths of the bright turquoise water that lay bare inches below their feet.

"Not yet," Adam replied. "We wouldn't want to get eaten by a giant alien fish."

"Pity," Carla sighed. "You could *really* use a bath."

Adam chuckled at that. "I'll get to it."

They sat staring over the water for long minutes, watching the bright red orb of the local sun inching slowly closer to the snowy peaks that ringed the valley. Sunlight shimmered brightly on the lake, warming their faces and exposed skin. The clear turquoise depths of the lake progressively deepened to shades of umber and rose as a brilliant sunset seeped into the clouds overhead.

"I don't know what we're going to call the planet," Adam said, "but I think we should call this *place* Sunny Valley."

Carla looked at him, her green eyes wide and shining in the rosy light. "It's perfect," she whispered, and then she leaned her head against his shoulder and they went back to watching the final rays of daylight fade.

Adam remembered watching sunsets like this one back on the ranch, but back then, those sunsets had been an omen of trouble, of impending nightfall, and of the stalkers coming out to hunt.

And yet here they were, in a different sunny valley, brazenly watching an alien sun slip below the horizon. So far, it seemed, no threats were lurking beyond that horizon except for the monumental task of starting over somewhere new.

But they had supplies, enough to last them six months, or maybe even nine with rationing, as well as plenty of know-how and expertise among the colonists.

And most importantly, they had each other. That was one resource that Adam would never take for granted. He'd lost Kim, Richard, Owen, and Harry, but somehow everyone else in their group was still alive and together.

Despite everything that they'd lost along the way, they'd survived and come full circle to a new home. A new Sunny Valley.

Adam smiled to himself as he thought about the future and all the good things that it would bring.

"What are you grinning about?" Carla asked.

"Well..." He trailed off and stared meaningfully at Carla's abdomen. "Have you ever thought about having a baby with me?"

"What?! I'm forty-one years old, Adam!"

"So? Plenty of women have kids in their forties. You wouldn't be the first. We should at least try."

Carla hesitated. "I don't know... we've got a lot of other things to deal with before we start breeding like rabbits."

"I agree, but something tells me after everything we've been through, surviving in a place like this is going to be a breeze."

"Don't get too cocky," Carla warned. "But... if everything's still going smoothly a year from now, I guess we can try for a baby."

Adam nodded. "It's a deal."

EPILOGUE

"Are you sure?" Adam asked.

Carla was lying with her feet up on a bed in the cargo bay of the lander, while Dr. Janssen conducted the ultrasound.

"There's no doubt about it," he declared. "She's pregnant." Janssen turned the screen of his portable ultrasound machine so that they could see.

Adam couldn't tell what he was looking at, but then he heard a familiar sound crackling through the machine's tinny speakers.

"Is that…" Carla's eyes filled with a shining film of moisture.

"The baby's heartbeat," Janssen confirmed. "Congratulations to you both. You're going to be parents. Again."

Adam smiled and laced his fingers through Carla's. She released a shaky breath and her other hand came to rest protectively on her abdomen, even though it wasn't yet protruding.

"This will be the twelfth pregnancy we've

had since we arrived on Haven," Janssen declared. "We'll have to crack out a barrel of Mayor Flores' finest ale tonight."

"I can't drink that," Carla objected.

"No, but *we* can," Janssen replied with a grin.

Adam smiled and nodded along with his sentiment.

Later, as they were leaving Janssen's clinic in the back of the lander, Adam guided Carla carefully through a dizzying bustle of activity in the colony.

Kids and dogs ran squealing and barking as they chased each other around the sod houses. Cooking fires smoked fragrantly, roasting local root vegetables, and meat from the slug-like grazers, as well as some of the more familiar crops that they'd brought with them —like corn, potatoes, and wheat and barley for Sophie's bread and the mayor's ale.

"Hey! How did it go?" Crystal asked, bumping into them as she ducked out of her cabin with baby Kimberly bundled in her arms.

"We're pregnant," Adam declared.

"What?!" Crystal exploded. "That's unbelievable! Here—" She handed Adam his granddaughter and folded Carla into a big hug. "I'm so happy for you," she said while rubbing her mother-in-law's back.

"Thank you," Carla replied.

Adam stroked his granddaughter's cheek with one hand, smiling fondly at her while she slept. She was already four months old but looked like she was six thanks to Connor's genes. Crystal hugged Adam next—side-on to avoid waking her daughter.

Connor and Bowser emerged from the hut, followed by Lola who came barreling between their legs with a couple of her one-year-old puppies. Bowser watched their antics with the vicarious amusement of an old man. He was getting up there, poor guy, but still kicking at fourteen, and that was a minor miracle all by itself.

When the conversation trickled into silence, Adam bid the kids goodbye and handed his granddaughter back to Crystal. Then he took Carla's hand and continued down the street.

"Where are we going?" she asked.

"You'll see," he said.

Emily emerged from one of the other houses up ahead with Corporal Tony Smith, the dark-skinned Ranger who'd helped her nurse Bowser back from his broken ribs.

They'd only gotten together recently, but no one had been surprised when they had. Both shared a mutual love of animals, having gone so far as to become vegetarians in the new world. Something about eating *alien* creatures had seemed even more appalling to them than eating the ones from Earth.

"*Just think about it,*" Adam remembered Emily arguing one night before the Sunny

Valley Council. *"To the local populations, we are like the stalkers!"*

The council hadn't voted to stop hunting, but Emily had won a minor victory by convincing at least a dozen other colonists to give up meat.

As for Adam, after having spent the better part of a decade raising cattle on a ranch, he still couldn't quite get himself to join team salad and potatoes. Those slug-like grazers weren't quite as delicious as beef, but they still made a mean steak or burger with the right seasoning.

They reached the pebble beach below the colony, and Adam led Carla back to their favorite rock. Carla eyed him curiously as he sat down. She slowly shook her head as she eased down beside him. "We're going to watch the sunset?" she asked, nodding to the distant, craggy line of snow-capped peaks where the sun was already splashing the sky with muted fire. "That's your big secret?"

A group of kids ran splashing into the water a dozen yards away with Bowser's and Lola's puppies snapping playfully at their heels.

"You don't remember, do you?" Adam asked.

"No..."

"We sat right here the day that we arrived, and I asked if you would have a baby with me. You promised that in a year if everything was going well, we'd try. Well, here we are, a year later, the colony is thriving, and you're already eight weeks pregnant."

Carla snorted and slowly shook her head. "I'm surprised you remembered that."

"Are you kidding? I was counting down the days until you finally agreed to it."

Carla smiled. "Well, someone's excited."

"Aren't you?"

"I am…" she replied.

"But?"

Carla heaved a sigh. "It feels wrong."

Adam eased away from Carla to regard her with a frown. "What do you mean?"

"Us, here, building this place." She gestured vaguely to the valley. "We're having babies, hunting and farming, and getting drunk on Mayor Val's ale, all without a care in the world —or the galaxy, which is probably a better expression these days. Meanwhile, back on Earth… we left millions of people at the mercy of the stalkers and the Specs."

Adam nodded gravely. "Yeah. We did."

"And that doesn't bother you?"

"It used to," he admitted. "You see this?" Adam lifted his bad leg and pulled up his pants so that Carla could see the gnarled scars and the lumpy ball of flesh where his calf muscle had been pieced back together by Army surgeons after a bullet had shattered his tibia and tore out the other side. "I survived Afghanistan. My entire unit was slaughtered, and the one guy that I managed to save later killed himself because he couldn't take being in a wheelchair. I was the only one who made it, and you know what I learned from that?"

Carla shook her head.

"I learned that you've just got to live. If you want to honor the people who didn't make it, then you've got to do everything that they couldn't. You've got to live and live well. Every smile and every laugh, that's you smiling and laughing for them. And I like to think that maybe they might be out there somewhere, smiling back." He flicked his eyes up to the heavens as he said that.

"After everything we've been through, you really think that Heaven is real?" Carla asked.

"I think it has to be," Adam replied. "We already found out that Hell is real, so why not Heaven?"

Carla smiled and leaned her head against his arm. "My husband, the idealist."

"Either way, this place is as close to paradise as damn is to a swear word."

"Damn is a swear word," Carla pointed out.

"See? That's the spirit." He bumped shoulders with her. "Either way, we've got a mission while we're here. Make every moment count. Be grateful for every sunrise and every sunset."

Carla sighed. "I guess that makes sense."

"You're damn right it does," Adam replied,

and then he turned and kissed her, conveying every ounce of life, passion, and determination that still raged like fire in his veins, lit anew each day that he woke up, grateful just to be alive.

GET JASPER'S NEXT BOOK FREE

STAR EMPIRES
(Coming November 2023)

Get a FREE e-copy if you post an honest review of this book on Amazon (https://geni.us/sanctumreview)

And then send it to me here (files.jaspertscott.com/starempiresfree.htm)

Thank you in advance for your feedback!

KEEP IN TOUCH

SUBSCRIBE to my Mailing List and get two FREE Books! https://files.jaspertscott.com/mailinglist.html

Follow me on Amazon:
https://www.amazon.com/Jasper-T-Scott/e/B00B7A2CT4

Follow me on Bookbub:
https://www.bookbub.com/authors/jasper-t-scott

Look me up on Facebook:
https://www.facebook.com/jaspertscott/

Check out my Website:
www.JasperTscott.com

Follow me on Twitter:
@JasperTscott

Or send me an e-mail:
JasperTscott@gmail.com

MORE BOOKS BY JASPER T. SCOTT

Keep up with new releases and get two free books by signing up for his newsletter at www.jaspertscott.com

Note: as an Amazon Associate I earn a small commission from qualifying purchases.

Star Empires
Utopia (November 2023) | Collapse (TBD)

Nightstalkers
Nightstalkers | Sanctum

Architects of the Apocalypse

Planet B | Worlds Collide | Apokalypsis

The Kyron Invasion
Arrival | New World Order | End Game

From Beyond
From Beyond | Signal | Survival

The Cade Korbin Chronicles

The Bounty Hunter | Alien Artifacts | Paragon | The Omega Protocol | Bounty Hunters

Final Days
Final Days | Colony | Escape

Ascension Wars

First Encounter | Occupied Earth | Fractured Earth | Second Encounter

Scott Standalones

Mrythdom | Under Darkness | Into the Unknown | In Time for Revenge

Rogue Star

Rogue Star: Frozen Earth | Rogue Star: New Worlds

Broken Worlds

The Awakening | The Revenants | Civil War

New Frontiers Series

Excelsior | Mindscape | Exodus

Dark Space Series

Dark Space | The Invisible War | Origin | Revenge | Avilon | Armageddon

Dark Space Universe

Dark Space Universe | The Enemy Within | The Last Stand

ABOUT THE AUTHOR

Jasper Scott is a USA Today bestselling author of over forty novels. With over a million copies sold, Jasper's work has been translated into various languages and published around the world.

Jasper writes fast-paced books with unexpected twists and flawed characters. He was born and raised in Canada by South African parents, with a British heritage on his mother's side and German on his father's. He now lives in an exotic locale with his wife, their two kids, and two Chihuahuas.

Made in the USA
Las Vegas, NV
20 October 2023

79436319R00395